Joe

His journey to a 'better life'

GUY HALLOWES

Published by OMNE Publishing in 2021 Guy Hallowes © 2021

Print and eBook production by OMNE Publishing

Cover by Designerbility

Joe is a novel. All the characters in the book are imaginary and bear no resemblance to anyperson, living or dead.

This book is available in print and eBook formats on Amazon and from all good bookstores.

TABLE OF CONTENTS

ACKNOWLEDGMENTS

I should like to thank Chris Lake and Zena Shapter and the members of the Northern Beaches Writing Group for their input, which improved the manuscript significantly as a result of their edits and recommendations, and to my patient wife Diana Hallowes, who read several drafts of the book and provided the final edit. Any errors are entirely my responsibility.

PART 1

Chapter 1: Happy Home

Occasionally in the dead of night, Joe would creep out of the hut he shared with his parents, Wacheera and Ellen. He liked the quiet, interrupted only by the gentle sound of their own and neighbours' cattle moving about, as well as the occasional night jar call and other familiar night sounds. Often moonlight would beam on the outlines of the great peaks of Sattimma and Kipipiri, which formed the eastern boundary of the Great Rift Valley, unless, as was often the case, Sattimma was draped in a mantle of cloud. Mount Kenya, although not visible from his vantage point, was just beyond Sattimma' s peak. Mount Kenya was where the Kikuyu God Ngai lived and kept them all safe.

Aged about nine, Joe was big and strong for his age. He usually had a bright smile on his face and liked to be everybody's friend. He normally ran around barefoot, although he did own a pair of tennis shoes, used only on special occasions. He had two sets of somewhat tattered shorts and shirts. In cold weather he sometimes wore a cloth jacket rescued from some *Mzungu* household.

In one of his nightly ventures, as he was minding his own business, two vehicles quietly drew up on the road nearby. They arrived silently and without lights. He crept closer. There were about a dozen men, wielding *pangas* (bush knives, a local version of a machete). He watched for a minute – they were obviously up to no good.

Joe rushed back to the hut. "Baba, baba – men out there," he gabbled. "What, where?" asked his now wide-awake father.

"Out there," Joe pointed. "Bad men, *pangas!*"

His father leapt out of bed and rushed out of the hut. He returned almost immediately, to grab his own *panga* and rushed out again.

Despite his mother Ellen's entreaties, Joe followed his father and hid behind a small copse of trees. The men wore what Joe thought were police uniforms. To his horror, one of the policemen took a wild swing at his father with his own *panga.* It sliced his father's head open and he collapsed in a pool of blood. The police all ran away.

Joe stood frozen, unable to think or understand what he had just seen. He ran over to his father's prone body and by the light of a nearby blazing hut he tried, unsuccessfully, to get him to move. After a few minutes, covered in his father's blood, he raced back to their own hut, where he found his mother under the bed.

"Baba, dead..." he whispered.

He was unable to get her to leave the hut until dawn peered over the horizon, two hours later.

Finally, Joe dragged his mother to where he had left his father. His head was sliced open like a melon and his brains were scattered all over the ground. Their neighbour and another man were lying close by, also dead. A neighbour's hut had burnt to the ground and was still smouldering.

His mother wailed desperately. She fell on his father's now cold body, while Joe tried to get him to move.

Still covered in his father's blood, Joe was for a brief moment able to collect himself together, and he ran to some neighbouring plot-owners to ask for help, who were by now responding to the events of the previous night, having heard his mother's desperate wailing.

The neighbours helped Ellen back to her hut and made sure that she was given breakfast, which consisted of *oogie* (mealie meal porridge) and tea.

One of the neighbours called the police on his *rununu*. They arrived a day later. Joe was terrified when he thought he recognised one of the attendant policemen as having been in the group that attacked his father.

The investigation lasted a few weeks; the murders were attributed to a person or persons unknown and the case closed with unseemly haste.

#

Over the next few weeks, Joe, although deeply upset himself, pulled himself together, managing to milk the three cows that needed milking, as he knew that was what his father would have wanted. His mother was unable to do anything at all, so the responsibility of looking after the animals – the few cows and three goats on their seven-acre plot – rested with Joe.

His mother only managed to provide meals for herself and Joe after the funerals of the three who had been killed in the raid.

Joe had no idea why his life had been so suddenly and completely turned upside down. He had been happy living on their seven-acre plot, where his father and mother, like many others with similar plots, lived. The land had been secured for them all from the British by the great Kikuyu leader Jomo Kenyatta at the time of *Uhuru*-Kenyan independence. He had helped his father with the animals on the plot and had run around playing games with the other boys of his age group, among whom he was always the leader. This often involved games of football, where Joe was the hero. When he had time, he attended the one- roomed school, where he excelled at arithmetic.

He didn't understand why his father had been killed. All he now knew was that he had to do his best to look after his mother, continuing to do the things his father would have done, like milking the cows.

"Why, Mum?" Joe sometimes asked. "Why did these people come and kill Baba?"

"It's that man Kigoro, who is the big man on the Council," Ellen would mutter. "He wants our land and the land belonging to others in this place."

Joe received no better explanation than that.

When Ellen appealed to her previously friendly neighbours, she was either ignored or they were now hostile. "Your husband," they told her, "brought all this trouble here because he tried to break down the dam that Mr Kigoro is building. You and your son must go away now."

"But that dam will stop the stream and there will be no more water for you or any of the people who have land here," Ellen yelled back.

"Mr Kigoro has said there will be water for us."

"And you believe that? You will be the next people he attacks."

"Go, we do not want to hear such things. Go away."

"That man Mr Kigoro has told us we must not try to help you," was another more sympathetic response, "otherwise we will be in big trouble too."

Ellen merely walked away.

She asked her father for help. He agreed to go and see Kigoro.

He re-appeared, very frightened, a few days later. "You will have to leave here. Maybe go to Nairobi. There is nothing I can do. Your husband got on the wrong side of a very powerful man, which was a stupid thing to do."

As far as Joe's Grandfather was concerned, Ellen's father had received a good bride price for her, and now he clearly did not want the burden of resuming responsibility for both mother and son.

On another night, Joe heard a noise outside their hut. There were three men opening the fence that kept the cattle in at night.

"Hey," yelled Joe. He rushed at the men.

He was given a great whack on the back with a large stick, which sent him flying.

"Get away, or you will get the same treatment as your father," a man yelled at him.

Joe gingerly picked himself up from the dirt and struggled to his feet.

It was the same man as the one in the gang who killed his father. He and some other men drove all their cattle away.

Joe phoned the police on Ellen's *rununu*. This time there was no response from the police.

The harassment continued. On one of the few days Joe had time to attend school, he returned home to find that their three goats had disappeared.

There was also a growing shortage of firewood.

"It's that Kigoro again," Ellen told him. "He has people cutting down all the trees to make charcoal to send to Nairobi."

Joe and his mother struggled on for almost a year after the murder. By then they were running out of food. "I can grow vegetables," Ellen informed Joe, "but not if there is no more water. And where will we wash? When that dam is finished there will be no water for us."

"And this is the last of the chickens," Ellen added at one of the last meals they had in what they had considered their idyllic little place, their haven.

Grandfather paid five hundred shillings into Ellen's *M-Pesa* account on her *rununu*. "You must leave. Go to Nairobi or somewhere," he told her again.

Other residents in the area had already moved. When one family, whom Ellen considered close friends, collected their few belongings and were waiting on the road for a lift, she asked them: "Where are you going?"

"Nakuru," was the answer, "this place is no good anymore. We sold the cows to Kigoro, but he didn't pay much." The man, his wife and two children clambered into a dilapidated saloon car and disappeared in a cloud of dust.

So, she decided they too would move. "Nairobi, we will go to Nairobi," she told Joe.

Chapter 2: Kibera

Joe and his mother walked the five kilometres into the village of Ol'Kalou, Ellen carrying on her head what she could of their meagre pile of belongings. Joe carried a small suitcase. He was already wearing his best shirt and shorts and, at Ellen's insistence, his tennis shoes instead of carrying them, which was his preference. They left everything else behind, including the bicycle, which neither of them was able to ride.

They had tried to ignore the torrent of abuse from one of their very hostile neighbours.

"You brought this on yourselves," they yelled. "That husband of yours was no good..."

"Where are we going?' asked Joe as they ambled along the dusty road.

"Nairobi."

"Where's Nairobi?"

Ellen shrugged. "I've never been there myself. All I know is that it is two bus rides away."

Joe was curious about the move, not scared. He had always held his own with his peer group and even with the older boys, and he presumed it would be the same wherever they ended up. He had very little idea why their lives had been disrupted so badly, or why his mother continued to talk fearfully of Mr Kigoro; but now it was Joe's duty to look after his mother, whatever that entailed.

From Ol'Kalou, they caught the bus to Gil-Gil, twenty-five kilometres away. The road had been tarred since the *Wazungu* left, but it had not been well constructed and delivered a very bumpy ride. Ellen paid the fares through her *M-Pesa* mobile cash account on her phone, and again from Gil-Gil to Nairobi. Some of the people on the bus were able to help her with directions to Kibera, where they suggested she make for a church called the Unity Wesleyan Church of God, run by Reverend Timothy Mweleli.

"This is not a Kikuyu name," protested Ellen. "Is this man trustworthy?"

"Not all the people in Nairobi are Kikuyu," said the woman sitting next to her, "but this man is a Christian. I am sure he will help you."

This was a new and uneasy experience for Joe and his mother. They had little knowledge of other Kenyan tribes.

"What is all this leading to?" Ellen muttered to herself.

"He is a Kamba," the woman said, "but all people are welcome to his church. You will see."

Out of curiosity, she and Joe had on the odd occasion attended St Peter's Church in Ol'Kalou, which was Christian. She told Joe she did not like the man who said he owned the place though, especially when he told her that the money she put in the collection box was not enough.

"Kamba," said Ellen doubtfully, "maybe that is better than Luo or Kalenjin."

Although only a distance of one hundred and twenty kilometres from Gil-Gil, the journey to Nairobi on a good tarred road took most of the rest of the day, because of the many stops. It meandered on from Gil-Gil through Naivasha. The road then took them up a steep escarpment, out of the Rift Valley and past a small chapel on the left side of the road. Joe and Ellen marvelled at the view, though Ellen wondered aloud if it wasn't a sign that she had altogether left her old life, for what she didn't know.

Joe was intrigued by his first journey on a bus. The other passengers were kind to him and they shared their food with him and Ellen, once Ellen had told her story. The woman sitting next to her even gave him a piece of *oogaalie* (baked maize meal cake), in a little dish so he could cover the *oogaalie* with a small amount of gravy. He started to look forward to his new life in Nairobi.

At dusk, the bus stopped on the outskirts of Kibera and another woman helped Joe and his mother off the bus. "I will take you to the Unity Wesleyan Church of God, which is just down the street," she said. "I must then catch another bus."

"Well, here we are," announced the woman, after a few minutes' walk. "You can stay in the church porch tonight; I expect the reverend will see you in the morning." She pointed up a set of steep steps.

"Thank you," Ellen managed to say to the woman's fast disappearing back.

Joe peered up at the huge edifice, made of solid blocks of dark stone. The church had a secure-looking corrugated iron roof, painted red. Ellen stared at the impressive sign and with Joe's help was just able to read it.

The church was locked, and it started to rain, so the pair prepared to spend an uncomfortable but dry night, in the ample porch.

"What now?" asked Joe. "We have no food."

"We'll be alright here, for tonight," answered Ellen, though she didn't sound particularly certain.

#

Just before seven o'clock the next morning, Reverend Timothy Mweleli found them there. This was not an unusual occurrence. At least three times a week he found a refugee of one sort or another on the front porch of his church and he wasn't in the least bit put out. His flock, as he thought of them, in the slum area of Kibera, were mostly poor and many of them had arrived as refugees from the rural areas.

At well over six-foot, Reverend Mweleli was tall for a member of his tribe. He was well-built and somewhat overweight, a feature that was not wholly disguised by the long black cassock he always wore, of course with his dog collar. His ensemble often featured a pair of car-tyre sandals on his large splayed feet. Despite the rough, clumsy appearance of the footwear, he actually found them to be comfortable. He also thought it emphasised the fact that he really was just one of his flock. A pair of light brown horn-rimmed glasses topped off the ensemble. There were slight flecks of grey in his crinkly hair, which he felt gave him an air of dignity and maturity.

"Ah, what do we have here?" he rumbled in Swahili.

Ellen jumped up. "Sorry, we were told to come here but the church was locked..."

"*Ah. WaKikuyu*?" asked the reverend. "*Ndio*," Ellen nodded timidly.

"*Na toka wapi* (where are you from?)"

"Kalou."

"*Ah, pande mbali sana* (a long way away)."

The reverend knew the location of Ol'Kalou perfectly well but pretended otherwise. He had for some time had dealings with a Councillor Kigoro, who was a major supplier to a business selling charcoal in Kibera, in which the reverend had a half share. "*Wapi mume* (where is your husband)?"

Ellen shrugged, "*Watu na uua* (people killed him)."

The reverend tried to look sympathetic, but he now had the information he wanted.

"And what is the boy's name?" he asked "*Njeroge*, but he is called Joe. I am Ellen."

As Joe was introduced, he scowled at the reverend and tugged at his mother's hand, trying to pull her away. Perhaps he sensed the nature of the reverend's questions? Either that or the boy was naturally suspicious.

To put them both at ease, the reverend unlocked the church and invited them inside, telling them his story as they went. He had been fortunate to have been educated at a mission school near his hometown of Machakos, the centre of the tribal area belonging to the Wakamba. Machakos is situated in a semi-desert area, a dry dusty place some forty kilometres to the south east of Nairobi. He was then ordained into one of the established Christian churches and served them faithfully for fifteen years.

What he didn't tell them was that he had always been mildly resentful of the expatriate priests appointed by the Church to oversee his activities. They had what he considered to be big houses and their children, if there were any, were sent home to *Ulaya* (England), a place he had never seen, to be educated. More and more he considered the Church he served as a *Wazungu* Church. With the advent of *Uhuru,* he could see that if he established his own Church, he would be much better off than before and maybe he would be able to educate his own children privately, either in Kenya, or indeed in *Ulaya*, like the *Wazungu*. Also, he would be able to set his own rules and not have to worry about anything the pesky *Wazungu* wanted. So, he had established the Unity Wesleyan Church of God in Kibera. He had little idea of what the name meant or its origins, having borrowed it from several other *Wazungu* churches.

What he did explain was that, initially he had preached outdoors, on one of the many patches of bare ground to be found in Kibera. His fire and brimstone style and the singing, inherited from another of the *Wazungu* churches and mixed with his own African style, soon attracted larger and larger congregations. He had managed to persuade the priest of one of those *Wazungu* churches, whose audience had dwindled to almost nothing as a result of his activities, to give him his own quite modest church. He had also inherited a source of funding from England, having persuaded the lonely *M'zungu* priest that he, Reverend Mweleli, was doing God's work and that God had clearly decided that *Uhuru* should apply to the Christian religion as well as to the government.

By the time Joe and Ellen arrived on his doorstep, his own church had been completely rebuilt and was now a large imposing building. He had also constructed himself a big house.

As he settled them inside the church, the reverend couldn't help but notice Ellen's slim, attractive figure. Her only garment was a colourful but quite thin dress reaching just below her knees, revealing her shapely breasts and strong legs.

"*Ngoja hapa,* (wait here)," he said to the pair. "I will be back later." He told them he had some plans to carry out, then left.

To the reverend's surprise, while his own church was being rebuilt, another African priest, whom he despised, had taken the initiative and started building a rival church not far from his own. Ruthlessly, he had arranged for one of his less reputable acquaintances to start a fire in the rival's partly constructed building. He then personally phoned the fire brigade giving them completely false directions, so by the time the fire trucks eventually arrived at the burning church, all they could do was to watch as the fire took hold and completely destroyed the 'pretender's' church, as the reverend thought of it.

Not long after that another African priest proposed something similar, but this time the reverend anticipated the move and persuaded the person in question to move to another one of the growing shanty towns surrounding Nairobi. He also showed the man the charred remains of the rival church that had burnt down. The man got the message and troubled the reverend no more.

The reverend's plans had a way of coming together.

#

Ellen spent some of her dwindling resources to buy a loaf of bread at a nearby store, which she and Joe shared for breakfast.

By mid-morning the priest returned. "There is a room in a house nearby. You can stay there. I will show you."

He helped by carrying their small bundle of belongings to a nearby house, made of concrete blocks and consisted of two small bedrooms and a kitchen. There was an iron bedstead in one of the rooms. "Well, this should be better than the church porch," he said. "There is some bedding and clothes in a storeroom at the church. The woman who runs it will be there later today. I will be back in a day or two to see how you are getting on," the reverend announced as he showed them their new home.

"See, the kind man has helped us, as the people on the bus said he would," Ellen said, relieved.

Joe said nothing. His instincts told him to completely distrust the reverend. This was unusual for Joe, as apart from the recent influences of Mr Kigoro, he had had normal trusting relationships with the people around him.

Once Reverend Mweleli left, the door of the other room in the cottage was opened nervously by what turned out to be another Kikuyu woman. "He will be back. I'm Wanjiru."

They started chatting and, within a very short time, Wanjiru had the whole of Joe and Ellen's story. Joe was even encouraged to sit on Wanjiru's lap, who sat on the bed. Joe was pleased there was another Kikuyu sharing, what to him, was quite a big house.

"As I told you, he will be back," Wanjiru informed Ellen, in a matter-of-fact way. "This place belongs to him personally, not the church. He will expect to lie with you when he returns. The way it works is that he will let you have the room for nothing for a month or two until he judges you are able to pay him some rent; then he will ask for rent."

"Where do I get money for that?" asked a bewildered Ellen.

"Like me, nobody will take you on for a job, if that's what you had in mind. You don't know anything. So, the reverend will expect you to lie with other men, who will pay you and then you will be able to pay him."

"What other men?' Ellen burst into tears. After a moment's hesitation she said, "I was quite happy with my husband and our life and small plot of land in Ol'Kalou. It seems this place is now just full of greedy men, with nothing in mind but their own riches. The only man I have ever been with in that way is my husband." She then wiped away her tears and looked at Joe. "We will get through this," she said fiercely as she hugged Joe, who had very little understanding of what they were talking about.

"The reverend will send men here, after that they will tell their friends and others will come."

Wanjiru laughed at the look of horror on Ellen's face. "It's not so bad. It's what I do. I can even pass some of the men who come to see me onto you." Wanjiru looked around. "Okay, let's clean this place up and then we will go to the church storeroom. I can give you some food."

They spent a companionable three hours thoroughly cleaning what was to be their room and the kitchen, when a well-dressed man knocked on Wanjiru's door and after a brief conversation went into her own room and shut the door.

"That's one thousand shillings, which buys food for the next week or maybe some clothes," said Wanjiru afterwards, flourishing a bunch of notes and smiling in triumph as she returned to help Ellen, before tucking the notes carefully into her bra.

Then they all went to the church storeroom and found a used and somewhat tattered mattress, some bedding and a selection of old clothes. The place was run by a severe-looking Wakamba woman, who said little and offered no solace.

During the next few days Joe and Ellen walked around the area. They established the location of the communal toilet and the one water tap that serviced the area. Wanjiru lent them a bucket. "You can collect water from the tap and wash in the kitchen."

#

According to Ellen's calculations, Wanjiru had three or four male visitors every day.

"You seem very calm about how you deal with these men," she observed.

"Yes. Mostly they just want sex, with no trouble. The same people come here every week, so I have got to know them a little bit. Occasionally a man has tried to beat me. Once I had to ask the reverend to sort the matter out, but mostly there is no trouble and there is more money doing this than working in a shop."

Ellen was tempted to run back to Ol'Kalou, but quickly rejected the idea. It was not practical, as they would continue to be harassed by Mr Kigoro and they were already running short of food. She also hoped that her precious Joe might do much better in the city. Through all the trauma and despite many sleepless nights, and after her initial shock at the circumstances in which she now found herself, she did not shed a tear. She had Joe to bring up and look after: Joe, her pride and joy. She would just put up with the situation and do what she had to do, as Kikuyu women had done from time immemorial.

Occasionally Ellen allowed herself the luxury of remembering the happy days she had enjoyed, living in Ol'Kalou: the excitement and joy of being told by her father she was to marry Wacheera. The fun they had all had during the wedding ceremony when she was the centre of attention during the noisy and energetic affair, lasting three days. And the anxiety of giving birth to Joe at home in her hut, helped by one of the local women.

"I have asked the dresser who used to work for the *M'zungu Doktari* in Ol'Kalou to come to the birth," Wacheera had told her. "The *M'zungu Doktari* left with all the other *Wazungu*, and this is the best we can do." There were some difficulties with the birth and the dresser told her she probably would not be able to have any more children, so now Joe was the one important person in her life.

Despite his reservations regarding the reverend, Joe did also show signs of being excited with his new situation. He told her that the cottage was better than their hut in Ol'Kalou, though he missed the animals. Although, by the time they had left, most of them had died or been stolen. He also said there were dozens of children roughly his age running about the area, with whom he could make friends. Initially he shared Ellen's bed, but that soon had to change...

Three days after they had settled in, Reverend Mweleli reappeared. "The boy will stay in the kitchen," he said.

By this time, Ellen knew what was expected of her, so she removed her dress and lay on the bed.

The reverend struggled out of his cassock, dropped a pair of boxer shorts to the floor, scrambled out of his car tyre sandals and without any further ceremony mounted her. Within minutes he had done his business and was ready to leave.

She disliked the experience but had decided this was the only way forward for her and her son.

The reverend was not violent and was quite matter of fact about the situation. "Wanjiru has told you how everything works here?" he questioned, as he got back into his clothes.

Ellen nodded uneasily.

"You can have two months rent free in this place; after that you will pay me five thousand shillings a month. Wanjiru will have explained how you can earn money to pay the rent?"

Ellen nodded.

"Some people I know will come here..." Ellen nodded again.

"Any questions?"

"School, is there a school for Joe?"

He laughed. "I will tell you at the church service on Sunday. You will always come to the service every Sunday."

Ellen reflected on her few brief visits to St Peter's in Ol'Kalou, without any enthusiasm. She had time to slip on her dress before the reverend opened the door of the tiny room to let himself out.

Joe, from the expression on his face, must have heard the squeaking of the bedsprings and the reverend's grunting noises, and known exactly what the man was doing to his mother.

"This is how we live now," was all she said, looking away, as that would have to be the end of it. What other choice did they have?

That Sunday, Wanjiru came bustling into Ellen's room, dressed smartly and wearing a pretty hat. "We must hurry, the service starts at nine sharp, but if we want good seats, we must get there half an hour early." Wanjiru looked Ellen up and down. "I can lend you a dress, but soon you will be able to buy nice dresses yourself."

Ellen spent a few minutes with Wanjiru and soon emerged in a very pretty dress, much to Joe's surprise.

With many others, they were then seated in the church fifteen minutes before the service started. Ellen was intrigued, she liked the singing and the fact that the service lasted almost two hours.

Afterwards, Wanjiru gave Ellen several packets of condoms. "You must ask the men who come to see you to put on one of these. Tell them it is for safety, so they don't get any disease. Not all of them will agree and some may want to pay you less..."

Ellen was very nervous when, a few days later, her first paying customer appeared at the door.

The man smiled. "The Reverend Mweleli sent me here," he said uncertainly. "He said I could lie with you."

Ellen looked at the youngish man dressed in a military uniform. She nodded. "Yes, for one thousand shillings you can lie with me." She surprised herself with the confident and straightforward way in which she dealt with the issue. She was happy that Joe was away on an errand. She let the man into her room and removed her dress, while the man completely undressed himself, somewhat to her surprise. After about forty minutes it was all over and the man paid her the expected one thousand shillings.

"I will be back next week," said the man. Ellen nodded.

The following day another man appeared at the door. This time Ellen was more confident and welcoming. She pretended she enjoyed the experience and soon she became altogether much more relaxed about what she did. In time, she treated her visitors as customers and made sure they took pleasure in the experience. Soon she had to get her customers to agree to visit her at agreed times so there were no clashes.

In time, as with Wanjiru, she had three or four customers every day, except on Sundays when she, together with Wanjiru and Joe, attended Reverend Timothy Mweleli's Unity Wesleyan Church of God. Her customers all paid her the expected one thousand shillings.

Very quickly Joe seemed to understand what the 'paying customers' were doing to his mother. Initially he was distraught. "Is this how we live now?" he yelled at her. "What would your father think? Is there not something else we can do to earn money?"

Ellen knew that she had to stand up to Joe. "What! You want to go back to that place in Ol'Kalou and starve? Do you want me to be killed like your father, then what will you do? I am here to do our best and to make sure you have a better life... I'm doing this for you!" She looked fiercely at Joe, knowing she had no other options.

Joe backed off and, after a few weeks, based on her apparently welcoming behaviour, he seemed to accept that this was their new way of life.

#

Joe did not accept their new way of life. "It is my duty to see if I can help her get away from this business; that is what I must do," he said to himself.

His first task was to make friends. Luckily, he made friends easily. During a very energetic pick-up game of football played in the street, he bumped into another Kikuyu boy, Waweru, slightly older than he was. Joe, as always, excelled.

"Where did you learn all those tricks?" Waweru asked.

"We played football most days at home in Ol'Kalou."

"I can show you round. Where is Ol'Kalou?"

Joe shrugged. He didn't really know. "Near Gil-Gil?" Waweru then took him on a short trip round the nearby area.

"There is the school, and the shops, one of which is run by a Kamba man, who charges too much – he is a friend of the man who runs the big church, Reverend Mweleli."

"I know Mweleli," Joe said quietly.

"Where do you live?" Joe pointed.

"My mum says those stone cottages were built by the *Wazungu,"* Waweru said. "We also rent from Mweleli." Which told Joe that Waweru's mum was also a prostitute beholden to the reverend.

Much of the rest of the slum was made up of a vast array of shacks, built from bits of timber, old packing cases, corrugated iron and even cardboard. They covered much of the open ground left in Kibera.

"Avoid the dogs," Waweru advised, as they passed a couple of mangy-looking animals.

The so-called roads in the suburb were just unmade dirt tracks, which often became washaways in heavy rain. There was little traffic. Joe had no reason to think this was unusual. He had hardly ever seen a tarred road until his and his mother's journey to Nairobi.

Whilst their own cottage had an unreliable electricity supply, Waweru pointed out that there were all sorts of 'informal' arrangements for power here, with what in many instances looked like bird's nests of wires hung from electric poles, and then extended to bare wires leading to nearby shacks. This turned out to be the source of the frequent fires in the shacks, especially during the colder weather. Many of the residents of Kibera used wood for cooking, purchased from the dozens of vendors in the slum. Other people used charcoal, which came in bags from the rural areas.

"Charcoal," Joe muttered to himself, "Kigoro again."

The wood and charcoal fires in the slum, as well as the authorities' attempts to collect and burn the piles of accumulated rubbish, meant the whole area was usually enveloped in a pall of smoke, creating a penetrating stench. Occasionally a strong wind provided some relief, blowing the smoke away to be quickly replaced with more smoke.

#

Ellen found that, as well as paying Reverend Mweleli his five thousand shillings each month, he expected her to satisfy his sexual needs whenever the mood took him.

Wanjiru became a good friend and they shared many confidences.

"It seems that the reverend does not pay you any visits as he does with me?" Ellen asked her one day.

"Not anymore. You are new and young, but he has many other places like this and people are coming from the rural areas all the time. At some stage, he may move on to another woman; when he does don't let him try to put the rent up, which is his usual trick."

Soon they found they had ample money with which to buy groceries, and paraffin for their small stove. Ellen taught Joe how to pay any surplus into her *M-Pesa* account on her mobile phone so she could buy new clothes for herself and for Joe from time to time.

After a few weeks, Reverend Mweleli asked Joe to join the choir, which he refused to do. In fact, in time Joe persuaded many of his football companions to boycott the choir and this sometimes extended to the church services as well.

In contrast, Ellen enjoyed the singing at the reverend's church and she learned the words of most of the songs from Wanjiru. She loved dressing up for Sunday services now that she could afford a new dress, and the contrast this afforded to the other days of her week. She did not understand anything about the God the reverend kept talking about, saying to Wanjiru, "This God they are talking about, I do not understand. Everyone knows the Kikuyu God, Ngai, lives on Mount Kenya. When they talk about this other God I always pray to Ngai; I know I must not upset him, otherwise he will keep the rain away and send locusts, or maybe he will make other bad things happen."

Wanjiru nodded. "Same for me. I always pray to Ngai when I am in the church. I think this God they talk about is a *Wazungu* God, anyway he is from *Ulaya* and knows nothing of the people here and this place. The reverend used to be part of a *Wazungu* church before. I think they must have taught him about this God. Anyway, this *Wazungu* God is better than a Kamba God. It seems that Ngai doesn't mind so much about the *Wazungu* God; I don't think he would like the Kamba God, if they have one."

#

One Sunday, when Ellen insisted they both attend, Joe and his mother settled themselves into their favourite seats in the church, when she suddenly went quiet and started shaking.

"What's the matter, Mum?' asked a worried Joe.

"Kigoro. It's that man Kigoro, see, in the front row there. We must not be seen. We will move to a seat at the back," said Ellen hastily. Without too much fuss, a still shaking Ellen and Joe moved to a seat at the back of the large church.

"Which one is Kigoro?" asked Joe.

"The man in the middle there, the one in a smart suit and dark glasses." Joe got up.

"Where are you going?" asked Ellen.

"I am going to have a good look at our famous Mr Kigoro," said Joe.

"No, Joe, he is dangerous, a bad man, be careful."

"He has never seen me..."

Joe got up and walked to the front of the church, carrying a few hymn books to make his presence look official. The reverend was just about to start the service. Joe found the man Ellen had described and handed him one of the hymn books. "Welcome to our church," he said to Kigoro in Kikuyu, who just nodded. Joe had a good look at the man.

"I will not forget that face in a hurry," he said to himself. "I will get you one day, that I promise on the life of my father," he muttered to himself as he walked back to join his mother.

Another man had also been sitting next to Kigoro, a short balding man, who wore a rumpled suit and had a less than clean tie on. The man had had a thoughtful but dour expression on his face. They were chatting, obviously comfortable with each other.

'A Luo,' thought Joe. 'Unusual. There must be money involved.'

Joe asked around after the service and one of the more knowledgeable women told him, "That was Mr Otieno Boniface. He runs a very big transport business, called Nyanza Transport."

'Ah, the charcoal,' thought Joe, 'but why come to the church service? It seems that the reverend is involved in more than just forcing women to lie with men for money...'

With Kigoro being a Kikuyu and Otieno a Luo, there had to be something much bigger in the wind than just transporting charcoal from the rural areas to Kibera. The information was stored away in his ample brain.

#

Early on at one of the regular church services, Ellen asked the reverend how she could enlist Joe into the local school.

"I will meet you and Joe at your house at nine tomorrow morning. We can then go to the school and I will help get Joe enlisted."

The next day, the reverend walked with them to the school. They went directly to the headmaster's office and without knocking he just entered the man's office. "New recruit for you, headmaster," he boomed.

The head was wholly intimidated by the reverend and within minutes Joe had been enlisted with all the requisite forms filled in. He was taken to a classroom and introduced to Phyllis, his new teacher, who Joe was pleased to see, was Kikuyu like him.

#

His mother left Joe in the school classroom and he was ushered to a desk. Joe already had a small pencil case, which contained two pencils and a red crayon – something he had brought from Ol'Kalou.

Joe looked around. The situation was much the same as the schoolroom he was used to, there were a few young children aged about six in the class, but all age groups up to fifteen or sixteen were represented, with an equal number of boys and girls. He liked Phyllis, a young woman of about twenty-five. She was smartly dressed; she was also very patient with her classes but did not tolerate any rudeness or ill-discipline.

During the first few days, Joe kept his mouth shut and listened to everything that was said. Attendance was somewhat desultory, much the same as it was in Ol'Kalou.

Over a few weeks, Joe began to participate more, with the encouragement of Phyllis. He felt most comfortable with arithmetic, which he had always been good at. During the breaks he teamed up with Waweru and they usually engaged in an energetic game of pick-up football, where Joe became a favourite, as he was one of the best.

Another of Ellen's customers, realising she had a young son, brought her a book of children's stories in English. Joe was intrigued. Initially he was unable to read it but, with Phyllis' help, soon got to grips with it. He asked Ellen to see if she could encourage other customers to bring him books, which some of them did. Joe was fascinated by the whole new world this opened up for him.

With Phyllis' help, by his eleventh birthday, he had taught himself to read properly, and although he had a strange accent, he had a rudimentary grasp of English and could just about converse in the language. Phyllis said Joe was bright, as he had no difficulty in dealing with anything that came up at school even though he attended barely fifty per cent of the classes. Phyllis helped him where she could. For his age Joe was big and strong; he was a natural leader, his physique helping to ensure his peers tended to look up to him.

Joe no longer had much time to reflect on how his life had changed since he and his mother had left Ol'Kalou. He could see that his mother, far from being the happy person she had been on their little plot, was now wholly in the thrall of the reverend. She was sometimes impatient with Joe and slapped him occasionally, something she had never done before. Joe was confused. There was no hint from anyone – the reverend, his mother, or others in the community – of what was right and wrong. It seemed that survival, at any cost, was what drove people. He kept his eyes and ears open and his mouth shut.

The school was completely chaotic, catering as it did for kids of all ages and abilities from five to eighteen. The older children, almost adults, were put in the lower classes because often they had had no education at all until they arrived in the city. They felt inadequate as a result and tended to bully the younger children. Assaults and rape were commonplace and were almost never dealt with satisfactorily by either the school authorities or the police. The community dealt directly with the more serious matters, with Reverend Mweleli taking a lead role in meting out punishment, which usually consisted of a severe beating; this of course helped recruit church members, which also helped to enhance his reputation.

Joe had several heated discussions with Ellen about the inconsistent nature of his attendance at school. "Don't you see, education is the one thing that could help you get out of this place." She waved her arms around.

Joe, having listened to Ellen and after some thought, concluded, despite his desultory attendance at the school, that education was indeed one possible route out of the degrading situation in which he and his mother found themselves.

So, after about a year at school, Joe had a conversation with Waweru. "We waste a lot of time here at school because it is not very well organised. Some of the teachers don't even come to school each day. I am going ask Phyllis if she could teach me at home for, say, two days a week..."

"Won't she get into trouble if she does that?"

"I don't think so. I overheard two teachers discussing this. That is what they do. If I can persuade Phyllis, will you join? I will ask her what she might charge, but it will be less if there are a few of us."

Ellen gladly agreed to give Joe money to pay Phyllis, to teach him privately, when he raised the issue with her. "At last," she said, "you are taking notice of what I told you before."

"You do not need to go to the school every day anymore," Joe said to Phyllis one day after school, when he managed to get her on her own. Phyllis was just packing her things up, still in the schoolroom. "Many of the other teachers take one or two days off every week."

She looked at him sharply

"I can come to your house, and you can teach me and maybe some others, without all the trouble and noise we have at the school." Joe offered to pay her two thousand shillings (twenty US dollars) a month.

Phyllis agreed and spent two days a week at home, teaching Joe and half a dozen other children privately.

Joe still attended the school on other days when he could. Attracted by his football skills, Joe had gathered and became the leader of a group of young boys from the school, all about his age. But he still worried about his mother and wanted to help her with money.

One of her early customers, Karanja, seemed to be very different and more approachable than the others, who were often military officers, priests or politicians. He was a short, wiry Kikuyu, who wore scruffy clothes stained with food and pungent with *bhang* (marijuana) smoke. It gave Joe an idea, and he decided to provoke a conversation with the man.

Karanja sat on the bare mattress in their room looking Joe up and down. Ellen was in the kitchen making tea, which she had promised to Karanja.

"Some of my mother's friends bring me books so I can learn," Joe told him. "Maybe you could bring me a book one day?"

"Don't they give you books at school?" Karanja asked.

"Sometimes, but they are not very interesting."

"Ask your mother for money – you can then buy all the books you want for yourself in the city."

Joe looked at Karanja. "I would like to earn money for myself, not take money from my mother. How do I do that? I think you could help me."

Karanja didn't respond, instead looked at Joe curiously, almost in another light. "I will think about what you propose."

Next Joe spoke to his friend Waweru on the subject. "This man Karanja. I know he sells *bhang* (marijuana*)..."* Joe said.

"So, what. What is your idea?"

"We can sell *bhang* here in Kibera. I think I can persuade Karanja to provide the *bhang.* Our friends at school can sell it..."

"Okay," said Waweru. "Let's talk to them."

#

His mother also had an idea about how to make their money stretch further. Once they had settled down in Kibera, she and Joe made several trips on the bus into the city, the first one with Wanjiru, who showed them the ropes; the two bus trips to the best supermarket.

"All my friends think this is the best place," she told them.

"See here," Ellen exclaimed after they had spent a few minutes in one of the larger supermarkets in the city, "these prices are much lower than that thieving Kamba shopkeeper, Mutua, charges in Kibera. Maybe we could shop here instead of with him."

Joe's flexible schooling arrangements gave him some extra time and he agreed with his mother that he could do most of the shopping. As often as possible he took the bus to town and bought what was needed at a much lower cost. On one occasion Joe had done the shopping and was sitting on the bus on the way home thinking about some homework that Phyllis had given him, when a man in a nearby seat got up, just as the bus was arriving at the next stop and stood next to Joe. Joe took no notice; the bus was often crowded. But as the bus came to a stop, the man grabbed Joe's bag of shopping, leapt off the bus and ran away.

Joe jumped up and tried to follow the man, but he tripped up on a loose paving stone and fell heavily. By the time he got up the man had disappeared and the bus had moved on.

A bruised but otherwise undamaged Joe forlornly explained to Ellen what had happened.

She shrugged. "Maybe shopping in the city is not such a good idea, after all," was her only comment.

After that Joe shopped in Mutua's store. He soon worked out ways in which he could buy a few items from the small local shop and then put one or two extra items into the bag without paying for them and without the proprietor noticing, which reduced the value of any savings he might have made by shopping in the city, especially after he took into account time and bus fares.

On one occasion, however, a few months after he had taken responsibility for shopping, Joe was in a hurry and was less careful about hiding what he had stolen from the shop.

The proprietor stopped him at the door, "Here, you little *mwivi,* let me look into that bag of yours."

Joe tried to escape but was held firmly and dragged round to the back of the store, out of sight of other customers. Mutua emptied the bag onto a table. He quickly isolated the stolen items and looked at Joe. Without saying anything more, Mutua grabbed a handy stick and spent five minutes giving Joe a severe beating.

Joe's screams attracted the attention of other people, who came to rescue him. He was eventually thrown out of the store with none of his purchases. Joe was battered and bruised but nothing was broken. His mother patched him up as best she could.

When Reverend Mweleli next appeared, she told him Joe's story. "I will speak to the man," he promised Joe.

Joe recovered but nothing was done. He purchased the household's groceries from another store and was more careful about hiding stolen items. Meanwhile Joe seethed with resentment about his treatment and what was obvious to him was that the man Mutua was overcharging.

Determined to get his revenge, Joe spent days carefully watching the store from every angle. Mutua's was set up as a supermarket, although it was quite small, and had only one cash point. Joe thought that was to save the expense of additional employees. The windows were all heavily barred, as was the door when the shop was closed.

To start with, Joe could see no weakness in anything Mutua did, so he tried to understand the pattern of the man's life. Once or twice a week a car was parked outside the shop and left there for no more than half an hour, after which his nemesis would appear and drive off. Joe then set a plan. He had determined that the car was left only on certain days of the week. He gathered up twenty of his group and they left school early, went to the vicinity of the store and waited.

As predicted, the car was delivered and within seconds Joe had inserted small sticks into the valves of the two rear tyres of the vehicle, which quickly deflated. The group waited and, as Joe had told them, Mutua emerged and hopped into the car. One of the groups then ran up and knocked on the driver's closed window, pointing at the rear tyres. To start with the boy was ignored but he became more insistent and eventually Mutua jumped out of the car to have a look. The boy then grabbed the ignition keys and made a run for it, with Mutua in hot pursuit. This was just what Joe had planned. Most of the group then chased after Mutua.

Three others, one with a bottle of petrol Joe had given him, poured petrol over the car's windscreen and roof. Another boy poured more petrol over its interior. A third boy with a crowbar Joe had given him, managed to remove the car's petrol cap. A lighted rag was thrown into the interior of the car and the small group ran away back to school. Soon there was a merry blaze inside the vehicle, which quickly engulfed the car; the windows shattered and the petrol tank exploded.

The group led by Joe caught up with Mutua just as he was about to catch the boy with the vehicle's ignition key. Joe tripped Mutua up with a stick. He fell to the ground semi-conscious, having banged his head on a stone; the children proceeded to beat the man half to death. Joe, in particular beat him several times on his buttocks in revenge for what he had done to Joe. Joe spat on him, as did all the other children. Joe felt satisfaction that he had got some revenge on the man but wondered if there would be any repercussions.

The group then scattered and, as with the other members of the gang, returned to school. The car key was discarded. The whole episode took less than three minutes. The car blazed away fiercely, to be finally extinguished by the fire brigade who arrived about thirty minutes after it started. Mr Mutua was tended by two of the personnel from the store and taken to hospital.

A few days later the police, having interviewed Mutua, came to the school and took Joe to the local police station. Before they did anything or asked any questions, they took Joe to a cell in the basement of the police building. One of the policemen held Joe down while another beat him severely with a *kiboko* (hippo hide whip), saying things like: "So you stinking Kikuyu, if you want to attack one of our people, this is what you will get."

Joe knew they were Kamba and, if the boot was on the other foot, he would have behaved in exactly the same way. He screamed as they expected him to, but he was determined not to say anything. They eventually cleaned the blood off his back and buttocks and took him upstairs to question him. He remained silent despite the many questions; then he asked them, "When did this happen?" They returned to the basement cell and repeated the beatings.

Joe collapsed and the police started to panic: "If we kill him, you will all be in big trouble." The senior sergeant had just arrived on the scene and was concerned about the way Joe had been treated. After much discussion the police eventually gave him the date of Mutua's attack.

"I was at school all day; go and ask Phyllis, my teacher," a very jittery Joe told them.

By this time, Ellen had been to the school and had seen Phyllis, Joe's teacher. She also went to see the reverend, who did nothing for a few days, since it seemed to suit him to have Joe beaten and locked up.

The reverend eventually went to the police station and persuaded them to at least visit the school and interview some of the teachers. Phyllis told them in no uncertain terms that Joe had been at school for the whole day in question.

"But that child often spends half his day away from school," the Kamba police constable protested.

"How do you know that? I suppose Mutua, that lying fool of a shopkeeper, told you," argued Phyllis, "I see Joe every day and he is a very diligent pupil. I remember that day, the day you are talking about, very well, Joe was here all day."

The police eventually reluctantly dropped the case and released Joe.

Ellen was horrified to see the condition Joe was in and spent several days tending to his wounds. She wondered what to do and asked Wanjiru.

"Just leave it alone," was her advice, "it's no good going to the police and the reverend won't do anything. If I know anything about Joe, he will find a way of getting his own back on all of them."

She was right. Joe was determined to make sure the proprietor of the store was aware that he had orchestrated the assault and that he would continue to take his revenge for the beatings he had received from both Mutua and the police.

So, once he had recovered sufficiently, he and three other boys from the school often went into the store. "Look this *posho* is much more expensive here than in Kariuki's store just over there. Maybe we should tell everybody to buy their *posho* at Kariuki's," they would shout.

Mutua, still showing the signs of his own beating, did nothing, he merely glowered at them from behind the safety of the counter.

They repeated this two or three times a week. While the children were there in the store many of the customers quickly left, not wanting to be involved in any trouble. Most were aware of the beatings. When asked why he didn't involve the police when he caught people stealing, Mutua answered with a laugh, "They do nothing; all they want is something for themselves. I did that a few times, when I caught people stealing; nobody was punished. All that happened was that I had to give the police things from the store. I was also made to wait in the police station for many days and my business suffered because of that. I can do nothing if I catch people stealing or I can punish them myself, those are my choices."

#

After the boys had been harassing Mutua for some weeks, Mutua came to see the reverend. "Can't you stop them doing this to me; it's ruining my business." He explained what the boys were doing.

The reverend had some sympathy with Mutua, a fellow Kamba, although, with an instinct for self-preservation, he had distanced himself from the whole episode of Mutua's beating and Joe's treatment by the police. He came to see Ellen. "I want to speak to your son Joe," he told her.

"Why, what has he done now? He's not here at the moment, but I will send him to you if you want."

"You must come with him."

"I am too busy earning money, so I can pay you rent," answered Ellen, "I will send him when he comes back from school."

Chapter 3: Joe

Having recovered from his beating by the police, Joe eventually paid a visit to the reverend as his mother told him to. He went on his own, despite the reverend's request for Ellen to accompany him. He was decently dressed in a khaki shirt and a new pair of khaki shorts. He had tennis shoes on his feet. There was little evidence of the severe beating he had endured, although he still limped – something that he was determined not to make visible to the reverend.

He knew he would be regarded as a supplicant and as such would be expected to present himself at the kitchen door of the reverend's house.

"He asked to see me, I'm no supplicant," he said to himself.

So, he boldly knocked on the front door of the mansion, which was opened by the reverend's wife. She was very surprised but before she could say anything Joe said politely in Swahili, "My name is Joe; the reverend asked to see me. I know he is here; I saw him come in."

After a brief hesitation, instead of telling Joe to go back and make his entrance in the usual way for supplicants, through the kitchen, she let him in saying, "He's in his study; I'll show you the way."

The reverend was seated behind a large desk. Joe was left standing.

"Reverend, my mother told me to come and see you," Joe said again, before the reverend could open his mouth.

#

The reverend looked at Joe, tried not to show his irritation that the boy had taken so long to come and see him, as he had ordered. He would do what he could to help the shopkeeper Mutua, a fellow Kamba. He had tried, not very successfully, to put Joe's beating at the hands of the police right out of his mind.

Here was this young boy only about thirteen years old, although the reverend had noticed that Joe was growing and filling out. His servants had told him that for his age Joe was very strong, he looked bigger than his age would suggest. However, his mother was a prostitute who lived nearby, in a grubby little room, at his pleasure; this boy should therefore have been completely in his power and should be here as a supplicant; but despite himself the boy scared him. He knew Joe could see right through him and thoroughly distrusted him. He wondered what, short of killing him, he should do.

"Joe," said the reverend in his most authoritative voice, "I need to speak to you about Mr Mutua – you know, the man who owns one of the shops not far from here."

Joe just nodded.

"Do you know who I am speaking about?"

"Yes."

"Do you know why I am speaking to you about him?"

"No."

The reverend tried not to show his irritation at the monosyllabic responses emanating from Joe. "Mr Mutua was beaten up recently."

Joe shrugged but said nothing.

"Don't you have anything to say about that?"

"No."

"Mr Mutua says you were involved; he says it was you who tripped him up, so others could beat him."

"I was at school when Mr Mutua says all this happened. Ask the police, and the teachers at the school."

The reverend was surprised Joe didn't mention the beatings he had received at the hands of the police. 'Most children would be whining about that beating,' he reflected.

"So, you had nothing to do with this?"

"No."

"Do you know who was responsible then?"

"No."

"Mr Mutua says that you go into his shop and tell people that prices are higher in his shop than other shops in the area."

"Mr Mutua charges very high prices for the things in his shop. I check them all the time. What I say is the truth. If you like, Reverend, you can go with me and we can check prices together."

"Mr Mutua is very angry with you."

"Many people are angry about his high prices, many people."

The reverend could see this talk was going nowhere and was about to dismiss Joe when he had an idea. So, he changed the subject. "Joe, there are a few things that need doing round the house here; I can pay you something for doing them, if you like."

Joe frowned, as if sensing a trap; then his expression shifted. Probably realising it was an offer too good to miss. "What things?" he asked.

"Washing dishes, some sweeping, maybe some work in the garden. The kitchen staff will direct you."

"How much will you pay me?"

"One hundred shillings an hour."

Joe shook his head. "Three hundred," he said.

The reverend was mightily taken aback. He was unused to bargaining with anyone, let alone young children. Generally, he dictated terms. He almost cut the discussion short, but that would mean that he, Reverend Timothy Mweleli, would lose an opportunity to get this vexatious child into his power. "One- fifty," offered the reverend.

"Two-seventy-five." Joe smiled, enjoying himself.

"Two hundred."

"Two-fifty," said Joe.

"Two-twenty-five. That is my final offer."

Joe hung his head, disappointed. "Okay," he said. "Start tomorrow," the reverend said.

"After school."

"After school," agreed the reverend. He knew perfectly well that with Joe, along with most of the other kids in the school, attendance was desultory, but he couldn't object.

#

Joe couldn't believe how well he'd negotiated a higher price for his work for the reverend. He'd feigned disappointment, but inside had been elated. For two hours each day after school, he attended the reverend's 'mansion' as he thought of it, worked hard and made himself useful.

The house far exceeded anything Joe had ever experienced. It had several bedrooms upstairs as well as two bathrooms, a separate toilet upstairs and one downstairs.

Joe asked one of the more sympathetic kitchen servants to show him how the toilet worked.

"You put the seat down and sit here," she laughed. "When you have done your business use this paper to wipe your bottom." She indicated the soft, white toilet paper on what Joe saw was a roll next to the toilet seat. Joe usually found an old newspaper or a leaf for the purpose. "You then flush the toilet, like this." She pulled a chain connected to a small tank above the toilet and everything was flushed away. "You must not leave a mess anywhere and when you only need a pee you must lift up the seat."

Joe was intrigued and compared it to what he was used to: the communal stinking pit toilets in the township or just doing his business in the street. It was unbelievable.

"The reverend and his wife do not like servants to use these toilets, so only use them when they are both out." She laughed again.

"What's this for?" asked Joe, looking in a room next to the toilet.

"This is where they wash themselves," she explained. "It is called a bath." She put the plug in and ran the taps for a minute.

"Do you wash here?"

"Again, only when the family is out."

Joe compared this arrangement with the bucket of cold water he and his mother had to make do with.

Downstairs there were several large rooms, one with a big table and chairs, which he was told was where the family ate their meals. Joe was used to sitting on the floor in their tiny kitchen and eating with his hands or, if he was lucky, using one of the few spoons he and his mother owned.

There was also a large room with what Joe could see were soft, comfortable-looking chairs; there were books in rows along one wall and pictures hanging in frames, a feature that was new to Joe. The reverend also had another room, the room where he had first been to see him, almost the same size as the room with soft-looking chairs, with a desk that Joe could see he used for writing.

Also provoking Joe's interest was a telephone, something Joe had never seen in his life before, although he was quite used to using his mother's mobile phone. In this room, there were also books in shelves and pictures on the walls. Joe got to know this as the study. The kitchen was well appointed with an electric stove and there were several rooms for servants at the back. All the servants' rooms were larger than the room he and his mother shared.

The reverend had three children, two boys older than Joe, and one girl who was younger. They all attended a school in the city and wore uniforms. Initially they ignored Joe, until one day when he was working in the garden, he rescued a football for them from a nearby tree.

"Maybe we should play a game," he suggested. "You two boys against me and the girl."

The boys looked at each other and agreed – anything to put the girl in her place. "I am Adam and my brother is Moses. The girl is called Mary," said the elder boy.

They set up makeshift goals at each end of the garden using Joe's and the boy's shirts.

Joe let Adam score the first goal, hoping he would then relax a bit, which he did. Joe then smiled at Mary and whispered a few words, "Just go where I point," he said. Joe, then using his considerable skills, outfoxed the two boys and twice put Mary in a position to score.

Adam then scored another goal, but Joe made two desperate saves from shots by the two boys, and then when they were all just about exhausted, he dribbled the ball into goal for the winner.

Even though they lost, the boys were amazed and delighted, as was Mary.

After that day they often played football, but only when the reverend was out, as he wouldn't approve of his children mixing socially with servants.

Joe's experiences helped him grow up quickly. He soon had good, but vague and distant memories of his early days on the plot near the village of Ol'Kalou, but he had put all that behind him. He had memories of helping his father, who taught him to milk the cows and tend the goats. But now the thirteen-year-old's sole focus and reality was Nairobi's slum Kibera, the tiny squalid room where he and his mother lived, and the constant stream of men who lay with his mother and paid her money – most of whom were better dressed than the residents of Kibera, which gave Joe a view that there was another better life out there.

'Something for the future,' he thought.

He knew his mother's activities would do neither of them any good in the long run, although the people in his life behaved as if it was all quite normal.

On one of his regular visits to Ellen, Karanja finally spoke to Joe again about earning money.

"A few weeks ago, we talked about you earning some money for yourself. If you want to earn money maybe you could sell this?" He produced a paper bag, which contained a quantity of *bhang*.

"How do I do that?"

"Roll the *bhang* into these cigarette papers and then sell them." There was a collection of cigarette papers included in the packet.

"There is another man, Munyao, here, who sells *bhang*; maybe he won't be so pleased when he sees me selling yours."

"Maybe I can help with that," said Karanja. "First you must tell me how you are going to move it."

"I have ten or twenty children at school who will help me."

Karanja's eyes lit up at this information. "Shouldn't they be at school?"

"You must tell me what I must pay you."

After a few minutes haggling over the price Joe was to pay to Karanja, there was further discussion about what Joe should charge his end users – but Joe declined to discuss what he would pay his sellers.

"You now need to sort out this man Munyao," said Joe, "who is Wakamba. I think he works for Mutua, the owner of one of the shops here?"

"Do you know this Munyao? Where does he live?"

"I'll show you. We need to go for a short walk."

He soon stopped and pointed out a man, lurking almost unseen in the shadow of a nearby building, just round the corner from Mutua's shop. Occasionally the man was approached and a furtive exchange took place.

"Munyao," Joe said. "Okay, we'll fix him."

"When should I start?" asked Joe.

"I will tell you in a few days."

Within a day Joe was unable to find any trace of Munyao. He soon had word from Karanja that Munyao had moved to another area. Joe had already approached all of his gang. They met in the street in the same place where Munyao had operated. "You all remember that a few weeks ago we talked about selling *bhang.*" He looked around and they all nodded. "You will buy this from me," he said giving them a price, "and sell it on." He gave them a selling price. "What I have given you is a small amount to start with. I can give you more when you have sold all that."

"Is this legal?" asked one of the smarter boys.

Joe had no thoughts regarding the legality or otherwise of what he was doing, neither did he consider rights and wrongs of selling drugs, or what harm that might do to the community at large. He had not been taught to think of such things.

"Look at us," said Joe. "We have nothing. And look around you – people like Reverend Mweleli, they all live in big houses and drive big cars. Will we ever live like that? The answer is a big fat 'no'. That is unless we do something about it, and this is our opportunity. Make the most of it. Those who don't want to help can go away now." Joe looked around and focussed on one or two members of the gang, whom he knew might hesitate. There was no movement, probably because they all knew they would be shunned if they walked away and would be bullied and possibly beaten up. Belonging to the gang was in itself some sort of protection for them and indeed their families.

Joe was never tempted to smoke any *bhang* himself, mainly because that would reduce the amount of the drug he had to sell.

Meanwhile, Joe diligently kept up with Phyllis and his private lessons, but he altogether stopped going to the school in Kibera. An extremely nervous new boy, Patrick, was introduced to her private lessons by Phyllis. Initially Joe's attempts to engage the boy were fruitless. Patrick just turned away. Joe found out later from Ellen that Patrick's mother had recently started to rent one of the reverend's rooms. He persuaded Ellen to speak to the woman to see if Patrick would eventually open up to him, Joe.

Joe waited while Patrick spent a few minutes alone with Phyllis and then walked with him on the way home. They talked of the lessons they had just had with Phyllis. Joe knew some of Patrick's story. "You are new here, you seem to have smart clothes, what brought you to this place?" he asked sensitively.

Patrick looked at Joe and then burst into tears. "My father had a good job with the railways, but then he lost his job. We don't know why. My father then went away, he said he was going to find a way to get to *Ulaya,* where everything is much better than here in Nairobi. But we haven't heard from him for six months, so we had no food and our house was taken away. So, my mother is..." Patrick turned away crying.

"How was your father going to get to *Ulaya?"* asked Joe.

"He told my mother that there were some Luo who would take him to Juba and then he would find a way to go further. He took all our money. He said when he got to *Ulaya* he would get us to come and join him."

"Do you want to make some money, to help your mother?" asked Joe.

Patrick nodded.

They went to Joe and his mother's room and he took out a small paper bag from under the bed. He gave Patrick the bag, which contained some *bhang*. "You can sell this." He gave Patrick a price. "When you have done that you can pay me. I have many of the boys at the school doing this for me. You can make money this way to help your mother."

Soon Patrick became a very committed member of Joe's gang.

#

The kitchen staff at the reverend's mansion were all Wakamba and might have been expected to exploit Joe, a Kikuyu boy, but Joe worked so well and diligently, saving them what they considered to be unpleasant drudgery. Joe always did a thorough job with anything he was given, and he was always cheerful, so with his charm and firmness, he soon had them under control. He learnt a few words of their language, which he didn't find difficult, since the Kamba and the Kikuyu share a Bantu ethnic root.

Most importantly he kept his eyes open: he made a mental note of all the visitors. If he didn't know who a visitor was, he asked the kitchen staff. One of the big surprises was the weekly visit of General Mwangi wa Kariuki, a Kikuyu. He always stayed an hour, had a cup of tea in the reverend's study, and was then escorted personally back to his chauffeured limousine by the reverend.

The general was always in uniform. He was only five foot six but well built, and Joe could see he kept himself fit. Joe thought the man was in his early fifties.

"If you like, I can serve the tea for General Kariuki," Joe said to the cook.

"Hm, yes, he's a Kikuyu like you," she said. Clearly the staff attitude to Kariuki was that he was just another wretched Kikuyu and they had no interest in the man, although he was a general in the army, so they were easily persuaded to allow Joe to serve the tea as he had requested, in the reverend's study.

#

General Kariuki was fortunate that he had been brought up in Kikuyu, a small village on the northern outskirts of Nairobi, and very close to a school that had been set up by Presbyterian missionaries to fill in what they correctly saw as an enormous gap in what the colonial government was providing in the way of education for the African population. Kariuki was bright and the teachers at the mission had persuaded his parents to enrol him. He was a diligent pupil and always did well. His father was a sergeant in the Kings African Rifles, but despite his obvious abilities, he knew that he could never be promoted beyond the non-commissioned ranks. All the officers were British. With the advent of *Uhuru,* Kariuki's father persuaded his son to join the army. Initially he had objected saying:

"Like you, I can never be promoted to become an officer, all the officers are *Wazungu.*"

"No. You are wrong. I speak to the *Wazungu* officers all the time. They tell me that now we have *Uhuru* this will change. Soon the army will encourage us Africans to become educated and then we can become officers. The British officer training place in *Ulaya,* called Sandhurst, is already taking people from Uganda and other places. It's too late for me but not for you..."

So Kariuki, having done well at school, applied and was accepted as an officer cadet at Sandhurst. Again, he did well there and after graduating was commissioned as a Second Lieutenant in the Kings African Rifles in Kenya. Some years after *Uhuru* this became the Kenya Rifles and the rapid 'Africanisation' of the Rifles made sure that Kariuki was at the forefront of promotional opportunities. Within fifteen years he had been promoted to the rank of 'general'.

With the advent of the Moi Government on the death of Jomo Kenyatta, Kariuki noticed that corruption levels increased dramatically everywhere. Although unmarried, because of his exalted rank he was put under pressure from his wider family to sponsor children at school and university. He was also asked to provide facilities such as schoolrooms for his home village. None of this was possible on his salary, so starting small he stole what he could. He eventually became responsible for the acquisition of material for the Kenyan armed forces where he soon found a secure and now well-trodden path to immense riches.

To the general's delight, after his first visit Joe exchanged a few words in Kikuyu with him, asking him how he liked his tea. The general and Mweleli usually sat in comfortable chairs, with a small coffee table between them in the reverend's study. He liked the boy and appreciated his efforts.

#

To start with, Joe only served the tea during the general's visits, but after a while, as both the reverend and General Kariuki became used to his presence in the study, he started to listen to conversations more carefully, and deliberately found things to do in the study to prolong his stay, like pouring additional cups of tea and handing round slices of cake.

Initially, the meetings between the pair were merely to establish trust; nothing of substance was discussed. After a while, from the snatches of conversation, Joe determined the two were getting involved in something substantial. They were now used to Joe being around, so he stayed unobtrusively in the background without leaving the room. As far as Joe was concerned, it was obvious that the pair assumed he would not understand anything that was said. They spoke in a combination of Swahili and English, since neither one of the pair spoke or understood the other's native tongue.

"Hii Pesa, na toka wapi?" (where does the money come from?) asked the reverend.

"Some soldiers are paid but they are not in the army," responded General Kariuki.

Joe did not understand this until the reverend, laughing, clarified the matter for him, "Ah so, the soldiers' wages, who are not in the army, are paid into your bank account."

The general nodded with a satisfied smile. "The *Wazungu* are also happy to pay commissions when the army places a big order..." he added.

The reverend laughed appreciatively. "The *Wazungu* taught us many things. This is much better than a grass hut and a bicycle," he said, waving his arms around indicating his house.

He continued, "So you need some help in transferring cash from here to a safer place, such as London."

"Yes."

Joe did not know where London was, but he was determined to find out.

The next meeting was quite different. The study was reorganised to accommodate a larger group. As well as General Kariuki, also present were Kigoro,

Otieno Boniface, who Joe remembered ran a transport business, and a large, fat *M'zungu,* who Mweleli introduced as Sir Oswald Higginbotham.

"I run a wealth management business in London," said Sir Oswald when he was introduced. He was dressed in a lightweight beige suit and colourful tie, clearly not remembering that Nairobi, sitting at six thousand feet above sea level, had a temperate climate.

Kigoro and Otieno were dressed in what Joe could see were new dark suits.

Mweleli was dressed in his usual cassock and dog collar but was wearing shoes. He opened the meeting, conducted in English for Sir Oswald's benefit. Unbeknown to the reverend, Joe now had a basic understanding of the language – enough to understand what was being said.

"This could be the start of a substantial opportunity for all of us," he said. "As you may know, many people from Kenya, Uganda and Tanzania as well as other places like Ethiopia, South Sudan and Eritrea want to leave and go to live in Europe. There is quite a lot of money to be made, facilitating this."

During the discussion Otieno said, "I can provide transport, of course."

"We can provide finance, and we have already helped Mr Otieno here with funding for much of his fleet," offered Sir Oswald, "you will need more trucks. We will of course be happy to provide the appropriate finance."

Otieno nodded.

"What would the charges be?" asked General Kariuki.

"One thousand per person, from here to Juba, another two thousand from Juba to the Libyan coast, and then another one thousand five hundred to cross the Mediterranean, all US dollars of course," answered Otieno.

"Where do these figures come from?" asked the general.

"These are the established rates, I have checked them again this week from my sources, and I have already taken some refugees to Juba," said Otieno in an irritated voice. "Only a few, here and there. There is room to increase the numbers."

"Where do the people get this sort of money?" asked the general.

Otieno shrugged. "There are many ways to make money, especially for women..." He looked down, knowing full well that a portion of the reverend's income came from the women to whom he rented rooms.

Kigoro appeared to be out of his depth, saying nothing until late in the discussion. "I can provide people; you can pay me one hundred US dollars for every person I introduce. I will send you the one thousand US dollars, less my one hundred dollars for each person. Maybe just send an empty truck to me in Ol'Kalou. I will tell you when I have more than twenty people, who have paid and want to go."

Joe looked at the man and thought to himself, 'I'll bet you anything he will charge the people something for introducing them to the scheme, unannounced to the wider group of course.'

The reverend and the general made similar offers.

Sir Oswald said nothing. His cut was to come from charging a premium for the money he lent the scheme on top of the premium he was already charging Otieno. Also, if these people sent money to the UK, he would probably be able to help manage any funds that accumulated in this way. He also expected to share in any profits made from the scheme.

#

The *bhang* business developed in leaps and bounds, much to the delight of Karanja and of course Joe. With his crew of Waweru, Patrick and recently joined Koinange and N'guku, they had managed to recruit sixty children from school to join their scheme. During one of their meetings N'guku had told the group: "My father was a mechanic in a garage in the city, he taught me many things about repairing vehicles."

"Where is your father now?"

"He was killed in a car accident; that is why we are now here." N'guku would not discuss what his mother did, but Joe knew she rented premises from the reverend.

Koinange was very reticent about talking about what had happened to him. "My father died," was all he would say. Joe knew his mother worked as a nurse-aid in a local hospital. Joe had found him to be quietly efficient.

Joe had short weekly meetings with his crew, sometimes in Ellen's room, at other times just in the street. Joe kept meticulous records of the quantities of *bhang* given to each crewmember and he balanced that against the cash that was returned to him. On one occasion there was a discrepancy with Waweru. Joe, with all the other crewmembers present, worked through everything thoroughly with Waweru. Eventually it turned out that someone had stolen some of Waweru's stock. "What is the fairest way of dealing with this?" Joe asked the group.

"He must pay," said Patrick. "No, not fair," added N'guku.

Joe listened to the various points of view in the group.

"We all believe Waweru's story, don't we?" He looked around. There were nods from the rest of the group. "The fairest thing is for Waweru to pay half and we will split the difference between the rest of us." Joe said. "Any objections?"

There were none. This drew the group closer together.

They all knew that Patrick was keen to see if he could find out what had happened to his father. "There are many people trying to go north to a country called Libya, and from there you can get a boat to go to one of those European countries, where everything is much better that it is here in Nairobi."

Nobody said much, but they all looked at Patrick.

Joe had never heard of Libya, but he would find out more. He also thought of the conversation in the reverend's study with Otieno, General Kariuki, Sir Oswald and Kigoro on this very subject.

Joe also approached Phyllis, his teacher, to participate in his *bhang* scheme. "Surely this is not legal," Phyllis had objected.

"No, but this is just a law the *Wazungu* introduced," Joe had countered. "A law preventing us from doing what we have been doing for thousands of years before the *Wazungu* came here." Joe was just parroting what Karanja had told him, but as always, he was very convincing.

Phyllis said she was intrigued, especially since all his suggestions had made her considerably better off, with no apparent adverse consequences. She also said he was very bright and had managed the school curriculum and anything else she chose to introduce with ease, as well as all his other activities, the extent of which she admitted she only had an inkling. In the end, she agreed to his scheme and, with Joe's urging, recruited several of the other teachers at the school.

Joe's relationship with Karanja continued to develop. He was by now Karanja's biggest distributor. So, he wondered if somehow, he could persuade Karanja to marry Ellen and get her out of what Joe considered to be their degrading situation. He decided to ask him, "This *bhang* business is making all of us quite a lot of money. Would you consider marrying my mother if she stopped her business with the Reverend?"

Karanja looked slightly surprised at the suggestion, coming from what he saw as a fourteen-year-old child. He said nothing though but merely nodded.

'I suppose that is a yes,' thought Joe.

However, Joe had not reckoned on interference from Reverend Mweleli.

#

Mr Mutua paid Reverend Mweleli a visit. "This Joe, that terrible child who sometimes works for you here..." Mutua was standing in front of the reverend's desk.

Mweleli was grumpily sitting behind it. He was getting tired of Mutua's complaints. "When he can spare the time from school."

"The boy never attends school anymore. He has chased away my man Munyao. You know the one who sells *bhang* for me on the street."

"Really? So, without the *bhang*, how will you pay my cut?"

"I don't know. He has all these *shenzi* Kikuyu children selling *bhang* in the street. I think I will tell the police."

"No, no, don't go to the police. They will just want money from you, it's the same when you complain about people stealing from your shop. Leave it to me, I will deal with Joe."

"I just want Munyao to be able to sell..."

"Yes, yes," said the reverend impatiently.

When Joe next appeared at the mansion, the reverend told him to come and see him in his study. Mweleli sat behind his large desk, Joe was left standing.

"Mutua has told me you have chased his man Munyao away, and your people are now selling *bhang* in the street here," said the reverend without wasting any time. As always, their conversations were conducted in Swahili.

Joe didn't respond. "Well?"

Joe remained silent.

"Maybe I should go to the police. They will lock you up."

Joe shrugged. "The police will never touch me again, not after the last time." The reverend looked at Joe warily. "So, who is selling this *bhang*?"

Joe looked puzzled and remained silent.

"The police may become interested, if Mutua goes to see them. I have influence with the police," continued the reverend.

"I have one or two close friends," Joe said, "selling small amounts of *bhang* to people they know. Maybe Mutua is still doing the same thing? His man Munyao has moved to Pumwani, I think."

"One or two?" shouted the reverend. "Nonsense, it must be more than that."

Joe was quite calm. He asked in quiet voice, "How much do you need to influence the police?"

"You must pay five hundred shillings a week," said the reverend.

#

Joe knew none of the money he paid the reverend would go anywhere near the police, and he was also certain he would be able to get Karanja to pay him at least double what he had now agreed to pay the reverend, since they would be able to extend their business without interference.

The meetings with General Kariuki continued, sometimes with one or two of the other conspirators, but often with just the general. On one of the meetings with just General Kariuki, the reverend had an Indian man, a Mr Das, in attendance for part of the proceedings.

"Shouldn't we ask the *toto* to leave the room?" asked Das in English. assuming Joe wouldn't understand.

"Not necessary," answered the reverend. "He's just an ignorant refugee from the rural areas, he won't understand any of this. He doesn't understand English."

It took all of Joe's will power not to look at the reverend. 'The bastard,' he thought, 'he just sees us as poor people he can exploit for his own benefit.'

The reverend explained to General Kariuki, also in English, "Mr Das imports things, so he is able to make payments to overseas banks without rousing suspicion. He can therefore send money for you to banks in England or Switzerland... I pay him twenty per cent..."

Joe realised the reverend had deliberately set the figure high, knowing he would be able to negotiate a kickback from Das for himself, if Kariuki accepted the plan.

Das spent thirty minutes in the meeting explaining that he was able to transfer money to London or other places outside Kenya, because he was a registered importer. He then left.

Joe was detailed to show Mr Das to his car, which was parked in the small church car park nearby.

After witnessing some of the conversations between the reverend and General Kariuki Joe began to realise how little he knew of the wider world: banks, computers, sending money to *Ulaya* (England or Overseas) and so on; he didn't even know where *Ulaya* was. He also understood that the conversations he had witnessed, if he could find out more, would put him in a very powerful position, since what they were discussing seemed possibly underhand or at least dishonest, otherwise why would they need to deal with the issue in such a clandestine way.

He could also see that the general seemed to be taking more than a passing interest in him personally, and he wondered how he might exploit that.

Most of the time the reverend escorted the general to his limousine, which was always parked immediately outside the reverend's mansion. At the conclusion of the meeting with Das, the phone rang when the time came for the general to leave, so with the reverend answering the phone, Joe swiftly opened the door, handing the general his braided cap. He escorted the man outside and opened the vehicle's rear door as he had seen the reverend do. With his heart in his mouth, he said, in Kikuyu, to the general, "The school here is very bad; maybe, sir, somehow you can help me learn other things?"

The general looked up, as he seated himself in the back seat of the limousine. He seemed surprised but quickly grasped what he thought was on offer, so he responded, before Joe shut the car door. "This car will come and fetch you at 3pm on Wednesday next week, outside Mutua's shop."

Joe then knew he had hooked his prey; it was just a question of how he would manage to exploit the situation.

Joe returned home in a jovial mood. He could see before he arrived that there was a commotion in the shack he shared with his mother. He found Ellen in a very bad way, being looked after by Wanjiru. Her face was all bloody and it looked as if she had a broken arm.

"What happened?" he yelled at Wanjiru, who was trying to look after Ellen. "Beaten up," was the terse response. "Hospital, she needs to go to hospital." Joe rushed out. He ran to Waweru's home, which was just round the corner.

"I need help," he yelled at Waweru. "My mother has been beaten up, find one of the others."

Waweru needed no further prompting. Joe returned home.

Ellen was lying on her bed, barely conscious.

"The others are coming to help," he muttered to Wanjiru. "Who did this?" Ellen somehow managed to give them a name, which Joe did not recognise. 'Must be someone new,' he thought.

A few minutes later Waweru and Koinange arrived in a battered old car driven by Karanja. Wanjiru explained what had happened, "We need to take her to the hospital," she said.

"My mum works at the Lucy Kibaki Hospital, which is a half hour drive from here. I will phone her," said Koinange.

They all managed to pile into the car, with Ellen in the front seat.

They were met at the hospital by Koinange's mum, who helped them through the admissions process. Ellen's arm was ex-rayed and she was given a bed in a large women's ward. Joe spent the night in the waiting room, periodically visiting Ellen. By the morning she seemed to be much improved, but Joe still hung around.

Joe was furious. Getting his mother away from the reverend and Kibera had now become a priority.

Joe briefly mentioned his arrangement to meet General Kariuki to Waweru, who had now become his confidant, someone with whom he could discuss ideas.

"I am hoping to be taught about computers and banks and things like that," offered Joe.

"What do you think the general wants from you?" Joe shrugged.

"Sex, he will probably want sex..." Joe looked uncomfortable.

"Waweru," Joe eventually responded, "we just need to find a way out of the mess we are in, with our mothers having to lie with men for money. I will do whatever needs to be done... if having sex with the general is part of that, then so be it."

"He may want you to suck his dick."

Joe nodded. "I know."

"This is the same sort of thing as your mother is doing... and my mother."

"Yes. I hope it will lead to something that helps all of us, instead of just allowing us to live, however poorly. I will tell you and the others what happens. If it leads nowhere then we will find something else." He then added fiercely, "I work in the reverend's house. You and I have no chance of living like that unless we do something else. I do not know what that 'something else' is. Yet."

#

"You must call the police," Wanjiru and the others urged Joe when he eventually returned home. "We know who did this."

"He will just bribe them and tell them he was somewhere else. I don't trust the police," said Joe.

Joe waited until the next day, to see if the reverend would take any action. He had continued to visit a still very battered and bruised Ellen in hospital and then arranged for Karanja to pick her up in his car when she was released. Nothing had been done after a week, so Joe, during one of the days he was due to make his regular payment to the reverend, approached him in his study saying, "Sir, you will know that one of my mother's customers beat her severely a few days ago..."

"Yes," was the reverend's short response.

"I know the identity of the man. He is a well-known businessman from Pumwani."

There was no response from the reverend. "Well, sir, what are you going to do about it?"

"I can't be expected to deal with matters like this. If I did, I would not have time for anything else."

"Sir, if you don't do anything about it, I can assure you I will, and you will regret it. For example, one of the things I will do is to make sure that there are no visits to any of the women who rent rooms from you. I know who they all are, of course."

A week later there was a grisly murder of one of the shop owners from Pumwani, which had a great deal of publicity in the local press. This was the same man who had beaten up Joe's mother.

When Joe next visited the reverend to pay his dues, he thought. 'I wonder if he will say anything about the murder in Pumwani.'

There was silence for a minute or two. Joe stood his ground, waiting for some sort of response from the reverend.

While he was waiting, he thought to himself, 'I have now managed to completely turn the tables on this evil man. From being wholly dependent on the priest for accommodation and with Mum being forced into prostitution to earn a living, I have moved to a position where the wretched man is now a partner in my *bhang* business. I also know quite a bit about his private life, involving transfers of money to *Ulaya,* unknown to him...'

Eventually the reverend looked up at Joe, saying, "Are you now satisfied?" Joe nodded and left.

For his own safety Joe realised he might soon have to distance himself from the reverend and Kibera. He had already had discussions with his mother and Karanja about Ellen giving up being a prostitute. From a previous conversation, Joe assumed that Karanja had already agreed he would marry her if she did that.

PART 2

Chapter 4: General Mwangi wa Kariuki

Joe was waiting outside Mutua's shop as instructed by the general. It was a week after Ellen had been beaten up and she was now resting at home, unable to work. The driver recognised him, but was surprised when Joe opened the front door of the luxurious Mercedes limousine and hopped in. Joe smiled at him and greeted him in his native Kikuyu. The car drove off.

"My name is Joe," he said to the driver.

"I know. General Kariuki told me. You can call me Elijah."

"Are you a friend of General Kariuki?"

"No, I am just his driver, but I come from the same village as the general."

"How long have you been his driver?"

"Ten years."

"That is a long time. Is that all you want for yourself, just to be a driver?"

"The general looks after me and my family very well. For a rich man like him it is his duty to look after all the people from our village. The village helped him to be educated and then he was sent to some place in *Ulaya,* to learn to be a soldier. When *Uhuru* came and the *Wazungu* left, he became a general in the army."

Joe remained silent for a few minutes. 'Mr Kigoro should have looked after my family the same way,' he thought. 'Instead, he killed my father and now we are just like the many other poor people here in Kibera. I will get educated and maybe I can become rich like the general and then I can get back our land.'

There was some further desultory conversation during the hour-long journey, in the usual heavy traffic, from the Kibera slum to the salubrious suburb of Muthaiga, north of the city.

Joe's eyes nearly popped out of his head when they arrived at the general's residence

A pair of heavy wrought iron gates opened as if by magic. Elijah laughed, showing Joe the button underneath the car's dashboard that he pressed to open the gates.

General Kariuki's mansion was even more imposing than the reverend's. The limousine made it's way up the long gravel driveway to an enormous three- storey house made of brown brick. Joe could see the house was partly covered by some sort of plant, which Joe later learnt was called ivy. The house was surrounded by beautifully mown lawns interspersed by well- kept flowerbeds. Joe could see at least three gardeners on their haunches, busily digging away. Joe marvelled at the sight – he had never seen anything like it. Two guards with fearsome-looking rifles patrolled as he was ushered in through the kitchen entrance, where he found a cook and three house servants, all Kikuyu. Joe greeted them shyly in Kikuyu, making them smile. He noticed a look of sympathy on their faces, making him even more determined that somehow this general was going to help him whether he liked it or not. The reaction of the general's servants made him more apprehensive. He was given a mug of hot, sweet milky tea and a thick slice of white bread smeared with strawberry jam, to keep him occupied during what turned out to be an hour's wait.

Then he was ushered into the general's study. The general locked the door, putting the key in his pocket. "Well, Joe, you wanted me to teach you some things. Can you tell me what you are interested in?" He smiled and sat down on a settee at one end of the room, which was part of a matching set, with two other comfortable chairs. The study was beautifully furnished: at one end was what Joe found out later to be a valuable antique desk. There were shelves full of books with confusing titles, and pictures on the walls. The room was carpeted from wall to wall. There was a small ensuite at the rear of the study.

Still standing Joe answered, "Sir, the school in Kibera is not very good. There are no computers, so we can't learn about those things and I know nothing about banks. I am sure you will be able to help me learn some of these things."

"Of course," answered General Kariuki, "I can teach you many things, but first you are going to do something for me." He removed his trousers and placed them carefully aside, exposing his large erection. "You will suck me until I tell you to stop."

After his discussion with Waweru, Joe was not altogether surprised and he did what he was told. The general was now lying on the settee making grunting sounds. 'Can I really go on with this,' Joe thought to himself. 'How long will it take to get what I want from this situation?'

"Do not stop," the general growled, "you will swallow it all, I do not want to make a mess." The general lay back for a few minutes when he was finished, with Joe, still fully clothed sitting beside him.

Joe managed to hide his distaste for what he had had to do. He managed not to be sick as he swallowed the general's emissions. He looked at the general.

"You will go now," said Kariuki. "Elijah will take you back to Kibera. Come back next week, there will be a man here who will teach you what you want to know." Kariuki stood up, putting his trousers back on before he unlocked the door.

Based on his discussion with Waweru and the looks of sympathy he received from the general's kitchen staff, Joe had known what would be expected of him when he visited the general, but he was horrified by the experience. He wondered if he would be able to continue. On the way back to Kibera he pulled himself together.

'This is the opportunity of a lifetime,' he thought. 'I have not been hurt in any way. What I am doing is horrible, but it is not dangerous. I have got myself into this position and I must just make the most of it. Opportunities do not come along like this very often.'

Joe managed to persuade himself that as far as he was concerned, he had got himself into the situation here in the general's house and he would exploit it for all it was worth, a price he had to pay, he thought, to somehow climb the ladder – whatever that meant. He was planning to gradually improve himself and get his mother away from what he now knew was a degrading business. If this was what he had to do, then so be it. As far as he could see, it was merely another example of the rich and powerful exploiting those 'lesser mortals', as they seemed to regard him and others like him. It made him all the more determined to rise above the position in society in which he found himself.

'I wonder how long this will go on?' he thought. 'No, I will not let myself think like that. I will always do what it takes, whatever the consequences.'

A routine was established: Joe was picked up by Elijah twice a week, once to service the general and once to spend an afternoon with a middle-aged Indian man, named Desai, who was an employee of Das, the man introduced to the general by the reverend. They met in the general's study, with the door open. Desai taught Joe everything he knew: how to operate the computer on the general's desk together with many of its functions, such as how to send e-mails, how to transfer money from bank to bank. He also taught him everything he knew about banking and finance and some basic accounting.

Soon Joe was given a backdoor key, which he used sparingly, but he found he was able to gain access to the general's mansion when the general and his household were away, something that happened periodically.

When the general was away on official business, the servants normally took the opportunity of his absence to go home to families in rural areas. On two such occasions Joe explored the garden looking for any weaknesses in the apparently impregnable fortress. He eventually found an almost totally overgrown path behind the borehole and water tank, which was close to one of the boundaries of the property, which led out to a small road behind the general's establishment.

'Probably created by the original *M'zungu* owner, for when they didn't want anyone to know he or she had left the premises. From the look of things, nobody in the general's household knows anything about this.'

#

A few weeks after Joe's lessons with Desai had started, General Kariuki happened to walk into his study as Desai was packing up. Joe had already left.

"How is the boy getting on?" asked the general.

"I have never seen anyone like him," answered Desai enthusiastically. "It's as if he was born to it, he just absorbs it all like a sponge. Where did he come from?"

The general shrugged. "He's just an urchin from Kibera. He told me he was born in Ol'Kalou, wherever that is."

"Well, he is very clever and incredibly determined. Most certainly worth cultivating."

#

During the twice-weekly meetings with Joe's intimate gang regarding the *bhang* business, Joe always shared with Waweru, Patrick, N'guku, and Koinange what had occurred in the general's mansion and what he had learnt.

What Joe had decided to put up with, as far as the general was concerned, meant his respect from the rest of the gang grew and grew.

"Do we have 'a way out of this mess' yet, as you have always described it?" Waweru often asked Joe.

"Maybe," was Joe's usual answer. A plan was forming in his mind, involving Kigoro and Otieno and moving to Juba.

Joe was also interested in the general's house, as well as his garden. Sometimes when he was alone there, he would explore it.

The general had explained briefly when Joe had showed some interest: "This mansion was originally constructed by a *Mzungu,* a Sir Northcott Macmillan who eventually became Governor of Kenya. I bought it when most of the *Wazungu* left. I have had a person from *Ulaya* help me restore it to its to its original condition."

On the ground floor, the mansion had an extensive kitchen, a very large dining room able to seat about two dozen people, which was attached to an anteroom that the general told Joe was used for pre-dinner drinks. Joe had no idea what that meant. There was also the large study, which Joe had become familiar with, as well as another bathroom and two toilets.

On the first floor was the general's extensive bedroom, with a large ensuite; private television room, in which stood another desk with locked drawers; two other bedrooms and a bathroom.

The top floor was almost a separate residence, with a small kitchen, two bedrooms and a bathroom. This place was occasionally occupied by members of the general's extended family. Joe's attendances were usually cancelled when these visits took place.

On one of his perambulations, Joe found a set of keys in a drawer next to the general's bed. This eventually led to Joe discovering a Glock 17 pistol and some ammunition, in a locked drawer at the back of a wardrobe in the bedroom. The weapon was covered in dust, indicating that it had not been touched for many years. Joe stole this weapon and later took it into the Ngong forest, a bus ride from Kibera to the south, and found out how it worked.

He then practised using it often; yet was also worried that the general might miss the pistol. For weeks after he had taken it, he was very apprehensive before visits to the residence, concerned he would be accused of stealing it. Nothing was ever said on the subject, however. Still, knowing it might in future be traced back to the general's house, he managed to swap the weapon, through a contact of Karanja, for a short barrelled.32 Beretta automatic. He had no idea of any law requiring him to license the pistol. He made certain through Karanja that he had access to more ammunition should he need it. Again, he found a place in the Ngong forest to test the weapon and to make sure he knew how it worked. Although Karanja was aware that he had the weapon, he asked him not to mention anything about it to Ellen.

Joe now clearly understood how some of Kenya's senior fellow citizens lived. Their lifestyle was in stark contrast to his own situation, with his mother being exploited by an apparent pillar of the church. Despite the success of his *bhang* business, he knew that unless he did something more about the situation, he would progress no further than where he currently found himself.

The reverend's meetings with the general, now every two or three months, always included Otieno, and sometimes Kigoro, with Sir Oswald on the phone. There was an occasional report of a truckload of refugees being taken to Juba, which everyone was pleased about.

"Why don't we step this up a bit?" said Sir Oswald during one meeting. "Perhaps one or two trips a month..."

"We must be careful of the police," answered Otieno. "I don't want to attract attention. There is this European Union agency called Frontex, which is beginning to be a nuisance, they work with local police to help identify activities like ours..."

The meetings in the reverend's study, so vastly different from his and his mother's lifestyle, and now General Kariuki, made Joe even more determined to somehow put himself in a similar position to the reverend and the general. He had no wish for revenge; the knowledge he gained merely created an insatiable appetite to get to the top of the heap by any means possible.

By this time, Joe had one hundred pupils at school and several teachers, who had been recruited by Phyllis, selling *bhang* for him.

During one of his weekly visits to pay the reverend his *bhang* money Joe said to him, "My mother has decided to leave Kibera. She is getting married and will now be living in Westlands." In point of fact, she had already left and they were both living in Karanja's house in Westlands.

The reverend was about to say something when Joe added, "She has asked if you would conduct a marriage service for her and her husband. She likes coming to the Unity Wesleyan Church of God, which she will continue to do every Sunday."

Again, before the reverend was able to say anything Joe added, "She will invite all the women you rent rooms to, as well as many others, so it will be a very big service." He didn't think he needed to add that that would materially help to promote the reverend's church.

The reverend appeared mildly irritated. "I normally charge a months' notice to those renting my rooms. But it sounds like a huge wedding, to which I could also invite guests." He didn't mean it as a question. Joe knew he intended to invite his various co-conspirators such as Otieno and the general, showing them how wide his influence was.

"Then it is agreed."

Joe also invited Phyllis and several other teachers from the school to the church service. Phyllis was also asked to the party at Karanja's house after the service.

The wedding was held a month later on a Saturday at eleven in the morning. The church was full and there were people patiently waiting outside. In the days before the wedding Joe had asked the reverend if he could set up the external loudspeaker system and the large screen to relay the service to people outside the church.

"The Church holds about five hundred people. I expect there will be about another five hundred people outside the church as well," Joe explained.

"You are able to organise such a crowd?"

"I am."

The reverend just looked at Joe, saying nothing; though there was an acknowledgement in his expression that accepted their relationship was about to change altogether.

Joe got his crew of Waweru, Patrick, Koinange and N'guku to get as many people to the service as they could manage; they in turn asked their *bhang* customers to attend if they were able.

"This is about much more than my Mum getting married," Joe told his crew. "This is about us, and I mean all of us getting out from underneath these people who exploit us, so we can find our way to a better life."

The reverend had persuaded General Kariuki and Otieno Boniface to attend. At Joe's request he did not mention the occasion to Kigoro.

"Why don't you want Kigoro to attend?" he asked Joe.

"My mother blames Mr Kigoro for chasing us away from our plot in Ol'Kalou. For this reason, she is scared of him."

"Alright, he lives far away anyway."

Sir Oswald had politely declined the reverend's invitation. "While I would very much like to attend an African wedding, I'm afraid that the date is not very convenient," he told the reverend during their phone call on the subject, which Joe overheard. "Thank you indeed for inviting me, much appreciated."

Because of the large gathering Joe, with his mother on his arm dressed demurely all in white, had trouble in pushing their way through the large cheering crowd.

Karanja was waiting anxiously at the front of the church, dressed in a suit and tie, which is what he, Ellen and Joe had agreed he would wear. Karanja had never in his life been inside a Christian church. One of his equally confused other dealers had agreed to be his 'best man'.

As a smiling Ellen and Joe made their way down the aisle, the recently installed church organ belted out 'Here Comes the Bride'.

Reverend Timothy Mweleli, looking his magnificent best, even wearing shoes for the occasion, stood at the front of the church grinning. He assumed that the general and Otieno, sitting in the front row, were suitably impressed. The reverend used his own version of the Anglican marriage service conducted in a mixture of Swahili and English.

"We are gathered here to witness the marriage before God of God's daughter Ellen to Karanja Githaiga. If any man knows any reason why this marriage should not take place, come forward now or forever hold your peace."

The Church was completely silent during the full minute the reverend stood there with his eyes closed, adding to the drama of the occasion.

As Joe had requested, led by the choir, they then sang two of Ellen's favourite hymns.

"Who gives this woman...?"

Ellen let go of Joe's arm and moved forward.

"Do you take this woman to be your wedded wife, forsaking all others?"

"I do," responded Karanja.

"Do you take this man..."

"I do," responded Ellen.

"The ring," muttered the reverend, which was duly produced and given to Karanja.

"Repeat after me," said the reverend, looking at Karanja.

"With this ring, I thee wed..." until finally the reverend said, "I now pronounce you man and wife."

Soon the ceremony was over and Karanja, Ellen, Joe and the best man retired to the sacristy to sign the register.

A smiling Ellen emerged from the church on Karanja's arm, again to the ringing tones of 'Here Comes the Bride'.

Guided by Joe, a group of Karanja's cronies had laid out trestle tables outside the church and were busy serving sweet milky tea and buns to the multitude.

"A bun and a cup of tea to anyone who wants it," Joe instructed.

A smiling Ellen and Karanja moved easily among the crowd. Ellen was popular having 'shown the way' away from a poverty-stricken life in Kibera to something better; the dream of almost all of the congregation. The pair spent more than an hour before Joe came to fetch them. Joe's crew had organised several vans to take about one hundred 'special guests' to Karanja's small house in Westlands, all of whom had gathered outside the shack that she and Joe had occupied for all the years they had lived in Kibera.

The reverend spent time moving among his flock, then took the general and Otieno to his nearby mansion for lunch.

The party at Karanja's was more of a traditional Kikuyu wedding, with people coming and going for three days. Joe, with help from Karanja's cronies, had brewed a very large quantity of traditional *pombe* beer and there was a copious amount of food, *ugali* (mealie meal cake), meat and vegetables.

At about eleven at night, Joe persuaded the drummers to desist. "So, we don't upset the neighbours." They started up again the next afternoon.

During the celebrations, Ellen went into the house and found an unoccupied corner. Joe sought her out during this period of reflection. "I was just thinking of my marriage to your father, Wacheera," she said, wiping a tear away. "And the joy of that occasion." She briefly reflected on their wedding, when she was a sixteen-year-old virgin, just making her way in the world.

Joe, with little understanding of what she was going through, said nothing but just hugged her. "You still have the title deed for the land we owned, don't you?" he asked eventually.

She nodded.

"Make sure you keep it safe. One day I will get the land back and I will deal with that horrible man Kigoro."

Ellen said nothing.

On the third day of the celebrations, the police came knocking. There were only a few guests remaining, and Joe and his mother had retired to their respective beds hours earlier. Karanja was well known to the police so they treated him respectfully. He offered them what was left of the *pombe* before he was persuaded to shut the party down.

"Your mother had a very big wedding," the general said to Joe during his next visit.

"Yes. Thanks to Reverend Mweleli," answered Joe. "She has attended the Unity Wesleyan Church of God, ever since we came to Kibera. She will always attend the Sunday service there, even though we now live in Westlands."

The general nodded, looked Joe up and down. Now sixteen years old, Joe was over six foot, big and strong from the work he had done in the reverend's garden and the regular games of football he indulged in, in the street and other open spaces in Kibera. He was almost an adult.

A few weeks later, the whole group of the reverend's co-conspirators, the general,Otieno, Sir Oswald on the phone, Kigoro, as well as the reverend himself, again gathered to discuss their people smuggling plan, to again see if, using Sir Oswald's words, they 'could step it up a bit'. Listening to them, this time the germ of an idea came to Joe, which he was reluctant to share with anyone at all.

Joe knew that Patrick's father had tried to move to Europe, but that Patrick had later found out that he was stuck somewhere on the Libyan coast, having run out of money.

First, Joe sought out Das, who he knew from Desai had an office in downtown Nairobi, where he had a display warehouse, promoting the goods he imported. Joe also knew that Das's main warehouse was some way away in one of Nairobi's main industrial areas. Desai had eventually been persuaded to give Joe Das's direct line.

"Please don't worry," Joe told Desai, "your lessons are some of the best things that have ever happened to me. I will tell Mr Das that of course."

"What do you need to speak to Mr Das about?"

"Something very private, it's to do with a friend of mine. It's better you don't know the details." Joe phoned Das from Karanja's house, when Karanja and Ellen were both out, and at a time when he knew Das was likely to be there.

The first few times there was no answer.

Eventually the phone was answered. Joe was relieved to hear the one- word answer, "Das."

"Mr Das, this is Joe Wacheera here. I just wanted to thank you for the lessons you have organised for me with Mr Desai at General Kariuki's house."

"Okay, he tells me you are getting on well."

"Yes, the lessons are very good, sir. Just what I need." Das grunted.

"Sir, I have a private matter that I would like to discuss with you in person. I won't take up much of your time."

"I'm very busy."

"Yes of course, sir, but this is very important and I only need a few minutes."

"What can I help you with?"

"I need to come and see you."

"Can't we just deal with it on the phone?"

"I don't think so, sir. It needs to be face-to-face."

"Is it anything to do with Reverend Mweleli or General Kariuki?"

"No sir, it's personal."

Das sighed. "When can you come?"

"Anytime, sir."

"Shouldn't you be at school?"

"I can get permission to be absent. I am a very good pupil; I get the best grades all the time."

"Okay. Tomorrow at 10am. I can spare you fifteen minutes. Do you know where to come?"

Joe gave Das the address he had been given by Desai. He knew exactly where to go since he had already checked the situation out.

"That's right," said Das.

"Thank you, sir," said Joe as Das put the phone down.

Joe was at Das's offices a few minutes before 10am the next day. Joe knocked on the door.

"Come in," was the grunt from the other side of the door.

"You're early," said Das, who was sitting behind his desk. "I can wait," answered Joe.

Das's office was a small boxy arrangement at the rear of his display warehouse. However, he sported an up-to-date computer, which he was busy typing away at, with one of the latest mobile phones sitting just next to it. He was wearing what appeared to be a new suit. "Yes, Joe, what can I do for you?"

"Like the general, I need to have some money in *Ulaya*," he said. By this time, the *bhang* business was earning Joe at least 50,000 shillings (USD$500) a week.

Das looked at Joe in utter amazement. "Why? Aren't you just a street urchin? How could you have money to send?" he asked.

"Like many people here in Kenya, it seems to be a good idea to have some money outside the country. The reverend does it, the general does it, maybe I should do it?"

"How much?"

"Ten thousand US dollars."

Das looked at Joe in amazement. "Where... okay, that is none of my business. I need twenty per cent if that is what you want."

"Seven and a half."

"What?" Das was astounded.

"I know you take twenty per cent of what the general sends. Some of which goes to the reverend. In my case there is nobody to pay off..."

There was a brief argument before they settled for nine per cent. "How will you get the money to me?" asked Das.

"I can give you a cheque, or transfer it electronically, as I was shown by Mr Desai."

"Cheque will do. At your age, you shouldn't even have a bank account."

Joe just smiled. Karanja had arranged the account for him. "I will have another one thousand US dollars every month. What is the best way of getting that to you?"

"Just transfer it to me electronically. Here, I'll give you the details of the account you should use." Das wrote down the details on a blank piece of paper and handed it to Joe. "No e-mails, just phone me when you have made the transfer."

"Thank you," said Joe.

As with his discovery of the Glock pistol, Joe had sometimes found himself alone in the general's house. With the general away, his servants often took the opportunity to return to their home villages. Joe made good use of this time and after very thorough, often frustrating searches, in the desk in the general's bedroom, he eventually found the details of the general's bank accounts in London, as well as all the access codes. He made careful notes of all the details.

Armed with this information, Joe found an internet café in the central city and with the skills taught him by Desai and the codes now in his possession, he was astounded by what he found. He was very excited but was never going to share this information with anyone else, anyone else at all.

Joe checked several times. The general's primary account had more than one and a half million pounds on deposit there.

On one occasion Joe had had a brief discussion with Desai about how to encrypt transfers of money outside the country. So, he did his research carefully. He found that if he established a VPN (Virtual Private Network) as well as using an anonymiser with a large number of users, nobody would be able to trace who was transferring money and where it was going.

In order to make the system fool proof, he asked Das to open an account in a private bank in Switzerland, which he did without question since Joe had, by this time, become a reliable client. Once the account had been opened, he tested the system by transferring funds to his London accounts. After several attempts and some experimentation, he was able to set a system up that did exactly what he needed.

After that, using a variety of different internet cafés, and using his recently set up system, firstly he managed to open up accounts in several other banks in London, to which he transferred small amounts from his newly opened Swiss account, the account to which Das was now regularly sending money, using the funds that Joe was providing every month.

Again, using the same system, carefully over time he made a few small transfers from the general's account to the new Swiss account. There was never any reaction from anyone resulting from this activity.

During his visits to the various internet cafés in Nairobi, Joe also researched what he knew about *Ulaya.* He was astonished at the variety of overseas countries he unearthed. He concluded that if he were to move away from Kenya, it had to be to an English-speaking country, so England became the obvious choice, since that was where his bank accounts were held.

He also thought about his conversations with Patrick, three years earlier, about his father travelling to Juba and his journey being arranged by a couple of Jaluo who owned a transport business.

"Sounds like Otieno," thought Joe. "He owns a transport business and is keen to take people to Europe."

He thought he would raise the issue with his crew, at one of their regular meetings, now held in Karanja's house. So, the next day, after he had collected the money they owed him and then distributed further supplies of *bhang* to each of them, and after having completed the detailed records, he always kept – of the cash collected and the *bhang* supplies distributed – he raised the subject. "You remember our conversations about how we can finally get away from corrupt people like the reverend and the general?" he said.

"The *bhang* business has made a big difference to us," responded Koinange, "what else can we do?"

"Some of the reverend's friends ship people like us to go to Europe and they are in the process of increasing the number of trips they do. One of them runs a big transport business; he may have had something to do with helping Patrick's father go to Europe. He was at my mother's wedding. Otieno Boniface is his name." Joe looked at Patrick to see if there was any kind of response.

Patrick shrugged.

"Maybe we should pay him a visit, just two of us to start with."

"If we go to Juba and then Europe, what happens to the *bhang* business?" asked Waweru.

"We can sell it to someone else I suppose. But we are not there yet. We must first go and see Otieno."

Joe and Patrick found their way to a large depot near what was now called the Moi Air Force Base. It had a big sign saying 'Nyanza Transport' over the gate. After gaining admission through the gate, they were allowed to wander through what both could see was a very well-organised operation, with large trucks moving in an orderly way through the compound.

They located the small office, up a short flight of metal stairs occupied by the owner of the business, Otieno Boniface, *"Na taka nini?"* (What do you want) he asked rudely in Swahili. He had a dour expression on his face and then the man did a double take. "Don't I know you from somewhere?" He looked at Joe, "Oh yes. Don't you work for Reverend Mweleli?"

"Yes," said Joe, "you were also at my mother's wedding a few months ago."

Otieno was a short fat balding Luo; and as with many Luo his front teeth had been removed, so he could be fed if he was infected with lockjaw, which was a real risk in days gone by. He was dressed in a shabby suit and wore a less than clean tie.

Joe said, "We have been told you are taking goods for the *Wazungu* to Juba. I thought maybe I could help in some way. With people."

Otieno looked at him suspiciously. "What do you mean 'with people'?"

"I know in the past you have arranged for several individuals to join trucks going to Juba," Joe said. "I also know you would like to do this on a more regular basis, although in general you run your business within the law; whereas taking people to Juba is outside the law. I could be just what you are looking for, doing the dangerous work on your behalf. You should not oversee more transports yourself, as it is too dangerous for someone like you. Running people in trucks to Juba is easy money, as long as they get there. Half the country wants to leave and go to *Ulaya*. I can help."

"Okay," Otieno said to Joe, after some thought. "Come back here in two weeks. You will go to Juba with one of my trucks. As well as the goods, we will be taking fifteen women and five children to Europe."

"Both of us please," said Joe.

Otieno nodded. "You will be both be paid one hundred shillings a day, which I will give you when you get back here. Look after the passengers. Ensure they get where they need to go."

"Okay," said Joe. He walked down the few steps from Otieno's office before he said anything to a bemused-looking Patrick. "The most important thing is to understand how all this works and we get to Juba," Joe whispered to Patrick. "Don't worry about the money."

When Joe and Patrick arrived at the depot two weeks later, there was a massive truck loaded up with relief aid supplies, and standing around the vehicle were fifteen women and five children, all of whom were Kikuyu. Joe was relieved to see the vehicle had a fixed covering over the load, leaving space above it. Most of the trucks in the yard had a big bold sign on both drivers' doors saying 'Nyanza Transport'. This truck had no insignia.

Otieno appeared. "Can you drive?" he asked Joe. Joe shook his head. "But I can learn."

Patrick shook his head.

"Do you both have passports?"

Joe waved the document at him; this was something he had acquired, with Karanja's help, during past weeks. Patrick had had a passport for some time, courtesy of his father.

Otieno grabbed both passports and had a good look at them. "Neither of you have been anywhere," he said abruptly.

Joe and Patrick looked at each other. They shrugged, saying nothing.

Earlier he had spoken to the general, who had been none too pleased when Joe had mentioned he would be away for a month. "Why, where are you going?"

"I need to go back to Ol'Kalou to see what I can do to get my mother's land returned to her. There will be many discussions..."

Joe had no intention of mentioning anything about going to Juba.

Chapter 5: Juba

The women and children were loaded on to the truck, sitting atop soft sacks of *posho* (maize meal).

"You too," Otieno waved at both Joe and Patrick. Two drivers hopped into the cab.

Joe had come prepared. He was dressed in a new pair of shorts and khaki shirt, trainers with no socks, and a cloth jacket, borrowed from Karanja. On his back he carried a small pack with a change of clothes and some food provided by Ellen. As an afterthought he had brought a football with him. The Beretta felt warm and heavy against Joe's skin, nestled in the waistband at the back of his shorts and hidden by the flap of his shirt tail.

Patrick was similarly attired, as advised by Joe.

Joe and Patrick helped the women settle down as comfortably as possible. They were scattered all over the load, as there was no proper place to sit. The women wore an odd selection of Western and Indian style clothing. They were anxious about the journey they were about to undertake, and were suspicious of Joe and Patrick who they saw as a couple of irrelevant '*kijanas*' (children) who probably would need looking after as well as their own children, but who would not be able to help them in any way.

Joe then talked to the children. "My name is Joe, what is your name?" he said to a ten-year-old boy, while spinning his football on the tip of his finger. He flicked the ball over to Patrick who headed it back to Joe, who was able to catch it again on the tip of his finger.

The boy was fascinated. Joe tossed him the football, which he was just able to catch.

"Mwangi." He clumsily tossed the ball back to Joe. "You like football?" asked Joe.

Mwangi nodded.

After that the ice was broken and all the children talked to Joe. The women also responded to Patrick and Joe, just as the truck started and lurched out of the depot and down the road.

"*Wapi Chakula?*" (Where is your food?) Joe asked, as the truck left the environs of Nairobi.

Some of the women produced small bundles of food, others looked helplessly on.

"*Maji?*" (Water?) he asked. There was no response.

They drove out of Nairobi and down the escarpment to the floor of the Rift Valley.

After two hours Joe banged on the roof of the cab and yelled, *"Choo"* (Toilet). They stopped near a copse of yellow-green fever trees on the side of the road. The women, with their children, all clambered down from the vehicle and scattered among the trees, chattering excitedly. One of the women in particular had lived nearby and was explaining where they were.

"There is not enough food for all those women and there is no water. You must buy food in Naivasha or Nakuru and provide them with water," said Joe to Okongo, one of the drivers.

"Otieno said nothing about food and water," was the response. This was the first trip of this nature either of the drivers had made. In the past they had been confined to other routes.

"So, you want some of these women to die before you get to Juba in four or five days?"

"Otieno told us we must be there by tomorrow."

"You know that's nonsense; these are people you are carrying, not sacks of mealies. If you were transporting goats or sheep, you would at least give them food and water. Phone Otieno if you have to or I will," said Joe.

Eventually Joe made the call.

"Otieno," the call was immediately answered.

"Joe here. From the truck."

"Is there a problem?"

"Yes. There is no food or water..."

"They should have brought their own."

"They were not told to do that."

"I am not providing food and water..."

"Do you want these people to die? They have paid you to take them to Juba. What is the idea, just to dump a whole lot of dead bodies somewhere?"

"They must go the short way; it won't take that long to get there."

"There is no fuel on that road. You know that; I know that. They must go through Eldoret and Kitale. Surely Mr Otieno, if you are going to take other people to Juba, you don't want to get a reputation for taking people's money and then leaving them to die? What about the other partners in this business – Kigoro, the reverend, General Kariuki, that fat *Mzungu,* who has lent you all that money..."

There was a short silence. "Let me speak to the driver."

Joe walked the few paces over to Okongo and handed him the phone.

There appeared to be a short one-sided conversation. Joe's phone was handed back to him.

Okongo glared at him.

They stopped in the nearby town of Naivasha where food was purchased and water collected

The vehicle trundled on through the rest of the day and the night. Joe made sure they stopped at least every four hours and saw to it that everyone had enough to eat and drink.

At one of the stops Joe said to both drivers, "Otieno said you would teach me how to drive, so maybe you, Odhiambo, can go in the back with Patrick, and Okongo can show me what to do."

They both looked at him with distrust. 'Who was this Kikuyu child, ordering them about?' they probably wondered. The conversation about the food and water and the instruction to go the long way to the border had clearly unnerved them, so they agreed. Once he had been shown the ropes on a straightforward piece of road, Joe was allowed to drive.

"I'm impressed," said Okongo after an hour of driving. "Let me take over for now, though – there is a tricky piece of road ahead."

Joe nodded with satisfaction as Odhiambo, who was then driving, took the main road to Eldoret. Mid-morning on the second day, Okongo stopped the vehicle in Kitale, ensuring there was enough food and water to last the rest of the journey, including the walk around the border post between Kenya and South Sudan. The four hundred kilometres from Kitale through Lokichogio to the border post just beyond the small village of Nadapal took them the rest of the day, with Joe continuing his instruction as a driver for some of the way. They arrived just before the short equatorial dusk set in, stopping five hundred metres short of the Kenyan side of the post. Joe was intrigued with the set-up – the dust, the mass of people and vehicles edging their way towards the barrier and the general air of chaos.

"Everybody out," instructed Okongo. "You can all eat now."

"I will walk with them and one of you drivers must come as well," said Joe. "I will now find a guide."

"You and Patrick can walk. Why do we need a guide?"

"Do you know the way across the border at night?" argued Joe. Okongo looked bemused. "How does this wretched *kijana* know all this?"

Joe then had a quick whispered conversation with Okongo. "The guide will cost us something. If Odhiambo walks with us he can pay the guide the money, which will make Otieno happy. I'm sure he doesn't want Patrick or me handling money. Patrick can then help you get Odhiambo's passport and my passport stamped."

"Why do we need to get those passports stamped?"

"If there is no proof that someone has left Kenya and then entered South Sudan, when he tries to come back to Kenya he won't be allowed through, so he will have to walk round the border post again."

Okongo grunted his understanding and agreement.

He then went to Odhiambo and there was a fierce argument for a few minutes, with Odhiambo pointing at his leg.

Joe just smiled. He now thought he had Okongo on side. If this caused some disagreement between the drivers, that was okay with him.

Joe then wandered around the unregulated crowds looking for someone to guide them; he thought he knew what he was looking for. There was a mass of people, from the many different Kenyan tribes, many women selling food and fresh fruit, often Kikuyu – the most commercial of all the tribes in Kenya. The Turkana women, all with elaborate brightly coloured bead necklaces and head bands, sold trinkets, including some of their elaborate leather work, but other easily recognisable tribes as well. The Luo, often with their front teeth missing, were also there, along with the athletic-looking Kipsigis, and some from tribes he didn't recognise – he assumed they were from smaller tribes based in the desert country of Northern Kenya. Also, the occasional policemen – all Turkana.

After half an hour mingling with the people, he saw a tall, proud-looking Turkana tribesman, with an old but well-kept .303 rifle slung over his shoulder; he was wearing shorts, which apart from the rifle, was his only concession to western civilisation. He had an orange-coloured blanket wrapped round his torso, and he was barefoot. Joe knew that the Turkana occupied most of this part of the semi-desert north-western Kenya and would be familiar with the whole area on both sides of the border. He was also aware of the fearsome reputation of the tribe, so treading very carefully he approached the man.

"*Jambo sana, askari,*" (warrior) said Joe, speaking Swahili.

The man looked him up and down, almost with contempt and was about to walk away.

"Bad rains this year," Joe added, "bad for your cattle."

"*Jambo,*" the man replied reluctantly.

"Would you like to earn some money?" Joe asked.

"What do you want?"

"Some people need to get to the other side."

"How many?"

Joe thought he had better be straightforward, so told him, "Fifteen women and five children."

"My friend must come as well." Joe nodded.

"Four thousand shillings."

"No, I will give you one thousand five hundred shillings. If you help us today, there will be many other people who want to come this way."

The man looked at him, frowning. "Two thousand – one thousand for me and one thousand for my friend. When should this happen?"

"Now, tonight, the people are already here."

"Two thousand?"

Joe nodded.

The man shouted at another man nearby, similarly dressed but without a rifle. He said something in his own language, which Joe was unable to understand. All three of them walked back to the truck. The women looked scared at the fearsome appearance of the two Turkana, who waited while Joe talked to Okongo.

"Otieno never said anything about paying for a guide, this is too much," protested Okongo.

"He's not going to do this for nothing as we already discussed. If you like I will speak to Otieno. You must remember he has many trucks all driving backwards and forwards to many different places. He's expecting us to work these little problems out ourselves, without having to ask him all the time."

With bad grace Okongo agreed to pay the two thousand shillings. He started to pull money from a purse in the cab.

"No," said Joe, "give the money to Odhiambo. One thousand when we leave and one thousand when we arrive at the other side, otherwise the guides may just run off into the bush."

Out of sight of the passengers, Joe saw Odhiambo give one thousand shillings to the Turkana guide, who told them to call him Kiyongo. "I will give you the rest when we arrive on the other side," said Odhiambo in Swahili.

Kiyongo looked at Joe, who nodded.

Patrick had helped to get all the women and children organised. If they had suitable shoes, he told them to wear them, if they had warm clothing, he told them to bring it, especially for the children, knowing that the desert nights could turn cold. The passengers' remaining meagre possessions were left in the truck.

Joe and Odhiambo gave Patrick and Okongo their passports.

"Otieno told me that if one puts twenty shillings in the passports that need stamping for me and Odhiambo, that is twenty on the Kenya side and twenty on the South Sudan side, there will be no problem," Joe said.

Okongo looked on with a scowl.

Joe, the two Turkana and a reluctant Odhiambo carried the water they had in water carriers, and the troupe quietly walked off into the dark in a line, with one of the Turkana in front and one at the back. Odhiambo and Joe stayed near the middle.

They spent two hours walking away from the road on an ill-defined path. The women carried two smaller children wrapped in traditional shawls on their backs. Where it seemed necessary, Joe and the two Turkana helped the smaller children by carrying them piggy-back for short periods. Whenever Odhiambo was asked to do his bit, he pointed at his leg, without saying anything. They stopped several times, partly to make sure everyone in the party drank water, particularly the children. During these stops, one or other of the Turkana went on ahead to see if there were any patrols in the vicinity.

During the second stop, Kiyongo hurried back to the group. He quickly led them further into a thicker piece of bush.

"Patrol," he whispered, "we must sit here for a few minutes to wait for them to go back to the border post. Keep the children quiet. I will track the patrol to see what they are doing."

He returned about thirty minutes later. "We can go now. They have gone back home."

The terrain was flat, with medium-sized bushes somehow surviving in the dry sandy soil. Joe knew the area was only about six hundred metres above sea level, much lower than Nairobi, which accounted for the warmer climate.

"Are there any lions or antelope around here?" Joe asked Kiyongo, who laughed.

"All these people here," he waved his arms indicating the border post, "now make sure that all the animals stay away, far away, although we did have a small group of elephants a few weeks back, which frightened everyone, and before that a large herd of buffalo. Before there was a big border post like there is now, this was a good hunting ground, with many animals," he added.

"What did they do for water?" asked Joe.

"There is surface water after the rains, but the lake (Turkana) is not so far away."

Three further hours were spent walking parallel to what Joe assumed was the road and then, after another two hours walk towards the road, now in the cool of the morning just before the dawn peeked over the horizon, they arrived at the road to Juba, and with Kiyongo urging the now exhausted women to hurry up, the South Sudan Border post became visible.

"We don't want to be seen," said Kiyongo, making them sit behind some bushes just off the road.

"There are no trucks going past," said Joe.

"There must be a problem, sometimes they keep the trucks in no-man's land between the posts at night. Maybe something to do with the South Sudanese border guards not being paid," observed Kiyongo.

Kiyongo then approached Odhiambo, demanding the balance of his fee.

"Ngoja, Gharry. Wait for the truck," said Odhiambo, glancing at Joe, who nodded.

Kiyongo sat disconsolately on the side of the road with his companion, away from the women.

As the sky lightened in the east, trucks started to rumble past. Okongo and his vehicle eventually emerged in the ever-increasing dust. Odhiambo paid Kiyongo the balance of the fee.

"We will be back," Joe said, "maybe in one month." Kiyongo shrugged.

The women by this time had all found the food left in the truck and were busy eating and chattering on the side of the road, with other trucks shuffling their slow way past.

Okongo started to get impatient.

Patrick handed Joe his passport. He showed Joe the stamp. "What about Odhiambo's passport?"

Patrick shook his head. "The Kenyan side was okay, but Okongo tried to play silly buggers on the South Sudan side and only gave the passport officer ten shillings. It wasn't stamped."

"We need to go," Okongo said to Joe. "Maybe there will be a big line-up at the refugee camp and we will only get unloaded and checked tomorrow or the next day if we don't hurry up."

This suited Joe; he wanted to really understand the set-up at the refugee camp and how easy or difficult it would be to move on north from there and indeed how costly.

"These people have been walking all night," he answered, "they need some rest."

The passengers were eventually all loaded up onto the truck by midday; all except one of the women. After a major search, another of the women came up to Joe saying, "She went back with one of the Turkana; she doesn't want to go to Juba anymore."

Joe told Okongo about the missing woman. He then bad-temperedly started the truck and set off for Juba, the capital city of South Sudan. They arrived at nightfall and, as Okongo had predicted, waited most of the night in a slow-moving line at the entrance to the refugee camp. When the officials in the camp became aware of the women and children in the truck, they were immediately unloaded, registered and allocated to an area. Joe then realised some of the officials in the camp could profit from the number of people seeking to go north from Juba. He assumed this was the reason they were so readily accommodated. He and Patrick both registered as refugees.

"Patrick, it might be best if you stayed here with the women and really find out how this place works. I'm sure we will be back here in a couple of weeks. How do you feel about that?"

Patrick looked slightly uncomfortable. "Okay, I suppose." Joe phoned Otieno.

"Why do you want to do that?" asked Otieno when Joe had explained to him what he had in mind.

"If you want to really extend this business taking refugees all the way to Libya and perhaps beyond, we need to understand everything. Patrick will spend his time getting all that information." Joe hesitated. "I will brief him properly. The women we brought here also need some protection – there is a lot of violence, with people stealing from each other..."

There was silence on the other end of the line for a moment. "We undertook to get people to Juba, not look after them for the rest of their lives," said Otieno angrily. "Anyway, Kigoro has now told me that he has twenty people who have paid him to go to *Ulaya*. We may need Patrick for that trip. Okongo says he has been a great help."

Joe wondered what Okongo was up to.

"I can provide Kikuyu people who can help with that trip. We will be back in Nairobi in a few days. We can discuss it then. I will alert those people. I think it is more important that Patrick stays here in Juba for the time being." He now realised that he needed all of his gang in Juba.

There was a brief silence on the line. "Okay. Let Patrick stay in Juba."

Joe then phoned Waweru and Koinange and explained to them, individually, that Otieno was planning on taking another group of refugees to Juba and suggested that they provide the help that he and Patrick had done on the first trip. They trusted Joe, so both agreed readily.

Joe, with Patrick trailing after him, spent much of his time walking around the camp, talking to as many people as he could. Conditions were much worse than Pumwani, Kibera or anywhere else he had ever experienced. There was some attempt at creating order, but because of the ever-changing population there was little sense of community and people were inevitably focussed on their own situations.

The camp itself was just a sea of tents of various sizes scattered about in unruly rows, as well as other forms of shelter constructed from pieces of timber, corrugated iron and cardboard. The area was fenced, but the fencing neither kept people in or out. There were some official-looking buildings at the entrance to the camp, which housed the registration office. There was also a massive storage shed for the food aid, busy almost all day and night, serving the continuous movement of people. Joe also observed a contingent of UN peacekeepers wearing their blue berets, providing some security.

Joe watched while a gang of people, from a tribe he did not recognise, in broad daylight raided a small encampment nearby and ran away with what looked like food and possibly cash.

Okongo and Odhiambo kept well away from the women and slept in their truck.

On the second night after arrival, another gang attempted to raid the encampment where Joe, Patrick and the women were sleeping in the open. There was some light. Joe pulled out the Beretta and fired one shot into the ground. The raiders scattered, except for one who pulled out what Joe could see was a sharp-looking, very long bladed knife. The man had one of the women in a firm grip round the neck, with the knife held at her throat. In the chaos Joe had managed to creep up behind the man before he said anything. He held the Beretta against the man's head.

"Drop the knife or I will blow your head off," Joe yelled.

The man did as he was told and tried to run off. Joe tripped him up, kicked him in the head, grabbed him by the arm and with a savage wrench dislocated the man's shoulder.

The woman collapsed on the ground unhurt. "Now, run," said Joe, "and don't come back."

They all watched as the man stumbled off, screaming in agony. Joe picked up the knife.

Patrick and the women watched in amazement. "They won't come back in a hurry," muttered Joe.

Dust spun in swirling eddies, coating everything in the camp in a film of red dust, despite the White Nile flowing through the city. Joe, Patrick and the women he had helped smuggle into South Sudan, were allocated to an area; though they were still in the open with no shelter, surrounded by the meagre belongings, so Joe found one of the camp officials, and spoke to him on his own outside the office.

"The people we registered with are just in the open. How do we get some tents?" Joe asked.

The thirty-year-old man looked at Joe. "How many?"

"Four."

He looked Joe for a minute. "I will need one hundred US dollars per tent. As soon as I have the money, cash only, you can come and collect the tents."

"Who do I pay?"

"You can give the money to me; I will pass it on."

"What is your name?"

"Brian Murphy."

"Okay, Brian Murphy."

Together with Patrick, Joe went back to the women, who by this time had learned to trust him.

"I can get you four tents," Joe told them, "but the man wants one hundred dollars each. It's the only way. I'm sorry, the tents should be allocated with no cost. The man is just looking after himself."

There was a flurry of conversation. After a few minutes, one of the women returned with two hundred and thirty US dollars in grubby five- and ten-dollar notes.

He found Brian Murphy. "Right now, I only have two hundred and thirty dollars; I'll get the rest later, but I want all the tents now."

Brian looked unhappy.

"If you give us the tents, it will be easier to earn the money – they provide some sort of privacy as you know," added Joe, counting the money out.

Brian frowned at Joe, then went to a shack fifty metres away from the official office and helped Joe collect four tents. They were well used and far from clean.

"I thought they would be new tents?" he said to Brian. "Do you want the tents or not?" was Brian's response.

Joe and Patrick carried the tents back to the women and spent the rest of the day cleaning them and helping to erect them. They had to give them all a good wash and in many cases the guy ropes and tent pegs were missing.

"What do we need?" asked Patrick. "I'll see what I can find around the place."

By the middle of the next day, they had managed to erect the four tents, which the women crowded into.

Joe then went looking for people who were transporting people beyond Juba, to the Libyan coast. He found a South Sudanese Dinka man called Jok, who said he was going to get a truck soon. As was typical of his tribe, Jok was very tall and very black.

"When?" asked Joe.

"You'll have to wait. There are no trucks at the moment," said Jok in very bad Swahili.

"When will there be trucks?"

The man shrugged. "Come back next week and we will see."

"Go to that man every week; and any others you can find. It may take some time to find a truck going north," Joe told Patrick.

Joe soon came across another Kikuyu named Kimani who, unusually and unchallenged, carried a well-maintained AK 47 rifle.

"What are you doing here?" asked Joe after the usual greetings.

"I need to go to *Ulaya* but I have no money."

"We will go soon," said Joe, "maybe you can come with us."

"I have no money," repeated Kimani.

"That may not be a problem," answered Joe. He introduced Kimani to Patrick.

"Keep in touch with that man," Joe said to Patrick. "I have made no promises, but we may need him if we manage to get on a trip going north.

Joe thought he could now see there might be a route for him to get to the 'promised land' of a first world country.

"Maybe for your own security and that of the women, I should leave the Beretta with you," Joe said to Patrick.

"I don't know how it works."

They found a patch of bush on the edge of the refugee camp and Joe gave Patrick a short lesson on how the gun worked. "Keep the safety catch on all the time," he showed Patrick how that worked, "and never have a round up the spout."

"Why?"

"If you bump it by mistake, the pistol may go off. It only takes a second to load a round into the breach." Joe showed Patrick how to load the pistol. "You just pull the breech back like this. See it then loads a shot from the magazine..." Joe made Patrick fire a couple of shots. "Always keep the weapon hidden. Hopefully you won't need it. People will run off if you just wave it about or fire a shot into the ground." Joe showed Patrick how to tuck the gun into his waistband.

For the sharp long-bladed knife he had taken off the unsuccessful raider, Joe had constructed a makeshift sheath from some material he had found. He tucked the knife into his waistband hidden by his shirt.

Once the vehicle had been unloaded, Joe assumed they would immediately depart for Kenya but he found the two Luo had discovered other attractions in the city of Juba and were in no hurry to leave.

"Come with us," Okongo cajoled, as they were about to leave the refugee camp and head into the city.

But Joe had had a call from Otieno. "What is going on?" he yelled. "Okongo is not answering his phone."

"We had some delays at the border post and there are many trucks here, I expect we will be on our way home in a day or two, when the truck has been unloaded."

"They normally unload the trucks straight away..."

"Not this time," Joe answered. "I'll get Okongo to call you as soon as we know when we are on the way back home."

He reported the call to Okongo.

Two days later they were on their way back to Kenya with an empty vehicle. They had no trouble at the border, despite Odhiambo's passport not being correctly stamped. There was room for all three of them in the cab.

"I need to practice my driving again," said Joe once they had cleared the border area.

To start with Okongo was nervous and gave Joe all sorts of unnecessary instructions such as, "You need to slow down a bit round this corner", and when they could see some cattle on the road, "slow down and get the truck into a lower gear". When it seemed Joe was well in control of the vehicle, the two Luo slept in the cab most of the way home, with the occasional break for a meal and to relieve themselves. Okongo took over the driving once they were on the final approach to Nairobi.

All three of them trudged into Otieno's office where Okongo made a brief report to Otieno, mainly to account for the money he'd spent. Okongo praised Joe's contribution.

Otieno asked Joe to wait behind, once the drivers had left to go home.

"You did a good job for me on this trip. We now need to talk about how we deal with Kigoro's people."

"I asked my people to come here today. They are just outside."

Waweru and Koinange were ushered into Otieno's office and introduced.

"Kigoro, the man from Ol'Kalou, has now paid me the money for twenty-five Kikuyu, men, women and children, who want to go to Juba," said Otieno.

"How many of each?" asked Joe.

Otieno shrugged. "They'll find out when they get to Ol'Kalou. Okongo and Odhiambo have gone home for a few days, but they will be back in two days. Can you two be available to go to Juba by then?"

"Yes, we now have passports," answered Waweru.

"Okongo and Odhiambo now know the ropes, I can brief these two if you like. If we are going to run a business taking people from Juba to the North, they should probably stay in Juba," said Joe.

"Okay, but we need to think about how we do that," said Otieno. He then stayed in the office and listened to Joe's briefing to Waweru and Koinange.

"Make sure there is enough food and water for all the people," said Joe to Waweru and Koinange, "before you leave here. If you need anything extra for the children then get it on the road. You will need to stop every three or four hours to let people out for the toilet and to eat."

He told them to make sure to take the long route through Eldoret.

"When you get to the border look for Kiyongo, who is a Turkana guide. He can take you round the border. He's easy to find as he carries a rifle over his shoulder all the time. The cost is two thousand shillings." Joe described Kiyongo.

"Make sure that your passports are stamped on both sides of the border post, even if you walk round the post with the passengers; if you don't get that done you may have trouble using the border posts if you want to come back," Joe continued. "Patrick stayed in Juba, so call him when you have left the border post. I will call him when you are on your way, and if you need any advice, please call me. Any questions?" asked Joe, looking at Otieno.

Both Waweru and Koinange shook their heads.

"Okay, I'll see you outside. I just need to talk to Mr Otieno for a few minutes." Waweru and Koinange left the office.

"You can run a business taking people to Juba," Joe told Otieno, "but maybe if you had a truck, or even two trucks based in Juba, you would make much more money taking people going North from Juba. There are people coming from Eritrea, Somalia and even some from Ethiopia, as well as Kenya and other countries, trying to get to *Ulaya*."

"Who would run such a business?"

"Maybe I could. First though I would need to make one or two more trips from here in order to understand everything. Also, I need help to get a driving licence."

"Okongo told me you were a very bad driver."

Joe laughed. "I drove almost all the way back here. Okongo was asleep most of the time. If you want, you can test me yourself..."

"Come back in a few days," said Otieno. "We'll see what we can do about getting you a licence."

Waweru and Koinange were waiting for Joe outside. They took a bus to Karanja's house in Westlands. Ellen was thrilled to have Joe back home. She provided a meal for Joe and his companions.

Joe told them about the trip.

"I am sure there is a business taking people to Juba and then Libya and then possibly beyond. We should all get together in Juba and then see where we go from there."

"What about the *bhang* business?" asked Koinange.

"I will talk to Karanja about that. Maybe we can sell it, as I have suggested before."

Joe was then silent for a moment.

"*Bhang!* That's a good idea. Take some *bhang* with you to Juba," said Joe enthusiastically, "say about twenty kilos, ten each. You will have to carry it round the border in your back packs, you don't want to be caught at the border post with that quantity of *bhang.* I am sure we can sell it in Juba. This will mean we have some funds in Juba."

Two days later, Joe returned to Otieno's depot at six in the morning to see off Waweru and Koinange. They were both carrying large backpacks.

"Tell the drivers nothing, and both of you should walk round the border post," Joe whispered to Waweru and Koinange.

There was another big truck in the yard, loaded with food aid for the refugee camp in Juba. Okongo and Odhiambo were standing next to the truck. Joe introduced them to Waweru and Koinange, who on Joe's instructions had come well prepared.

"Kigoro is expecting you to be in Ol'Kalou sometime this morning," said Otieno. "So, if you are ready, please be on your way," he said to everyone.

Waweru and Koinange hopped onto the back of the truck with their back packs, and it moved off.

"Let me see how well you drive," said Otieno to Joe, "then we can see how we get you a driver's licence."

The truck they had taken to Juba was still in the yard. Joe took the keys and Otieno clambered into the passenger seat. They drove around the busy streets of Nairobi for a while.

Otieno said nothing until they returned. "You must take a test, but I'll speak to the man testing, I may have to pay him something. There will be no problem. You must study the highway code." In the office, afterwards, he handed Joe a rather tattered copy of the code.

Within a few days, Joe had a license to drive a large truck.

Joe spoke to Waweru several times during the latter's trip north. "The *bhang* still undetected?" asked Joe.

"Yes. I am pretty sure that the truck is actually carrying some packages, probably *bhang*, which are hidden underneath the food. The drivers keep trying to make sure whatever there is remains hidden."

Joe returned to Westlands.

"Karanja, we need to talk about how we manage the *bhang* business," said Joe. "Most of my people are either in Juba or going there. At the moment, as you know, the operation has provisionally been handed over to others, but we need to formalise the situation. You can either pay us a lump sum, which I will share with my people, or you can pay me something each month, as we do with Reverend Mweleli," Joe added.

"Are you going to stay in Juba?" asked Karanja.

"Maybe. But we will probably see if we can make a business going north to *Ulaya.*"

"Why should I pay you anything?" argued Karanja.

"Most of your sales are through contacts made by me and my crew. That is still the case. We have developed a very good business, which we don't want to abandon. We can leave you with those contacts or not. Your choice."

They eventually agreed that Karanja would pay a monthly amount to Joe for three years, which Joe would share with his people, after which he, Karanja would own the business.

Chapter 6: The General Again

After his return from Juba, Joe re-established his routine with the general, except that now Elijah picked him up from Karanja's house in Westlands, once to service the general and once to resume his lessons with Desai, both still at the general's residence.

Joe was surprised that the general had allowed the relationship to continue for as long as it had.

"I thought you were going to be away for a month," the general said afterwards.

"It's more complicated than I thought," said Joe. "I will have to go back to Ol'Kalou a few times, I think."

"Do you need any help from me?"

"Thank you, sir – at the moment I have all the help I need. I will come back to you if I may," he said, adding as an afterthought, "if I get into trouble."

The general was not fooled by Joe's rejection. Joe could see from the expression on the general's face that he thought Joe was about to move on to another phase in his life.

Their previous relationship continued, but Joe was now focussed on making quite sure he had all the details of the general's personal financial affairs, to which he already had access from his previous investigations. He continued to transfer increasing amounts of money via his Swiss account, from the general's main account to his own accounts, now scattered across several banks in London.

"Now we have the truck taking Kigoro's people to Juba," said Otieno, in an urgent phone call. "I have another truck going in a few days. I want you to take it. This time there are thirty people, all Kamba."

"Is this food for the *Wazungu* aid people again?" asked Joe.

Otieno looked at Joe. "You seem to think everyone except you was born yesterday. The answer is 'yes.'"

"How many drivers?"

"You and a Kamba man."

"I will bring another of my Kikuyu colleagues, he also speaks Kamba." Otieno clicked his tongue, irritated, but said nothing further.

"It's the land business again, I will be away for about ten days this time," Joe told the general.

The general waved him away impatiently.

The Kamba driver was named Mbiti and Joe had asked N'guku to accompany them, as he had arranged with Otieno. The idea was that N'guku would stay in Juba with the rest of his crew. Joe said to Mbiti, "Your name means hyaena, doesn't it? You had better not behave like a hyaena or I will shoot you," he smiled, "or maybe just leave you in Juba."

As with Waweru and Koinange, both Joe and N'guku had large packs, which included a quantity of *bhang*.

As Otieno had told him the truck was full of aid, mainly *posho*, with the thirty men, women and children perched uncomfortably on top of the load. Joe ran the trip based on his experience of the previous journey. When he arrived at the border, he went looking for Kiyongo, his Turkana guide, whom he found after a day's wait.

"I have been busy with some of your friends, Waweru and so on," offered Kiyongo, "this time I need two thousand five hundred shillings, because there are more people."

Joe didn't argue.

Joe had seen Mbiti eyeing the women on the trip a bit too eagerly, so Joe told him to drive the truck through the border, to get him out of the way.

"I have checked all the papers," he said. "N'guku will go with you. We will see you on the other side. Go now and you may get through today; last time the truck had to wait at the South Sudan side most of the night." He handed N'guku his own passport, making sure he knew what to do to get it stamped. Joe carried his pack round the border. They decided that N'guku's pack would remain hidden in the truck. None of the trucks had ever been searched and they thought the contraband would be safe.

The refugees were escorted across the border without incident, with the Turkana still being cautious; from time to time, they directed their charges to hide, while they reconnoitred their passage. Joe and the Turkana helped by carrying the children, if they were flagging.

The passengers were hidden in the bushes beyond the border with Joe standing on the road. Mbiti, N'guku and the truck were one of the first vehicles to appear. Joe flagged them down and they quickly loaded the group onto the truck. He paid Kiyongo.

"Will you be bringing any more people soon?" asked Kiyongo.

"Yes, probably, maybe one truck a week," said Joe.

"Many people, is there something bad in Nairobi?" observed Kiyongo. Joe shrugged.

"It's still early," said Joe to Mbiti and N'guku, "if we keep going, we may not have to wait too long in the queue at the refugee camp. People will just have to eat in the truck."

Joe took over the driving. "I know the ropes," said Joe to Mbiti, who looked surprised.

At the camp, Joe walked across the dusty ground, eyes flicking left and right as he satisfied himself that all his passengers were accounted for. Once he had sighted every last one and was satisfied, he went to the aid station to complete the usual formalities.

N'guku was registered as a refugee. Joe already had his papers.

"See if you can find Patrick and the others," Joe said to N'guku, "while I deal with everything here, I have already texted them that we have arrived. We need to have a quick meeting. I will be returning to Nairobi tomorrow and will probably be back next week with another truck."

Joe thought Mbiti would play games and try to delay the return journey to Nairobi, so he managed to filch Mbiti's passport, from his jacket.

Joe then went looking for the Kikuyu women from the previous trip. He found Patrick and the rest of his crew in the area where he had left the first group of passengers. Kigoro's Ol'Kalou group were also with them.

The women from the first trip greeted him like a long-lost friend.

"*Habari,*" they said almost in unison.

"Habari. Mzuri sana," Joe responded.

"Two people have gone in a truck, going North. The others are still waiting," said one of the women.

"How much do they have to pay?' he asked.

The women looked at each other before one of them answered, *"Mia mbili* (two thousand) *Americano*," he was told.

He wondered if they were telling the truth and how they raised that kind of money. 'Ah,' he thought. 'Maybe drugs, obviously prostitution. I wonder what else?'

"How far will that money take you?"

"*Ulaya*."

He wondered whether there wouldn't be further payment requests before they arrived anywhere near Europe, based on what he had heard from Otieno during one of the reverend's meetings.

Joe, Patrick, Waweru, Koinange and N'guku made time for a meeting.

"There was no problem at the border. Okongo and Odhiambo definitely brought some *bhang* and possibly other drugs with them," said Waweru.

"They seemed to have bundles of cash when they left and they were very excited."

"What have you done with our stuff?"

"I found a couple of bars in Juba who will take anything we can give them. Very high prices. Even your friend Brian seems to be in the business." He tried to hand Joe a wad of cash.

"Keep it for us," said Joe. "We may need it when we go north. N'guku and I also brought another twenty kilos with us. You can sell that for us as well."

Joe paid a visit to the South Sudanese man, Jok, he had seen on the earlier visit and told him about the people he had just delivered to the camp, as well as Kigoro's group.

In atrocious Swahili Jok told him that he would be arranging a truck in the next week or two.

Joe briefed Patrick. "You need to deal with Jok. We all need to be taken on as assistants. See if you can agree a wage."

There was no sign of Mbiti at the appointed time for departure.

So, as he had planned, having refuelled, Joe drove back to the border on his own. He passed through both sides of the border without difficulty.

Otieno was pleased and surprised when Joe appeared at the depot at least two days before he was expected.

"That hyaena Mbiti was nowhere to be found when I wanted to leave, so I left him in Juba," explained Joe. "Maybe he'll find his own way back here?" Joe removed Mbiti's passport from his jacket and waved it about. "I'll keep this then, for the time being, to see if I can find Mbiti on another trip." Joe fully briefed Otieno.

"There will certainly be another trip for you in the next few days. I am going to step up our business in this area; it's very profitable," said Otieno.

"There are more and more people collecting in those camps near Juba and wanting to go north," said Joe, "but there are not enough trucks. I think if we had a truck or two in Juba, I could find a way of making a business taking people from there to the big *maji* – the one the Wazungu call 'The Med'.

Joe explained in some detail how he thought such a business could work: "I will need to go on at least one trip from Juba to Libya, just to see how everything works."

"What would we charge, per person?" asked Otieno.

"I have been told two thousand US per person, but maybe that's on the low side. I think we'll be able to charge more like three thousand."

Otieno raised his eyebrows.

"Also, you could take things other than people to Juba and beyond."

Otieno was silent for a moment. He looked at Joe, smiled, and shook his head. "You really do think we were all born yesterday... Anyway, to get back to what we were discussing," Otieno continued, "I'll think about what you said. Maybe I'll get you to stay in Juba for a while, to see if we can make a business based there."

"I already have four of my colleagues in Juba, as you know. We are talking to a man who organises trucks, going north. With your permission we should join his trip."

"We will take two trucks on the next trip, which will be in a few days and my brother Odongo will go with you." Joe could see Otieno was excited by the proposal, despite his usual reticent, dour expression.

At home in Westlands, Joe spent time checking his London accounts, using a new smartphone he had persuaded Karanja to get for him. He topped them all up from the general's deposit account, using a variety of internet cafés in the city and sending it all via his Swiss account, and making certain he had about one hundred thousand pounds in each of ten accounts.

Joe really wanted to know whether the general was aware that two thirds of his ill-gotten gains had now disappeared. He was in two minds about a visit to the general. His initial reaction was to leave the man well alone. Curiosity got the better of him; the thought that if the general suspected Joe of being involved in the theft of funds from his London account, he might find a way of trying to get the money back.

So, Joe paid what turned out to be one last visit to the general. Unusually Joe phoned Kariuki, something he rarely did.

"Yes," said the general, having answered his mobile. "I will see you at ten o'clock. The servants and gardeners have all gone home, since I am going to be away for a while, but you have a key so let yourself in."

Joe hesitated. 'I wonder if this is a set up,' he thought. 'He just wants me there on my own. Maybe I should just forget the general and take the trip to Juba.'

In the end, Joe decided to go and see the general.

He took a bus and walked the short distance to the general's residence. The place was eerily quiet. There was nobody in the garden. None of the general's cars were visible. Joe let himself in through the kitchen door, which was empty of people. The place was beautifully clean with everything put away in its place. He walked the few paces to the general's study. The door was open and the general was sitting on the couch waiting.

The general seemed to be just the same as he always was. Joe serviced him as usual, then everything suddenly changed. Just as he finished, General Kariuki grabbed Joe by the shirt. In his fury the general had not bothered to put his trousers back on.

"You thieving little shit! You've stolen..." the general screamed, he grabbed Joe by the throat with both hands.

Joe tried to get away but, in the struggle, they fell off the couch with the general on top of Joe. The general was very strong and was overwhelming Joe, continuing to throttle him. Joe could feel himself weakening. In desperation, Joe made a grab for the long-bladed knife he now always carried in a sheath under his trousers and stabbed wildly at Kariuki. Joe's desperate lunge hit the general in the groin.

The general's grip loosened and he slid down into the growing pool of his own blood on the floor. Joe had struck an artery and blood started to jet out over Kariuki himself, the furniture and all over Joe.

Joe pulled away and jumped up, watching the general getting weaker and weaker.

"Help me you little..." the general lost consciousness.

Almost in shock at what had happened, Joe was unable to move or do anything, as the general, his nemesis, died within ten minutes.

In a daze, he instinctively jerked himself into action: the house was empty, he was certain he had not been seen. In the bathroom attached to the study, he removed his clothes, wiped and washed the long-bladed knife clean, showered and washed all the blood off himself. He found and put on a set of casual, ill-fitting clothes belonging to the general. He went through the kitchen, making sure he left no fingerprints anywhere, and collected some heavy cleaning cloths. He left his own bloodied clothes where they lay, making sure there was nothing contained in the pockets or anywhere to identify him. Finding the passport taken from Mbiti, he wiped it clean of all fingerprints, using the cloths he had picked up in the kitchen, and then he left it in the shirt pocket of the clothes he had just taken off. With the cleaning cloths he had found in the kitchen, he made doubly sure he wiped the bathroom down as clean as was possible, removing any trace of his own fingerprints.

Joe then looked about for signs of any other people, wiped the door handles down, and made his escape out through the kitchen and the rear entrance.

PART 3

Chapter 7: Back to Juba

Still in a daze Joe went home to Karanja's place in Westlands and changed into a set of his own clothes. There was no sign of either his mother or Karanja. He just about remembered to pick up the heavy backpack, now filled with *bhang*, which he had carefully packed for the journey to Juba, checking for his passport, which he put into his jacket pocket; he then took a bus to Kibera, and dumped the clothes borrowed from the general in the street in an area where he knew there were many Kamba living. He did not return home but spent the night in the Ngong forest. He spoke to nobody. Looking around, walking, on the bus, on his way back to Otieno's truck depot, everything seemed quite normal, nobody reacted to him in any way.

'Why did you have to kill the general,' he muttered to himself, 'stupid, stupid, stupid.'

He didn't give the general himself a second thought, only the action. As far as Joe was concerned, the general had used his obvious talents to steal his country blind and exploit his fellow citizens wherever possible, all for his own ends. Both the general and the reverend thought that what they were doing was to steal from the *Wazungu*. They had never really understood that they were actually stealing from themselves, from their own country.

When he arrived at the depot, just before 5.30am, he was greeted by Odongo, Otieno's half-brother. Otieno was not there.

"I'm glad to see you are on time," said Odongo gruffly.

Joe hardly knew the man but remembered what Okongo had said to him on their first trip, "Otieno is alright, but watch out for Odongo, he's stupid and thinks he knows everything."

"I'm ready to go," said Joe. "I have arranged for a young Kikuyu boy to come with me to help with the passengers. We just need to load all the passengers."

There were about fifty Kikuyu men, women and children, all huddled together against the cold, in one corner of the depot chattering quietly. Two large trucks, already loaded with food aid were standing nearby.

"That truck is mine," said Odongo aggressively, as Joe walked over and had a look into the backs of both trucks.

"Okay," said Joe. "I suppose that truck is the one loaded with *bhang* or some other contraband," he muttered to himself. Joe took it upon himself to get the trucks loaded, trying to ensure that families stayed together.

Odongo left him to it.

With everyone loaded up they left the depot at 6am on the dot.

Taking two trucks turned out to be more difficult than just one. Joe and a Kikuyu, named Kago, drove one truck with Odongo and another Luo driving the other. Odongo thought that having a young boy to help look after the passengers was unnecessary. Joe had a young boy helping the passengers on his, and insisted on going what Odongo thought was the long way through Eldoret and Kitale. Despite Joe's entreaties, Odongo went what he considered to be the short way. "We'll see you at the border," said Odongo cheerfully when they parted ways.

"They'll have trouble," Joe told his companion Kago, "maybe run out of fuel and there are no places to buy food."

Joe arrived at the border as expected; there was no sign of Odongo. He thought for a minute, 'Should I wait for Odongo? No, he will have got himself into trouble and I'll be waiting here for a week. I wonder if I should phone Otieno. No, they made the bed; let them lie on it.'

"We'll go through the border and then come back here, once we have delivered the load to the refugee camp in Juba," he eventually announced.

He found Kiyongo, his Turkana guide, and made Kago and the boy carry his backpack round the border with the passengers.

With small bribes, both his and Kago's passports were stamped, on both the Kenya side of the border and the South Sudan side, showing a date two days earlier than the date of the general's death. The boy had no passport. Joe was relieved to see that the border officials barely registered Joe's request; they were obviously used to accommodating people's requests and lining their own pockets as a result. It was the same on both sides of the border.

They picked up their passengers as usual on the South Sudan side of the border. Joe paid Kiyongo the balance of his fee and within a day the vehicle was unloaded in the now familiar refugee camp. Joe found his crew and handed over the bhang in his backpack to Waweru.

"That should add to the cash stash," he said smiling.

"Jok will be leaving in a week," said Patrick. "We are all engaged as assistants on his truck. "You need to be back here by then."

There was still no sign of Odongo. 'The stupid fool must have got himself into trouble,' Joe thought.

He was still trying to think about what to do about it when his phone rang. It was Otieno.

"Where are you?" asked Otieno.

"In Juba, at the refugee camp. We have unloaded and are waiting for Odongo, but there is no sign of him. I was wondering what to do."

"Odongo got himself into trouble. Why did you let him go the short way? You know there is no fuel on that road..."

"I told him not to go that way, he took no notice. He made it clear that he was in charge."

There was a short silence.

"I have sent a rescue truck with fuel, so Odongo will be on his way by now. He doesn't understand what to do at the border, so I want you to drive your truck back to the border, leave it on the South Sudan side, with Kago. You should then go through the border, find Odongo and help him through. Just make sure the passengers get through to South Sudan in good order. You can then take Odongo's truck through to the refugee camp and Odongo can drive your truck back here with Kago."

"Right," said Joe. "We'll go now. You must tell Odongo to wait for me before he does anything."

'Otieno obviously doesn't know anything about the contraband that Odongo has in his truck,' thought Joe.

He went to find Kago, who was sitting with the boy, uncomfortably in the shade, next to the truck. "When..."

"We'll drive back to the border," Joe said to Kago. "You will stay in the truck and wait for me." There was no possibility that Joe could go through the border post again so soon. 'I need to be certain that it seems that I was in Juba before the date of the general's death, and did not return to Kenya,' Joe said to himself.

"I will walk round the border with the boy, since he has no passport," he said to Kago, "and then get Odongo through the border posts. Otieno wants you and Odongo and the other Luo driver to take our truck back to Nairobi. You'll have to pick the boy up once you are through the post. I will walk back."

They returned to the border post. Joe waited until dusk and then he and the boy headed off through the bush to walk round the border post. By this time Joe was familiar with the route and had no trouble. At dawn, he and the boy joined the mingling crowd and Joe went looking for Odongo.

"I've been waiting here for a day," grumbled Odongo, "what took you so long?"

Joe did not respond directly. " I just need to find my guide and then we can unload the passengers and get you through the border. How are the passengers? Will they be able to walk for seven hours through the night?"

Odongo shrugged.

"I suggest you give the passengers a meal, and look after this boy, who you need to pick up on your return," said Joe.

Within an hour Joe found Kiyongo and Kiyongo's companion. "The charge is now three thousand shillings," said Kiyongo. "Okay," said Joe. "I'll make sure you get paid."

"Otieno never said anything about paying, can't you just walk the passenger's through to the other side," said Odongo.

"No," said Joe "we need the guide. It's worked for us many times already. I'll phone Otieno if you want."

Odongo grumpily just gave Joe the money.

Joe and the passengers, with the help of his Turkana guides, arrived on the South Sudan side of the border post just as the yellow dawn was breaking. They were as usual hidden in the bush just off the road.

Leaving the passengers in the care of the Turkana, Joe went and found Kago. "Any sign of that bloody fool Odongo?"

"No. I've checked. Trucks have been coming through all night." Joe then phoned Odongo.

"Where are you?" asked Joe.

"We've had a bit of trouble on the South Sudan side of the border," muttered Odongo.

"I suppose they found your *bhang* stash and any other stuff you were carrying?"

"How do you know about that; nobody knows about that?"

"Mr Odongo, the way you were prancing around in the depot in Nairobi, it was obvious that you were carrying something. Just give them whatever they have found and pay them whatever they ask and I expect they will let you through. The passengers are in a bad way with all the delays. We need to feed them and get them to the refugee camp."

"You, you must have told them I was carrying something," Odongo said. He had to find someone else to blame for the nonsense he had made of the trip.

"Don't be ridiculous. I didn't actually know you were carrying anything and I have not been through the border post itself for almost a week now. There are dozens of trucks similar to yours; they would never have been able to identify your particular vehicle. Anyway, do what I say or you will end up in jail and the food aid will be confiscated; imagine what Otieno would say about that. I don't suppose you told Otieno that you were carrying *bhang,* so he won't be very pleased on that subject either."

Odongo muttered something incomprehensible and the phone was put down.

Joe phoned Otieno and told him the whole story. "I'll let you know when he arrives here Mr Otieno, but he really has made a big mess of everything, mainly by not being prepared to listen to anyone."

"You say he was carrying *bhang,* he never told me that."

"Yes, and possibly some other stuff as well. He will obviously try to blame me for the fiasco, take no notice. I will get him to return with Kago as soon as I see him..."

"You didn't take any *bhang* on any of your trips?"

"No, of course not. It would be a stupid thing to do."

"Okay, tell me when he arrives." The phone went down.

During Joe's perambulations round the border post waiting for Odongo, he managed to pick up a copy of a Nairobi paper, 'The Standard'. Plastered all over the front pages was the story of the murder of General Kariuki:

'GENERAL KARIUKI STABBED TO DEATH IN HIS OWN HOME'

Joe stared at the headline; it was almost as if it was an accusation directed straight at him, Joe.

'One of Kenya's senior generals was yesterday stabbed to death in his own home,' the newspaper continued. Then there was a long story about the general's career and how successful he had been.

At the very end of the piece the paper added, 'General Kariuki had become very wealthy. Sources have suggested that this wealth may not have been accumulated by wholly legitimate means.'

A government spokesman, when asked to comment on the source of the general's wealth said, 'One of our leading generals has just been murdered, he was well known for his honesty and straightforward dealings. His philanthropy was also well known and respected. To suggest anything else is criminal. The government is in touch with his family and is considering a State Funeral for one of Kenya's leading post *Uhuru* figures.'

Joe read all he could on the subject.

'It is believed that the police wish to talk to a Kamba man regarding the murder,' the newspaper continued.

Joe put the newspaper in a nearby bin. He was relieved to see that the reported date of the death of the general was after the official stamps in his passport of his arrival in South Sudan. He went and sat by himself and tried to stop shaking. The newspaper article had made him relive the whole episode of the death, the aftermath and his own escape.

Two hours later he finally saw Odongo's truck, carefully making its way in amongst the noise the dust and other trucks. Joe was relieved to be able to put the death of the general to the back of his mind and concentrate on what was in front of him.

He waved Odongo down and directed him to a parking spot next to where his own truck had been parked, which was in a safe area off the road, away from prying eyes.

"I'll just get the passengers," Joe said to Odongo.

He went and fetched the passengers, some of whom needed to be helped. He paid Kiyongo. He helped all the passengers clamber into Odongo's truck. They were well hidden, so it was not obvious what was going on.

"Please eat and drink," he said to the passengers. "We'll only be in Juba tonight."

Joe checked the load and was relieved to see they had enough fuel to get them to their destination.

A somewhat contrite Odongo had watched Joe going about his business without saying anything. He was sitting in the shade of Joe's truck.

"We'll be going now," said Joe.

Odongo looked at him. "Why did you tell Otieno about us being stuck at the border post and about the *bhang?"*

Joe shrugged. "You should have told him yourself. Why didn't you?" Odongo just glared at Joe.

"Mr Odongo. I suggest that you wait for a few hours. You need to make sure that the shift has changed before you go through again or they might ask for more bribes and don't forget to pick up the boy."

"You think you know everything, just like all the bloody Kikuyu, they all think they know everything," yelled a furious Odongo.

Joe backed off, said goodbye to Kago, got into the loaded truck and drove off joining the queue of vehicles going north.

He phoned Otieno.

"Mr Otieno, I have left Odongo with the empty truck at the border. He has Kago and the Luo driver who came up here with him. I have told him to wait for a few hours to make sure the shift changes before he returns. You obviously know the reason for that. But he is not listening, so he might do something silly again. Also, you must remind him to pick up the boy, who came up here with me, who is waiting on the Kenyan side of the border."

Otieno said nothing.

"Also, I have been taken on by a South Sudanese who has a group of refugees who want to go north."

"Okay, you have been busy, phone me when you have more information." Otieno hesitated. "You know the police are looking for you, they say they need to speak to you," he said.

Joe's gut tightened. "Speak to me? Did they say what it was about?"

"No, not really, but there is this murder of General Kariuki..."

"Murder, how terrible. As you know, General Kariuki occasionally came to visit Reverend Mweleli, as you did, of course. He was also invited to attend my mother's wedding..." Joe tried to speak as normally as possible.

"The papers are talking about a Kamba man as their chief suspect. They don't know his name."

Joe waited, but Otieno didn't say anything about Mbiti's passport being found at the scene of the murder. Hopefully he had no recollection of Joe being in possession of it on the previous trip, or if he did, he prioritised Joe being in Juba.

As soon as Mbiti's name was publicised, of course, Otieno would know that he, Joe, was implicated in Kariuki's murder.

Chapter 8: Joe in Juba and Sudan

On his own, Joe drove the truck to the refugee camp in Juba. He had found a Luo mechanic whom he had met on an earlier trip and he asked the man to look after it for the owner.

"I know Mr Otieno," said the man.

"I will tell Mr Otieno that I have asked you to take care of his truck. I will suggest that he phones to tell you what he wants you to do with it."

"Why, where are you going?"

"North," muttered Joe.

The man nodded.

Joe then phoned Otieno. "I said I would phone you to update you on our progress."

"Who is looking after my truck?"

"It's with a Luo mechanic I've found here, who seems to be reliable. I will send you his mobile number," which he did there and then.

"You are not taking my truck to Libya?"

"No. The South Sudanese man I mentioned has his own truck. As you know Mr Otieno, I have myself and four Kikuyu colleagues here in Juba. We have all been taken on as assistants, since many of the passengers on this trip are Kikuyu."

"Okay, don't spend too much money."

Joe laughed. "We're all being paid, so I will spend very little money."

Joe did not mention he had his own resources, mainly from the sale of *bhang* in Juba.

"Odongo arrived here as I expected, together with the other drivers and the boy," offered Otieno.

"Good. No more trouble at the border, then?"

"No. Thanks to you. I was able to persuade him to wait at the border as you suggested. He had no more trouble."

Otieno rang off, seemingly happy.

Joe was relieved that Otieno made no further mention of General Kariuki's murder. Before he left, Joe phoned his mother on her mobile. "Mum, Joe here..."

"Where are you?"

"I'm in Juba and have been here for some time."

"You just disappeared. We saw that your backpack was missing."

"There was very little notice. You were not at home and Otieno was in a hurry, so I just left. I'm sorry I didn't phone sooner but I've been very busy. We had trouble with one of the drivers."

There was a brief silence on the line.

"There has been a terrible murder here, it's all over the papers."

"What are you talking about, Mum? What murder?"

"I thought you might have heard. General Kariuki was murdered, sometime in the last few days. I thought you would want to know."

"What! Who murdered him?"

"They don't know, but maybe they are looking for a Kamba man." There was another short silence.

"When are you coming back home?" asked Ellen.

"I'm not coming back just yet. I am taking refugees for Otieno to Libya."

"Are you ever coming back?"

"I'm going to *Ulaya*, Mum. I just don't know. Is Karanja okay?" asked Joe, trying to change the subject.

"Yes, he's fine. The *bhang* business is doing well. All the arrangements you and he put in place are working. He pays your share directly into your bank account here."

"Yes. I've been getting it." There was another silence.

"I will be able to call you from time to time," said Joe. "The trip to Libya is very long; there is mobile phone coverage only some of the time."

Joe was glad to get away from any further discussion relating to the general.

There were some tears from Ellen before they rang off. She said she was used to putting up with life's burdens; losing her precious son was just another one.

Back in the Juba refugee camp Joe caught up with his companions, Patrick, Waweru, Koinange, and N'guku.

"As I have told you, Jok, the leader of the expedition has accepted all of us as assistants; he is particularly pleased that N'guku is a qualified mechanic, so can be responsible for any breakdowns, with Koinange as his assistant," Patrick told him.

The trip was sponsored by Jok and a North Sudanese called Suleiman. "I don't suppose those are their real names," Joe whispered to Patrick. "Does it matter?" Patrick shrugged.

Jok was a taciturn man, practically silent, tall and well built, well over six feet, with the very black skin typical of the local Dinka tribe.

Joe found Suleiman more accommodating and could converse with him in a mixture of English and Swahili. Suleiman was short and wiry at about five feet six. He always wore a less than clean turban and seemed to Joe to be the smarter of the two partners.

Joe had just acknowledged (celebrated would be the wrong word – he did nothing to celebrate the occasion) his seventeenth birthday; he assumed the date was approximately correct, being the day given him by his mother and listed in his passport, though most would have assessed his age at nearer twenty – his size and personal maturity reinforced that impression.

Joe had no fear as far as the journey was concerned, the expedition was just another of life's adventures. He was determined to learn as much as possible and to really understand the difficulties and dangers such a trip entailed. He would have to learn some Arabic. He would also have to learn how to manage his way through difficult situations, how to bribe people when necessary and how to take a stronger line if needed.

Joe did not confide in anyone about the death of General Kariuki, and he was greatly relieved that none of his companions made any mention of the man's demise.

'I suppose they were all in Juba by then,' he thought to himself.

When he was busy, Joe was able to put any thoughts of the death of the general right out of his mind, but often at night he woke in a sweat, often in the middle of a recurring dream in which the general had come to life and was about to strangle him. He also knew that Otieno would try to get his pound of flesh when he found out that Mbiti's passport was in the clothes left in the general's study.

Joe helped N'guku load the spares for the truck: tyres, tubes, puncture mending equipment, heavy jacks, long ropes.

"We will need these when the truck gets bogged, which it will," explained N'guku. "I have spoken to one person who has made the trip as far as Khartoum, and he told me that parts of the road are very bad if we go that way."

N'guku also loaded a variety of spares for the vehicle and a very large toolbox, attached to the underside of the vehicle.

Joe looked at N'guku as if to ask whether it was all necessary.

"This is not a new truck. It will break down..." was the best answer he received.

During a casual conversation, Joe had also acquired a pair of night vision goggles for three US dollars from a man selling them in the camp, which he also put in the toolbox.

N'guku gave him a curious glance but said nothing.

"Patrick, could you see if you can find Kimani, you know..."

"Yes, the man with the *bunduki*. He keeps telling me that he wants to go north."

"You still want to go north?" Joe asked Kimani when Patrick had found him. Kimani nodded. Joe was pleased to see he still had his AK 47.

"Please show me how that works," said Joe. They went off into the nearby bush where Kimani showed Joe how to load, aim and fire the rifle. They fired a few shots using a nearby tree for target practice.

"We are going north," Joe gestured at the truck, which was still being loaded. Kimani nodded.

"I will pay you, not Jok," Joe added.

Jok was furious when he saw Kimani helping Joe's Kikuyus load the truck. "No, no, too many..." shouted Jok in his incoherent Swahili.

"Kimani will help," said Joe mildly. "There will be no pay. He brings his own food and I hear sometimes people have had trouble with the *Janja*; they will run away when they see Kimani with his rifle."

Jok looked suspiciously at Joe, but kept silent, indicating tacit approval.

Joe loaded the food, which mostly consisted of *posho*, although there was a small quantity of hard vegetables such as potatoes and carrots, plus the water that Jok had provided for the forty passengers; to Joe the quantity seemed inadequate, but when he mentioned his concerns to Jok all he got in return was a fierce look and a guttural grunt, which Joe interpreted as a signal to keep his mouth shut.

Joe, with Kimani's help, added more food to the load on his own account, making sure it was kept separate from what Jok had provided. Joe took it upon himself to supervise the allocation of food. All the costs Joe incurred were written down for Otieno's account; as far as Joe was concerned, he was still working for Otieno.

Jok managed to gather the forty passengers round the truck.

"They pay *mia tatu* (three thousand) *Americano*. Stamp on hand. You check," he instructed Joe. "If stamp on hand, you load," Jok said.

About half the passengers had travelled to Juba on Otieno's trucks.

"We are happy you're still involved," one woman said to Joe. "We don't always understand that man Jok very well."

Jok, Suleiman and another Dinka driver settled themselves in the front of the truck; the rest of them, including Joe, were made to sit in the back. There was no seating, people merely settled themselves as comfortably as they were able in and around their own belongings. As well as the passengers who had been brought on one or other of Otieno's trucks from Nairobi, there were six men from Eritrea, seven from Ethiopia, the six Kikuyu men: Joe, Waweru, Koinange, Patrick, N'guku and Kimani, and the balance were South Sudanese wanting to escape the civil war now engulfing their new country.

They drove out of the refugee camp, almost unnoticed among the myriad vehicle movements in and out of the place.

Whenever they stopped, if Joe had a chance, he questioned other travellers about the road going north, and kept a wary eye on a map he had found in the Juba refugee camp. Initially he got very little response since few people seemed to speak Swahili.

The third time they stopped for a short break, he was told by a man herding cows: "Road very bad this way, plenty mud. Better to go west," the man pointed

Joe mentioned this conversation to Jok, as he could see they were going almost due north; and asked why they hadn't gone west through Mundri and Mvolo, which would have avoided the nearby Sudd swamp, where the river Nile meandered into a low-lying area, moving sluggishly through a mass of vegetation. Joe knew the Sudd stretched some four hundred kilometres north of Juba.

He received a very garbled explanation, "*daraja* (bridge), Luri." By which he was led to understand that the bridge was down at Luri, which was just outside Juba.

To start with, Joe and his companions were pleasantly surprised to see the road was tarred, but as with many roads in Africa, the tarred stretch soon deteriorated to bad dirt and in one place they were obliged to disembark all the passengers, and Joe's men and the male passengers were made to push the truck through a very muddy patch. They caught sight of the Nile from time to time, mainly glimpses of water flowing slowly through large stretches of the slow- moving plants, which looked like floating lilies.

Passing Terakeka through a variety of road conditions, they made their way to Rumbek after two days of hard slog. Joe wondered what the rest of the journey would be like. Another two days and they were in Wau, with the road conditions being just as bad. Joe was wondering what it would be like further north, when Jok decided to stop the vehicle at a fuel stop near the Wau railway station.

Some of the journey took them through remote unpopulated areas. Joe was intrigued by the variety of wild animals and birds they disturbed. Joe was aware of what most of the animals were, but he had never seen any of them before, all his information had come from books. There had been no wild animals left in Ol'Kalou, although there were a few birds and certainly no animals or birds in Kibera.

On the journey through both South and North Sudan, they saw dozens of antelope, large and small; he was unable to identify any of the individual species. He saw lions feasting on a zebra kill, and once they had to wait for a herd of elephant to cross the road. One of the larger elephants made as if to charge them.

"Put a shot in the air," Joe said to Kimani, which he did and the herd quickly disappeared into the bush.

Most of the people in the truck were in the same position as Joe and had never seen any animals in the wild. Until the incident with the elephants, as with Joe and his crew, they were all absolutely captivated and there was much 'ooing' and 'aaing' among the passengers.

Joe took dozens of photos on his smartphone, which Jok allowed him to recharge in the cab of the truck.

During the bumpy ride, which he and the rest of the passengers were quite used to by now, Joe noticed that the area close to the river looked fertile and in places there were people growing crops. A short distance from the river, the vegetation deteriorated into stunted thorn trees and then in some places deteriorated further into sandy desert.

Once in Wau, Joe and Kimani raced off into the railway station after making sure the truck would remain where it was for another half hour. After a lengthy discussion with the station master, who spoke Swahili, Joe discovered it was possible to travel by train from Wau to Khartoum and then Wadi-Halfa, which was their ultimate destination in Sudan. Joe handed a startled Kimani several grubby small denomination notes adding up to one hundred US dollars.

"Take the train to Wadi-Halfa; you should change trains in Khartoum. Here give me the rifle and take this," he handed Kimani the Beretta. "We'll find you in Wadi-Halfa. Just make sure you understand everything – the cost of the fares, how to avoid paying fares, how long it takes, how many people you have to bribe to get through the border between South Sudan and the rest of Sudan, and anything else you think is useful."

"What's all this for?"

"I'll explain it later. You will be very well paid if it all comes off, just use your brains and come back with useful information."

Kimani still looked confused.

"Look, trying to ship people around in a truck with all these bad roads is crazy," explained Joe. "I just want to see if the train works properly. The fares are not expensive."

"What happens after Wadi-Halfa?"

"We'll see. Suleiman will tell us, I think."

Jok was surprised to see Joe now toting the AK 47 when he returned. *"Wapi* Kimani?" he asked.

"He will join us later," said Joe.

Jok looked at Joe suspiciously, but the journey continued, with the road varying from newly constructed tar to bad dirt and then almost impassable muddy tracks.

"I have asked Kimani to see what it is like travelling by train from Wau to Wadi- Halfa," said Joe, during a meeting of his gang of Kikuyu. He showed them on his map. "Maybe a better way is to use the train, and it may be cheaper. It would mean we would need a truck or trucks in Wadi-Halfa, for the rest of the journey."

There was a brief discussion. Joe was trusted and rarely questioned.

"That animal Jok," said Waweru as the meeting continued, "almost every time we stop, he drags one of the Kikuyu women off into the bush and rapes them. This is bad news and sooner or later there is going to be big trouble. We need to stop this." He spoke in Kikuyu, which meant that Jok and any of the other Dinka on the trip would be unable to understand.

"Why do you let him do this?" Joe asked one of the Kikuyu women.

"He will kill us if we don't do as he says. We want to go to *Ulaya*; maybe this is just something we must put up with," was the tearful answer.

Joe thought of his mother and what she had had to endure. "I'll see what I can do," Joe promised

When they arrived at the border between South and North Sudan, late at night, Joe accompanied Jok and Suleiman to the hut that constituted the border post. A few US dollars changed hands and the truck was let through without any fuss; the same thing happened at the North Sudanese side. The officials didn't move from their hut and none of the people in the vehicle were asked to disembark.

Joe made a note of the grubby little towns they passed through: Al Muglad, An Nahud, Kusti, and then on to Khartoum.

During one of the stops, they were some way off the road and Jok as usual had dragged one of the women off into the bush, followed by one of the Eritrean men who, unknown to Jok, had befriended the woman. Joe thought there would be trouble, so he followed at a safe distance, carrying the AK 47, which never left his side anyway.

After a few minutes' silence Joe heard shouting, so he ran towards the noise. In an open space, surrounded by bushes Jok was kneeling in the grass, without his trousers, his hands up and pleading with the Eritrean man who was about to deliver a coup de grace with a very large knife. Joe took aim and, despite his lack of experience, shot the Eritrean in the head. Joe hesitated for a moment, horrified at what he had done. The man's body, grotesquely twisted, lay still on the ground and there was blood and brains all over nearby bushes.

The woman stood frozen. "Quick," he said to her, "get Patrick and tell him to bring a spade. Go now, hurry! And bring a first aid kit," he said as an afterthought.

Joe ran over to where a traumatised Jok was still sitting on the ground and looked at several stab wounds on Jok's arms and neck, one of which was bleeding profusely. Joe took off his own shirt and ripped it up to make bandages. By the time Patrick and the woman had returned Joe had managed to stem the flow of blood. Jok was sitting uncomfortably on the ground, still without his trousers. Between Joe and the woman, they managed to bandage Jok up and they bundled him back into his trousers. Patrick was busily digging a grave for the Eritrean.

"We should kill this bloody *shenzi*," said the woman in Kikuyu, indicating Jok, "he was going to rape me."

"No," said Joe, "at the moment we need him, but I promise you, you will be safe from now on and this man will be punished for what he tried to do to you."

Jok was unable to understand the conversation.

Joe and Patrick picked up the dead Eritrean and dropped him unceremoniously into the shallow grave, but not before Joe had thoroughly searched him, taking three thousand US dollars and the man's passport from his pockets. They found nothing else of value.

Joe gave five hundred US dollars to the woman. "You saw nothing, you know nothing," he said to her in Kikuyu, which they knew Jok didn't understand. "If you say one word about any of this you will get the same treatment." He pointed at the dead man now being covered in sand by Patrick.

Joe said to Jok, fiercely, "This is all to do with you. If you touch another woman on this trip, or any other trip, I will shoot you. Do you understand?" He waved the barrel of the AK 47 in Jok's face, who looked terrified.

Joe and Patrick half carried, half dragged Jok back to the truck.

Many anxious faces surrounded them as Joe and Patrick emerged through the bush and asked for help to load Jok into the back of the truck. Joe asked all the men in the expedition to gather round at the front of the truck. They assumed mistakenly that he was going to tell them what had happened. He pointedly loaded a round into the breach of the rifle, saying quietly to the four Kikuyu men in the group, in their own language, "This is where we take over." He made everyone sit down, except the Kikuyu.

He sought out Suleiman, who was half hidden behind the truck. "Stand here with me," he said to the man. Suleiman reluctantly obeyed.

"Put your hands on your heads," Joe instructed all the passengers. One of the Dinka men demurred. Joe fired at the man's feet. "The next one will be into your thick head," he said in English, which he knew the man understood. The man then complied.

"Okay," he said to the Kikuyu, again in their own language, "search them all. Take away any firearms, knives, anything that can be used as a weapon. You will not touch money or passports. I am only interested in weapons. When you have finished, search the truck, and their personal belongings thoroughly. Anyone who disobeys will be shot." He put another shot into the air to emphasise the point.

Within a few minutes, several knives, two pistols and a panga had been gathered. "Okay, do that again," he instructed. Three more knives were unearthed. "Now search all these people, one by one so I can watch, including the women."

One man had a Glock 17 tucked into his waistband. "Who the fuck do you think you are?" Joe asked. "Next time..." he patted the AK.

"I need to search you too," Joe said to Suleiman, which he did. The knife he found on Suleiman was added to the collection.

"I have now taken over the expedition," Joe said to a terrified and scared-looking Suleiman. "If you cooperate, you can make some money. If not..." Joe made an unmistakable gesture as if to cut his throat.

Suleiman remained silent.

The knives were all securely locked in to N'guku's toolbox, as was all the spare ammunition for the pistols. The Glock and the other two pistols were shared with N'guku, Waweru and Patrick.

"I'll get you a pistol in Wadi-Halfa," he said to Koinange.

The women tried to organise a meal, but by now the provisions Jok had provided had almost run out.

Joe clambered onto the back of the truck. He approached Jok and kicked him in the ribs, waking him. "You have run out of food," said Joe, "but I have plenty. Just pay me first and we can use my supplies." Jok tried to protest. Joe merely kicked him again on one of his wounds.

"How much?' asked Jok. "One thousand US."

After Jok gave him five hundred, which resulted in another kick, Jok produced another five hundred, mixed in with some worthless Sudanese currency. Joe then delivered another couple of kicks. The rest of the money was then produced.

During the meal, Joe had a long, productive discussion with Suleiman. As it turned out, Suleiman was fed up with Jok's antics and could see that an association with Joe could benefit him, certainly in the short term and possibly beyond that. Joe knew he would need a person like Suleiman, who spoke Arabic and who was familiar with the people and situation in North Sudan, if what Joe had in mind was to work.

Immediately after the coup, Joe personally conducted an extensive search of the vehicle and of Jok himself. He found all the papers belonging to the truck, and all of the cash from the fees paid by the passengers, which Jok had brought with him. Joe hid it all in the locked toolbox, which only he and N'guku had access to.

Waweru and Koinange approached the Kikuyu women on the trip.

"We have now taken over this trip. Could you please help to prepare the food? Something Joe is now providing, something he will do until we get to the Libyan coast," said Waweru.

The women got into a huddle.

Soon three of them got back to Waweru. "Yes, but when we get to Wadi-Halfa we need to get food that we can eat. Also, we need proper gas cookers."

So, the Kikuyu women prepared food for all, that night and for the rest of the trip.

At night, the passengers all settled as best they could in and around the truck, mostly sleeping on the ground with what cover they had brought with them. Joe ensured that one of his Kikuyu was on guard right through the night.

"I will take the 2am to 5am shift," said Joe, "after that we should all be on the move, with breakfast. We should always be on our way by six."

After the incident with Jok, one of the young Kikuyu girls in the group, Wambui, and her mother moved their sleeping position next to Joe's area, he supposed for security reasons. This continued for the many nights it took to get to Khartoum. Joe didn't respond immediately to Wambui's overtly sexual overtures. Wambui's mother looked at Joe suspiciously.

Joe reflected on the situation. He was briefly tempted. He did weaken once and once only; Wambui made sure the whole expedition knew of her encounter by making a great deal of noise as she climaxed. He regretted his action and decided that all Wambui and her mother were doing was to look after their own interests. He was now the leader, so any sexual relationship with anyone would change the dynamics of the group. It was in his interests to keep his distance and to treat all the people now in his care as equally as possible. In any event, he had never before touched any of the women in the group. He made sure his Kikuyu comrades in arms recognised the issue and behaved as Joe instructed.

The rest of the trip through Khartoum and then on to Wadi-Halfa, took ten gruelling days. On the way to Khartoum Joe established a regime where the original Dinka driver and Suleiman sat in the front with N'guku. One of Joe's Kikuyu alternated with N'guku. Joe and the rest of his crew remained in the back, keeping an eye out for any trouble or dissent.

At the end of each day, usually during meal preparation, but sometimes while everyone was just gathered round the truck, Joe took it upon himself to brief all his passengers on the progress they had made and what to expect the next day, making it clear that they should come to him privately with any problems.

"Keep well in touch with all these people," Joe told his own cohort, "not just the Kikuyu, and make sure that we nip any trouble in the bud before it develops, and come and tell me anything, anything you hear."

"I will look after the Eritreans," offered Koinange. "And I the Ethiopians," said Patrick.

"And I the Dinka," said Waweru.

"That leaves me and Joe to deal with the Kikuyu," said N'guku.

Before they had arrived in Wadi-Halfa, the passengers gradually warmed to Joe, firstly the Kikuyu and then most of the others. The women in particular were relieved, since none of them were raped during the rest of the journey. Also, they became aware that the food they were eating was now what Joe had provided.

Once they had by passed Khartoum, Suleiman advised taking the road from Khartoum via Dongola, which tracked the Nile all the way to Wadi-Halfa. "The road was properly surfaced a few years ago," he told Joe, "so it should be all right. I even saw some maintenance crews the last time we came along here."

It took almost three days to travel the one thousand kilometres from Khartoum to Wadi-Halfa.

"Railway station, tell the drivers to go to the railway station," Joe instructed Suleiman, who looked at him curiously, "Kimani will be there."

"Where the hell have you been?" asked Kimani when he saw Joe and the truck. "I've been here for almost a week."

"Difficulties," answered Joe, "we had some problems, I'll explain later. What about the border? Have you tried to go over? You've had plenty of time."

"I've been talking to as many people as I can find. They all say: 'Don't go into Egypt. Cross the Nile here and make for Libya.'"

"Okay, how do you do that?"

"There are people who can take the truck and all the people across the river. There is a ferry, about fifty kilometres south of here; he will be able to do what we want."

"What about petrol?"

"We'll need a tanker. I've found one which we could clean up."

"Who owns it?"

"Don't know. I am sure someone will turn up when we start doing things to it."

"We need to take Jok to the hospital," said Joe, changing the subject. Kimani looked at Joe quizzically.

"He got hurt. He will not be coming any further with us."

Joe was intrigued with what Suleiman told him was the ancient city of Wadi-Halfa; for centuries, it had been a stopping off point for expeditions further south.

"The British used it as part of their explorations into Sudan," Suleiman explained. "It is close to the southern end of Lake Nasser, where the river Nile was dammed by the Egyptians. There is a Chinese-owned fish processing plant, which has just commenced operations."

Joe was learning new and important things on a daily basis as he went along. He found the place was unbearably hot, with daily temperatures hovering above the mid-forties Celsius. Most of buildings were low rise with flat roofs. Joe briefly examined the ferry terminal that Kimani had told him was not the way to go, unless they all wanted to end up in an Egyptian prison. He decided they would get out of the place as soon as possible, having ensured they had enough food and fuel to take them into Southern Libya.

After a long discussion with Suleiman, Joe sent all the Dinka staff back south; from the money he had taken off Jok, he paid their train fares to Wau. "After that you can try to catch a lift from another vehicle returning to Juba." Joe told them. He paid them slightly over the odds, for the time spent on the journey up to that point, knowing that Jok would have paid them as little as he could get away with. Joe thought he might need them in the future, although he was beginning to have second thoughts about the value of the trip, which they were now about halfway through.

"They can bring people from Juba to Wadi-Halfa and then my North Sudanese can take over from here," announced Suleiman.

"No," said Joe, to Suleiman's surprise. "The Dinka can drive trucks from Juba to Wau and then we will bring everyone here by train. Kimani has found someone who can take the truck and the people over the river." He then added more thoughtfully, "We will need more trucks and more people up here though. We'll need Arab speakers as drivers from this point on, which is where you can help."

Joe phoned Otieno from Wadi-Halfa and told him the story of the trip so far.

"The police have been round here on several occasions, looking for you. It's about the murder of General Kariuki. They have publicly stated that the passport they found with the general's body belonged to Mbiti. I remember you showed me that passport, when you returned from one of the trips to Juba. I have not told the police anything about that, yet."

Joe's gut tightened. He didn't know whether Otieno was telling the truth or not about police visits, but he desperately did not want the police to link him with the possession of Mbiti's passport, so he decided to play along with Otieno.

"As far as I am concerned this trip is now being financed by you, Otieno, although I have taken all or most of the funds Jok, the previous leader of the operation, received from the passengers. So, the business belongs to you. As always, I will account to you for all the sums received and spent on your behalf."

Otieno grunted as if content he now had Joe back in his grasp.

After some haggling, Joe got Suleiman to agree that his and Joe's share of the final profit would be fifteen per cent each. Otieno would get the rest. Joe didn't care about his share – he had a great deal of money in London. All he wanted was to cover his tracks as far as possible. He knew he would need an untraceable new identity when he arrived in England.

They were quite unable to find the owner of the tanker, so Joe and Kimani hitched it up to the truck and towed it to a small garage Joe had found. Over two days, N'guku and one of the other Kikuyu cleaned it up, repaired the tyres and the spare, and then filled it with water to satisfy themselves that there were no leaks.

Meanwhile Joe, Suleiman and Kimani paid a visit to the ferry operator, whose name turned out to be Clinton. With Suleiman translating, Joe explained what he wanted and said that if all went well, he expected to be transporting five hundred to one thousand people every year to the north.

Joe and Kimani examined the dilapidated and rickety ferry carefully. It was a large flatbed vehicle carrier, with a shallow draft. In many places the safety rails round the edge of the vessel were missing. It was rusty and looked as if it had been in place for several decades. Joe insisted that Clinton start the engine. He also insisted that they took a brief return trip into the middle of the river. Much to Clinton's discomfort, Joe took the trouble to point out the obvious defects in the vessel: "The engine looks as if it is about to break down," Joe observed, "with all the smoke coming out, and this thing lists to one side, not to mention the whole thing is rusty and looks as if it might sink at any time."

Clinton said nothing.

Returning to the dock, Joe asked, "How much?"

"Two thousand," was Clinton's response in Arabic. Suleiman translated.

Without blinking Joe peeled off two thousand Sudanese pounds. Clinton looked at him in horror.

"Dollar. US Dollar," he gabbled.

Joe continued to hold out the two thousand Sudanese pounds.

"Tell him we only deal in Sudanese currency," said Joe. From what Kimani had told him, even with a full boat, the man barely made two thousand Sudanese pounds for a return trip.

They eventually settled for three thousand Sudanese pounds, to be paid once the trip over the river was complete.

"Kimani, you stay here and make sure that this fellow is still around when we need him."

Kimani nodded.

Joe and Suleiman returned to Wadi-Halfa, Joe also managing to buy another five AK 47s, all for less than ten US dollars each. He used the rifles to arm his Kikuyu colleagues. He then spent a few hours traipsing round the various service stations, accompanied by two of his Kikuyu companions. He eventually negotiated a twenty per cent discount for a full tank of petrol for the truck and the tanker from a back-street operator, with the promise of returning in a month or so with more business.

Before they could go anywhere though, they were approached by a group of half a dozen policemen, tearing round in a battered-looking Toyota pick-up truck. They came to a screeching halt in front of Joe and his companions.

"Joe!" the Sergeant in charge yelled.

Joe said to his companions in Kikuyu, "I know what this is about. One of you will have to pretend to be me. It's bloody Jok again. I'll get you out of this double quick, I promise you, but I need to be able to deal with the situation."

Koinange stepped forward, giving his AK 47 to Joe, and was arrested by the police and driven off.

Having found Suleiman, he, Joe, and Patrick went to the hospital, which was a labyrinth of old buildings put together haphazardly. After many delays, they eventually found their way into a private ward where Jok was recuperating. Joe firmly shut the door of the ward and locked it. Nobody in the hospital took the slightest notice of two armed men wandering about.

Jok looked terrified when the trio approached. "Okay, Jok, what do you want?" Suleiman asked him in Arabic. Joe still had Koinange's AK 47 and the Beretta.

Jok pretended not to understand.

Joe pulled out the Beretta, saying to Suleiman in Swahili, "I think we should just finish him off now, something we should have done back there..."

Jok said something in Arabic to Suleiman.

"He says you should have been arrested by the police," Suleiman said in English so Jok wouldn't understand.

In Swahili Joe said, "I'm just going to shoot this bastard, unless he tells me what gives."

Jok mumbled something in his poor Swahili to the effect that he wanted his money back.

Joe waved the Beretta about. "Forget that. We are still less than halfway through the journey."

"I need money to get home," wailed Jok. "How much?"

"Ten thousand US."

Joe pointed the Beretta at Jok and cocked it. "How much?" he asked.

"Five thousand," said Jok.

"He'll probably have to pay the police something," advised Suleiman in English.

"Three," said Joe. Jok nodded.

Joe tossed him his mobile phone. "Phone the police and tell them to release the man they think is me, who they have in custody."

There was a rapid-fire conversation in what Joe assumed was Arabic.

"Okay," said Suleiman, "they will release your man outside the hospital in ten minutes."

Joe grabbed his phone back from Jok.

Joe said to Patrick, "Go down. When you see our friend, Koinange, take him and get the hell out and load everyone onto the truck. Make sure the tanker is attached and that both the truck and the tanker have been topped up with petrol. Phone me and then go to the ferry. Suleiman, please lend him your phone."

Once Patrick had left, Joe said to Suleiman in English, "I'm going to move this asshole to another place in the hospital. The police will be more interested in their share of the money than anything else, so they will be delayed here, looking for him, while we scarper. I'm sure the idea is to take Jok's money and then see what more they can get out of us." Joe found two white coats in an unattended nurse's station next to Jok's ward.

Wearing the white coats, they wheeled Jok out of his ward in his bed. The AK 47 was hidden in the bedclothes. They locked the door behind them and took Jok to a nearby lift. Amid Jok's protestations they wheeled him into the lift, which they took to the basement. Quickly looking around, Suleiman found a way to get Jok into the boiler room, where they bound and gagged him and partially hid the bed, with Jok still in it, behind one of the boilers. They shut the door and left their white gowns on the bed. Joe tossed three thousand US Dollars on to the writhing Jok.

Joe, having retrieved his AK 47, led Suleiman to the back entrance of the hospital, where they waited for what seemed an interminable time for the promised phone call.

When Joe's phone rang, it was Patrick who said, "We have loaded everyone onto the truck."

"Go to the river. We will meet you there. Any signs of police?"

"Police? No. No police." They hung up.

"Taxi to the river," said Joe to Suleiman.

Suleiman went outside and within a few minutes returned in a taxi.

"Fifty US to the river," said Suleiman to Joe, who fished a fifty dollar note from his pocket and waved it about. "Hurry," yelled Suleiman.

They arrived at the river to see that all the passengers and the truck and trailer had been loaded onto the ferry. Joe paid the taxi driver and told him to get back to Wadi-Halfa and say nothing.

Suleiman introduced his three North Sudanese drivers. "All unarmed," Joe insisted.

"No," said Suleiman. "They must bring rifles. We may have to fight the *Janja*."

"Give me all the rifles then," insisted Joe. "If we have to fight the *Janja* I will give them their rifles back."

After a discussion between the drivers and Suleiman, the rifles were given to Joe, who had them locked in the toolbox. Suleiman looked unhappy at the development.

Joe looked around.

Clinton standing next to the ferry was waiting expectantly; he had two of his staff on the ferry itself.

Joe looked at Kimani. "Any trouble?" he asked.

"No, but we need to watch out. They may try something on..." Clinton approached Joe, demanding the fare.

"When we arrive safely over the other side, I'll pay you in full," Suleiman translated.

Clinton hesitated.

Joe approached him, cocked his AK 47 and fired a shot past Clinton into the river.

Clinton jumped a mile into the air. "Crocodiles," explained Joe. He eyed Clinton. "Just get a bloody move on," he gestured. There was no need for a translation.

Clinton, his two assistants and Suleiman climbed onto the ferry followed by Joe, N'guku, Kimani, Patrick, Waweru and Koinange, all armed with the recently acquired AK 47s. Suleiman's drivers were already on board.

Halfway across, the engine sputtered and slowed down. Joe went close to Clinton and this time fired two shots into the river, which passed a few inches from Clinton. The engine miraculously sped up again. The crossing took about half an hour. The passengers and then the truck and tanker were disembarked. Joe paid Clinton his three thousand Sudanese pounds and climbed onto the truck with his entourage.

"Look, look over there," said Suleiman. He pointed to a small group of what looked like policemen on the far bank of the river.

Joe clambered down off the truck and walked over to the ferry: he cut the fuel lines and ripped out the alternator from the engine, which he threw into the river.

Clinton protested wildly, waving his arms about and yelling something in what Joe thought was Arabic.

"Stay here for a couple of days," he told Clinton. He pointed to the far bank. "Police."

Clinton continued to protest. "Here," said Joe, "this will help fix the engine," he handed Clinton one hundred US dollars.

"We'll be back in a couple of months," Joe shouted to a mesmerised Clinton.

Suleiman translated but most of what he said was lost in the breeze. It was hot, but the dry heat was tempered by the river.

"They won't follow," Suleiman observed, referring to the police. "They have restricted fuel allowances and their vehicles wouldn't make it anyway."

Joe pulled out one of the maps he had secured in Juba. "Just remind me of the journey," he said to Suleiman. "It's firstly Selima Oasis and then Uweinat on the Libyan border?"

Suleiman nodded.

"How many days?"

"Maybe six," said Suleiman.

"Will they phone the police in Selima?" asked Joe.

"Probably not. Different jurisdiction." Suleiman shrugged, pointed due west. "Selima Oasis, we must keep an eye out for the *Janja*."

The track was sandy, but they were able to make good time. Joe, standing in the back of the truck, kept watch for any signs of life.

They had only left the Nile in mid-afternoon, but Joe urged them on until dark in order to put more distance between themselves and the river.

Desolate did not begin to describe the landscape. It was just an endless expanse of sand with an occasional rock formation carved by the steady westerly wind. Joe saw nothing, certainly no humans, but no sign of any other beings either.

They stopped as dark fell and they moved the truck slightly off the track, where the Kikuyu women prepared a meal for all.

Joe was relieved they had got away with no further damage to the expedition. Most of the passengers were by now very much on his side. They were now individually coming to him or one of his crew with issues. They had seen that Joe had somehow negotiated his way through several very difficult situations. They had all paid substantial sums to come on the trip and they could see that Joe was their best hope of making it. For his part, Joe wondered how much more difficult it would be to negotiate the rest of the trip. He wondered if there wasn't an easier way...

By the light of the moon, Joe addressed the throng:

"As you can all see, Jok is no longer with us," he said. There was a loud cheer from almost everyone.

"He and his assistants have returned to Juba. We had some difficulties in Wadi-Halfa, but nobody was hurt. We will honour the arrangements made by Jok to take you to the Libyan coast. I don't need to say any more, but if you have an issue, please talk to me or one of my men. Any questions?

"No more payments?" asked one of the Kikuyu women, who was beginning to trust Joe.

"No. We will take you to the Libyan coast. If you want to go to *Ulaya* it will cost you more."

The next day and some hours into the journey to Selima Oasis, he caught sight of what he thought might be palm trees, or maybe some sort of mirage.

Suleiman was in the truck cab. Joe leant out and tapped him on the shoulder and yelled over the engine noise, "Selima?" He pointed. Suleiman told the driver to stop and he clambered in next to Joe. He looked through his binoculars and nodded.

"As I told you there is small police post here. We will go to the edge of the oasis and then you and I need to talk to the people there."

"No other people?"

"No, sometimes some Bedouin on their way through, otherwise nothing."

"What do the Bedouin do here?"

"Trading."

"What trading?"

"You'll see, if they are here today."

Within a half hour they stopped in a dune on the edge of the oasis, but out of sight of any people in the oasis. The passengers sheltered from the dry heat under the vehicle.

Joe and Suleiman walked into the settlement. There were scattered palm trees and a large pond. A North Sudanese flag was attached to what looked like an ancient ruin among the palm trees.

"Police," said Suleiman, pointing.

Beyond, there was a large group of Bedouin, busy loading newly filled water carriers onto protesting camels squatting on the ground. The men were dressed in their traditional white kanzus, which reached their ankles; on their heads they wore the square-looking keffiyeh. There were women, also dressed traditionally in blue thobe wrap-around robes, with their heads covered, as required by religious tradition in Islam. They were tending cooking fires.

Joe then noticed something else: a group of about twenty black people all chained together, sitting huddled a little way from the main group. Taking a closer look, Joe also spotted a reasonably well-dressed European woman, smoking and sitting separately and quite comfortably under a palm tree. The woman gave no sign that she had seen them. Suleiman pretended not to notice Joe's gesture asking who they were.

Joe then asked the question directly, "Who are they?"

"Slaves," answered Suleiman. "Going to markets in Khartoum and on the Red Sea coast. We've been doing this for centuries."

"Doing what?"

"Slaving. The tribes select who will be slaves and then sell them to the Bedouin. The West tries to stop it, but they can't."

"And the white woman?"

Suleiman again pretended not to hear. Joe repeated his question.

"Sometimes these people are employed to transport aid workers or tourists that have been kidnapped. The kidnappers get very big money from Western governments to release them. Travelling with the Bedouin is a way of hiding them." Suleiman looked at Joe. "Don't say anything to the police, or anyone else, about that or any of your other questions. Anything at all. The police will be nervous and will get a big payout from the Bedouin, for both the slaves and the kidnapped woman."

Joe nodded. 'Might make our job a bit easier,' he thought.

They entered the police post. Within minutes they were ushered into a back office, where they found a very nervous-looking man dressed in a police uniform sitting behind an old table, which was devoid of even a scrap of paper or a pen.

The two men spoke in Arabic. By now Joe could understand a few words of the language, a skill he kept from Suleiman. Joe had also started to learn something about Islam. 'It's a bit closer to African traditions,' he thought.

The man behind the desk was obviously anxious to deal with Joe and Suleiman and their business, as quickly as possible.

"The man wants ten US dollars per person," Suleiman eventually told Joe in Swahili. "He says we can collect water, but we cannot stay in the oasis."

"Tell him if we can't stay here, we will only pay five. Also, tell him that we will be back here every two months or so."

There was another brief conversation in Arabic.

"He says he will accept seven, but he wants us away from here before dark."

Joe nodded. He handed Suleiman one hundred and forty US dollars. "That's for twenty of our passengers."

Suleiman handed over the money, which was pocketed without another word. They were ushered outside quickly and there was a flurry of words from the police chief.

"We have two hours," Suleiman told Joe.

"Okay," instructed Joe. "Your drivers and my Kikuyu guards will collect all the water carriers we have; fill them up here and then we will be off."

While this was going on, Joe gathered his thirty-nine passengers and told them what was going to happen.

"We'll camp in the desert a few kilometres from here."

Soon all the water carriers had been filled and loaded and all the people had clambered back into the truck. They found a rough track that skirted the perimeter of the oasis and they were again on their way; now towards Uweinat, the border between Sudan and Libya. After a few kilometres, Joe indicated that they should drive into the sand dunes and off the rough road, where they would camp.

The women in the group set up gas cookers and prepared a meal for all.

"We'll do three-hour watches. First watch is me, Patrick and one of the Arab drivers, and so on through the night," he announced. He gave one of the confiscated rifles to the first Arab driver.

Joe maintained the strict watch routine he had set up on their first night out of the Selima oasis. The second night Kimani was part of the midnight watch from eleven to two in the morning. Halfway through his watch, he noticed what he thought was a few flashes of light to the northeast of their camp, and woke Joe to tell him. They sat and waited to see if what Kimani had seen was repeated. It was. This time much closer to their camp. Joe woke Suleiman and returned the confiscated firearms to the other Arab drivers. Joe said to them, "don't shoot until I shoot." He made all ten of his force fan out so each one had visibility of the men on each side of them. They walked slowly through the thick sand. Joe put on his night vision goggles, which he had retrieved from the toolbox. To his amazement, he saw a dozen shapes less than three hundred metres away scrambling towards them.

"Down," he instructed.

The men next to him dropped to the ground and Joe could then see all his men following suit. He continued to watch the progress of the people approaching. There was one figure who, by his gestures, appeared to be directing the others. Joe knew that if he fired a shot all his men would follow suit, which was fine by him.

Joe waited and when the apparent leader kept still for a few seconds he fired one shot, aiming at the man's legs. The man fell over, screaming, this was followed by all of Joe's people firing shots directly at the would-be attackers. From the screams Joe was certain that some of the attackers were hit, which provoked shouts of panic. The men hurriedly picked up their still screaming leader and at least two others as they beat a hasty retreat. Joe thought that the attackers had left one body behind.

Joe fired two more shots directly at the rapidly retreating erstwhile attackers. "*Janja,*" Suleiman muttered unnecessarily.

The camp was wide-awake when they returned. Despite the dark night, the women had started to prepare breakfast, and as the eerie light of dawn emerged, they were on their way again. Joe in his usual way briefed all his passengers, hoping to keep them calm. The next few days would be very tricky.

Joe and Suleiman were sitting in the front of the truck as they approached the border between Sudan and Libya at Uweinat. They were fortunate that the approach to Uweinat was over a slight hill so they could view the border area from a few hundred metres away without being seen.

Two border posts were clearly visible. The area seemed to be utterly deserted, although after a while a man emerged from the nearest post. He walked a few metres and urinated into a stunted bush, then returned. Scanning the area, Joe could also see, partially hidden behind some scraggy-looking bushes and half a dozen huts, what appeared to be women sweeping.

"There are two border posts here: North Sudan and Libya," Suleiman informed Joe.

"You know these people?" asked Joe.

Suleiman shrugged. "I've been through here before, but the people change sometimes."

"Okay," said Joe. "I suggest you go with one of your drivers and see what you can do, one deal covering both posts, this side and the Libyan side. We don't want to be stuck in between the two posts..."

Suleiman looked at Joe and was about to say something when Joe said, "We need to keep hidden, so we will stay here until you signal us." Joe then added, "You must also remember that we hope to bring many other people through here, so do a sensible deal, something we can live with..."

Suleiman looked up to the heavens saying, "It's hot, hot." Which it was. Joe shrugged.

The vehicle was backed away, and they managed to find some shade under an overhanging rock. Patrick was left to keep watch on Suleiman's progress. The Kikuyu woman, who was now in charge of the food, handed out small amounts of *Ugali,* which she had kept after the previous meal. Joe joined Patrick on watch. It took Suleiman and one of his Arab drivers half an hour to walk to the border post. The man they had seen earlier emerged and initially his angry gesticulations indicated he was telling Suleiman to go away, but after a little while Suleiman was allowed to enter the post. The driver was left standing in the sun.

A few minutes later, Suleiman and the border guard emerged and together they walked to the other post. There was a brief conversation. Suleiman and the border guard then disappeared into the Libyan side of the border. Suleiman then emerged and waved.

Chapter 9: Libya

Still under the overhanging rock, the vehicle was loaded. Joe made sure that his armed Kikuyu were clearly visible, with the passengers hidden inside the truck, behind the tarpaulins.

When they arrived at the post a triumphant Suleiman said, "One thousand US, both sides."

Joe made a point of going into each post and thanking the two people inside, in very rough Arabic, as he handed over five hundred US dollars to each one.

They drove on, arriving in Al Jawf, the Kufra Oasis, just after dark.

Suleiman found a boarding house able to accommodate everyone. Joe's Kikuyu were left to deal with the passengers.

"I must find the police chief," announced Suleiman. "I'll come with you this time," said Joe.

Suleiman nodded.

N'guku had found a garage, with the help of one of the Arab drivers.

The police chief had been advised by the Libyan border guards to expect them; tea was brought. Suleiman introduced Joe. There was a longish conversation between Suleiman and the police chief. Suleiman translated for Joe's benefit. Joe had a feeling that some of the conversation was lost in Suleiman's translation.

The chief was well-prepared, being well dressed in his official police uniform. He had a stack of official-looking forms on his well-appointed wooden desk.

There was another brief discussion between Suleiman and the chief.

"These are all official resident's forms," Suleiman told Joe in Swahili, assuming the police chief would not understand. "They have all been properly stamped and signed. All we have to do is to fill them out," he smiled, "in Arabic."

Joe didn't flinch. "Sounds like a job for you and your drivers. What's the cost?"

"Fifty US for each form."

"Ouch," said Joe.

"Do you speak any English?" Joe asked the chief, after a moment's thought. The man nodded.

"We are going to bring about one thousand people through here each year."

"One thousand?" queried the chief, looking at Suleiman, who nodded uneasily. "How much you pay?" asked the chief.

"Eight," said Joe.

The chief shook his head, smiling. "Twelve."

They eventually settled for ten.

The chief handed over fifty forms, all indeed stamped and signed. "There must be an expiry date," Joe said to Suleiman, again in Swahili. Suleiman looked through all the forms, trying not to appear anxious.

He looked at Joe, again saying in Swahili. "How did you know? The expiry date is tomorrow."

Joe ignored the question. "Someone has made a small mistake here, one of your assistants, I suppose," he said to the chief in English. "We just need to fix the date here, one year from now. Suleiman, maybe you could change the dates on all the forms and the chief can just countersign all the changes."

The chief looked at Joe with an irritated expression on his face, but he did what was asked. There was a brief flurry of conversation between Suleiman and the chief in Arabic, some of which Joe understood. Suleiman and was about to say something, when the chief said to Joe in English, "You must give me one of your women."

Joe didn't miss a beat. "Married women? Next time I travel through here maybe we will have some unmarried women." He continued to look through the forms, checking that they were now in order.

"Who are they married to?" asked the chief.

"Me, Mr Suleiman here, other men on the truck. You want virgins?"

The chief nodded, unhappily. "You must all leave tomorrow. Bosses from Tripoli..."

"Yes, that's okay with us."

There was another brief conversation in Arabic, between Suleiman and the chief, with the chief looking at Joe with distaste.

They shook hands with the chief as they left his office. Joe handed over four hundred US dollars.

"The money doesn't include everyone?" questioned Suleiman, once they had left the police station.

Joe shrugged. "The whole thing is a charade, just to squeeze us. Don't worry."

"We leave tonight," added Joe, as they left to return to the boarding house. "We'll be halfway to the coast by the time that bastard wakes up; it's only about seven hundred kilometres to Ajdabiya; the man at the garage told N'guku it's a good road. That man," he said referring to the police chief, "is going to try to stop us on some pretext or another. Pay the boarding house for two nights and don't tell them we're leaving, but indicate we'll be back in a few months."

Suleiman made an excuse and then walked back into the police post on his own. Joe frowned, wondering what Suleiman was up to.

On returning to the boarding house, Joe went to find N'guku. "Those repairs must be completed by no later than midnight. We'll be leaving tonight. Just help me keep an eye on Suleiman," added Joe, "he's behaving strangely."

N'guku didn't argue. He never argued with Joe.

Joe rounded up all his Kikuyu crew and told them to be careful of Suleiman.

Just as they were about to leave, a police vehicle drove up in a rush. Two officers jumped out, hurriedly handcuffed Joe and loaded him into the vehicle. Suleiman smirked as they drove off. Joe was dumped into a filthy cell. There was one other man there, who turned out to be one of his Ethiopian passengers. Joe was not searched.

By midnight the truck had been loaded and all the passengers, except the one Ethiopian man and of course Joe, had been accounted for.

#

Back at the boarding house, Suleiman wasted no time. He said, "We must get going, right now as Joe told us."

"What about Joe?" asked N'guku, who was on full alert because of the warning from Joe.

"He'll be joining us later," said Suleiman.

Joe's Kikuyu crew all gathered around N'guku, concerned about what had happened to Joe. They were all still armed. "Just play along," he said in their own language. "Something is going on; we may have to take out Suleiman and the Arab drivers, who are all now carrying their rifles."

Suleiman didn't try to pay the boarding house; mostly because he had no access to the toolbox, where the money was kept, but also because he was in a hurry to consolidate what he thought was his new position.

So, they set off, without Joe and the missing Ethiopian.

#

Now in his filthy cell, Joe spent a few moments collecting his thoughts. The jail appeared to consist of a lot of iron bars made into cells, so even in the dim light Joe could see right through the jail from end to end. He said to Bikila, the Ethiopian, in Swahili, "Why are you in here?"

"Don't know," was the response in English, "I just went for a walk and was picked up by the police. Maybe all they want is money?"

"Don't worry. Let everything settle down and I'll get you out of here. I think you are right about wanting money. While we're here, why are you on this trip? Why do you want to go to Europe?"

"The government stole my business."

"What sort of business?"

"Motor repair business. I am a trained mechanic."

"How did the government steal your business?"

"A minister's brother wanted the business, so they invented all sorts of lies that put me in trouble and in jail... I managed to escape jail and here I am."

"Do they feed people in here?" asked Joe, after a short silence.

"No, people's family have to feed anyone locked up here. The guards sometimes bring water."

"So, you have had nothing to eat at all since being locked up here?"

"The man in the next cell gave me the remains of what he had; he left just before you were dumped in here. He paid the guard something."

"How many people are in here?"

"Maybe one hundred or more."

"How many guards at night?"

"Two. Don't worry they will come and maybe ask for money."

The conversation stopped for a few minutes, while Joe listened to the noises in the facility, which consisted of mostly wails and screams and sometimes mumbled conversations.

As darkness descended it became almost impossible to see anything. There was one dimly lit bulb at the end of the passage and the occasional flash from a torch as one of the guards patrolled, an event that seemed to occur infrequently.

"Do you speak Arabic?" Joe asked Bikila.

"Some; enough to get by."

"See if you can attract the attention of the guards."

Soon both guards appeared. There was a short discussion between the head guard and Bikila. "They want one thousand US."

"For both of us, not each."

There was another short discussion. "Okay," Bikila said.

"They must open the door of the cell before we give them the money."

The guards entered the cell and Joe didn't hesitate. With his strength, and taking the guards completely by surprise, he knocked one unconscious with a single punch and he stabbed the other one. With Bikila's help he tied them both up with their belts and strips from their clothing. There were shouts of encouragement from the other prisoners. Joe grabbed the keys from the guards. He and Bikila left the cell, ignoring the guard's firearms, and locked the guards inside, leaving no money. He then unlocked several neighbouring cells, tossed the keys to one of the freed prisoners and then left. As they ran outside. Joe phoned N'guku, who answered immediately. "Don't say anything, just listen. We were in jail, something to do with Suleiman and the chief of police here. Just see if you can delay progress any way you can. We'll be with you soon. Don't let Suleiman anywhere near the toolbox or the money."

Leaving the chaos of the jailbreak behind them, Joe said, "Bikila, we need to find a car. One you can hot-wire, to get it started."

They walked along a few streets with Bikila looking for an old car. "Here's one," he said.

Within a minute Bikila had forced open the locked door of an old Volkswagen beetle and within another five minutes the engine roared to life. With Bikila driving they managed to find their way out of Al Jawf and, keeping their eyes open for their truck, drove slowly through the neighbouring town of Jiao. There was very little traffic on the road and no sign of the truck.

A few minutes outside Jiao they saw the lights of a big vehicle on the side of the road – it was indeed the truck. The passengers were all milling around, with N'guku trying to look busy with his head underneath the bonnet.

Joe hopped out of the beetle some fifty metres behind the truck and in the dark. He walked up to the truck, behaving as if nothing was amiss. N'guku was one of the first to see him. Joe lifted his index finger to his lips indicating that N'guku should keep quiet. He then made a gesture asking, 'Where is Suleiman?' N'guku pointed to the other side of the truck.

Bikila in the meanwhile, as Joe had asked him, left the beetle and walked over to what seemed to be the largest gathering of passengers. He described how he had hot-wired the beetle and driven off to find the truck. As asked, he made no mention of Joe.

With most of the attention being paid to Bikila, in the half-light Joe crept up quietly to N'guku saying, "Are you and the crew still armed?"

"Yes."

"Where is Suleiman?"

"Over there with his drivers, the other side of the truck."

"Just watch my back. I'm going to give them a bit of a fright, I hope."

"What hap..."

"I'll tell you in a minute, just let me deal with this."

Joe walked round the side of the truck. He spotted Suleiman almost immediately, in deep conversation with his three Arab speaking drivers. So, in the dark, Joe was able to approach to within a couple of metres without being seen.

"Hello Suleiman, how nice to see you all again."

Suleiman jumped up in total amazement, as did his drivers.

N'guku and the four other Kikuyu had also approached in the half-light. They raised their AK 47s, and cocked them as one, with N'guku saying, "Sit down again or you will get what's coming to you." Nobody understood what had been said but the message was clear; they all sat down again.

"How?"

"Oh, they just let me out. No problem. Big misunderstanding," explained Joe. "The chief of police is keen to see you though, he would like you to return to Al Jawf. Your decision, of course. You are welcome to continue the journey with us if you wish."

Suleiman just sat there with his mouth open.

"I see your drivers all have their rifles with them still. I think we should return to the previous regime, so if you would all hand your weapons to my colleagues, we will lock them up in the toolbox, as we did before."

Under the watchful eye of N'guku, Joe's Kikuyu removed all the rifles, one by one, from the drivers. He removed the magazines from the rifles and made the rifles safe.

"Just pat them all down for pistols and so on," Joe instructed.

The passengers had in the meantime all gathered around. Joe said to them, "Just a small problem with the police in Al Jawf. We can now continue our journey."

Suleiman looked furiously at Joe, yelling, "We wish to go back to Al Jawf, to see the police chief."

"Fine," said Joe. "You can take the car we borrowed. I'm sure they'll be happy to have it back."

Joe sought out Bikila and said to him quietly, "Just make sure the car only gets them a few kms down the road, make it run out of petrol or something."

Bikila smiled and spent a few minutes doing what he had been asked to do.

An enraged Suleiman, having by then gathered together his belongings, jumped into the beetle with one of his drivers. The two others declined to go with him. Joe and the passengers watched them drive off.

"Won't they just get the police in Al Jawf to come and take us all back to Al Jawf again?" asked N'guku.

"I don't think so," said Joe.

Within a few minutes of continuing their journey, they came across a roadblock made of poles and a set of tyre spikes. It was lit with hurricane lamps and people waved flags at them to stop.

Joe together with Jordan, one of Suleiman's drivers, hopped out of the cab with one of the resident's forms. As yet, only a handful had been properly completed with the passengers' names in Arabic. There was a quick conversation in Arabic. The people in the roadblock seemed to be in a hurry, since there was now a queue of several vehicles heading south.

"Twenty this time, maybe a bit more as we approach the coast," Joe muttered to his Kikuyu crew. "They had no interest in the forms. I'm actually not sure that any of them could read, but they were all heavily armed."

Three more roadblocks along a reasonable road through the desolate sandy desert, and they were in Ajdabiya by mid-morning. They found a quiet street and parked.

"Find a boarding house," Joe said to Bikila and Jordan, who seemed to want to be helpful. "Away from the coast and in a backstreet. We don't want to attract any attention. I'll say here with the truck. Then I have other plans."

An hour later Bikila returned, directing them all to a large ramshackle house in a small laneway. The passengers all excitedly found places in dormitory style rooms, where there were rough beds covered with thin blankets. The men were segregated from the women and children. Joe said to everyone in Swahili, "Don't go far away. We'll be back in a day or so."

He said to Kimani and Koinange, "You are in charge here. Set up a watch regime and make sure everyone stays together. Also, find a couple of different number plates; our vehicle still has plates from Sudan. Make sure that nobody has a mobile phone. Jok removed all the mobile phones earlier."

The difficulties with the whole journey from Juba had created grave doubts in Joe's mind about the long-term viability of taking people from Juba right through to the Libyan coast. He thought he might have upset too many people on the way, such as in Wadi-Halfa and Al Jawf. So, he started to think of other options. He desperately needed to keep Otieno on side.

"What are we looking for?" asked Jordan, as they drove off westwards. He, Joe, N'guku, Patrick and Waweru were all part of the group, all armed. Here and there were gangs of armed men, whom they avoided.

"A boat. Something we can take the people across with."

They drove up and down the coast for a few days, stopping off periodically to check on their passengers. Kimani changed the number plates of the truck.

The group became impatient. "What are we trying to do?" they asked Joe. "Just getting a feel for the place. I'm now ready to move."

Leaving the others in the truck, Joe went and sat in a coffee shop in the small port of RaS Lanuf, east of Sirte, where he had seen men wearing Libyan military uniforms. He got chatting as some of them who spoke English. The main topic of conversation was how much they were owed in back pay. Within an hour, most of the military had left the place, except the man who Joe thought was in charge.

"You want go over?" the man said in broken English. He pointed vaguely north. He was a quite short but well-built Arab man in a neatly turned-out uniform. He had some sort of insignia on his shoulder lapels

"Yes, I have a boat, I just need cooperation."

"How many?"

"The boat can carry one hundred and fifty."

The man looked surprised and appeared to be thinking. "Okay, you pay seventy-five thousand US. I protect," he said eventually.

"How?" asked Joe.

"We have patrol boat."

The pair wandered over to the harbour and the man, who said his name was Ali, pointed out a decrepit-looking patrol boat.

"Do you know the harbour master?" asked Joe. "Of course. He, my cousin."

"You must introduce me."

"Okay."

They walked over to an old tattered-looking office building, situated in a backstreet just off the port with a sign in Arabic, which Joe assumed indicated that it housed the said harbour master.

Ali knocked on the door and they entered a small neat office. The man in uniform behind the desk got up and greeted Ali with a kiss on both cheeks. They said a few words in Arabic, which Joe now partially understood. There was a rapid-fire conversation of which Joe only understood a few key words. He heard the word 'fish' a few times.

"This my cousin Ibrahim," Ali said to Joe. "He fix you up. I go now. I see you in thirty minutes on patrol boat."

Ali left.

Joe was surprised at the turn of events, but said to Ibrahim in broken Arabic, something he had been working on. "I need to be able to berth my boat, here in RaS."

The conversation continued in Arabic, with some English if there was a need for clarification.

"What are you going to do with the boat?"

"Fishing. Mostly fishing."

"Okay. No forms, all cash. One thousand dollars a week." Joe looked horrified. "Two fifty," he offered.

The argument went backwards and forwards. They eventually settled for four hundred. Joe paid Ibrahim for four weeks.

"You can refuel, here in RaS," said Ibrahim.

Joe assumed that Ibrahim had a finger in the refuelling pie. "Price?" Again, after a short argument they settled on a fixed price.

"All cash. Only US dollar." Ibrahim reaffirmed the arrangements.

They shook hands. Joe knew he would have to keep an eye on Ibrahim, but he hoped that his relationship with Ali would help to maintain the arrangement.

Joe returned to Ali, who was on his patrol boat, smoking. "All, okay?" asked Ali.

"Yes, of course, thank you."

"Where is boat?" asked Ali.

"I will fetch it now."

"Okay," said Ali. "One week from now. Eight o'clock at night."

Before he left Joe pointed to the insignia on Ali's shoulder lapels. "Is this for captain?" he asked.

Ali laughed. "No, I now commander. All patrols boats from RaS, my responsibility."

Joe nodded. He thought he had probably chosen the right partner for the next phase of his venture.

"I need to buy the boat I have found. Can you come with me?" he said to Ali. Ali smiled. "Why not."

Joe hustled back to the truck, accompanied by Ali; and directed them to Sirte itself, where he had found a fishing boat, which he knew would carry at least one hundred and fifty passengers. Surprisingly, it was named 'Ellen'. He and N'guku went into a small grubby office accompanied by Ali, who he saw as a guarantor of what he, Joe, had in mind.

"You speak English?" Joe asked the man identified as the owner. "Some," said the man in accent-less English.

"I'm looking for a boat like this. Is it for sale?"

"Yes."

"How much?"

"Four hundred K, US."

Joe shook his head. "I'd better go somewhere else."

"How much can you pay?"

"Ninety K. The boat is worth nothing. Security problem." He waved his arms about.

"Two hundred."

After further arguments they settled for one hundred and twenty-five thousand US dollars.

Joe handed out ten thousand US dollars as a deposit. The man looked askance at Ali.

Ali nodded.

"I will pay the rest over the next two weeks," said Joe. The man looked at Ali again, who nodded.

Joe retained two of the boat crew, which pleased the owners of the boat, since they saw that as further security guaranteeing payment. The crew claimed they understood the coast and knew where Lampedusa Island was to be found, the largest of the Italian Pelagie Islands, and where they might find the best fishing grounds.

Joe had the fishing boat filled with diesel and he, Ali and N'guku, accompanied by the two crewmembers, spent a day sailing it east back to RaS. Joe returned briefly to the boarding house and asked Bikila and Kimani to see what could be done to gather up another one hundred or so refugees.

Chapter 10: Mediterranean Crossing

Ali was pleased with Joe and the quality of the boat, which even from a casual observation was in much better condition than his own patrol boat. N'guku gave the fishing boat a quick once over, finding nothing much was wrong. He offered to have a look at Ali's patrol boat, which he did, spending two days servicing it.

From the time that the 'Ellen' was docked in RaS Lanuf, Joe ran a strict watch regime. Each watch was three-hours starting at dusk; the schedule included Joe himself.

Without much trouble, Kimani and Koinange managed to gather another one hundred and twenty refugees, so the boarding house was overrun with people.

"Have they all been told what they will be charged for the crossing?" asked Joe.

"One thousand five hundred US per person."

"Right. We'll take them fifty at a time, in the truck, when they have paid. I have a stamp, which I have had since Juba, and some indelible ink, which we will use to make a mark on the hand of all those who have paid."

It took a day to transport all one-hundred and fifty refugees to the fishing boat. Joe saw the name 'Ellen' as a sign that all would turn out to be fine.

Several people tried to board the truck without paying but were turned back. Some said they only had one thousand dollars or less. They were firmly told to go elsewhere.

Wambui and her mother also claimed not to have sufficient funds. "How much do you have?" Joe asked. The mother handed over two thousand US dollars. Without another word, Joe took the money and stamped their hands. He hoped no one else had seen what had transpired. He had a slight feeling of guilt regarding his one sexual encounter with Wambui, and Wambui's mother continued to look at Joe with suspicion.

Joe and his crew had taken to dressing in a Libyan way, often wearing a fez, and he grew a beard and let his hair grow. He had several outfits, including a sleeveless leather jacket and he had several pairs of long white trousers. To a casual observer, he soon looked like one of the locals.

By 9pm on the appointed day, they had one hundred and fifty people safely sitting on the deck of the Ellen. Joe had wads of US dollars in a strongbox in a locked cabin on the boat. One of his Kikuyu guards, Kimani, armed with his AK 47, was locked in the cabin with the cash. N'guku, Waweru, Koinange and Patrick, all armed, were stationed at strategic points round the deck of the Ellen.

Ali signalled, and the little flotilla set off. The weather was benign and Joe's crewmembers indicated it would stay that way. Joe had a reasonable idea of the direction and distance to Lampedusa, the small Italian island just off the coast of Tunisia. Ali's patrol boat, which accompanied the Ellen, had a radar device, so they were able to avoid the one naval ship of unknown provenance in the area.

Ali directed them to a deserted beach on the south side of Lampedusa Island. Just as the dawn broke, they sailed the Ellen to within one hundred metres of the shore. Joe then personally jumped into the sea, indicating it was safe to go ashore, and that this was Italian soil. The water came up to his chest. The passengers were then quietly offloaded into the sea, making sure the children were in no danger. They set off once they could see that all the passengers were safely on the beach. They were now in Europe. Joe tried to ignore the gestures of Wambui and her mother, which Joe thought indicated that Wambui was pregnant.

Joe phoned Ali on his mobile. "Fishing for two days and then Tunisia."

"What about my money?" asked Ali.

"It's here. You can come and get it if you want."

"Why go Tunisia?"

Joe shrugged. "Better fish prices. Proper banks."

"I come."

They soon saw a small rubber dingy, powered by an outboard motor, dropped over the side of Ali's patrol boat. Ali clambered on to the Ellen.

"Is the patrol boat going back to RaS?"

"Yes."

"Can it take four of my men back to RaS?'

Ali nodded.

"We need another 150 people for another trip as soon as possible," Joe said to N'guku, Koinange, Waweru and Patrick as they carefully climbed down onto the dingy.

"Do you want your money now?" asked Joe.

"I come with you Tunisia. Patrol boat going RaS."

"Okay," said Joe, "fishing first."

On the way to Tunisia, they were intercepted by a naval destroyer, who were part of a multi-national force attempting to intercept people smugglers crossing the Mediterranean. The British crew insisted on boarding the Ellen.

"What are you doing here?" Joe was asked.

"Fishing."

The officer in charge of the boarding party looked doubtful. "Likely bloody story," he muttered.

"Go. Have a look." Joe opened a hatch, which was indeed filled with fresh fish.

"We had a report of a boat fitting your description offloading refugees onto a beach in Lampedusa."

"Search the boat if you wish."

"Not a dicky bird," reported one of the sailors in the boarding party, as he came back up onto the deck.

"Where are you from?" the officer asked. "You don't look like a Libyan to me." Joe shrugged, saying nothing.

"Just be bloody careful, we'll be keeping an eye out for the likes of you," the officer in charge said to Joe before he returned to the destroyer.

Ali had kept well out of the way while the search was on.

Two days later, the Ellen nosed into the harbour at Sfax, a major commercial port south of Tunis. Joe locked his long-bladed knife and the Beretta into the cabin in the fishing boat. The first down-payment for the Ellen and some spare cash for continuing operations was left in the cabin, with Kimani still looking after it. He took the remainder of the funds garnered from the trip with him.

They were directed to a small fish market, where their catch was enthusiastically received.

"Come with me," Joe said to Ali once they had been paid for the fish and the boat was temporarily tied up on the quay.

Joe explained to Ali, "I'm going to pay cash into bank accounts in London, from several banks here. Everything has to be less than ten thousand dollars, so it falls under the radar. I can certainly pay you what is owed here, but I can help you open an account in London if you want."

Using the VPN/Anonymiser system he had set up in Kenya, Joe transferred several amounts of just less than ten thousand US dollars to an account he had set up for Otieno in London. The money was sent directly, Joe didn't think it necessary to direct it through Switzerland.

"I must pay my people," said Ali, "but I think about what you do. Maybe next time."

A day later, still in Sfax, once he was away from Ali and his colleagues, Joe phoned Otieno in Nairobi on his mobile phone. "Where the hell are you?" Otieno asked Joe in Swahili.

Joe could tell from Otieno's voice that he was not well.

"I thought you had disappeared or got into some sort of trouble," Otieno continued.

"I'm in Tunisia."

"What are you doing there? Where is my truck? Where is all the money you are supposed to be making?"

"Your truck is still in Juba, as I have explained, but we have another truck here which now belongs to us." Joe laughed and then explained what had occurred and what he was doing. "Just check those bank accounts I've opened for you in London, and that's just the start," he added. "I sent you encrypted details yesterday. And you now own a very nice fishing boat," said Joe after a short silence.

"What do I need with a fishing boat? When are you coming back here?" asked a mollified but still irritated Otieno.

"Are you alright?" Joe asked before they rang off. "You sound ill."

"Nothing to worry about," was Otieno's response.

Two days later Joe phoned Otieno again, having given him a chance to review his bank accounts.

"I'm not coming back," said Joe. Otieno was silent; he had just checked his UK bank accounts. "I had thought we would be bringing refugees all the way from Kenya," Joe continued. "But the journey from Juba is ridiculously difficult." He explained what had happened in Al Jawf but neglected to say anything about the incidents in Wadi-Halfa. "There are thousands of refugees here. We don't need to bring any more. All we need do is to ship them in the boat I've now purchased. You will make more money than you could ever imagine. What I sent you yesterday was after paying for the fishing boat."

Otieno was silent a moment. "How long will you be there?"

"I don't know, the security situation here is very difficult and dangerous."

"What about my truck in Juba?"

"I left it with a Luo mechanic there, as I told you. Maybe he could return it to Nairobi for you, or just ask him to sell it. It's probably worth more in Juba. Just let me give you the mechanic's mobile number again." Joe read out the number.

Otieno grunted. "The police still want to talk to you about the death of General Kariuki."

Joe said nothing.

"I have not told them about Mbiti's passport," continued Otieno. Joe said nothing.

They rang off.

Joe returned to RaS via Sirte where, accompanied by Ali, Joe paid the first instalment of what he owed to the previous owners of the Ellen. "I'll pay you the rest in a couple of weeks," he told them, now speaking in his rough Arabic.

Joe had picked up some Arabic in the weeks spent travelling from Juba and this had improved somewhat since arriving on the Libyan coast, so unusually for a foreigner he was able to understand much of what was being said.

Once the first trip was over, Joe could see he had a modus operandi that worked. In view of the business with the general, Joe had to make absolutely sure that Otieno was still on side. To Joe, Otieno was the one possible weak link in his story, if anyone chose to ask too many questions regarding his whereabouts at the time of the death of the general. He knew that at some time in the future he would want to return to Kenya, even if it was just for a visit. He also suspected that Kenya had an extradition agreement with the British, so if there was ever a case against him and he ended up there, it was possible that he would be sent back to Kenya by the British authorities.

Joe asked the two of Suleiman's drivers who had remained with him, what they wanted to do. Both wanted to go home and were paid off. They had had no word of Suleiman.

Joe was annoyed with himself. He totally blamed himself for the position he was in, regarding the death of the general. He still occasionally had the dream where the general was trying to throttle him. He knew that, without that problem, he would have no hesitation about going to England to make something of his life; instead, he was saddled with shipping refugees to Europe. He would have to keep all his wits about him. The unstable security regime in Libya made life difficult. It also created the opportunity to make other mistakes, with heaven knows what consequences. Joe decided that before he could make a move to Europe, he needed to have Otieno completely on side, preferably with him retiring to his tribal home south of Kisumu in Kenya, on Lake Victoria. There, he would be well out of the way of any police enquiries.

'If I don't do what he says,' he thought to himself 'Otieno will go to the police and tell them about Mbiti's passport.'

During the journey to Libya, and from his experience of shipping refugees across the Mediterranean, Joe could see that corruption was endemic in all the places he had travelled through, otherwise people like him would not be able to operate. He hoped it might be different when he actually arrived in Europe, although he wondered about the activities of Sir Oswald Higginbotham.

When Joe returned to RaS, his crew had collected another one hundred and fifty refugees in the boarding house.

Before the next trip developed, his crew approached him.

"All this money you are now making. What about us?" said Patrick as a spokesman for the crew. "We are doing all the work and taking all the risks."

"I was coming to talk to you about that," said Joe, feeling uncomfortable. He was never going to tell them, or indeed anyone else, anything about the death of General Kariuki, or the threat that Otieno presented. "I just needed to make sure the whole process worked. On the next trip I will pay twenty thousand US into accounts that I will open for each of you in London. We'll see what happens after that. You have to understand that I am paying for the Ellen from the funds we get from the refugees and Ali gets his cut."

The crew had always trusted Joe, so accepted the situation.

The second trip worked much as the first one had. A small sum was paid into Otieno's London account. Ali was persuaded to open a London Bank account. Joe opened bank accounts in London for each member of his crew and paid the promised twenty thousand US dollars into each of their accounts, in amounts of less than ten thousand.

Joe did not phone Otieno. The fishing boat was paid off.

'I wonder how much longer I'll have to do this,' he thought to himself. 'It's dangerous, and my people will want to move on with their lives.'

When they returned to RaS Lanuf, Joe found that the matter had effectively been taken out of his hands. Waweru and Kimani met the Ellen on the quay, looking anxious. They boarded the Ellen as soon as it docked.

"Everything okay?" asked Joe. "You both look as if you have just seen a ghost."

"In a way we have," said Waweru, "we have just seen Suleiman..."

"So?" responded Joe.

"Let me finish," continued Waweru. "He is with what appears to be that group of Bedouin, the people we saw in Selima Oasis, and they definitely have the white woman, the one we saw there, with them. Also, they are heavily armed."

"Are you sure? I thought they were going east, we were going west."

"I'm sure it's the same woman," said Waweru. "I made a point of taking a good look at her at Selima. It's definitely the same woman, looking a bit more dishevelled and her clothes are dirtier. I don't know about the men, it's possible they are a from a different group altogether."

Kimani nodded in agreement.

"Again, so what. What has that got to do with us?"

"The owner of the boarding house has told them about us, and that we have a boat that can take the woman over the Mediterranean, safely. Apparently, they will only get paid once they drop the woman off somewhere in Sicily."

"Sicily? That's much further than Lampedusa. Do we really want to have anything to do with this?" asked Joe. "Carting refugees around is one thing, but having anything to do with white western hostages will get us into a whole heap of trouble; if our involvement alerts western powers that we are shipping refugees across the Med, they will come down on us like a ton of bricks."

"Maybe we should talk to Ali," suggested Kimani. "Also, Suleiman is looking for revenge..."

"Ali's not here, just yet. I will talk to him in the morning," said Joe, already thinking. Shipping refugees across the Med couldn't last forever, no matter what their colour. At some point, he would have to think of a new way to earn money. Maybe even a legitimate one.

Again, however, developments effectively took over.

#

In the very darkest part of the night, Waweru, on watch, noticed a man creeping about on the quay. He stayed alert but took no action. 'I hope whoever it is will just move on,' he thought.

Waweru then saw the man stop right next to the Ellen. He cocked his AK. "Go or I will shoot," he said quietly. He did not want to attract attention.

"I need to speak to a man called Joe. It's very urgent," the man whispered back.

"Come back in the morning. He's asleep now. Just go away." Waweru waved his rifle at the man.

"I can't. I must speak to Joe now. It's about that white woman who's being held hostage by the Bedouin. I'm not with them, I'm from British security."

Waweru looked around. 'I wonder if this is some sort of trap.' He was unable to see any other kind of movement in the shadows of the dark buildings near the quay. 'Maybe not,' he said to himself. "Stay where you are, I'll get Joe." Waweru dashed down the gangway, woke Joe and hurriedly explained the situation.

"British security?" Joe sounded intrigued, even though he had previously said he didn't want anything to do with the situation. "I'll be up in a minute," he responded.

Waweru dashed back on to the deck. The man was still standing in much the same place, next to the boat. He lowered a gangplank. "Come up." He pointed his loaded rifle at the visitor.

A well-built quite tall man in his mid to late thirties stepped onto the deck, he was dressed in green army fatigues, was bareheaded and appeared to be unarmed.

"Wait there," Waweru gestured, hoping Joe would appear soon.

#

Joe soon appeared dressed in his long white baggy trousers, a white shirt and a sleeveless leather jerkin. He nodded at Waweru.

Joe noticed a hard edge to their visitor. 'Someone I need to take seriously,' he thought.

Waweru collected deck chairs for them to sit.

"What do you want?" asked Joe abruptly, once they were all sat down in the dim light.

"I'm from British security. I want to talk to you about the white woman, who's being held hostage by the Bedouin."

"I know about her. I'm not sure I want to have anything to do with the situation," Joe responded.

"The Bedouin think they are going to get a large sum of money from us when they return her to us. They will be disappointed. Giving money for hostages just encourages hostage-taking."

"Who is this woman?" asked Joe. "She's one of our agents," said the man.

"Why don't you rescue her yourselves then?"

"No. Too many diplomatic complications."

"What is her name?"

"Anne Smith."

'That is almost certainly not her name,' Joe thought to himself. "What do you want from us?" he asked.

"You take refugees across to Italy. We want you to do the same for Anne Smith. But only for Anne Smith."

"What's in it for us?"

"We'll pay you. We understand you charge fifteen hundred dollars to take someone over?" The man looked at Joe.

Joe laughed quietly. He shook his head. "There is this woman in the hands of a heavily armed gang of Bedu, and you want to pay the standard amount? Obviously, you know as well as I do that that is ridiculous. Sicily is also much further than our usual route. Also, I have to take all this on trust. How do I know you are from British security?"

"How much do you need?"

"Well, I will have to pay..."

"We know you are in cahoots with elements of the Libyan coast guard."

"Hm, let me continue, I will have to pay them off. If we do this, we probably won't be able to continue doing what we do. It's already very dangerous and being involved in rescuing this woman will turn us into targets. I suppose you are expecting us to eliminate the Bedu, as well as rescuing the woman? Also..." Joe took a deep breath. Perhaps this was the answer to his question about what to do next? A new plan? "Would this help to earn us British citizenship?"

"I am unable to guarantee that, but we would put in a good word for you."

Joe did some rapid mental calculations. 'Maybe doing this could earn us some money and also somehow assist in getting us British citizenship?' he thought to himself. 'And get us out of this situation, which we are unlikely to be able to go on with much longer. Despite Ali, we will probably become a target for one of the lawless groups running around. We could likely get ourselves far, far away, somewhere to earn money more safely...'

"What is your name?" Joe eventually responded. "And please don't call yourself John Smith. We would need six hundred thousand US to even think about it," said Joe, "as well as proof of your identity. Something we can use in Britain to help us gain citizenship there. I also need to talk to my colleagues and the Libyan coast guard."

The man didn't react in any way to Joe's proposal.

Joe got up and much to the man's consternation took a flash photo of him with his smartphone.

"That wasn't necessary," said the man as he got up to go. "You can trust us."

"I trust nobody," said Joe. "We might see you tomorrow."

The man nodded, then went down the gangplank and disappeared into the dark.

The next day, Joe, Waweru and Kimani went to see Ali, who had just returned to his patrol boat, berthed nearby.

He explained the situation, including the visit of the man the previous night. "How much money will they get for this white woman?" asked Ali.

"Rumour is that the Bedu think they will get two million US," answered Joe. "Based on what I was told last night, they won't get anything at all."

"Two million US dollars!" exclaimed a very surprised Ali. "If no money, maybe they kill woman?"

Joe shook his head. "I told him that if they were prepared to give us six hundred thousand US, we would think about it. If you don't want..."

"Six hundred thousand, maybe we should take. Get rid of Bedouin," said Ali.

"How?" asked Joe

"You got guns..." He shrugged. "I will send someone, negotiate a price to take them Sicily, to collect them their ransom. Secure. No fuss. Then, when we on boat, we get rid of them, overboard, keep woman, collect six hundred thousand US."

"What about Suleiman?" asked Joe. "Who Suleiman?" asked Ali.

Joe briefly explained.

Ali shrugged. "Show me, Suleiman. I get police to lock up." Ali and Joe then got into a huddle to plan the details. "Fifty, Fifty," offered Ali.

Joe shook his head. "If we are going to do what we plan, it will be too dangerous for us to come back here. So, you take twenty-five per cent and the Ellen."

Ali looked at Joe. "Forty."

They eventually settled for thirty-five per cent plus the Ellen, and the truck. They shook hands on the deal.

"How many Bedouin with the woman?" asked Joe. "Five," answered Waweru.

"Okay we will agree to transport them across, with three on patrol boat and two on the Ellen, which must include the boss," said Joe.

"Why boss on Ellen?" asked Ali.

"He and the woman might have some codes or sign off process. They must be together, otherwise it won't work," said Joe.

"We have about twenty refugees waiting to go over," said Kimani, "what do we do about them?"

"We'll take them all, usual price. Fifty thousand US for the woman," said Joe.

"I don't suppose the Bedouin have that sort of money," said Waweru.

Joe shrugged and looked at Ali, who smiled. "They can pay us from their ransom."

Joe, Waweru and Kimani returned to the Ellen and explained everything to the others. They spent a long time discussing the precise details of what they needed to do.

The next night they decided to maintain the same security arrangements with Waweru on watch. Earlier Joe had asked Patrick and N'guku, dressed in dark clothing, to stay in the shadows of buildings in the area, which was quiet at that time of night. Their job was to keep a watch out for any vehicle movement, and especially the British man who had paid them a visit the previous night. Joe shared with them the picture he had taken of the man.

The man appeared as he had done the previous night at 2am. He was carrying a briefcase.

Waweru called Joe, who was ready, and the three sat quietly on the deck of the Ellen.

"We will agree to your terms," said the man, much to Joe's surprise. 'They must be desperate,' he thought.

"I will give you half the money, three hundred thousand US now, and the rest when you deliver Anne Smith within two weeks, safely, to an address I will give you of a small hotel in Syracuse, Sicily. I also have a phone number you should call when you arrive."

Joe had anticipated such a move. "This is not quite what we spoke about... and we want a clear idea of your identity."

The man handed Joe a warrant card, which appeared to be from one of the British security services.

"You can take a photograph of this... I can't do any better than that."

Joe did as suggested. The warrant card certainly had a picture of the man in front of him. "I take it that, when I approach this organisation, if I ever get to Britain, they will recognise the name, Michael Baker."

The man didn't bat an eyelid. "Yes, of course."

"What about the money?"

"I have three hundred thousand US dollars, in cash, in used notes here now..."

"Can we count it?"

The man who called himself Michael Baker, handed Joe the briefcase.

Joe handed the case to Waweru. "Count it please, make sure the notes are used and that the numbers on the notes are completely random. We will not accept any notes that are sequentially numbered."

While the cash was being counted Joe went to a corner of the deck, where he could not be overheard but where he could still keep an eye on Waweru and their visitor. He phoned Ali.

When Joe returned, Michael Baker was still sitting there, apparently relaxed, though Joe could see he was on full alert. It took a full hour for Waweru to count all the money.

"All in order?" Joe asked Waweru in Kikuyu. Michael Baker looked at Joe sharply.

Waweru nodded.

"Okay, we'll accept the arrangements," Joe said to Michael Baker. "Just text me the phone number I need to call when we arrive in Syracuse." Baker did as asked. Joe then added, looking the man in the face from an inch away, "You had better make sure that the cash you provide in Syracuse is also in used notes and not sequentially numbered. Also, don't think of doing anything to put your hostage's life in danger, just to save money. We'll see you in Syracuse."

Baker did not blink. They shook hands and the man calling himself Michael Baker, leaving the briefcase with Waweru, went down the gangplank and disappeared behind one of the dockside buildings.

Joe waited on the deck for a few minutes to see if Patrick and N'guku had noticed anything significant regarding their visitor.

"We saw your man get out of a van with diplomatic number plates," reported N'guku. He and Patrick had returned to the Ellen, a few minutes after Baker had left. "Your man, after a short look around, then walked quickly over to the Ellen and returned two hours later, without the briefcase. There were two other people in the van as far as we could see. I have pics of all of that."

"Diplomatic plates," said Joe. "That's interesting. The rest of it is unremarkable, although the pictures may turn out to be useful."

The cash was locked in the cabin with Kimani in charge. The six of them then discussed what should be done with the cash.

"We have fifty thousand for each of you," said Joe. "What about you?" asked Patrick.

"And fifty thousand for me."

"We can't carry that amount of money around with us."

"No. It will take a week or more to get the hostage and all the Bedu sorted out, convince them to use our charter, so what I suggest is that we do some fishing and then go to Sfax, where you can pay in all or part of your fifty grand into the bank accounts, I have opened for you in London. When we get back the Bedu should be ready to travel."

Joe then told Ali that he would be away for a few days. "What you do?"

"Fishing. We'll become a target if we stay here too long."

During the night, the Ellen edged out of the harbour, spent a few days fishing and then made their way to Sfax, where, using a variety of banks, they all paid whatever amount of money each of them decided on to their London accounts, all in amounts of less than ten thousand dollars.

One or two of Joe's gang initially needed some help from Joe.

Joe himself paid all of his share into his London accounts. He would use the cash paid by the twenty refugees for his immediate needs.

In less than a week, they were back in Ras Lanuf, where Ali had finished negotiations with the Bedu.

Joe then arranged through Waweru and Patrick that the Bedouin and their hostage, the white woman, would be delivered to the Ellen after dark once the twenty refugees, all wearing suitable life jackets, had been loaded onto the boat.

"Suleiman?"

Ali made a gesture holding his hands together as if they were handcuffed. Joe nodded his thanks.

"Where money?"

"I'll give it to you when we get to Sicily."

Kimani, Patrick, Waweru, N'guku, and Koinange all boarded the Ellen with the refugees. They were all armed with their AK 47s and were hidden in strategic locations around the vessel. They were all wearing life jackets, as was Joe.

"We may need to get rid of the Bedouin, before we get to the other side," Joe told his crew. "Only fire when or if I give the order."

A very nervous group of six Bedouin, all heavily armed, arrived at the dock at the appointed time. The white woman, handcuffed and with leg irons, shuffled along as well as she was able. Ali was with Joe.

Joe looked at the woman with interest. She was tall, slim and many would have regarded her as good-looking, but Joe noticed a hard edge to her demeanour.

'Probably very suitable for a British agent, if that is indeed who she is,' thought Joe. 'I would not trust her an inch. All we represent is a vehicle that is able to rescue her, at the lowest possible cost, and the British won't give a damn what happens to us after she is back in their hands.'

"Where is Suleiman?" Joe asked the apparent leader in his very rough Arabic, to check his story matched Ali's.

"Gone. Maybe police. Two days ago." The man shrugged.

Joe looked at the man and decided to play the full set of charades with him. "What is your name?"

"I, Fahed," answered the Bedu leader, pointing to himself. "Joe," said Joe.

"Fifty thousand US dollar to take the white woman over," Joe pointed vaguely in a northerly direction.

"I'll pay when I get hostage money," Fahed replied.

"Fine. But woman must not be tied up. The other passengers will be scared if they see that."

The man ignored Joe and dragged the woman towards the Ellen. Ali intervened. "No. Do as Joe says," he said in Arabic.

"You," Ali said to Fahed, "and two others as well as the woman will go on the Ellen." He pointed. "And those three will go on my patrol boat," he pointed to the other three Bedouin accomplices.

The Bedouin leader looked suspicious.

"Security. I, Ali will provide security for the safe transfer over to Sicily. Without me this boat will be stopped by European security and you will all end up in jail."

Joe caught a glimpse of Ali glancing at him with a half-smile on his face.

The leader reluctantly ordered that the woman be unshackled and his three compatriots followed Ali obediently onto the patrol boat. Joe provided them all with life jackets.

Joe then arranged for the woman and Fahed to board the Ellen, together with two other Bedouin. They were housed on the deck among the other passengers. In the dark, while they were boarding, Joe managed, for a few brief seconds, to separate the Bedouin leader from his hostage. The deck was lit dimly.

"Don't worry," he whispered to the woman, who looked relieved at the sound of spoken English. She looked dirty and unkempt and, although she was outwardly calm, Joe could see from her eyes she was on full alert.

"They will try to kill me when they get the money," she whispered.

"How?" Joe was unable to finish his question.

Fahed pushed his way back to take control of the woman and, looking angry, dragged her to the edge of the group of refugees, nearer the guard rail, just as Ali's patrol boat moved away from the dock alongside the Ellen, driven by N'guku.

The crossing was of course much longer than their previous trip. It gave Joe time to circulate unobtrusively to the various hiding places accommodating his Kikuyu crew. He asked them one by one to walk past the hostage and take photos of her whenever they could. This he also continued to do at regular intervals.

"We need to confuse the woman," Joe told his crew. "I don't want her to be able to recognise any of us afterwards. Just in case."

The other accompanying Bedouin had mixed themselves in with the crowd of refugees.

Joe took no notice, he was focussed on Fahed and the woman.

When they were halfway across Joe spotted a set of bright lights looming over the horizon. Italian border patrols? He quickly called Ali. "Looks like a frigate. If they catch us with refugees, we'll go to jail. What are we going to do?"

"You put refugees in sea. I stop to pick up and give refugees to frigate. I claim I rescue them?"

"They will drown..."

"No, they have life jacket. I pick up quickly. We will keep the frigate busy. They will have to stop."

Joe signalled to his crew. "Dump a few of the passengers in the sea. Ali will pick them up."

There was hesitation from his crew members.

"Now," said Joe, waving at the fast-approaching lights of the patrol boat. "It's our only hope."

Each one of the Joe's crew quickly picked up one refugee, which included one of the Bedouin and, amid screams of fear, dropped them over the side of the Ellen.

"I'm going with them," yelled Waweru, following the four unfortunates over the side.

Joe kept his eyes on Fahed, who kept a firm hold on the woman during the fracas.

Instinct made Joe look into the milling crowd of refugees for a second. He dived to the deck as the remaining Bedu fired a burst from his weapon in Joe's direction. Pain seared through his right shoulder. Kimani shot the man dead with a burst from his AK.

Fahed lifted his own weapon. The woman pulled away to hide herself among the remaining refugees.

There was a shot and Fahed dropped down dead on the deck. The refugees panicked and rushed haphazardly all over the deck.

Joe got up, trying to stem the flow of blood from his shoulder. "Grab and hold the woman," he said to Patrick.

By this time the frigate was approaching rapidly. Ali had his searchlights on highlighting people struggling in the sea.

Joe made a quick call to Ali. "I'll see you on the beach."

Joe signalled to N'guku. All the lights on the Ellen were switched off and the boat, now completely dark, surged away from the scene. Joe staggered up to

N'guku. "Go south," he yelled. The Ellen did a U-turn and ran south. The frigate stopped beside Ali's patrol boat.

Koinange found a first aid kit and bound Joe's shoulder, stemming the bleeding. "Maybe just a nasty flesh wound," he told Joe.

Once the lights of Ali's patrol boat and the frigate were out of sight over the horizon, Joe, still clutching his shoulder, said to N'guku and the two crewmen, "Okay, now head for the beach near Syracuse."

The deck lights on the Ellen were switched on again. Patrick and Kimani moved the bodies of Fahed and the other Bedouin away from the still terrified refugees.

"Ali can deal with them. I'm sure there is a religious process...," said Joe.

"I don't believe this," said Kimani peering at the face of the 'other' Bedouin. "It's Suleiman. It's bloody Suleiman."

"Damn, damn, damn," said Joe. "Ali double crossing us? "

Just as the dawn broke, they found themselves approaching the designated beach. Ali's patrol boat was already there.

The Ellen was beached and the still terrified refugees were unloaded on to the sand. Joe was relieved to see a very wet Waweru among them, but there were only three of the four refugees that were dumped into the sea. Ali had two of his men with him; the rest were on the patrol boat.

"You couldn't pick up all refugees from the sea?" questioned Joe.

Ali shrugged. "Dark, only found three and one of yours, one Bedouin ...poof."

"Why didn't you give them to the frigate?"

There was no answer.

"Sulieman, he was on our boat..." Ali shrugged.

There was a short silence.

"I want my money," yelled Ali.

"We'll get it from the British," answered Joe. "The British! I want my money now," yelled Ali. Joe's crew cocked their weapons.

"I'll show you how to get your money. I have no money here."

"Show, how?" he yelled.

Joe's crew lifted their weapons, all pointed at Ali.

Waweru put a shot over Ali's head, which missed him by a foot.

"Get your people back on the patrol boat, or we will open fire, you have ten seconds to drop your weapon."

A glowering Ali did as he was told. Koinange picked up Ali's rifle.

Ali looked at Joe, then gave his men the signal to return to the patrol boat. "Frisk him," Joe said to Patrick.

Patrick found a small derringer in an ankle holster. He handed it to Joe.

"Frisk him again," Joe ordered. "Clean," said Patrick.

"Take cover, take the woman," said Joe quietly to his crew, who then went and hid behind some rocks, dragging Anne Smith with them. The refugees scattered.

"Tell your men to take the patrol boat away out to sea. They can come back when we have the money," Joe said to Ali.

When the patrol boat left the beach, Patrick said to the refugees, now having hidden themselves among the rocks near the beach, "There is a road up there." He pointed. "Turn left at the road, towards Avola, police will find you. This is Italy, they have to treat you as refugees."

After the refugees started to walk down the road, Joe said to the woman, "Are you prepared to tell me your real name? I presume it is not Anne Smith."

"Anne will do for the time being," was her trite answer. She had recovered her hard-edged demeanour.

"We shouldn't stay in a group," Joe said to his friends. "Patrick and N'guku, you stay with me, until I get the remainder of the money from the British. The three of you make your way to Britain. I have given you directions. You all have cash. Cut your hair and shave and get western clothes. Dump your weapons. Try not to be picked up by the police or you may end up in a refugee camp and may not be able to get to Britain at all. Look after yourselves, you are all smart and bright. I hope to see you all there sometime in the next few months."

He embraced them one by one. "Thank you and I hope to see you in London."

Koinange handed Joe a small first aid kit. "You must change the dressing every day or it will become infected," he said

The three trooped off into the dark. "What now?" asked Anne.

"We now have a longish walk," Joe announced, with a disconsolate Ali, hovering. "I have an address where I have to meet our British colleagues, who hopefully will have the balance of the cash I was promised. I will then release you, Anne Smith, if that is indeed your name, to the British authorities. It's about fifteen k's" added Joe, "which will take us, say, three to four hours. How are your shoes?"

"Worn out," responded Anne, glancing at Joe.

To everyone's surprise Joe took off his own shoes and gave them to Anne. "Socks, we need socks," said Joe.

Socks were found and given to Anne. The woman looked surprised.

"I spent most of my first dozen or so years without shoes..." Joe shrugged.

"Are you going to be okay for a fifteen-k walk?" Patrick asked Joe, indicating his shoulder.

"I think so. We'll see."

Joe gave all his other colleagues a thirty-minute start, and then with Ali in front followed by Patrick, the woman and then N'guku, with Joe holding up the rear, they walked off into the dawn, with Joe, Patrick and N'guku still carrying their weapons.

Joe used Google maps to identify the hotel where he was expected to meet the British.

"Fat chance," he said to himself. "They really must think we are a bunch of mugs."

By midday Joe had found a small, run down-looking hotel a few hundred metres from the hotel the British had identified. On his own he approached the run-down hotel's check-in desk, leaving his companions sheltering under a nearby tree. He gave Patrick his AK 47.

The clerk handed him a registration form, which Joe ignored.

"Five hundred US," he said to the clerk in English. "No police, no checks, three nights, one room."

The man behind the counter blinked once.

Joe handed him the money in cash, correctly assuming he would pocket most of it.

The clerk handed Joe a key and pointed. "Room at the back, very safe," the clerk muttered.

Joe waved at his colleagues and they found the room. Battered furniture, thin sheets.

"Just what we need," thought Joe.

"Don't I get a room to myself?" asked Anne.

Joe looked at her. "No," he said harshly, "and the patrol boat has not returned to Libya. If you and your colleagues play any games, you will go straight back on that boat and you will end up being abandoned in Libya. So, keep your mouth shut and do as you are told."

Anne went white. "I need the toilet," she said. "Go then, leave the door open," said Joe.

He was able to keep half an eye open on what Anne got up to.

"Don't trust the woman, not one inch, and don't go to sleep, and the same applies to Ali, he may try to play games as well," he said quietly to Patrick and N'guku, "and don't get into conversation with either of them. I am going to see if I can find the British contacts. We can go from there. I'll be back in a couple of hours. Do not open the door to anyone except me," he said as he went out.

Joe found a barber, where he had a haircut and shave. He found a small clothing store where he purchased a mid-range set of clothes. He had borrowed Patrick's shoes, so he replaced them. He dumped his Libyan outfit in a garbage bin nearby. He also made an arrangement with another equally seedy hotel in the vicinity, to move there. As with the previous hotel, he paid them 500 US dollars and pocketed the key. Out in the street, he phoned the number he had been given by the British.

"I have rescued your hostage," Joe said once the phone was answered. "I will wait for your phone call telling me you have arrived at the hotel." He shut the phone off before there was any further conversation.

Joe collected some takeaway food and returned to the hotel. He carefully washed his wound and changed the dressing.

"Anne, you can have one of the beds, Ali, the other. One of us will be on guard, the others can sleep. I will sleep on the floor."

Early the next morning there was a call on Joe's mobile, it was the contact number he had been given. He returned the call only after he had left the hotel and went to a vantage point he had identified, which gave him a good view of the entrance to the 'British' hotel.

"We'll be at the hotel in a few minutes," said a voice. "Okay," said Joe. He cut the call and waited.

Soon a van with diplomatic plates appeared and parked in the shade next to the hotel they had identified.

Joe again phoned the contact number.

"Hello," said an English voice. A heavyset man in green battle fatigues got out of the van. He was holding a mobile phone to his ear.

"As I told you, I have rescued your hostage," said Joe. "You need to produce the funds we agreed upon and then we will release her."

"Where are you?"

"Watching you," said Joe.

The man looked around anxiously. Two other men emerged from the van, also dressed in green battle fatigues

There was silence.

"One of my men will come and count the funds you are proposing to give us. If everything is in order, he will tell me and I will release the woman," said Joe. "He can count the money in the van."

"Where are you?" the man repeated his question.

"Watching you," said Joe. "If what I said is acceptable my colleague will be with you in fifteen minutes."

"You should be in the hotel."

"I'm not in the hotel and nor is your hostage." Joe remained silent after that.

The man had a short conversation with his two colleagues.

"I need to speak to the lady, just to make sure you are not bluffing."

"Five minutes, I'll get her." Joe returned to their hotel. "Here is Anne Smith," he said into the phone after redialling the number. Joe handed her his phone.

"This is Anne Smith speaking..."

"I need your security identity number," said the voice. "71362AD," she said quickly.

Joe wrote down what she had said. "Okay, speak," said the voice.

"Don't play games with these people," Anne said in a controlled voice, "they know what they are doing and they are absolutely ruthless. I have personal experience of that. After all, they did rescue me from the Bedouin, who probably would have killed me, whatever they may have told you."

"We'll get back to you on this number," said the voice. The phone was returned to Joe, who cut the call.

"Ali, you can now go to that van there." Joe pointed to the van, which was just visible from the hotel window, partly hidden by a small copse of trees. "You can keep all the money they give you; it should be three hundred thousand. You can then call the patrol boat and they can fetch you. That is all the money we promised you."

Ali looked pleasantly surprised and to Joe's relief did as he was told.

The sliding door on the left-hand side of the van opened and Ali was allowed to look inside. The man who had answered the phone stood a metre away from him.

To Joe and his two colleagues' utter amazement, there was a burst of sub-machine gun fire from inside the van and Ali was lifted off his feet and fell down a dead bloody mess.

"Jesus," said Joe. "Patrick, tie the woman up, gag her and stuff her under the bed. We need to get out of here."

"All lights off. N'guku, help me tie this trip-wire across the room."

This was followed a minute later as they saw three men, dressed in green battle fatigues, all armed with sub-machine guns, dash across the few hundred metres that separated the van from the crew's hotel.

Joe and his colleagues just made it out of the room and were racing across the nearby road when they caught a glimpse of the three men running into the hotel complex. Luckily the men were focussed on what they were doing, so they did not see the backs of the escaping trio. They ran to the other hotel Joe had booked.

"Okay, stay here. I'll be back," said Joe. "The British double crossers obviously have a device that can identify our position using my mobile. So, no phones."

He returned to his original vantage point in time to see the three men, supporting Anne, returning to their van.

She was hurriedly bundled into the van before it raced off. Ali's body was left where it lay in the street.

Joe returned to the hotel.

Patrick and N'guku were all packed up. Joe told them what he had seen. "We need to split up," said Patrick.

"Where are you going?" asked Joe.

"Back to the Ellen," was Patrick's response. "I have some unfinished business in Libya. My father..."

"Here. Take this," said Joe handing his weapon to Patrick, "I won't be needing it."

He hugged them both. No words were said. They all left the hotel together.

Patrick and N'guku took the first taxi that appeared and Joe the following one.

"Taormina," Joe said to the taxi driver and handed him a one hundred dollar note. The taxi drove off quickly.

After almost an hour and a half the taxi driver said, "Up or down?"

Joe looked confused. "What does that mean?" he asked.

"Main town up above. Better hotels near sea. Quieter."

"Okay, thanks," said Joe. "Down."

PART 4

Chapter 11: Pastures Green

He checked in, with a false name. "Passport," said the clerk.

"Stolen," said Joe. "I must contact the embassy to get a replacement."

The well-dressed middle-aged lady shrugged. "How will you pay?" she asked.

"Cash," said Joe. He handed her two hundred dollars in small denomination notes. "I'll pay the balance when I leave," he said.

Joe was given a key and went to his room. He looked at his wound. "Shit," he said to himself. "Looks like it's infected." The wound was very red and swollen.

Joe returned to the receptionist, who looked up. "Is there a doctor nearby?" he asked.

"Yes. Can you tell me what the matter is?"

"I'll tell the doctor."

The receptionist looked at Joe suspiciously as she made a call. There was a quick conversation in Italian, which Joe did not understand. "Expensive, you will have to pay in cash," she said as she out the phone down. "A five-minute walk and he can see you now." She gave Joe directions.

Joe made his way to the doctor's surgery, which was very well appointed. He gave his name to a receptionist. 'Must be a set up to deal with tourists,' he thought. He was immediately ushered in to see the doctor.

"I will need payment before I treat you," said the doctor before Joe sat down. Joe nodded. "US dollars, okay?"

"Si. Four hundred."

Joe peeled off four hundred dollars from a wad of cash and gave it to the doctor.

"What's the problem?" asked the doctor as he pocketed the cash.

Joe removed his shirt, stripped off the dressing on his wound and showed the doctor.

"Hm, bullet wound," said the doctor. Joe said nothing.

"I'll clean the wound, then take this prescription to the chemist – there is one round the corner, and come back here in two days," said the doctor. "Take the antibiotic pill three times a day, with food."

Joe nodded, and the doctor cleaned the wound carefully and refreshed the dressing.

'I bet the bastard's next move is to call the police,' Joe thought to himself as he walked back to the hotel. 'There's no way I am going to some refugee camp.'

"Thank you," he said to the hotel receptionist. "I have just had a call and I need to check out."

The receptionist nodded. "I need another hundred dollars."

Joe handed over the money, returned to his room and left. He caught the rack railway to the top town, found a chemist who fulfilled the prescription without question. Joe then wandered the back streets for thirty minutes until he found a small, seedy-looking hotel and, as he had done in Syracuse, he went to the reception, which was attended by a poorly dressed, indolent young man.

"Five hundred. Three nights, no questions," Joe said.

Without a word Joe was handed a key and the young man pocketed the cash.

Joe found the room and by now he was not feeling very well at all, so he took a pill and tried to sleep.

Joe did spend three nights in the seedy hotel, periodically popping out to local cafés for a plate of pasta and a coffee. He kept a careful watch out for any police presence. He checked the times of buses to Messina.

For the first time in months, he also phoned his mother in Nairobi. "Mum, sorry it's been so long..."

"Joe, Joe, Joe," she cried. "We thought you must have run into trouble. Are you alright? Where are you?"

"Mum, I'm fine. We did have a bit of trouble, but I'm fine now. I'm in Italy."

"You don't sound very well."

"I'm fine."

"Italy. I thought you were going to *Ulaya*."

"I'm on my way there. I hope to be there soon."

"How are all your friends, Waweru and so on?"

"They are fine. We have split up for the time being. We'll see them in London. How is Karanja?"

"He's okay. I think he needs help with the *bhang* business."

"What sort of help?"

"It's too big. There were five of you. He is on his own now."

"I'm not sure what I can do from here. I'll speak to the others though..."

"I have some other news which may interest you."

"What news?" asked Joe.

"That Luo man Otieno, the one who took you to Juba."

"Yes."

"I was told, yesterday, that he died two weeks ago." A flood of relief swept over Joe. "Died. How?"

"In hospital. I was told he was very sick."

"I'm sorry."

There was silence for a few seconds. "Mum. How are you? Are you well?"

"Yes. I'm fine thank you. When are you coming home?"

"I'm going to *Ulaya*. Hopefully, I won't find any people like the reverend there." There was an uncomfortable silence. "Mum, I'll call again soon."

Later he called Waweru. "Joe, where are you?"

"In Italy. Where are you?"

"We went to Rotterdam. Looking for a way to get across to England now."

"How."

"There are truck drivers who will take us across. Kimani has already gone over."

"And you two?"

"Maybe. Koinange says he wants to go home."

"Karanja is not coping with the *bhang* business, so if he wants to go home, maybe he could go and help Karanja. I'll text you Karanja's number. Also, Karanja has just texted me the mobile number of a man, Mwangi, who has lived in London for ten years now. You should contact him when you arrive. I will send you the number."

"When will you get to *Ulaya*?" asked Waweru.

"Two weeks maybe."

They rang off. Joe texted Mwangi's and Karanja's numbers to Waweru. There was no answer from either Patrick or N'guku.

After three days, feeling a little better, Joe caught the bus to Messina, arriving later in the morning. He spent some time making certain he understood the security arrangements relating to the ferry from Messina to Reggio di Calabria. He then purchased a one-way ticket and spent the two-hour journey sitting comfortably on the deck of the crowded ferry.

The next phase of Joe's journey involved several buses to Naples, a train to Rome and another one to Genoa. Yet another train took him to Lyon in France. His shoulder ached at times but wasn't as painful as before.

He'd been told, during his sojourn in Libya, that the Schengen arrangements between various European countries meant that there was no border check between Italy and France. Joe was relieved to find this was actually the case as the train sailed through what was clearly the border between the two countries.

Joe eventually arrived at a large, busy truck stop, some seventy-five kilometres short of Calais, where he had learnt there were certain British truck drivers who could be persuaded to hide him in the passenger compartment of their vehicle, for a substantial fee of course. He would then be dropped off somewhere in the English countryside, or if he was lucky in London. Joe spent two days in the truck stop. Nobody took much notice of him. The place was busy twenty- four hours a day, but he was able to make up for some of his lost sleep by nodding off in a corner of the bustling café attached to the stop.

During one of his longer sleeps, Joe became conscious of a large, overweight, middle-aged man dressed in a blue overall, sitting beside him noisily slurping a cup of coffee and munching on a baguette, which Joe could see contained ham and other less stable fillings, which kept falling on the floor. The man said nothing but when he became aware that Joe was awake, he pushed a scrap of paper in front of Joe, which said: 'London?' It also had a vehicle registration number and then 'ten minutes'. The man noisily finished his meal and then wandered off without saying anything.

Joe picked up his backpack and went to the toilet, where in a locked stall he arranged for most of the thirty thousand US dollars he had with him to be safely ensconced in the money belt he had acquired in Italy; he kept just four thousand dollars in his trouser pockets, two thousand in the left-hand pocket and two thousand in a back pocket. He still had the Beretta handy in the right- hand pocket of his jacket and the long-bladed knife. Walking off into the crowded parking lot, it took him a few minutes to identify the vehicle indicated. The large man from the truck stop was standing next to a well-maintained B- double.

"Lookin' for a lif' mate? As all you darkies normally are."

Joe nodded and with his backpack he clambered into the open door of the vehicle.

They drove a few kilometres down the road before the truck driver said anything. "Foive grand US and I'll be dropping yer off in London Town," he muttered.

"Two and a half," answered Joe.

"Oi'll drop yer off right 'ere and now, if yer go on loike that."

"Okay. Three," said Joe.

"Three five."

"Done," said Joe.

"Wher' yer from?" asked the driver after a short silence. "Do you know anything about Africa?" asked Joe.

"No' much. Took the wife on a package tour to Kenya, a year or two back. Sum place called Diani, saath of Mombasa."

"I come from Kenya," offered Joe, "but I've never been to the coast. Lots of visitors go to the game parks in Kenya though. I've never been there either."

"The wife wants to visit game parks. She loikes the David Attenborough programmes on the telly."

"Who's David Attenborough?" asked Joe.

"Yer don' know of David Attenborough? Mate yer do 'as a lot to learn. 'Es world-famous. 'E makes programmes for the telly abaat wil' animals."

Joe smiled. "Where I lived, we didn't have television."

"Kenya? A bi' backwar' then. We 'ad a very noice 'otel."

"By your standards, Kenya may be backward. Big men have all the power."

"I thought i' was a democracy, at leas' that's wha' the brochure said."

"I never voted for anyone," said Joe thoughtfully.

"Yer speaks good English," said the driver, "bu' yer 'as a very strange accent."

"I know. I'll do something about it once I get to England."

"Why do you wan' to go ter England?"

"I've had enough of the crooks in Kenya."

"Plenny crooks in blighty."

"Blighty?"

"Yer does 'ave a lot ter learn. Jus' another word fer England." Joe said nothing.

"Wot yer gonna do 'ere?" the driver added.

Joe shrugged. "Not sure yet. I've driven large trucks, a bit older than this one though."

"Licence. Yer'll need a licence."

"I'll get a licence then."

Joe had been pleasantly surprised at the lush, well maintained countryside and the prosperous-looking towns he had passed through both in Italy and in France. He grew more and more confident in his quest for a new life. Compared to his homeland, and all the places he had been through before arriving in Europe, he couldn't believe how green everything was.

A few kilometres before entering the port of Calais, the truck driver who still hadn't mentioned his name, told Joe to get into the sleeper compartment at the rear of the cab. "Jus' cuvver up wi' that silver paper fing I use for keepin' the sun off. There'll be a couple hours wait at the port I expec'. Then the train. They check docs before we get inter the port. Then maybe customs at Folkestone. The train only takes abaat thirty-foive minutes, so yer stay put until I give yer the okay."

Joe paid the driver half of what they had agreed. " I'll give you the rest when you drop me off in London."

He got a peculiar look but no further comment from the driver, as the cash was pocketed.

Joe fell asleep almost immediately. He was vaguely aware of the truck moving around and then he thought they must be on the train. After an interminable wait he sensed the truck driving off at a normal speed. It then stopped.

"Okay, yer can come aat now," he heard the driver say.

As Joe emerged from the back of the cab, the driver held out a large knife. "Righto smartass. Yer can now pay me all o' what yer owes me, an' all the cash yer 'ave... Oh shit!" exclaimed the driver as he found himself staring into the barrel of Joe's Beretta. He dropped the knife.

Keeping an eye on the now terrified driver, and keeping the pistol pointed at him, Joe crept out of his hiding place, saying quietly, "Just get into the driver's seat and get going, or I will plug you. Drive towards London and drop me off at a mainline train station, and no more silly buggers," Joe added, still pointing the weapon at the driver.

The truck driver looked fearfully at Joe and did as he was told. They drove on in silence for forty minutes, when the driver pulled up outside what Joe could see was a sign saying, 'Maidstone Railway Station'. "Yer can ge' a train inter Lunnen from 'ere," he said shakily.

Joe pulled the balance of the fee out of his pocket, dumped it onto the seat next to the driver and without another word opened the truck door and hopped out with his backpack, putting the Beretta in his jacket pocket as he did so. He watched as the vehicle drove off.

He'd been told he should make for London's East End, where he wouldn't stand out as there were many refugees in that part of the city.

He asked the woman in the Maidstone South Eastern Railway ticket office what was the best way to go. The station was clean and tidy, with numerous new-looking trains travelling both ways, driven by electricity. He compared this with the station at Ol'Kalou, where there was one train each way each day. The Kenyan trains were mostly driven by steam and were wood fired.

"Waterloo, then take the Drain to Bank and the Central Line to Bethnal Green."

Joe laughed. "What's the Drain?"

"Direct line from Waterloo to Bank."

Joe took a few US dollar notes from his pocket saying. "Can I pay with this? I haven't had time to go to the bank..."

"Sorry, only pounds..." was the answer.

The ticket office woman gave him a very suspicious look. She unobtrusively moved to pick up the nearby phone.

Joe then realised he had made a very bad mistake by drawing attention to himself. He walked out of the station and ran to a nearby cab rank, where he had seen a black cab on his way into the station.

"I'm in a hurry to get to Bethnal Green," he told the cabbie. "But I only have US dollars on me, if you'll take those." He waved a one hundred US dollar note in front of the man.

"No problem," was the answer, "and that's what it will cost you, one hundred US."

Joe got into the back of the cab. The meter was turned off. "What's your hurry, anyway??" said the cabbie.

"Sick mother," Joe answered.

"Where are you from?" asked the cabbie.

"Bethnal Green," Joe answered. "Look I'm sorry, I just need to make a private call."

The cabbie partially shut the communication window. Joe firmly shut the window properly. The cabbie, turning his head around glanced at Joe briefly as if to say, 'Be like that'.

Joe then called Waweru. "Where are you?" asked Joe

"I'm talking to your friend Mwangi..."

"You in London?" asked a surprised Joe.

"Yes."

"Where?"

"Somewhere in the east."

"Look, I am in a taxi heading for Bethnal Green. How far are you from there?"

"Not far."

"Can you both meet me at Bethnal Green underground station in an hour?" There was silence for a minute.

"Yes. It's only a short walk from where we are."

Joe sat back in the taxi. With the little time he had to look around him, Joe was astonished firstly at the pretty green countryside from the port of Folkestone and the greenery even in the more built-up areas. The place was busy, with huge volumes of traffic tearing about the narrow streets.

Sometime later, with the taxi scrambling through the heavy London traffic, Joe found himself standing on the pavement next to a sign that told him he was at Bethnal Green underground station. It was just about lunchtime. Joe was surprised at the number of people busily rushing about. It was still summer, so people were dressed casually. He particularly noticed the many young women and girls in the crowd, on their own, just going about their business. The smell of diesel hung in the air.

Two black men walked towards him; Waweru and another man who Joe assumed was Mwangi.

Joe hugged Waweru, who introduced Mwangi.

Mwangi was dressed as a tradesman, although his clothes were clean. He was typically Kikuyu, medium height, dark brown skin and well built.

After a few words of greeting Joe asked Waweru, "How long have you been here?"

"Yesterday. I got here yesterday. I only met Mwangi this morning."

"Are you hungry?" asked Mwangi.

"Yes, starving, I haven't eaten much today. I also need somewhere to stay. Where are you staying?" Joe asked Waweru.

"Street. I slept on a park bench last night."

"We can go to a cheap café nearby or there is a pub around the corner that is also okay," offered Mwangi

"We'll try the pub," said Joe.

The pub had an inexpensive roast offering with four choices of meat and, as far as Joe could see an astonishing array of vegetables.

"Yorkshire pud?" the woman dressed in a clean white uniform, standing behind the counter asked, smiling.

Joe looked uncertainly at Mwangi. "Go on, it's okay."

Joe nodded at the woman. "Thank you." Waweru followed suit.

The trio managed to find a corner table, but there was little conversation while both Joe and Waweru tucked hungrily into their meals. Mwangi ate more steadily. Joe was persuaded to order a half pint of beer, which he didn't like much. He gave Waweru a sip, who pulled a face.

"Not like the beer in Kenya," observed Joe. "It's warm."

"I'll pay," offered Joe, after they had finished their meals, "but I've only got US dollars, which seems to attract the wrong kind of attention… oh and some Euros."

"How much do you want to change?" asked Mwangi. "Maybe three hundred US."

"Give it to me."

Joe handed over three hundred dollars and Mwangi dashed out, to return a few minutes later with some British pounds and a receipt.

"There's a Bureau de Change nearby. No problem."

Joe counted the money and checked the exchange rate and the total printed on the receipt.

He showed Waweru.

Mwangi looked at him curiously. "I'm not questioning anything," said Joe, "I just wanted to understand the process."

Mwangi nodded.

"Do you know where Kimani is?" Joe asked Waweru.

"Birmingham. Mwangi here suggested he went to a friend in Birmingham," answered Waweru, "he has a room there and there is space for me as well."

"It might be better if you both went to Birmingham as well," said Mwangi. "I have contacts there."

"No," said Joe, looking at Waweru. "You remember I talked about that fat *mzungu* who was involved with the reverend, the general, Kigoro from Ol'Kalou and Otieno of course."

"Yes, of course."

"Sir Oswald Higginbotham," said Joe, "he runs a business here in London. I am going to see if I can get a job there. Maybe just as a messenger to start with and we'll see how we go. Mwangi, I will need some advice from you on various things when I have sorted myself out."

"Sure. Anytime," said Mwangi, seemingly surprised that Joe already had a plan.

"What happened to Koinange?" asked Joe.

"He returned to Kenya," answered Waweru. "He said he needed to go back to look after his mother. He went to the airport in Holland and bought a ticket back to Kenya. His Kenyan passport meant there were no questions. Also, Karanja was pleased to hear from him. He needs help to run the *bhang* business."

"How did he pay for his ticket?" asked Mwangi. "And what's the *bhang* business?"

"Joe gave us all a share of the money we got from rescuing that British hostage," Waweru shrugged.

Mwangi looked curiously at Joe.

Joe quickly gave Mwangi a shortened version of the rescue of Anne Smith and explained what was meant by the *bhang* business.

"We hope the hostage rescue might help us get British citizenship more easily," explained Joe.

"So, you're not just a bunch of desperate refugees?" Mwangi said, impressed. "But you're not thinking of running an illegal drug business here?" Mwangi added anxiously.

"No, no," said Joe, "never."

He looked at Waweru, who nodded.

"How is that bullet wound in your shoulder by the way?" asked Waweru.

"I'm not sure," answered Joe, "it became infected and I had some treatment in Italy, but it still aches. I really need someone to look at it."

"Bullet wound?" asked a surprised Mwangi.

Joe gave him a brief explanation of what had occurred on the Ellen, during the rescue of Anne Smith.

"Hm," said Mwangi, "you'll have to use my NHS card. I have registered with a doctor but I've hardly ever used it. Provided you are black I suspect they won't worry." Mwangi made a call. "They can see you tomorrow. I'll show you where to go."

"How do I get to Birmingham?" asked Waweru.

"Train from Kings Cross, I can take you there," answered Mwangi.

"Is there a cheap boarding house or hotel nearby, where I can stay for a couple of nights while I look for somewhere more permanent?" Joe asked Mwangi once he had paid for the meal.

Mwangi nodded and made a call on a mobile phone. "There's a place just around the corner. Forty quid per night..."

"Quid?"

Mwangi laughed. "Pounds. They sometimes use the word 'quid'. It's a sort of slang."

The next day Mwangi picked Joe up and took him to the entrance of the doctor's surgery. "I'll wait at the Wentworth," said Mwangi. "By the way it's all free, you pay nothing."

Joe walked in to the surgery, a clean, ordinary, workmanlike office. "I have an appointment to see the doctor, my name is Mwangi..."

To Joe's relief the receptionist asked no questions saying, "Doctor won't be long."

Joe looked around the reception area. There was what looked like a surveillance camera in one corner. He got up and left, and five minutes later was sitting opposite Mwangi at the Wentworth. He ordered a beer.

"That was quick. Is everything okay?" asked Mwangi.

"I saw they had a spy camera in the reception area. I don't think I can go through with this. What happens if the doctor says he has to report the matter to the police?"

"So, you didn't see the doctor then?"

"No. I was using your name of course, so they might have decided to come looking for you. I think we would then both be in real trouble."

"Okay, thank you. You may be right."

"Any other suggestions?"

"Not really. There are private clinics in a place called Harley Street, who may be able to help. I don't know any more than that though."

They finished their beers and Joe returned to his boarding house.

Chapter 12: Joe in London

Joe rented a small, poorly furnished room in Tower Hamlets in the East End. He could see after a few days that he would fit in easily in the area – there were Africans, Arabs from the Middle East, Chinese, Indians, and Pakistanis, with whom he was familiar as there were many people from the subcontinent living in Kenya; as well as the local Cockney English of course.

Checking various advertisements in the local newspaper, he eventually engaged a middle-aged widow, Mrs Braithwaite, who was established in nearby Bethnal Green, to conduct elocution lessons for him, every day of the week, including Saturdays. He made it clear from the start that any questions regarding his origins or identity would not be welcome. He told her to call him Joe, giving her a false address when she asked. He reluctantly gave her his mobile number. He had purchased a 'burner' phone, but kept his Kenyan mobile, since that was the number, his crew had. "I need these lessons to make sure I fit in better," he told her during an early lesson. "I want to be identified as English born." Mrs Braithwaite was entirely sympathetic to such sentiments. "I wish a few more of our migrants had the same attitude," she said to him.

He consolidated the amounts in his bank accounts into three separate accounts and he ensured they all had his new address. Most of the money stolen from the general, as well as what was left of the money from his hostage rescue, was left on deposit, despite low interest rates.

Joe also spent time studying the British financial press and tried to make himself familiar with the stock exchange. He had learnt something of stocks and shares from Desai during his lessons at the general's mansion. He acquired a laptop and enlisted in an online financial analytics course. He used public transport. He cooked for himself most of the time except for his regular meetings with Mwangi, whom he pumped for information, whenever possible. He never physically visited any of the bank branches where his money was deposited.

Once he had acquired a laptop, he researched what Mwangi had described as 'private clinics in Harley Street'. After several searches he found a few names, he thought were promising. Using a public phone, he phoned the first number.

"Doctor Sims rooms?"

"I need a very private consultation. No names. A bullet..."

The phone was put down. The same thing happened with the next two calls. The next call was different. The receptionist put Joe through to a female voice.

"Dr Smith here. I understand you need treatment for a bullet wound. How serious is it?"

"It happened some weeks ago. It was treated, but it still needs some attention."

"Are you mobile. Can you get here?"

"Yes and yes," said Joe. "I need to make it very clear Dr Smith, I need complete anonymity and I am prepared to pay in cash."

"Of course."

She gave Joe an address, which was indeed in Harley Street. "Three pm Saturday. That's tomorrow. You will see a bell at the entrance labelled Dr Smith. We are on the ground floor. I'll be alone."

"Thank you. I look forward to seeing you."

Joe found the address easily enough, having walked from Regents Park tube station. He was thirty minutes early, so sat in the sun on the pavement of a café a short distance from his intended address.

On time, Joe rang the bell as instructed. A minute later a tall, pretty well-dressed black woman opened the door. "Dr Smith?" he asked.

"Who else?" she answered with a smile. "Please come in."

They went into a well-equipped surgery. Joe was relieved to see a number of certificates on the walls indicating that Dr Smith was qualified.

"What can I do for you? You said something about a bullet wound."

Joe removed his shirt and showed the doctor his wound, which was still red and sore.

"How long ago..."

"Six weeks. It was treated." He explained the situation.

"What were you doing, if you don't mind me asking?"

"Rescuing a hostage. A British agent."

"I won't ask any more questions. It looks nasty." The doctor took a scalpel out and opened the wound. She squeezed out a mountain of pus.

"Certainly. You were right. This thing needs attention." She squeezed out a bit more pus and then dressed the wound. "Are you allergic to penicillin?"

"What's penicillin?"

The doctor laughed. "Obviously not." She gave him what turned out to be a painful injection.

"How far away are you? Can you get to me easily?"

"I can get here easily enough."

"Wednesday 7pm okay?"

"Yes, of course. How much do I owe you?" asked Joe.

"One hundred, this time."

Joe looked surprised as he handed over two fifty-pound notes. "Is that too much?"

Joe laughed. "Compared to what I had to pay the bloke in Italy, it's very modest."

Dr Smith shrugged. "You are obviously an illegal." Joe nodded.

"My father was an illegal. I understand the pressures. I don't want to pry, but if any of your colleagues need medical help, they can come here. Always after hours."

"Thank you. I will certainly do that. See you Wednesday."

Joe returned twice more, until he and Dr Smith were satisfied the wound was in the process of healing.

Joe told Mwangi of his experiences with Dr Smith. He also looked her up on Google. It turned out her father was a Nandi from western Kenya.

Joe made a point of phoning both Patrick and N'guku once a week. Occasionally he was able to record a message on voicemail; more often the call just rang out.

Acquiring a genuine British identity was more of a problem. His contact with Mwangi introduced him to the Kikuyu and other African diaspora in London. Joe soon established himself as a regular at the Wentworth Arms in Mile End, partly for his regular meetings with Mwangi and partly to use their Wi-Fi system. It was close enough to where he was living, and convenient for Mrs Braithwaite's elocution lessons, although it was a forty-minute walk. In one of these discussions, Mwangi told him how he had obtained British citizenship.

"Firstly, I had to be accepted as a refugee, which was difficult, but I managed it. Then there is a process of obtaining permanent residence, which involves passing all sorts of written tests, particularly proficiency in English and then you also have to have some local knowledge, like who is your local Member of Parliament." He shook his head. "I wonder if all English people know who their Member of Parliament is? Anyway, there is then a waiting period and, provided you don't end up in jail, you are given full citizenship, which I now have."

Joe knew that if he went down that path, he ran the risk of being shipped back to Kenya, making all his efforts over the past few years worthless. He did not want there to be any trace of his origins in Kenya, since, although he had no knowledge of the law, he thought it was at least possible there was some arrangement for people like him to be shipped back to Kenya if there was any suspicion of his involvement in the general's death.

After a few weeks of meetings with Mwangi, Joe again raised the subject of his own quest for citizenship. "I need to short circuit the process, I simply can't wait that long," he said to Mwangi. Joe was never going to tell anyone about his involvement in the death of General Kariuki and even with Otieno now out of the way, he was not going to take the risk of being identified and then possibly shipped back to Kenya. He still had the occasional dream of the general throttling him.

Mwangi was eventually persuaded to give Joe an address in Finsbury Park in North London.

"Be very careful of these people," Mwangi said to Joe. "They are not nice people and may try something on..."

Joe had been told to go to the Finsbury Park address after midnight. So, on the day of the appointment, Joe, while it was still light, went to the address he had been given, which turned out to be a tower block. It was obvious that the address was on the top floor. To Joe that had the potential of being a trap. He almost turned round and went home. But there was nobody about so, after looking around carefully, he dashed up the stairs to the top floor, where he saw two of the flats were obviously unoccupied with front doors hanging on their hinges. A brief look inside the flats showed a few sleeping bags – obviously squatters, currently absent. Several needles were lying about among the debris. The other two flats appeared to be legitimately occupied. As he was about to go back down the stairs one of the doors opened; there was a very young man, almost a child, standing there, holding a revolver. "What the fuck do you want?" he said in a squeaky voice.

Joe could see the revolver was not loaded as all the chambers facing him were empty. He walked over to the boy saying, "That thing is not loaded." He grabbed the gun and pushed the boy away back into the flat, all the way into a dilapidated chair, and said, "What is this place all about? What do they do here and what are you doing here?"

There was no response from the boy.

Joe opened the revolver confirming his suspicions that it was not loaded. Instinctively, he knew he should just leave and find another way to establish his citizenship; but he thought, 'it's just a young boy, maybe I can pump him for information'.

Joe wandered into the kitchen and opened the fridge, which contained nothing and was not switched on. It seemed that the flat was not really occupied, it was just used for whatever nefarious activities this gang got up to.

"Do you want to earn some money?" he asked the boy, who nodded enthusiastically.

"Then meet me at the café just a few streets from here. Do you know the place?" he gave him the name and address of the café.

The boy nodded.

Joe handed him a five-pound note. "This is just for starters. I will be there on Tuesdays at ten o'clock in the morning. What is your name?" asked Joe.

Before there was any answer, the door of the flat burst open and six men rushed into the flat. Joe jumped up and smashed his fist into the faces of the first two, who went down like poleaxed steers. The other four backed off. The boy escaped into the kitchen.

Joe dropped the revolver and pulled his Beretta out of his jacket pocket. The four men pulled out wicked-looking knives. Joe pointed his pistol, threateningly. "Back off, back off or I will shoot," he shouted.

"A bloody gun," yelled one of the men. "He's gonna shoot!" They started to back off.

Brandishing the gun, Joe herded the four men into the kitchen and locked the door. The man on the floor struggled upright, weakly.

"Okay, my friend. You are going to answer some questions," said Joe to him. "Hospital, I must go to hospital."

"Answer my questions and then your friends can take you wherever you want." The man moaned.

"You made an arrangement with me to help me acquire British citizenship, and all you can think of doing is to set up this ambush, what's going on?"

The kitchen door creaked, the others pushing against it.

It was too risky to stay longer. He gave the man on the floor a good solid kick to the stomach, which doubled him up; and then he fled through the front door. He had the presence of mind to take the front door key with him, which he had noticed was still in the latch. As he left the premises, he locked the front door and pocketed the key. There was a massive crash as he rushed down the stairs, which he assumed was the kitchen door being broken down. He was in the street within a few seconds. He checked to see if there were any other gang members waiting around and then quickly, unobtrusively, walked to Finsbury Park tube station. He dropped the key of the flat into the first garbage bin he saw.

A very shaken Joe returned to his Tower Hamlets flat and wondered what he should do. He wondered whether Mwangi had deliberately set him up, then dismissed the idea.

'It's not in his interests for me or anyone else to come to grief,' he thought to himself.

A day later he phoned Mwangi and told him what had transpired. "They are just a bunch of crooks," Joe told him angrily. "There was no chance that they could have provided me with a path to British citizenship, you must have known that."

"I'm really sorry about that," said Mwangi, apologetically. "I don't know them very well. Obviously, I will never recommend them again. I heard there was some sort of a fracas."

"Yes," said Joe, "there was. I was lucky to get out of the place unharmed."

"I'm sorry," said Mwangi

Joe said nothing for a few seconds and then said, "The issue of citizenship for me still exists. Is there anything else you can suggest?"

"Possibly, but very expensive. I will let you know. In the meantime, you should get yourself some passport photos. You can get them taken at any photo shop."

Joe got his passport photos taken; then the Tuesday after his affray in the flat in Finsbury Park he went to the café he had nominated for a meeting with the boy. The boy was sitting down nervously, looking around. Joe spent ten minutes scouting the area, making certain he was not about to be ambushed again. He also set up an observation post from where he could watch the boy, who was obviously of Indian or Pakistani origin. Just as the boy was about to get up and leave, Joe sat down in front of him, giving him a fright. His lips were split and he had two black eyes, one nearly swollen shut.

Joe ordered two coffees.

"What happened to your face?" asked Joe.

The boy shrugged. "They fuckin' done me over didn't they? Thanks to you. Beat me up. I was blamed for lettin' yer into the flat."

"How did they know I was there?" asked Joe.

"They ga' me a phone. All I 'ad to do was press a button and they said they would come in a few minutes, which they did."

"Who were they?"

"Money first."

Joe pulled out two tenners, but when the boy tried to snatch them, he put them away again. " I will pay you and pay you well, but I need to know what you say is valuable to me."

The boy looked at Joe. "The firm's name is Park Slavers. They bring people into Lunnen, steals their paper..."

"Paper?" asked Joe. "Passports," said the boy. Joe nodded.

"They then send the paper away agin and use it ter bring sumwun else in."

"Go on," said Joe.

"Wun of the men you thumped is the firm's leader. Name is Ibrahim."

"What happens to the people when they come here?"

"They stay in sweatshops, which belon' ter the firm, and they 'ave ter work for 'im in some sort of factry. Or brofels, wimmen are forced to be prossies."

"All that round here, in Finsbury Park?"

"Some, they also have a place in Milton Keynes and in Sheffield."

"You still haven't told me your name," said Joe.

"Jerker, you can call me Jerker." 'Street name,' Joe said to himself.

"They promised to arrange some sort of citizenship for me."

"That's wha' they tell everywun. All they wus gonna do was to capcha yer and put yer in a sweatshop."

"Why do people stay with them, why don't they run away?"

"If they run off, Ibrahim sumtime tells police, illegal immigrant or sumfink, or jus' 'as them beat up an' brought back to the sweatshop or whateva."

"What happens then?"

"I don't know."

"Right. All that is very interesting. Can you give me Ibrahim's address?" Joe wrote down what he was told. "Are you still working for Ibrahim?"

Jerker nodded.

"Do you know any of the addresses of the sweatshops or brothels where these people are kept?"

"Not this time. I will find out and tell you another time."

"Text me on this number, when you have more information." Joe gave him the number of another burner he had acquired for this meeting.

Joe handed over twenty pounds and Jerker dashed off.

"About your citizenship, I think I have something for you," said Mwangi, at their next meeting, once coffee had been brought for both of them by Jo-Ann, one of the waitresses.

Joe was briefly distracted by the young, pretty, buxom blonde waitress. She was wearing a short skirt showing off her long slim legs. Joe paid. "Please keep the change," he said, giving her a quick smile.

"Ta," she said with a grin.

"Okay, what's that?"

"Here is an address in Peckham. It's just off the high street. You'll find it easily enough." He handed Joe a piece of paper on which there was an address and a phone number for a Mr Patel. "I have called Mr Patel; he will be expecting a call from you."

"Thank you," said Joe. "No hanky panky this time I hope." Joe's vocabulary had increased as a result of his lessons with Mrs Braithwaite.

Mwangi looked surprised at the turn of phrase.

"No, five of us will be around, just to make sure there are no difficulties," said Mwangi. "You won't see us, though, unless you get into trouble."

Although Joe had done nothing much to support and help the group in the short time he had been in London, they had come to trust him and wanted him to be a part of their community.

Having called ahead and made an appointment for the next day, using his oyster card Joe took the London underground District Line to Whitechapel then the London Overground to New Cross Gate rail station. A walk to the Sainsbury's at New Cross Gate followed, from which he took a P13 bus, which terminated at the Peckham bus station, and finally he walked for a few minutes to Peckham High Street. He found the address, down a side street squeezed between a pub on the high street and a hairdresser further down a side street. It was a small rather dirty-looking three storey building, with a sign saying 'HR Patel, Solicitor' on a wooden door on the ground floor.

Joe knocked on the door at 10am precisely, which was the agreed time of his appointment. He went in before there was any answer. A small man of Asian appearance was sitting behind a steel desk, wearing dark glasses. Joe noticed that the office was very tidy. Two filing cabinets stood against one wall and there was a stack of papers on the desk. A door behind Mr Patel opened and a middle-aged woman, who appeared to be English, handed him a cup of tea and then withdrew, closing the door behind her, after saying, "Will that be all, Mr Patel?"

"Thank you, Brenda, nothing more at the moment."

"Mr Wacheera?" asked the man.

Joe nodded.

"Please sit down," he indicated the one visitor's chair on the opposite side of the desk. "My name is Patel, what can I do for you? Mr Mwangi indicated that it was something to do with British Citizenship."

Joe nodded.

"It is quite a long process Firstly..."

"I know what the process is," Joe interrupted. "I arrived here illegally and don't have the time to go through the whole process of registering as a refugee, applying for permanent leave to remain and then eventually applying for citizenship."

"I see. Any other reason for wanting to avoid the non-traditional route?"

Joe ignored the question. "Mr Patel. Is there another way? My colleague Mwangi indicated that there might be another way."

After a short silence Mr Patel said, "Maybe, but it is not completely straight-forward. Also, it's quite an expensive operation..."

"What do you mean by that?"

Patel looked at Joe, as if trying to assess him. "For a completely new identity," said Patel eventually, "with a British birth certificate, a national health card and a British passport, I will need fifty thousand pounds, in cash."

"I see."

"Do you have that kind of money?"

Joe studied the man a moment, then eventually said, "Yes."

"I will need it all up front before I do anything."

"Forget that. I can pay you a deposit, and then we can proceed from there."

"That isn't how I operate."

Joe shrugged. "Then you can go and get fucked."

"Okay," Mr Patel sighed. "I need ten up front – it's necessary. I have expenses too. And then the rest later."

"I only have five on me today. I'll give you the rest in cash when you deliver," Joe offered.

"This is most irregular," Mr Patel blinked furiously. "But you do come recommended." He then said, "Okay. Do you have a passport photo?"

Joe handed one over. "I will also need some sort of written confirmation that I have paid you five thousand pounds and also confirmation of what you will deliver."

"I can sign a services agreement with you that appoints me as your legal counsel."

"Okay," said Joe.

From a drawer in his desk Patel produced a very short agreement, with no letterhead, appointing Patel as Joe's legal counsel.

'Looks like a worthless piece of paper,' thought Joe, so he insisted that the details of what they had agreed were included in the document.

"Do you have a stamp with your name and address on it?" asked Joe.

Mr Patel impatiently opened one of the drawers in his desk and produced a rubber stamp. He retrieved the document he had given Joe, stamped the document, signed it and handed it back.

Joe spent a minute reading it all again. He nodded, as he put it into his pocket. "Now the five thousand pounds deposit, Mr Wacheera."

Joe pulled money out of his pocket and counted five thousand pounds out on to the desk in twenty-pound notes.

Although Patel watched Joe, he then counted the pile himself. "Just making sure," said Mr Patel. "Be back here in a week's time at exactly 10am with the forty-five thousand you owe and I will deliver what I promised."

Joe proffered his hand, which was ignored. Joe left. Mwangi joined him on the bus returning home. "Everything under control?"

"Yes."

"Did you pay the man?"

"Yes, just a ten per cent deposit. I'll pay the rest when he delivers."

"Well, keep an eye out. He's been known to play tricks in the past."

"Like what?"

"I don't really know more than that."

While Joe waited a week, his elocution lessons continued with Mrs Braithwaite.

He was also often in one of the booths in the Wentworth Arms reading the financial pages of The Times. He also read the Financial Times from cover to cover every day and once a week he picked up The Economist. He made copious notes, engrossing himself in analysing companies of interest. During one analysis, Jo-Ann, who had always been so friendly and helpful, came into his booth, crying.

Joe got up. "What's the problem? Is there anything I can do?"

"It's that bloody Len, he's playing around again."

"Who's Len?" asked Joe.

"My boyfriend, he plays for West Ham, just the reserves at the moment, but he thinks he's good enough to make the firsts."

"Here, just sit down a minute. Wipe your tears. What has Len done?" Joe was struggling. He knew West Ham was a local football club, but he knew nothing about them.

"He had a trial with the firsts and now he thinks the sun shines out of his blind eye and he's fucking that bloody Maureen again."

Joe took out his handkerchief and wiped her tears. He wasn't really sure how to cope.

Gradually Jo-Ann recovered. "I'd better get back," she said.

'She's a sweet girl,' thought Joe, 'but the last thing I need is any sort of involvement with her.'

Before one of his regular meetings with Mwangi, Joe was again engrossed in the accounts of a company of interest.

"What's all that about?" Mwangi asked when he arrived.

"Just keeping myself informed, so when I get a job, I will understand what's going on."

Mwangi looked impressed.

Finally, the day to meet Patel arrived. Joe had drawn out the remaining money in cash, in amounts of less than ten thousand pounds, from his various bank accounts. At the appointed time, he confidently went to the grubby little building where he had found Mr Patel the previous week. The sign on the door had disappeared.

He tried the door; it was locked. Peering in the window, Joe could see that the place was quite empty. He walked around, making sure he had the right address. He walked round to the back of the premises and tried the back door, which was also locked. He put his head into the hairdresser and asked the woman at the reception desk if she knew what had happened to Mr Patel.

"Who is Mr Patel?"

"The solicitor next door."

"They haven't been there that long. I did notice that there was a sign on the door a few weeks ago but I didn't take much notice."

"He has an assistant; Brenda I think her name was. Did you have any contact with her? Maybe she had her hair done here."

"Nope," was the dismissive response. "But you could try the pub on the high street."

"Thank you."

Joe went to the pub, which had just opened. There was one patron, sitting at a corner table of the old-fashioned pub, nursing a pint of beer. Seeing an older man behind the bar and assuming he was the licensee, Joe said, "Sorry to bother you, but I had an appointment with Mr Patel, the solicitor, just next door to here, but now the place seems to be empty..."

The licensee suddenly became animated. "Dodgy, that lot. The police were round here a few days ago asking the same question. They must have scarpered during the night. They were here one day and gone the next. Never had anything to do with the bloke. Actually, I never set eyes on him. He was only there a few months. I only noticed the place was empty when the cops showed up, coupla days ago now."

"Any idea where he might have moved to?" The man shook his head.

"Thanks," said Joe as he left.

He phoned Mwangi and explained the situation. "I'll see what I can find out." Mwangi answered.

"Looks like I pissed away five grand," Joe muttered to himself as he turned to go to the bus stop. He then noticed a woman, pacing up and down, looking anxiously at her watch, outside the door of what had been Mr Patel's office. He walked over. To his surprise, it was the woman Mr Patel had addressed as Brenda.

As he approached Brenda looked up, and she seemed to recognise him. "Oh, thank heaven, it is Mr Wacheera, isn't it? I'm probably a bit late but Mr Patel only told me about your appointment ten minutes ago. We moved premises a few streets away just the other day. I'll take you there."

As they walked, Joe said, "Bit unusual, isn't it, to move so suddenly? Couldn't you have told me when I came to see you last week?"

Brenda shrugged. "It's how he works. I'm not complaining. He treats me well."

They entered the ground floor of a small block of flats and walked up an unswept stairway. Brenda opened a door, and there was Mr Patel, still wearing his dark glasses, sitting behind the desk that he had occupied in the previous premises. All the other furnishings appeared to be the same as before.

"Thank you, Brenda. Yes, tea would be nice," said Mr Patel. Brenda went out. "Mr Wacheera, I have everything you will need for your new identity, including a full bio of the man you will become. First the payment."

Joe tried not to show his irritation. "The people in the pub told me the police are looking for you."

"I'm sure they are, that's why we moved," answered an unperturbed Mr Patel. "They don't have anything on me, but I especially don't want to answer any of their questions."

"I would like to see everything you have promised; I'll pay you after I'm satisfied you have delivered what you promised."

Mr Patel said nothing, just took a file out of one of the desk drawers and gave it to Joe, who looked through it. There was a British birth certificate in the name of Joseph Arnold, and a British passport in the same name but with Joe's photo. The passport had a number of stamps in it indicating visits to South Africa and Kenya. He had been told that passports were not stamped in most European countries. He carefully read the extensive bio.

Joe nodded at Patel. He packed the file into the backpack he was carrying.

"Mr Patel, I am going to pay you twenty thousand pounds today. Because of your behaviour, and in view of the fact that if there is any kind of problem, the probability is that I will have difficulty in getting hold of you, I need to check that this all works. So, come to the Wentworth Arms in Mile End, five weeks

today at ten o'clock in the morning. If everything is in order, I will pay you the balance of what I owe you." He handed over a wad of notes and a card with the name and address of the Wentworth Arms. "This is twenty thousand pounds, count it if you like."

Mr Patel didn't say anything, but Joe saw he was frantically scratching about in another of the desk drawers. Joe was ready when Patel produced a pistol. "You will pay all..."

Joe lifted the desk up and shoved it at Patel, whose chair fell backwards. A shot went off into the ceiling, as Patel banged his head on the floor, rendering him unconscious. Joe then pushed the desk on top of Patel, trapping him underneath, then he walked over and picked up and pocketed the pistol, which had fallen onto the floor. There was no sign of Brenda. He dumped the promised twenty thousand pounds on to the floor next to Patel, then ran down the stairs.

He quietly went to the bus stop and hopped on the first bus that arrived. In an hour he was back home in Tower Hamlets. He dumped Patel's pistol at the first opportunity, making certain that he was alone when he did so. He was shaken. He phoned Mwangi to tell him what had transpired, but there was no response.

Joe re-examined the documents he had been given by Mr Patel. His new identity was that of one Joseph Arnold, a black man. He was given a complete identity: a birth certificate, a passport, and a complete history of the man, including schooling and previous membership of a gang in nearby Lewisham; he was even supposed to have spent time in jail for robbery. There was no information on Joseph Arnold on Google or any other search engine facility. There was even a reference from a previous employer. When Joe checked, there was indeed such a company in the North of England. There was an address but no phone number. When he checked he was satisfied that the company existed at the given address. He didn't really know what sort of checks were made on such references since he had never had a job before. He just hoped that the checks would not be particularly thorough for applicants for the lowly position of messenger, which was where he thought he would start.

After a few days, since there seemed to be no repercussions relating to the incident with Mr Patel, Joe decided it was time to test his new identity. He took a train to Dover and purchased a day ticket on a ferry to Calais. His passport was barely glanced at both on the British and French sides of the English Channel. On his return the passport was scanned by the British system in Dover, but again there was no response from anyone in authority there.

Joe told Mwangi the whole story by phone.

"The trip across the channel to France was probably unnecessary," Mwangi told Joe. "You could further cement your identity by registering to be put on the electoral role and in time you will need to register as a taxpayer."

Joe popped into the Wentworth, hoping to see Mwangi face-to-face.

"He just left," Jo-Ann told him. She was dressed in her street clothes and it looked as if she had just finished her shift. "Fancy a movie?" asked Jo-Ann.

Joe had never been to a cinema in his life. "Sure, yes I'd like that, but what about Len?" he said quickly.

"They're playing up north, Manchester, I think... There's the latest Star Wars on at one of the cinemas in Mile End Lane. It's only a short walk," Jo-Ann added. "Maybe we could get tickets and then there's a McDonalds nearby..."

Joe was all at sea. "Sounds lovely," he said. Joe paid for the movie tickets and he watched what Jo-Ann ordered at McDonalds and chose the same. He paid for both their meals. "Ta," said Jo-Ann.

"You live nearby?" asked Joe.

"Yeah, I live with my Mum. She's a cleaner and usually works nights. Between us, we do okay."

During the meal, which Joe did not enjoy that much, although he could see it was cheap, Jo-Ann chatted away about her hopes for the future. "If Len gets into the firsts, we'll do alright, might even be able to buy a house or a flat somewhere."

"Did you go to school nearby?" asked Joe.

"Yeah, did a couple of GCEs, but then Dad pissed off and I had to help Mum by getting a job. I've been at the Wentworth now for a couple of years, before that I worked in a local cafe."

"Would you ever go back to school?"

"Nah, can't, Mum wouldn't cope..."

The movie was a complete eye-opener for Joe. Although he was aware of cinemas in Nairobi, he had never been. He was slightly bemused at being in a room full of people sitting in the dark watching a film that showed a world of which he had no conception at all.

"I would ask you home," said Jo-Ann, "but Mum told me she had an early shift..."

"That was lovely," said Joe as he kissed her on the cheek. He walked Jo-Ann to the bus and waited until her bus came.

She waved. "See you at the Wentworth," she said as the bus drove off.

Chapter 13: Employment

During the few months Joe had spent sorting out his personal situation he had carefully researched Higginbotham's, the firm run by Sir Oswald Higginbotham. To his surprise, advertised on the website, he saw they were looking for what they described as a messenger. He phoned the office manager and went in for an interview to a very new building on London Wall. Higginbotham's occupied the lower six floors of the building.

Joe was ushered into the office manager's newly furnished small office. He presented the man with his carefully prepared CV, based on the identity of Joseph Arnold, provided by Mr Patel. He had included the reference provided by Patel.

The man briefly went through the CV, item by item, with Joe. Joe was surprised by the lack of any real interest shown by the man. He asked no intrusive questions.

Halfway through the interview, an obviously more senior man put his head round the door.

"Messenger interview," said the office manager quickly.

"My name is Oscar Fitzpatrick," the new arrival said to Joe, who stood up expecting to shake his hand, which was ignored. "Could you wait outside for a moment," Fitzpatrick said to Joe.

Joe left the office and stood in the corridor with the door slightly open so he could overhear all that was said.

"Gives a very good impression, speaks perfect English, he's very well dressed," the office manager said to Fitzpatrick.

"Okay," said Fitzpatrick, "he's black, which probably suits us. Helps with all this bullshit about diversity."

"What about the importance of confidentiality?" asked the office manager. "That's the reason we don't use outside services..."

"Most of our black brethren are not well educated," interrupted Fitzpatrick. "He won't understand a word of anything in the documents he'll handle. So that base is covered. He doesn't stink. Take him on and don't pay him too much."

"Maybe I should go elsewhere," Joe said to himself, "they're just like the reverend and others. At least I know where they are coming from and how to deal with them."

Fitzpatrick hurriedly left the office and brushed past Joe, without saying a word. His interviewer called Joe back into the office.

"We have decided that you are the ideal man for the job," said the office manager. "We will send you a letter of appointment in due course."

"Can you tell me the salary and the hours you work please?"

"The hours are 9am to 5pm. Your wages have not yet been decided but will be included in the letter I have referred to."

"Okay thank you," said Joe. He got up, shook the office manager's hand, and left.

At his next meeting with Mwangi Joe showed him the letter of appointment from Higginbotham's. "The salary is below the minimum wage as you can see, but I have accepted the job. I need to have a track record here in England and this is at least a start. Frankly the cursory nature of the checks made by the company tells me something about the operation. All they are really interested in is cheap labour."

"Yes, most of us have had to accept a lower wage just to get employed," responded Mwangi. "You have managed to get as far as you have much more quickly than most."

Joe decided that since his British citizenship seemed to be in order and he had secured a job, he would pay Patel without further ado. "Would you be able to take the cash and make the final payment to Patel?" Joe asked Mwangi, "I don't really want to go near him again, if I can help it."

"Sure. Just give me the cash and I'll pass it on," responded Mwangi.

Once he had accepted the job, Joe moved into a larger flat in the same area, where he installed a computer, a high-speed copier, and a shredder. He also installed a land line and a Wi-Fi system. Before he went to work at

Higginbotham's, he made what now had become his regular monthly call to his mother in Nairobi.

"I have a job," he said. "At the place run by that big fat *mzungu* Higginbotham. You will remember he came to the reverend's church once or twice?"

"How could I possibly forget? What are you doing there?"

"I am a messenger," responded Joe.

"Messenger!" said Ellen. "Just a little *karani,* can't you do better than that?" Joe laughed. "Give me time, Mum, give me time. My first day is tomorrow. How is Karanja?"

"Much better, now that Koinange is involved, Karanja tells me that the *bhang* business has picked up again. Karanja buys all the *bhang* from growers all over the country and Koinange has the sales well under control, most of the children at your school in Kibera sell for him."

Joe rang off. 'Somehow we rescued ourselves from that disaster at Ol'Kalou and we are both living good lives again,' he thought to himself.

On his first day at work, Joe waited in the reception area at Higginbotham's as soon as it opened at 8.30am.

"My name is Joe Arnold, I'm new here and I was told to wait here for the office manager," Joe said to the pretty receptionist.

"My name is Tracey," the receptionist smiled. "Welcome. He always arrives dead on nine. Would you like a cup of tea or something while you wait?"

"No, I'm fine, thank you very much," he smiled. "I'll just read some of the literature here."

Joe sat in reception and waited and watched as the staff wandered in. During the half hour he sat in reception, he identified most of the senior staff. Just as the office manager stepped into the foyer, a chauffeured limousine stopped outside. The driver opened its car door and Sir Oswald Higginbotham emerged, dressed in an expensive suit. He bundled his way into the foyer. Everybody in sight, including Tracey, greeted him effusively. Tracey glanced at Joe, with raised eyebrows and a faint trace of an ironic smile on her face.

"Might be an ally of sorts," thought Joe. He approached the office manager, who had made way for Sir Oswald.

"Oh, yes, Joe Arnold," he said. "I was expecting you, come along. I will show you around." They went up in the lift to the sixth floor. "Sir Oswald's office is up here. His PA doesn't seem to be about. We'll try later."

They proceeded down floor by floor, where Joe was introduced mainly to senior managers' PAs. Tall, strong and well-dressed, Joe made a good impression with most of those he met, especially the women.

"The business has a senior manager reporting to Sir Oswald for each department: British Investments on the fifth floor, US investments one floor below, European Investments on the third. There's a small department dealing with African investments, mainly South Africa. We have computers, accounts and personnel on the second floor. You will have to pay personnel a visit sometime today. We are on the first floor. Mr Fitzpatrick, whom you have met, is on the second floor, I'll see if he's in."

They went to a spacious office and found Oscar Fitzpatrick sitting behind a large wooden desk. Fitzpatrick stood up, saying to Joe as he reluctantly shook his proffered hand, "Welcome. If there's anything you need, you know where to come."

"Thank you," said Joe, as they shuffled out.

'It all seems quite busy and efficient,' Joe thought.

He was shown to a large office on the first floor, which had a few desks and several large copying machines. Two desks were occupied by two older white men introduced as messengers, Bill and Jim. They did not seem to be busy.

"This is your desk," the office manager showed Joe to a metal desk, which was devoid of anything. "As I said, you should firstly go to personnel. The way we work is that each messenger has particular responsibility for an area. You will be responsible for the fifth and sixth floors, Bill and Jim share the other floors."

Joe spent a few minutes with personnel. He gave them his address and signed his appointment letter. He was given a card that allowed him to access every part of the building.

'That's a surprise,' thought Joe. 'They don't seem to take security very seriously.'

Within a few minutes of settling into his desk, he had a call from one of the PAs on the fifth floor. "Urgent delivery," was all she said.

Joe rushed up to the fifth floor. "Hello, I'm Joe. What can I do for you?"

"Samantha," the young woman smiled at Joe. "Could you please copy this for me and then take the originals to this address." She handed Joe a large stack of papers. "Please bring the copy back to me, but these people are in a hurry for all this, they need it by midday, so make the delivery first and then bring me the copies." She handed Joe an address in a nearby street.

Joe had no sooner returned to his desk when there was another call, this time from Sir Oswald's PA. "How urgent is this?" asked Joe. "I have a job..."

"Very urgent," was the response. "Okay, I'll come up."

He locked the papers he had received from Samantha in his desk drawer and rushed up to the sixth floor where he was met by a severe-looking middle-aged woman, sitting behind her computer outside Sir Oswald's office.

"Joe," he introduced himself. "How can I help you?"

The woman looked surprised. "Are you the new messenger? You seem very well-spoken."

Joe smiled. "Yes, I just joined today. You had something urgent for me?"

"Yes. It's not quite ready yet. Sir Oswald says he needs to change something."

"I'll come back in thirty minutes. I have a package that needs delivering urgently."

Without further ado Joe left, completed the previous task he had been set and returned to the sixth floor after about forty minutes. "Is the package ready yet?" he asked the woman, who was yet to disclose her name.

"Not quite," responded the woman. "How long?" asked Joe.

At that moment Sir Oswald appeared from his palatial office, seemingly ready to go out.

"Have you ordered the car?" he asked his PA, taking no notice of Joe. "Yes sir, he's waiting downstairs. What about...?"

"Oh, that's not urgent. Maybe tomorrow," Sir Oswald responded. "I won't be back today." Sir Oswald made his way to the lift and disappeared.

Joe looked at the woman and shrugged without saying anything. He returned to his desk and completed several other tasks, which involved copying documents and making deliveries. He glanced over each set of documents before dealing with them. Most were innocuous matters of routine. One set of documents, though, appeared to be details of an upcoming takeover bid where Higginbotham's had insider information, which would only be made public in a few weeks' time. The documents contained instructions to a stockbroker to acquire, in small quantities, stock of the takeover target, all in the name of Higginbotham's. Joe surreptitiously made a note of the pertinent details on his phone.

Later, at home, he spent the evening looking up details of the company that was the subject of the takeover bid.

'Looks sound enough,' he thought. 'I suppose the instruction to purchase small quantities is to avoid drawing attention to Higginbotham's activities.'

He looked up the company making the acquisition. It was a large, well respected business.

'I wonder where Higginbotham's got the information on the takeover,' Joe thought to himself.

The next day Oscar Fitzpatrick came to see Joe. "Sir Oswald's PA has complained about you."

Joe shrugged and told Fitzpatrick what had happened the previous day. "Frankly, Mr Fitzpatrick, what she said was urgent yesterday still isn't ready, and she would have had me standing there all day doing nothing. I had a number of other jobs, which I needed to complete. I told the woman I would treat her request as a priority as soon as there was something to copy and deliver. What's her name by the way?"

"Dorothy, you can call her Dorothy. We've had trouble like this before."

"Please don't bother yourself, Mr Fitzpatrick. I'll deal with the issue." When he had a spare moment, Joe went up to the sixth floor, where he found Dorothy idly sitting at her desk.

"Good morning, Dorothy, maybe we got off on the wrong foot yesterday. If Sir Oswald is out, I wonder if we could pop out for a few minutes for a cup of coffee?" he said.

Dorothy looked very surprised and for a moment Joe thought she was going to reject him. Then she smiled. "I have been here for ten years and this is the first time anyone has ever asked me out for anything. Yes, that is a very nice suggestion, of course I'll come."

They went out to a coffee shop nearby. Joe fetched coffee and a bun for each of them.

"Very naughty, that bun," said Dorothy smiling. "What did you do before Higginbotham's?" asked Joe.

"I was married and we have two children, but my husband died and he left us almost destitute, although we managed to keep the house, so I got this job.

We knew Sir Oswald and his wife socially so I suppose he took pity on me." She wiped away a tear.

"I'm sorry. How old are the children?" asked Joe.

"Boy and girl, both at university. Doing well, they both live at home."

"What are they studying?"

"Girl, physics; boy engineering."

"Tough subjects," observed Joe.

They spent most of the next forty minutes talking about Dorothy's life and family. She didn't ask a single question about Joe's situation or about her complaint to Oscar Fitzpatrick.

"I will always treat anything to do with Sir Oswald as an absolute priority," Joe said to Dorothy on their way back to the office.

Dorothy nodded.

He accompanied Dorothy to her desk and then returned downstairs.

A few days later Fitzpatrick bumped into Joe in a corridor. "What did you do to old Dorothy, fuck her or something? She's now as sweet as pie about you."

Joe shrugged. "Coffee. We just had coffee together. She seems to be fine now."

Every three or four months afterwards Joe made a point of going out for coffee with Dorothy.

The rest of the time, he kept his head down and made sure he did as good a job as possible, bearing in mind his experiences with the reverend. He was always on time and was often seen around the office after hours. Soon the people at Higginbotham's came to trust him and he did little chores for some of the more senior people, such as fetching their lunch and delivering and collecting dry cleaning. He also delivered the occasional personal message for Oscar Fitzpatrick, always to the same address, less than a ten-minute walk from Higginbotham's.

He also still regularly met the boy, Jerker, now always on a Saturday, who continued to provide him with very useful information on the gang that Ibrahim ran. As he had done in Libya, Joe always made extensive notes on what he had been told. Without any notice, however, Jerker failed to appear for four weekends in a row. Joe mentioned this to Mwangi, who was not able to find out anything more than Joe already knew. Joe had no real idea why he maintained the contact. 'Though, could come in useful sometime in future I suppose,' he thought to himself.

Over the next few months, Joe became aware that much of what he handled at Higginbotham's was highly confidential and it often contained very useful information. If time permitted, he read everything that came his way. If he thought it could be useful, he secretly photographed one or two relevant paragraphs on his phone, and then did some further research online at home.

"Why don't they send all this stuff by e-mail?" Joe asked the office manager on one occasion, once he had been at Higginbotham's a few months.

"God no!" was the answer. "We wouldn't want any of this shit floating round on e-mail. Sending packages by messenger preserves confidentiality."

"Hm, okay," said Joe to himself.

He always had regular meetings with Mwangi, now after hours at the Wentworth. "Can you get hold of Waweru and Kimani?" asked Joe. "I haven't heard from them and they are not answering their phones."

"Yes, I expect so. Certainly, through my contact in Birmingham."

"Could you get them to e-mail me, please?"

"What do you need them for?"

"Well, there's this messenger business at Higginbotham's. It's completely useless and inefficient. If you and they were interested, maybe we could contract the business and, if that works, we could do the same thing with other potential customers. I'm sure we could save the business money and do a better job."

"I am interested," responded Mwangi. "I'll get the others to contact you. There were several others in the group that came over with you; what happened to them?"

"Koinange went back to Kenya," responded Joe. "I try phoning N'guku and Patrick from time to time. So far no luck."

Joe was in his usual booth at the Wentworth. Jo-Ann had brought him his usual beer. "If you are not busy tonight, we could do another movie," she suggested.

"Yes lovely. I would like that."

"Why don't you pick me up at home?" She gave him her address.

Joe went home, showered, and changed into a fresh set of clothes. He took a bus and found the address Jo-Ann had given him easily enough.

She shared a basement flat in a small rundown-looking block of flats not far from the Wentworth, with her mother. "Mum's out at the moment," she said, as she kissed him 'hello' on the cheek.

Joe sensed that there was more on the agenda than a movie. Jo-Ann was dressed in a very short skirt, was barefoot and wearing a loose shirt with most of the buttons undone. Joe could see that she was not wearing a bra. "I've ordered in a pizza. It arrived just before you did."

"Lovely, I like pizza." He had tried it once.

"Beer?" offered Jo-Ann.

"Thank you."

The flat had a small lounge area, poorly furnished with a settee and two unmatched 'comfortable' chairs. The room also sported a large screen TV in one corner. There was a ragged carpet on the floor. Joe could see a short corridor, which looked as if it led to a bathroom and two bedrooms. The place reeked of poverty.

They ate the pizza sitting next to each other on the settee, with Jo-Ann sitting very close to Joe.

"We have a little time," said Jo-Ann. "Mum will only be back after midnight."

Joe soon got the message; he leant over and clumsily kissed Jo-Ann on the lips. Within minutes they had stripped each other of every vestige of clothing and Jo-Ann had led Joe to a large bed, which occupied most of the smaller of the two bedrooms. They made frantic love. Jo-Ann then went and fetched the remains of the now cold pizza. Within an hour they made love again. There was very little conversation.

Joe looked at his watch. "You said your Mum would be back at midnight, so I had better be off. We'll catch the movie another time." He dressed and kissed a sleepy-looking Jo-Ann on the cheek.

"See you at the Wentworth," she whispered.

Joe was not enthralled with the experience, so put it out of his mind. Jo-Ann and her mother were clearly in a classical poverty trap – little education, two jobs, barely keeping their heads above water. If her boyfriend Len ever made it to the first team at West Ham, which was doubtful, he would move on and abandon Jo-Ann. 'Sweet, sweet Jo-Ann,' he thought. "She will probably just follow in her mother's footsteps and wake up when it's too late. That's just never going to happen to me.'

Joe spent hours most nights at home devouring information he had scooped from the office. He also did his own research on the same companies through the internet. He started to compare what he thought might happen to the stocks with actual results in the market. He soon found his own forecasts becoming more and more accurate.

With this new knowledge, Joe decided to invest on his own account and established a relationship with the local branch of a stockbroker in Woodford Green. To start with he invested small amounts. The proprietor, Fred Smiley, took little notice to start with, keeping their interactions functional and straightforward. But after a while he asked more questions.

"You seem very well researched," he said to Joe over the phone. "You make sound investments. Twice now, you've invested in stocks that, within weeks, have become the subject of takeover bids."

"Yes, I have made substantial profits."

"I think I will take your lead on the next investment you make."

"That is of course up to you."

Smiley did indeed make a few investments on his own behalf, based on what Joe had done, most of which resulted in his making considerable profits. So, once Joe thought Smiley understood that Joe's investment strategy was sound, he paid him a visit.

Fred Smiley was a slightly overweight man in his mid-thirties. He seemed open and friendly. His office was small but it was well run and everything he did was properly documented. Joe had never had any questions not immediately and correctly answered. Away from the bustle of the city, his office also suited Joe's purposes. He did not want there to be the slightest hint of his activities, beyond his job at Higginbotham's. After introducing himself he said, "You will have seen that my investments are well researched and, in most cases, have paid off."

"'Yes," answered Smiley. "I'm very glad to be meeting face-to-face at last."

"I'm in the process of establishing a substantial client base, mostly small investors," Joe told him. "They will all invest individually on recommendations I make to them. I'm in a position to put all that business through you, if we can come to some sort of arrangement?"

"How many people are we talking about?" asked Smiley.

"A few dozen to start with, but I expect that to grow into several hundred over time."

Smiley blanched. "A few hundred?"

"Yes."

"I am not prepared to discount my brokerage fees."

"I don't want you to. All I am asking for is a sixty per cent share of the fees you garner because of the business I introduce."

"Sixty per cent?" said a horrified Smiley.

"Yes, you won't have to do anything except exercise the trades I give you." They eventually settled on fifty-two and a half per cent.

"Two other things," said Joe. "I'll be tracking all the trades I introduce so don't try anything on, I'll know immediately."

Smiley just looked at him. "And what is the second thing?"

"I will be trading through a series of nominee companies, the details of which are never to be disclosed to anyone."

"No problem. I am curious, though, how you have become such a hot-shot investor?" Smiley eyed him suspiciously.

Joe needed to throw him off the scent. "I have been studying financial institutions," he told him truthfully, "since I was a teenager. It took a lot to learn what I know, and at great sacrifice."

Smiley held up his hands in defeat. "In that case, all I need to do is execute whatever trade there is to make, according to individual instructions, nothing more."

Joe left, satisfied, and began choosing targets for his newly formed investment advice business very carefully. Mainly well-dressed businesspeople. Despite many rejections, he soon had a coterie of small investors, all of whom did well on his advice. In turn they had introduced other investors.

Back at Higginbotham's, despite the apparent division of responsibilities set out originally by the office manager, more than half the Higginbotham managers and PA's now used Joe for any jobs they needed doing. Joe supposed that was because he was always did what was asked of him, cheerfully and without complaint.

During one brief interaction with Fitzpatrick, the latter asked, "How are you getting on?"

"Fine," said Joe. His experiences suggested that he should never pass up an opportunity such as this to pursue his own agenda. "The other two messengers are talking about retirement," said Joe. "More and more of the stuff they do is coming my way, which I am quite happy about. But should you want to make a change, if you awarded me an exclusive contract for messenger services here at Higginbotham's for example, I am quite sure it would save you money." Joe shrugged. "Not that I suppose messenger services is high on the list of priorities here..."

Fitzpatrick just blinked, but Joe could see that what he had said registered with the man.

From time to time, Joe was required to deliver a package to a Higginbotham's investment advisor, Clive Anderson. He occupied an office on the fifth floor. Tall, slim, and good-looking, Clive was always well turned out in expensive suits from what Joe could see was a Savile Row tailor. His short blond hair was always maintained without a hair out of place. Mostly Joe gave the article in question to a PA whom Clive shared with two other analysts. On more than one occasion when the PA was absent, Joe popped into Clive's office and left the item on his desk. Clive never looked up.

From his research, Joe discovered that Clive's father Ron had inherited a small construction business in Sydney, Australia, from his own father, which he had ruthlessly developed by building shoddy blocks of flats, in Sydney and Melbourne. Ron must have cut every corner known to man, and even invented a few of his own, to make the profits he had. In order to avoid any legal unpleasantness, he probably made suitable payments to various local politicians and bureaucrats, as similar businesses did in Kenya.

Clive and his sister Isabel had both been educated at the very best private schools in Sydney. Ron eventually sold his business to a rival operation in Sydney, for what seemed a very good price. He then moved the family back to England, and Clive had spent the last two years of his schooling at an equally prestigious school in the home counties of England.

From time-to-time Joe had heard Clive talking to other senior members of staff.

"Oxford, yes... upper second, the old man had banked on me getting a first... Hm, a year at the London Business School... Bullingdon Club, good contacts."

Joe also learned that Clive had captained the Oxford cricket side and was a regular member of the first fifteen Rugby side. He seemed to be very keen to tell everyone of his record. Maybe his Australian background meant that he felt not quite a member of the English upper class? They might have some things in common.

So, on one occasion when Clive's PA was away, Joe dropped a document on his desk, saying casually, "Wouldn't touch that one with a ten-foot pole, it's a bum steer."

Clive looked at Joe with a very surprised expression; it was as if his dog had spoken to him, with a clear upper-class English accent. "What would you know about it?"

"Three reasons," answered Joe. "The financial results seem contrived to me; they have excessive borrowings and all the publicity they have generated makes the thing look dodgy. This lot are up to no good."

"How do you know any of that?"

"I make a note of the companies and people we deal with here and do some of my own research; it's amazing what one can find out from open-source channels."

Clive shrugged.

"It would help me to know whether you think my research is useful, by showing you some examples. I think it might even help you, if I am actually on the right track; it might save you a lot of time." Joe could see from the expression on Clive's face that he was about to dismiss him out of hand. 'Probably just thinks of me as an uneducated low-class peasant,' Joe said to himself.

But then Clive's expression changed. "You know, something my father always said, 'Never ignore the little guy; they often know a helluva lot more than we give them credit for'. But... not here. I can't have people seeing me hobnobbing and poring over documents with a mere messenger."

Joe understood his dilemma. "It's all right," he said, smiling. "I have somewhere in mind, and I'm sure none of your acquaintances would even be aware of this place."

"Okay. But I'm afraid I don't know your name."

"Call me Joe. If you are interested, what I suggest is that we meet at Mile End underground station on the Central Line at, say, seven tonight, or any other night. We can then go to a nearby pub."

As Joe led Clive into the crowded Wentworth Arms that evening, he was greeted in a friendly way by Jo-Ann. "Over there, there's a table over there, Joe.

Those two just left." Joe had been using the pub as a recruiting venue for his investment advice business, so Jo-Ann knew he liked the quiet corner tables. "What can I get you? I'll bring it over." She smiled at Joe.

"Two pints of Best, thanks Jo-Ann." He gave her the money.

"You seem to be well known round here," Clive observed as they sat down. "I look after the staff a bit, it pays," said Joe.

Jo-Ann brought the drinks in double quick time. Joe added some coins to the change proffered and handed it to Jo-Ann as she wiped the table down. "Ta, always the perfect gentleman." Jo-Ann smiled and moved away to serve another customer.

Joe produced two copies of a brief page and a half report, one of which he handed to Clive. "This is a report I've done on the company we talked about," he said. "I would like your opinion on it. I'm trying to develop my skills in this field, so if you would be as critical as you can be that would be very helpful. In my opinion, the business is a dog, despite the extensive publicity they have generated. As you see I've recommended short selling the stock. I certainly would not recommend buying into the business."

Clive read the report, twice.

Without saying anything Joe could see from the nods and grunts that as far as Clive was concerned the report was up to scratch.

"I have all the back-up info if you need it: earnings, projected balance sheets and cash flows. From what I can see the business is dodgy and they are into some dodgy and risky strategies," Joe added. "There's plenty more where that comes from."

"It's good," said Clive without much enthusiasm. "If you send me the back-up stuff, I'll let you know what I think."

Joe was not fooled by Clive's cautious approach. He was clearly excited by what he, Joe, had produced. He had attracted his prey. So, they finished their drinks, quietly left the pub and Joe left Clive at the tube station.

A few days later, Clive phoned Joe. "Yes, your appraisal was correct. What else have you got for me?"

Every week or two Joe and Clive then met at the Wentworth Arms or occasionally at another pub in the area. Clive was paranoid about being seen having a drink with a messenger, and he certainly didn't want it known that a large part of his output was soon being produced by someone else. Joe knew that what he passed on to Clive was easily up to the standard of anything else at Higginbotham's, since he frequently had sight of other analyses, including some done by Clive's peers. Also, Joe overheard occasional commentary about Clive's output, such as 'Must work all day and night' and 'great stuff'.

"Where did you acquire these skills?" asked Clive, during one of their early meetings.

"It's all self-taught," was Joe's answer. "It's amazing the info that's available on the internet."

"Where do you live?"

"Nearby, it's an easy commute to the office."

On another occasion, Clive said to Joe, "Much of the analysis you have done has gone down very well at the office. It's right on the mark."

Joe always assumed that Clive presented the analysis Joe had given him as his own work.

"Where did you go to university?" asked Clive.

"I went to the University of Hard Knocks, the University of the World, if you wish; I had some very good lessons from a man who taught me the basics of finance and accounting. I have progressed from there."

"School? You appear to be well educated."

Joe thought for a moment. "Pembroke House." The name of a private primary school not far from Ol'Kalou, run by the *Wazungu.* He didn't think Clive would have heard of it.

"Never heard of it," said Clive with a dismissive wave of his hand. "Now, what do you want from me, moving forward?"

"Not a lot. If I may, I will continue to give you my analyses of companies that interest me. I would be grateful if you would please critique them for any flaws they have, so I can learn. In time, we will see if they are of value to you and the business."

"Where is all this leading?" asked Clive. "Maybe I could ask you to do other stuff, like assessing risk and investment bundles?"

"Sure. That would increase my skill set."

Their meetings continued. But, a few months later, Joe was surprised to see Clive arrive accompanied by an extremely beautiful woman. "My sister Isabel," said Clive awkwardly before they sat down and ordered drinks. "She's at Oxford."

Isabel was tall, at nearly six feet, with dark brown hair worn down to her shoulders, an intelligent and pretty face, and a slim trim body. She smiled at Joe as he shook her by the hand. She was wearing a skin-tight pair of jeans and a pink shirt with several top buttons undone to give anyone interested an eyeful. She certainly turned the heads of most of the males in the pub. Some of the women too.

"Please to meet you," Joe said smiling. Their eyes connected, for longer than usual. Without anything further being said, he sensed a kindred spirit, very clever, and single-minded.

"So, what are your conclusions?" asked Clive, looking at the latest of Joe's analyses.

"Very good for the longer term, but there's no hurry. The price will follow the market for a while and then gradually outperform it," responded Joe confidently.

Clive popped into the toilet.

"Isabel," Joe said, "I would like to see you again; I'm sure we have many common interests. Here is my card."

Smiling, Isabel scribbled her mobile phone number on it and handed it back to him. "Call me anytime," she said.

"I will, I certainly will," said Joe. He watched her looking at him for a moment, a half-smile on her face. Joe thought it might be better if Clive was not aware of their exchange, at least for the time being.

PART 5

Chapter 14: Isabel

Joe wanted to see more of Isabel, but he was unsure what her reaction was likely to be, until, during one of their regular meetings, Clive happened to say, "Isabel was very impressed with you and the analysis you provided. I actually share some of what you give me with her. She wanted to know more; said you had her number?"

So, with his heart in his mouth, Joe phoned Isabel. "Hello," he said. "It's Joe, you know we..."

Isabel laughed. "I know who you are! I'm glad you called."

Joe breathed a sigh of relief. He could hear the smile in her voice. "Thank you. I have to admit I was a bit nervous to call, wondering what your reaction would be." He laughed. "Would you like to meet? I can come to Oxford or we can meet when you are In London?"

"I'm in London at the moment. What do you suggest?"

"I would like to be able to talk to you, so maybe dinner in a pub somewhere?"

"Okay. If you like I'll book at The Engineer in North London. It's a gastro- pub."

"That would be wonderful. What's a gastro-pub?"

"It's a sort of slightly better class of pub, they are supposed to serve decent meals. I've been there once. I'm sure you'll like it. Seven?"

"Lovely. I'll come straight from the office."

"Thanks. Look forward to seeing you again."

'Gastro-pub,' Joe said to himself. 'Sounds like a sort of stomach-ache pub.'

Joe arrived a few minutes early and was relieved to see Isabel already there, sitting at a table and looking at a menu. He went over and was about to shake her by the hand when to his surprise she stood up and kissed him lightly on the cheek. Unthinkingly he put his hand to the spot.

Isabel smiled. "Lovely to see you again."

"You look really beautiful," said Joe. She was dressed again in skin-tight jeans and a tight blue blouse. Joe was dressed as usual in his one and only modestly priced suit.

"Thank you," she said smiling.

Joe looked at the menu carefully. "What's polenta?"

"Maize meal. It's an Italian dish. Not my cup of tea, but it's perfectly okay."

"*Posho,*" said Joe. "We called it *posho.*"

"Oh, what language is that?"

"Swahili. I was brought up in Kenya."

"Wow! That's a surprise. You sound almost Oxbridge."

"I took extensive elocution lessons when I first arrived. You say almost – obviously I still have some work to do."

"I think I will have snails to start and then one of the fish dishes. What are you going to drink?"

"Snails?" said Joe in a horrified voice.

"Yes, they're usually excellent. I've had them here once before. You can try one of mine."

"I'll have tomato soup, rump steak, well-done, polenta and vegetables," said Joe firmly. "I've got used to the beer, so I'll have a beer."

"*Well-done* rump steak. It's much fuller of flavour if you don't burn the meat to death." Isabel laughed.

"We always cooked any meat we had very well in Kenya. It makes sure that any trace of tapeworm is completely killed."

Isabel laughed and laughed. "Tape worm, you really don't have to worry about that here in England, but certainly have whatever makes you comfortable."

Isabel had a glass of Pinot Grigio. "I come down to London about once a week, during the term. I'm reading physics at Balliol," she told him. "I take my degree this year, and I intern at Wates, a large construction company, something Daddy arranged; but I am going to do an MBA at the London Business school next year, which takes a year and then who knows..."

"Could you explain physics and internship please?"

"Physics is the study of matter and energy and the interaction between them."

"I'm still none the wiser."

"I suppose a better explanation is how the universe works."

"And internship?"

"It's an unpaid junior position. They give me jobs that help me understand how the company works. I really like it."

Joe laughed. "Unpaid. Sounds a bit like Higginbotham's."

Their meals arrived. Joe gingerly ate one of Isabel's snails. "It's alright. A bit rubbery... Where do they come from? Do people just run around the rural areas picking them up?"

"I think they are specially bred."

"Specially bred. Where I come from snails eat everything in sight. Madness." They both laughed.

"Why do you stay at Higginbotham's?" asked Isabel. "From what I've seen of your work you could be a great success in the City. What you produce is better than most. "

Joe wondered how much he should tell her. "It's all a bit one dimensional. I'm learning all the time. I don't really know how to run a business," said Joe. "Yet," he added.

"You could just have a few clients on the side. It's what Clive talks about but I don't think he would risk his relationship with Higginbotham's to do that."

"Hm, I do that already, just a few clients at the moment. I need to find a way of expanding." He didn't tell her he now had more than a hundred clients, run from a one-room office in Bethnal Green, where he employed two clerical assistants. Joe thought he would try to put her off this line of questioning and said, "I am in the process of taking over the messenger service at Higginbotham's. The arrangements are almost finalised. When that happens, I will expand it to other businesses. I have people in place who can do that for me."

"A messenger business. Sounds like small potatoes compared to the potential of the investment advisory business."

"Yes. There is a small Kikuyu diaspora here in London. As much as anything, I am doing it to provide employment opportunities for them. Many have limited skills."

"Kikuyu?"

"The tribe I belong to in Kenya."

"Is that important to you?"

"Yes. They helped me when I first arrived. But it is also a tribal tradition, which I would like to keep up; one's tribe is what you are, one's reason for existence, flesh of my flesh, blood of my blood. There are others who came here with me, they need help as well."

"I like that," said Isabel quietly.

"Where do you stay when you are in London?" asked Joe.

"Mum and Dad have a flat in South Kensington. They're not always there, but I can use it anytime. Provided I don't make a mess."

Joe could see that Isabel was surprised that he didn't ask if her parents were currently staying in the flat.

The main meal was served.

Joe said nothing. He ate some of the polenta. "It's okay," he said. "Just a bit fussy. We had mealie meal plain, either as porridge or as a sort of cake."

He broke the easy silence that followed as they focussed on their meals, by asking: "You have used a couple of odd expressions that I don't fully understand, like 'not my cup of tea' and 'small potatoes'. It's obvious what they mean, I suppose. Do you know the origins of these expressions?"

"I doubt many people could answer that question. I'll look them up and let you know, next time I see you."

"I'm happy to know there will be a next time." They chatted on until closing time.

"I'll call a Uber," Isabel announced. "Where do you live?"

"Tower Hamlets, it's suitable for messengers." He laughed.

"Oh, yes. Not too far from the pub where we first met."

Before she got into her Uber, Isabel leant over and kissed Joe. "That was a lovely evening. We must do it again; please don't wait three weeks before you call me."

"I won't."

They met every week for the next three weeks, mostly in pubs. Joe admitted to her that, despite his apparent sophistication in the world of share trading, he was all at sea when it came to social situations, so she made him as comfortable as possible when they were together.

During the meal, this time at The Bunch of Grapes on the Brompton Road, Isabel said to Joe, "I should tell you that Clive is becoming a bit paranoid about you, because at least half his output at Higginbotham's is now provided by you, he's worried about what will happen down the line. He is totally focussed on his own situation of course, as he always has been, no thought as to what you might want out if the relationship."

Joe looked at her. He could see they were beginning to trust each other. Everything she said confirmed his own assessment of the self-serving, sense of entitlement that was Clive.

"Thank you," he said. "I expect I will be able to look after myself."

At the end of their meal, which Joe paid for, Isabel said to him, "My flat is just round the corner. The parents are away at the moment, though they said they might be back later tonight or tomorrow sometime. Why don't we go home and have a coffee or something?"

"That would be lovely."

They walked hand-in-hand towards Isabel's parents flat, which took about ten minutes.

"I'm going back to Oxford tomorrow," she said on the way, "and won't be back for a couple of months. Finals are at the end of June and I need to put all my energies into getting the best result possible."

"I could come up to Oxford for the weekend sometime, if you aren't too busy?"

She hugged him. "I was hoping you would suggest that. The weekend after next might be best. Something to really look forward to. Here we are," she announced, pressing a code into the security pad at the front door. They went up a few floors in the lift and Isabel opened the door of a flat on the top floor.

The flat was part of a luxurious new block, carpeted throughout, tastefully furnished, everything blended in perfectly. Joe's memory of the general's house was of beautiful items crowded together untidily, like someone had bought into a culture which was not fully understood. This place was different.

"It's beautiful," he said.

"I'll put the kettle on and show you round," said Isabel.

Joe absorbed it all. One large bedroom with a bathroom attached. Another three big bedrooms and two bathrooms, something that Isabel referred to as the laundry. There was also a small study. "Dad's hideaway," said Isabel. She showed him a very large and well-appointed kitchen. The dining room had seating for twelve guests. She finished the tour in the large, beautiful lounge, with a giant smart TV dominating one wall. "You can't see much in the dark, but there is a balcony out there." She pointed. "It overlooks a small park, owned by the surrounding property owners, one has to have a key to access it."

Joe was not intimidated. He briefly compared it to his own grubby little flat, but then thought to himself, 'This is obviously what's possible.' He wondered if there was any way he could cooperate with Isabel to achieve his dreams.

"Isabel," he said. "I would like to kiss you properly, but you need to show me how. Africans do not kiss, they think it is unhygienic." He pulled her towards him and they kissed.

Isabel responded enthusiastically. "Well, that was lovely," she whispered afterwards. "Forget the coffee," she led him to a large couch in the lounge and the kissing deepened.

Joe unbuttoned her shirt and undid her bra. He fondled her breasts and started to undo her jeans.

"No, not here," said Isabel, rising to lead him into the bedroom.

"Wait," Joe said, stopping. "This is absolutely wonderful, but if I am to continue to behave myself, I think I should go home."

Isabel smiled and led him to the front door instead.

They had another long kiss before Joe left. "I really look forward to the next time. I will think of you all the time and every day," said Joe, as he descended the stairs.

During the next two weeks, Joe finalised the negotiations regarding the Higginbotham messenger services with Fitzpatrick and met with Mwangi, Waweru and Kimani to bring them on board. They had a somewhat rowdy reunion at the Wentworth, where they spent most of the evening reminiscing. Waweru and Kimani rushed up to Joe and hugged him.

"How was Birmingham?" Joe asked them.

"Not so great," Waweru told him, "casual jobs, not well paid, we just knew we had to be patient."

"Citizenship?"

"On the way. Legally we are allowed to work."

Joe eventually explained what he was negotiating at Higginbotham's. "You will all be properly paid," added Joe. "Initially I will fund the business from my own resources, until the operation turns a profit. We will also need to make similar arrangements with other people in the city; Mwangi and I will do that. We will use bicycles to make deliveries, which is much quicker and you need to understand the geography of the streets, particularly in the one square mile of the city. We also need to think of other businesses, such as cleaning offices," said Joe to his excited audience. "And it can't just be us Kikuyu in the business. As we grow, it will be important to have English people with us," said Joe.

They all agreed.

Fitzpatrick, however, wasn't happy when Joe asked for Mwangi, Kimani and Waweru to be given security clearance for Higginbotham.

"What's all this about?" asked Fitzpatrick. "We are not about to take on half the population of Africa!"

"You won't be taking on any of them, they are employees of a company I have set up, but from time to time they will need access to your offices to service your requests. They will have to use the copying equipment here as well."

"How will we communicate with them? From what I understand they won't be based here."

"By mobile phone," said Joe. "Every call will be answered immediately, during office hours, and we will respond within a few minutes of receiving each call. All your PAs will be fully briefed."

Eventually the contract was signed.

Joe and Mwangi then visited other businesses in the area. Within months they were servicing ten operations and, much to Joe's relief, the messenger business was profitable.

Joe also made his usual phone call to his mother Ellen. Unusually Karanja answered the phone.

"Where's Mum?" asked Joe.

"She's out," said Karanja. "If you call again in a few days, I'm sure she will be here."

'That sounds really odd,' thought Joe. "How is the *bhang* business?" he asked.

"Very good. As you know I have Koinange with me now, and just the other day your friend Patrick returned to Kenya and joined us also."

"Patrick?" said a surprised Joe. "I've been trying to get hold of him for a couple of years or more. Is he alright?"

"Yes. He said something about rescuing his father in Libya or somewhere."

"What about N'guku? He was with Patrick."

"He has not mentioned N'guku."

"Okay, I will try to phone him myself."

"We need to talk about the ownership of the *bhang* business."

"Yes. You want me to give it all back to you?" said Joe. "That's fine, I will tell Waweru and Kimani, and N'guku when I find him. There is no need to sign anything, just stop paying every month."

When it came time to visit Isabel again, Joe took a train from Paddington. He was mesmerised by the flat green lowlands between London and Oxford. When the announcer declared the next stop to be 'Oxford', Joe called Isabel.

"Where are you staying?" she asked.

"The Studio."

"I know it. I'll meet you there. Fancy sort of place..."

Joe said nothing. He wondered whether he shouldn't have booked something cheaper.

Joe found The Studio easily enough. He had a quick shower and changed into a pair of grey slacks and a red open-necked shirt, which he thought would be more appropriate for a student's night out. Isabel arrived as he walked into the lobby. Again, she looked stunning: skin-tight jeans, plenty of cleavage, hair tied back in a pony-tail. Smiling, they were soon kissing, locked in a deep embrace.

"I've booked in a nice little restaurant a few minutes' walk from here," she said as they came up for air. "A bit of a change from the pub scene," she told him. "I hope you like it."

He wondered what the food would be like. Despite the pub experience, he hadn't really got past steak and chips. Most of the food the British ate seemed tasteless and insipid, although he had enjoyed the meals they had shared.

"Okay," he said, "let's go."

Joe's heart sank when he saw the menu: Oysters, mussels, something called pate de foie gras.

"I think I need some help here," said Joe smiling, "perhaps you could take charge of ordering the meal?"

"We need to get you off this meat and potatoes malarkey. Maybe we could try you on duck as a main course."

"Duck?" he said suspiciously. "Ducks are scrawny, diseased birds, not fit for human consumption."

She laughed. "No, it's very nice, especially the way they cook it here. I'm not trying to poison you, you know. You are much too precious for that."

"Okay," he smiled. "Duck with chips and some veg."

"They may want you to have mash, and the veg may be a bit of a token, but we'll try that. Now to start, I'm going to have oysters. I'll give you a couple to see how you get on."

"Maybe just soup, it says tomato soup here," he said jabbing his finger at the menu. Her relaxed way made the whole exercise fun. Joe was persuaded to eat one oyster and he had a taste of Isabel's sole. He thought he could get used to duck. "A bit like chicken," he said. He had a taste of her wine, which he didn't like, so he had a beer. By the end of the meal, Joe had completely relaxed.

"Clive has become almost wholly dependent on your analyses, you know," Isabel said. "He's become even more paranoid about it. I haven't always got on well with Clive, he still seems to think that I am around just to do his bidding," Isabel offered.

A man just leaving the restaurant approached their table. "Hello Isabel, just though I would pop over and say hello. I was wondering when I could see you again?"

"Oh, Peter. I would like to introduce you to my friend, Joe."

"How do you do," said Joe.

Peter ignored him.

Looking absolutely furious, Isabel was silent for a moment, then she stood up. "Listen, Peter, frankly you can fuck off. Your behaviour is totally unacceptable. I never want to set eyes on you again. Is that clear?"

The man looked puzzled. Clearly embarrassed he quickly left the premises. "Well, that sorts that little problem out," she said.

Joe raised his eyebrows, saying nothing.

"I dated him a few times. He's an arrogant little prick."

'Impressive,' Joe thought to himself. 'Despite everything she really is her own person.'

There was a short silence.

"You have a most interesting background. Can you tell me a bit more?" asked Isabel.

"As I mentioned earlier, I have a small operation advising a group of friends and acquaintances on what shares to buy and sell. I have done pretty well for them since I started. Better than those invested with Higginbotham's anyway. I also invest in my own account..."

"Hm, interesting. How many friends and acquaintances do you have?"

"Just a few, but it's grown a bit in past months. I'm wondering what do about it all. I have also just signed the contract for the messenger business at Higginbotham's and we are working on a few more similar contracts."

"Why do you stay at Higginbotham's?"

"It's a good source of information, if you know where to look; I now only pop in once a week."

"Sailing a bit close to the wind, aren't you?"

Joe frowned. "I don't understand the reference; I am learning all the time. What does that mean?"

Isabel laughed. "What I meant was, isn't what you are doing quite risky?"

Joe smiled. "I've taken much bigger risks. In fact, my whole life has been a risk; I might even tell you about it some time. 'Sailing too close to the wind', I will store that away for future use."

"What about Clive?"

Joe shrugged. "What about him? The analyses I do for him has helped me hone my skills. I obviously use the same analyses to service my own clients. On the rare occasion he has anything useful to add I include that in my own document."

"As I have told you, Clive is becoming dependant on your input."

"What do you think I should do about that?"

"You still meet him at least twice a month. You've said you now only go to Higginbotham's offices about once a week. You could see him less often, and if this is what you want to do, gradually disengage..."

"Okay, that's helpful. I'll probably do that."

They left the restaurant when they had finished their meals. "Come back to my place," said Isabel, "it's only a short walk."

Joe needed no second invitation. He found she had a small studio flat quite close to the town centre.

"My father could afford to fund a bigger place," she said apologetically, "but he said something like 'it's good to struggle a bit, makes you hungrier', so this is what he says I'm due."

Joe laughed, reflecting briefly on how he and his mother had lived in Kibera.

"Coffee?" asked Isabel.

Joe shook his head. "I just want to kiss you again."

The kiss became more than a kiss. Isabel allowed Joe to slowly undress her. What he saw was a truly beautiful woman: her pretty face, her slim well-looked after trim body. The dark patch between her legs... She helped him extricate himself from his own clothes and soon, with their clothes scattered over the flat, they were making love on Isabel's large double bed.

"Wonderful, that was wonderful," Isabel whispered afterwards as she snuggled up to him.

There was a short silence.

"I see it's true then," said Isabel, giggling as she looked down to admire the lithe, strong, dark brown body next to her.

"What's true?"

"Your member. It's a lot bigger than I expected."

"Bigger?"

"Yes, the myth is that black men have bigger pricks than whites."

"I have never seen an *M'zungu's* prick."

"What's an *M'zungu*?"

"White man. It's what we called them in Kenya."

They were silent for a few minutes, rejoicing in the feel of each other's bodies. "I could do with a bit more of your large black member," murmured Isabel.

Joe laughed. "You need to be careful of your terminology. Certainly, you can have as much of my black member as you can take, but do you know what a black mamba is?"

"No, but I'm sure that I am about to find out," she giggled, clutching his growing erection.

"I have what you describe as a black member. A black mamba is an aggressive and very poisonous snake. Never confuse the two, you might get more than you bargained for."

They made love again and once more during the night.

During one of their interludes, Isabel said to Joe, "That waitress at the Wentworth Arms, the one who served us."

"Yes, Jo-Ann." Joe looked at her quizzically.

"She was taking more than a passing interest in you personally."

Joe wondered how much to tell her. 'If this relationship with Isabel is to go anywhere, I had better tell her everything,' he quickly thought to himself. "Yes. We went to the movies a few times and, yes, since this is what you seem to be asking, I have ended up in her bed once and once only." He went on. "She lives with her mother, no sign of the father. Her mum has a cleaning job, mostly at night. If you want to see evidence of the working poor, those two are a classical example. Two jobs, just making do. Jo-Ann has a boyfriend, who plays football for West Ham. He has aspirations to become part of their regular first eleven and Jo-Ann sees him as a solution to their long-term financial future. When the boyfriend misbehaves, a not infrequent occurrence, she comes and has a cry on my shoulder. That's about it. Decent girl, Jo-Ann, left school too early, no real skills and no real prospects. Sorry I seemed to have gone on a bit."

"Thanks for telling me that. That's okay, I see what you mean by the working poor."

Joe said nothing.

The next day, Isabel tried to show Joe some of the sights of Oxford. After showing him the Bodleian Library and several of the prominent Colleges, including Balliol, her own college, she said to Joe, "I can see you are not really engaged in all this..."

"I like your college, it's obviously a great privilege to be there. Also, I was interested in the fact that the library, what's its name, Bod something..."

"Bodleian."

"Yes, Bodleian, is over four hundred years old and has about thirteen million books and other items in it, but I am conscious of the fact that the so-called civilisation this represents was used to suppress us in Kenya. Maybe it could have been put to better use."

"I see what you mean."

As they walked past Oriel College Joe stopped and looked up. "Have you any idea who that bastard is?" Joe pointed at a statue at the college entrance.

"Yes, of course, Cecil Rhodes..."

"I don't want to make a fuss, but have you any idea what he represents as far I am personally concerned?"

"I do, but tell me, you had better get it off your chest."

"White supremacist above all, probably a bit of a crook... I could go on."

"If you wish. I don't disagree, but you can't change history. His statue will stay, it reminds everyone what he did and what he stands for. On the positive side he did leave a lot of money for something called a Rhodes Scholarship, which has helped to complete the education of people from my country, Australia, here in Britain and indeed the United States and other countries. Scholarships now include women and," she looked at him smiling, "dare I say it, black people."

Joe couldn't help laughing.

"You are a clever girl," he leant over and kissed her, "popped my balloon." He laughed again. "Ah, did you apply for one of these scholarships?"

"It wasn't relevant, I came here to study physics." She shrugged.

Joe caught the train home on Sunday. He wondered, as he stared at the landscape blurring past him, what would come of the relationship. He liked Isabel, but the *M'zungu* concept of being in love was foreign to him. He wondered how far he could trust her and whether he had already told her too much about his activities. They had discussed his relationship with her brother Clive, and how he would deal with that, so he knew that she was on his side. He also knew he should be moving on from Higginbotham's. Looking at the situation in the cold hard light of day, he wondered whether a partnership or a relationship with Isabel would help or hinder the process. He still had a lot to learn and understand about the society he now lived in.

There were other worries in his background too, which recent events had masked – the death of General Kariuki, his past as a people smuggler, his drug crimes – he wondered how likely it was that these things would catch up with him. He was only too aware of the differences in the standards of living between what westerners called the third world and the developed world. Living as he was in the African community, there were always people from his homeland coming in. It might only be a matter of time before someone recognised him. Also, his contrived identity. Certainly, an association with Isabel, if she fronted an organisation he might set up, would lend him legitimacy while keeping him in the background. He had absolutely no intention of coming as far as he had only to rot in jail.

'For all their fine things and feelings, the West is just another dog like me, but one with bigger teeth,' he thought angrily.

He also knew there was nothing on Earth that could stop him wanting to continue his relationship with Isabel. He would continue to see her, even though he would have to watch himself.

Joe's world was turned upside down when he next phoned Ellen back in Nairobi. The phone was again answered by Karanja in a very shaky voice.

"Hello Karanja, how are you? Can I speak to Mum please?" Joe was surprised to suddenly hear Patrick's voice on the line.

"Hello Joe, I'm here just looking after Karanja. I don't know how to tell you this gently, but Ellen died in hospital last week. We had the funeral yesterday."

Joe was almost too shocked to speak. "Died. What are you talking about? She was fine when we spoke two weeks ago." The news was just too shocking, Joe had trouble understanding what he had been told. He eventually pulled himself together. "Died, what did she die of...?

"AIDS, she had AIDS," responded Patrick.

"Can I speak to Karanja again please?"

"Hello Joe," said Karanja in a weak voice when he came back on the line. "Your mother was diagnosed with AIDS some time ago. We agreed that she was not going to tell you... she was very firm about that. She did not want you to come back to Kenya, she said there was nothing you could do."

"Couldn't you have told me when she died?"

"Ellen was quite clear, even during her last days, she said she did not want you to come back to Kenya. 'Tell him after the funeral' were almost her last words."

"Why?"

"She said you had made a new life for yourself in *Ulaya* and if you came back here the police would probably arrest you. She was very proud of what you were doing."

"Arrest me? What for?"

"The police still want to talk to you about the death of General Kariuki."

"Ridiculous," said Joe. "I was in Juba when he was killed."

There was silence on the line.

"Is there anything I can do?" Joe eventually asked.

"I don't think so," said Karanja. "As I said your mother was very proud of you, especially the way you got her away from that life in Kibera."

"Thanks to you too," said Joe.

"Ellen was very important to me, you must understand that, she really looked after me, I don't know what I will do now," said Karanja, crying.

Patrick came back on the line. "Joe, I'm sorry, really sorry," said Patrick. "You must understand that Karanja did exactly what Ellen asked him to do."

"Okay," said Joe. "Look, all this has shaken me up a bit, but we do need to have another conversation. I have been trying to get hold of you since we went our separate ways, in Italy. Where is N'guku by the way?"

"I'll call you in a week or so. I think N'guku should be with you soon." They rang off.

Joe was absolutely devastated. He had no idea who to turn to; his relationship with Isabel was still in its infancy and she had no knowledge of his history and the journey that had got him to where he was. He was not that close to Mwangi, despite their cooperation.

He eventually phoned Waweru.

"I need to see you and Kimani," Joe said after some perfunctory greetings. "You sound terrible," said Waweru. "What's the problem?"

"It's personal," responded Joe. "I'll tell you when we meet."

"Kimani and I will see you at the Wentworth at six, it sounds serious."

When Joe arrived at the Wentworth, he quickly saw that Kimani and Waweru were seated in a booth, talking animatedly to another man, who looked like an older version of N'guku. It was N'guku.

Joe rushed up and hugged them all.

"What, where?" Joe said, looking at N'guku, who was incoherent. "We'll talk about all that later," said Waweru.

Jo-Ann brought them drinks and they ordered food. "You called me," said Waweru, "it sounded serious."

"Yes," said Joe. He told them all about the death of his mother and how he had been left in the dark. "I just needed to talk to someone. I don't know what to do."

"There is not much you can do now. It seems your mother had it all sorted out, brave lady," said Waweru.

"There is no purpose in returning to Kenya," said N'guku. "You may be arrested, whether or not you had anything to do with the death of General Kariuki."

Joe had never told a soul about Kariuki and how he had died. He was almost in denial now that he had anything to do with it.

Jo-Ann served the meal.

"I've been trying to get hold of you and Patrick for what seems like years," Joe said to N'guku, "there was never any answer."

"It was too difficult," said N'guku.

"Where were you?"

"All over the place, mainly Libya. Patrick was determined to track his father down. We did find him, and he's back in Kenya now. He's in a very bad way."

"I spoke to Patrick earlier. He was helping Karanja," said Joe, "something that I should have been doing."

"Too late now," said Waweru.

Towards the end of what turned out to be a rowdy but joyous reunion, the conversation turned to when Waweru and Kimani had arrived in England.

"You and Mwangi obviously helped us when we arrived, but we never understood why we were dumped off in Birmingham. Wouldn't we all have been better off if we had stayed together?"

Joe looked uncomfortable. "I didn't understand the society I had suddenly arrived in. I felt I desperately needed to work through what had to be done to get a British identity. At the time I thought it would be better and less risky for all of us if I worked through it on my own. That is how it has turned out. I have put us all in a position where we all have jobs and with Mwangi's help we can all move on from where we are. We own the messenger business and we can get into other businesses such as cleaning offices." Even to Joe that did not sound convincing. 'We should probably have stayed together,' he thought. "What help do you need?" Joe asked N'guku.

"British identity and employment. I still have some funds from the rescue of that woman in Italy."

"Mwangi will help with that," said Joe

The discussion broke up just before closing time. N'guku left with Waweru and Kimani.

Joe went home, with a greater understanding of his need for the support of his friends.

Chapter 15: Oscar Fitzpatrick

Joe had always found Oscar Fitzpatrick unpleasant to deal with and, before Mwangi became too well-known at Higginbotham's, he asked him to follow Oscar for a few weeks to see what he was up to.

Mwangi reported to him, "Oscar visits a place called Atlantic Investments every day, usually at lunch time, but also sometimes after work. Often, when he returns to Higginbotham's, he looks very pleased with himself and on other occasions he looks worried." He gave Joe the address of an office a few minutes' walk from Higginbotham's establishment.

Joe then spent a few days researching Atlantic Investments. 'Hm,' he said to himself, 'he's hidden it quite well'. Through several holding companies, Oscar was the sole owner of Atlantic Investments. A brother or cousin or something ran the business for him. Joe scrolled through several more screens and carefully filed all the information he could find on Oscar and Atlantic Investments. "You never know," he muttered to himself, "might come in useful one day."

Joe did not have to wait long. Some months after he had come to the arrangement with Oscar Fitzpatrick regarding the messenger service, Oscar asked to meet him in a pub near the office. In contrast to Clive, it appeared that Oscar had no concerns about being seen with Joe by any of the senior management of Higginbotham's. He wasted no time. Once their drinks had been acquired, Oscar said to Joe, "I have been talking to an old friend of mine, Fred Smiley."

"Oh yes, I have put quite a lot of business his way. I think I am one of his bigger clients."

"Where does all your research come from?"

"I do it myself. Ask Clive Anderson. I pass much of what I do on to him. I suppose that a large proportion of what he puts forward actually comes from me."

"Where does the original info come from?"

Joe frowned. "The internet has all the info needed to do that kind of research."

"Isn't there more to it than that?"

"Meaning what?"

"I'll be quite blunt," said Fitzpatrick. "You must have nicked some of the info in your research, from confidential sources at Higginbotham's."

Joe looked at him without saying anything for a full minute. "Mr Fitzpatrick, you have a saying in the English language, 'People in glass houses shouldn't throw stones'. Be very, very careful where you go with statements like that."

Fitzpatrick looked surprised. "What's that supposed to mean?"

"You know very well what that means, Mr Fitzpatrick. I know more about most of the senior people working at Higginbotham's than anyone else in the business, and that includes you."

"Are you trying to blackmail me?"

"You asked for the meeting, not me."

"I'll remove the messenger service business from you."

"Okay with me. It's neither here nor there in the scheme of things. In terms of our agreement, just give me a formal notice that you wish to quit, and we'll take it from there. 'Sir' won't be pleased, as your costs will undoubtedly increase."

"Fuck you."

"Mr Fitzpatrick, unless there is anything else, we'll leave it there if you don't mind."

Joe got up to leave. He hadn't touched his drink. He proffered his hand to Fitzpatrick, which was ignored. Joe left the pub, with Fitzpatrick sitting there fuming, but with a worried look on his face.

A few days later Joe went to see Fred Smiley. They dealt with several routine matters and then Joe asked, "Do you value the business I pass on to you, Mr Smiley?"

Smiley blinked. "Yes, of course. You are one of my most important clients..."

"Do you know Mr Fitzpatrick? He also works for Higginbotham's."

"Yes, I've known him for years."

"Do you do any business with him?"

"No, not really. He has his..." Smiley stopped what he was saying, his face went pale and his hands started to shake.

"I know about that," said Joe.

Smiley looked shocked but said nothing.

"You were obviously indiscreet in a recent discussion you had with him. Fitzpatrick made a clumsy attempt to blackmail me recently, because of that conversation. The fact that my name came up in the discussion does you no credit. If you value our mutual business activities, then I suggest you cut all contact with Mr Fitzpatrick."

Smiley's expression again looked shocked, but then it shifted to acceptance. Over the years, their relationship had grown from patronising indifference to mutual admiration. Joe's business was extremely important to him now.

"Okay. I'm sorry. It won't happen again." Joe nodded and left.

Chapter 16: Joe and Isabel

Joe and Isabel continued to meet, often at her flat in Oxford, until she graduated with a first in physics; and then in her parent's flat in South Kensington, always when Isabel's parents were away. Joe was usually allowed to spend the night.

"You look awful and exhausted," observed Isabel one evening, soon after Joe had learnt of the death of his mother. "What's the matter?" asked a confused Isabel.

"My mum died and I've only just been told." Joe sobbed. "She died. of AIDS. They didn't tell me."

"Oh Joe, I am so sorry, just come here." Isabel led him to the couch and hugged him. "You poor boy, please tell me if you can."

Gradually the story poured out.

"She was so unselfish, didn't want me to know until it was all over. I should have been there..." he cried. "She was still young, early forties."

Isabel said nothing but continued to hold him. "You could have called me," said Isabel.

"I know, I now wish I had, but I haven't told you much about me. There are some things that you might find difficult to come to terms with."

"It can't be that bad."

"For a classy western woman like you, it is beyond bad."

"Try me."

"I will, I certainly will, but not now."

Joe gradually relaxed and Isabel took him to her bed, where she undressed him and herself, and they made the gentlest love that either of them had ever known.

Isabel went once and only once to Joe's flat in Mile End, when she was in London and her parents were staying in their flat. After the opulence of her parents' flat, Joe wondered what Isabel's reaction would be to his abode. He became conscious of the unswept concrete stairway as they walked up the two flights, the partly lit corridor where most of the light bulbs were broken and the modest flat itself, with its battered second-hand furniture. The only decent pieces of equipment were Joe's PC and printer, his copier and small shredder.

Isabel was happily taken to Joe's bedroom. They made love. Joe was thankful that he had put fresh sheets on the bed.

"Can I borrow your phone?" asked Isabel. "Mine is out of charge."

"Sure. Just give me yours and I will charge it up." Joe was conscious that Isabel made several calls. He tried to take no notice.

Isabel was wandering around the flat naked, examining everything.

"Why do you continue to live in this shit-hole?" she asked. "With all your activities, surely you can afford something better?"

"What's wrong with it?"

"Well, everything – the shared washroom; the filth; the neighbours – they're all tramps. I don't feel all that safe on my own in the streets here either. There's no view, and the pubs and restaurants are awful."

"I don't even notice it." He laughed. "You should've seen the place me and Mum shared for so many years in Kibera..."

"Yes, you need to tell me more about that place, but there's no need to stay here. What do you do with all your money?"

"I invest it."

"In what, shares?"

"What else is there?"

"Property."

"I know nothing about property."

"I'll tell you what, I'll do some research. What kind of loot are we talking about?"

He looked at her. Did he trust her? Yes, implicitly. So, after a moment's hesitation he gave her a figure. "That's about half my assets. I've gone to cash over the past few weeks, although I've kept investments in a few of what I think are exceptional companies."

"Jesus," she said. "Look, I need a bit more of your black mamba, or whatever you call it, while I get my head around that."

"Member," he reminded her as he rolled her uncomplaining onto her back, "and stop thinking; it may spoil the experience."

"Wonderful, that was just wonderful, where did you learn all that?" Isabel said afterwards.

"Learn? I have never formally learnt anything in that line. Put it down to natural African talent!"

"You are the only African I have ever slept with... Should I try a couple of others?" she joked.

"Hm, they'll have only seconds to live if they get within ten feet of you, so I wouldn't recommend it."

"Mm, do you love me that much?"

"This *M'zungu* idea of love, it's not well understood in Africa. Sometimes I hear the *Wazungu* men in the office on the phone to their wives, telling them they love them; but the next thing, they are fucking one of the secretaries. I even interrupted one having it off with his PA over the boardroom table."

Isabel laughed. "Well, at the moment, I am certainly in love with you. When I am away, I can't think of anyone else, and not all of it's about black mamba..."

"Member," he corrected her.

"Member," she continued. "We have such fun together and I just love the serious conversations we have. Your experiences are quite unique. And then I go all wet when I think of black mamba. Anyway, how do you feel?"

"I think of you all the time. I look forward to seeing you. I can't say I have ever felt this way about anyone before. I really look forward to our weekends. Do you think this love feeling, as you call it, will go on forever?"

"Probably not. There needs to be other aspects to help cement a relationship."

"Like what?"

"I will be finishing up at the London Business School within the next few months. I am quite certain a partnership between you and me would knock the spots off the investment community here; but we both need to be happy about that, and I need to know a bit more about your mysterious background."

"You'll have to explain 'knock the spots off'."

"Later. I need more..." She didn't finish. "Are you happy about the idea of some sort of cooperation between us?"

"Yes. I've been thinking along those lines myself, but what about Clive?"

"Clive? He won't have anything to do with it. Nothing."

"That is what I hoped you would say."

Still lying in bed, Isabel said, "When we first met, I guessed you weren't just an impecunious, impoverished peasant, which seems to be the image you want to project, so I've booked in a really nice, smart restaurant near Covent Garden for tonight, and before that I've booked us into Brown's Hotel."

He looked at her suspiciously.

They dressed and Isabel spent time on her make-up.

"I'll pay," she added, smiling. "You need to dress in one of your suits, and bring your laptop, and a few clothes."

As they walked down the stairs Joe was even more conscious of the drab, unattractive place he lived in. As they left the building Joe said, "We can take the tube to..."

"Tube? No." Isabel hailed a passing taxi. "Brown's," she said.

"I've almost never used a taxi in all the years I've been here," said a protesting Joe, though he had the grace to pay at the other end.

Joe had never seen anything like Brown's, and he took in every detail, the elegant entrance, with the Union Jack fluttering above, the beautifully furnished reception, the well-turned-out staff all flitting about looking busy and efficient.

He was about to carry Isabel's suitcase up to the room, together with his own, when they were both snatched away by a hovering porter. He carried his laptop.

He noted everything, storing it all away in his memory, including what he considered to be the gargantuan tip Isabel handed the porter.

"I booked a suite," said Isabel as they wandered through the luxurious set-up, "for three nights. As we discussed I am hoping that we might be able to thrash out the basis of cooperation between us- even a partnership."

"Three nights? I have..."

"How many years have you been working as hard as you do?"

"Three, almost four. "

"Okay, so it's time for a break – we need time if we're to make sense of what we're talking about. Mwangi can surely manage the messenger operation?"

Joe nodded.

Joe wandered round the luxurious suite – the bedroom with its large double bed, the ensuite with its fancy bath and separate shower. He set his laptop up in the well-furnished lounge area, which had a small dining table and a set of comfortable chairs.

They made love and then had a shower and dressed for the evening.

"I have never seen such a beautiful woman," Joe said. "You look quite wonderful."

Isabel kissed him lightly on the cheek. "Thank you. Even in that shitty suit, you look really great too," she said smiling.

"I got it at Burton's. It cost..."

"I know where you got it and I know what it cost. If anything comes of our discussions, we may have to go a bit upmarket, but that's for another day."

"Taxi?" asked Joe, as they left the suite.

"It's a lovely evening and we have forty minutes. Maybe we can walk."

"What? Trying to save money now?" He laughed and looked down at her shoes. Isabel at six feet never wore high heels. She smiled.

They walked hand in hand down Piccadilly, through the Circus and Leicester Square, across Charing Cross Road, chatting easily. "You know your way around," observed Joe.

"Dad brought us here for holidays when we lived in Australia," was Isabel's response. "He loves London, that's why he came back here, so I got to know the centre quite well. Since knowing you, I've come to realise that there are some less attractive parts of this wonderful city," she giggled and kissed him lightly on the cheek.

"Sheekey's," announced Isabel as they arrived. "I was lucky to get a table."

Joe looked at her, wondering if he was being bulldozed into something he was not quite ready for. Regardless of that feeling, he just could not get enough of the fascinating, confident woman who marched up to the reception desk. "Table for Anderson."

"It's a very special table," she was told. Isabel nodded.

By now Joe was more confident in his choices although he always consulted Isabel before ordering.

"I would like you to try the wines I order. They will go well with your meal." Joe nodded. "Every time I'm with you, I learn something new."

Isabel laughed. "Just watch me, I've hardly started."

Joe examined the prices on the menu; nothing shocked him any longer but he smiled to himself.

"What's the joke?" asked Isabel.

Joe laughed. "I just quickly added up what the next few days will cost..."

"Don't spoil it Joe..."

"No, I'm enjoying myself, being with you is very, very special." He hesitated for a moment, looking at Isabel intently. "I've just realised that what we will spend over the next few days would have lasted Mum and me more than twelve months..."

"You're not serious?"

"Sadly I am. Can I add something?"

"You're going to anyway, so go ahead."

"This city is very much first world; almost the centre of it so to speak. The first world seems determined to grow and extend its wealth and standard of living, although the government here constantly pisses money away like there's no tomorrow. For this to happen, the so-called third world must remain at the bottom of the heap."

"Yeees," answered Isabel, clearly wondering where all this was going.

"Unfortunately, with communications as they are, the third world understands this all too well. For all sorts of reasons – corruption, bad government, governments servicing selected elites, high population growth, conflict and so on – more and more third world people who see no possible improvement in their own situation will try to move to the first world. I'm a good example. The first world will be swamped. One day I will tell you about the journey I took to get here. There are millions like me."

Isabel gazed at Joe, apparently fascinated. "I discover more hidden depths about you almost every time you open your mouth. While I was at Oxford, I attended meetings on many different subjects, covering philosophies from the crazy far right to the loony left. But you, you speak the truth from the heart. So, I understand. Is there anything we can do about it?"

Joe smiled. "You understand intellectually, but you have no idea of what precipitates the decisions people make to leave their home country, places they were familiar with… and then the risks they take to get into Europe." He shook his head. "They are not normal, the experiences for those who survive makes them very tough, very tough indeed. The first world is soft, soft as shit, and has no idea what is going to hit them and no idea how to deal with the situation. I have some ideas how we might influence things; any discussions we have about the future must include consideration of this."

"It will, I promise."

There was a short silence as they both enjoyed their meals. They had almost finished when Isabel said, "You see that big man over there, he keeps looking in our direction. I thought he was perving at me, but it's you he seems more interested in."

Joe nodded and smiled. "I've been aware of his interest for a few minutes now. That's the big white chief, Sir Oswald Higginbotham, no less. I wonder if he recognises me. I think I'll just go over and say hello."

"Why not?" answered Isabel, then she said, "Hm, you're not going to have to bother, it looks as if he's coming over here."

Sir Oswald approached, saying to Joe, as he got to the table, "Do I know you? You have a familiar face."

"Joe Arnold, I run the messenger service at Higginbotham's." Joe stuck out his hand, which was taken reluctantly.

"Messenger service, we must be paying you too much to afford a place like this."

"I'm happy to say I'm not paying." Joe then graciously introduced Isabel to Sir Oswald. "Isabel has a business proposal she thought I might be interested in." He hesitated for a moment, "To be clear, sir, we run a contracted messenger service for Higginbotham's; your messenger costs are considerably lower than they were when you ran the service yourselves."

"How do you manage that?"

"Well, currently we run a service for Higginbotham's and a dozen other businesses in the city. You must wonder how we manage to cut the cost to you. There's no spare capacity any longer; we only have messengers at your place when they're needed. There are now no messengers sitting around reading papers, for example. Also, some people only want a part-time job. It's the same with all the other businesses we service, and the service is much better for everyone." He looked at the man, trying to ascertain his on-going interest in the conversation. "I started with you a few years ago, and then came to an arrangement with Oscar Fitzpatrick. He says it's his job to keep an eye on costs."

"Ah, I thought I recognised you. You are a man after my own heart in a way. Is your business viable?"

"Viable?" said Joe, with a surprised look on his face. "Yes. I make sure of that."

"I might see you in the office then?"

"I pop in about once a week, to make sure everything's running smoothly," Joe said as Sir Oswald returned to his table.

"Hm," said Joe, after a moment's thought. "I'll bet you ten quid that I'll be asked to discount my fees when I next go into the office. I'll prime Mwangi. The messenger business can't be very high on the list of Higginbotham priorities. If he does ask for a discount, I'll resign the contract immediately; I guarantee we'll be back there within six months." He laughed. "Just like the fucking reverend, he can't pass up an opportunity to screw one of the little people."

"Hm, I don't bet, but who's the 'fucking reverend', as you so charmingly put it?"

"I'll explain later, probably together with a lot of other stuff you need to know... Kiss me, Isabel,' said Joe.

She did, attracting a few curious glances from nearby diners, including Sir Oswald. "We have a lot to catch up on."

They finished their desserts and relaxed further over a cup of coffee. "Well, that's better than chewing on a piece of raw sugar cane, I suppose," joked Joe.

Isabel just shook her head. "Will we need more than three nights at Brown's? There is a mountain of things I don't know about you and the list seems to grow with every waking minute."

Joe whispered in her ear. They quickly left the restaurant and hopped into a taxi. Isabel had paid the bill. They spent the rest of the night and half the next morning making love.

While he was in the shower Joe reflected happily to himself. 'This *M'zungu* woman is in the process of taking over my life. There is nothing I can or wish to do to change that. I wonder if she really understands what she is getting into though, with all the baggage I carry...'

Over a late breakfast delivered to their suite, Joe said to Isabel, "If anything, the last few hours have been more meaningful and more passionate than ever, and I've certainly never experienced what I'm experiencing now. Over the past few months, I have never ever enjoyed getting to know someone like I have with you, it's been wonderful."

"You took the words out of my mouth," said Isabel as she kissed him.

Joe looked at Isabel. "If we're going to take our relationship further, both personal and business, I need to come clean with you. What I'm going to tell you will scare the shit out of you and some of the story, particularly from a westerner's point of view, is very ugly indeed, worse than you could possibly imagine. I will tell you absolutely everything, so what I am doing is to put total trust in you; potentially it makes me very vulnerable." He paused, gathering his thoughts.

Isabel said nothing.

"From the moment I met you, Isabel, I could see there was something special between us; we really are kindred spirits," said Joe, "despite you coming from obvious wealth, and me coming from the depths of despair in darkest Africa. Individually we might do very well in this environment but together we'll conquer the world. There are going to be rough patches, so we need to keep faith… It's a long story, so please be patient."

Joe started to talk. He talked and talked, well into the night, with Isabel staring at his face, interjecting to ask him to explain a word or a place, weeping at times, blenching at others. When Joe spoke of his father's murder, she reached across the little table and took hold of his hand, and rarely let go for the rest of his account.

Later, in bed, Joe was still talking, tracking his progress from two-bit drug dealer to people smuggler. It was as if once he'd opened the locked vault of his memory and mind, he could not stop. Even in the darkness of the night, he could still see her eyes, wide with sympathy and attention, even when he confessed to his multiple acts of evil. It was as if the whole universe had shrunk into the little cocoon of intimacy they shared in their grand suite, the whole world now made of only a pair of gentle eyes, and the hand that held his own

It took the rest of that day, well into the night and most of Monday for Joe to tell his story. They went for walks in nearby Hyde Park; they both cried at times. For meals, they made do with room service. They didn't make love, just cuddled each other in bed when they became too tired to continue.

"So, it's not all about, um, just making money."

Joe shrugged. "I wouldn't have done any of the people smuggling stuff if it hadn't been for the incident with the general. Otieno had me by the balls and I had to do what he asked or face him going to the police." Joe rambled on, "I've told you about Mum's death. I still feel guilty that I wasn't there for her."

There was silence for a few minutes with both Joe and Isabel trying to collect their thoughts.

"Sorry, reliving all that made me feel sorry for myself, which is the last bloody thing we need. One of the things Mum and I never did, we just got on with it."

"Joe, we need to get away from all this for a few days," said Isabel. "Thank you for telling me all that, it will be the basis of the absolute trust we will have in each other. I have a lot of ideas on how we could go forward, but I am not going to burden you with any of that right now. How would you feel about a few days walking in the Lake District? It really will clear the air and then we can get down to brass tacks," said Isabel after a few minutes reflection.

"Ah, another lesson in the English language. You'll have to explain 'brass tacks' to me, and where the hell is the Lake District?" Joe smiled.

In the end, they spent ten days in the Lake District. Isabel made certain they were both properly equipped for some serious walking. They took a train to Manchester, Isabel insisted on first class. "It's a waste of money," wailed Joe, "Almost twice the price of an ordinary fare."

"Stop behaving like a peasant," smiled Isabel. "We're going to enjoy ourselves and that includes you, just get used to it."

"I am a peasant..."

On the way, Isabel said to Joe, "I've booked into a couple of decent places. We'll walk every day and then be able to come back to a hot bath and a decent meal. You're paying for all of it."

They rented a small car in Manchester. Isabel drove, since Joe had no British licence, firstly to Kendal, where they had lunch in a pub, and then on to a decent hotel near Keswick. Isabel had done her homework, so they walked every day, often long walks taking five or six hours. They walked regardless of the weather. "If we worry too much about getting wet, we'll never do anything," she said.

Joe didn't complain, and he delighted in the exercise and the scenery. "I've never seen anything like this before," he confided in Isabel after a few days. "I had no idea it existed."

"Another time we can be more adventurous, but that would involve camping out or staying in walker's huts."

"Huts, that sounds more like my style." Isabel just smiled.

On one of the longer walks, Joe looked at Isabel. "There's nobody around, we haven't seen another soul for more than a couple of hours." He edged towards her, and she looked at him suspiciously.

"Here, you want to make love here?" she questioned. "I must admit I've been thinking of black mamba for the last hour..."

"Member," he said as he stripped her trousers off and rolled her over in the soft grass.

"Mm," said Isabel laughing. 'I've never been fucked wearing boots before. That was lovely, I could do that again."

"You will, soon," said Joe, basking in the warm sun.

By the time their ten days was over, they had both completely relaxed and the trauma of Joe's revelations was pushed to the back of their minds.

They drove back to Manchester, where the uncomplaining Joe happily sat in the first-class train back to London. They rebooked at Brown's.

During their sojourn in the Lake District, apart from regular calls from Mwangi and his Bethnal Green office, Joe had a call from Oscar Fitzpatrick. "Where the fuck are you?" he asked. "I've been trying to raise you for days." Their relationship had returned to normal. There was no further mention of Fitzpatrick's attempt to blackmail Joe.

"Lake District," Joe responded.

"What are you doing there?"

"Stumbling about in the heather, Mr Fitzpatrick," said Joe laughing, "that's what everybody who comes here seems to do."

"Very funny. I need to see you."

"Certainly. Mr Fitzpatrick." Joe gave Oscar a date.

"Can't you make it sooner? I'm being hassled by the boss."

"I really can't. I'm sorry. I know what it's about; we can back date anything we agree."

"Okay," said Fitzpatrick.

Joe phoned Mwangi. He laughed as they rang off. "It's what I guessed," he said to Isabel. "Sir is looking to screw me. I'll have them all tied up in knots with what I've agreed with Mwangi. You owe me ten quid."

"I never took the bet on." Isabel smiled.

"Changing the subject," said Isabel, "I haven't mentioned this before but now that I have graduated with a first, which Dad is very pleased with, he has bought me a very decent flat, near where they live in South Kensington. We can move in there, if you like, and you can give up that ghastly place of yours."

"Just like that?" said Joe. "Very nice."

"Well, not just like that. I had to work my arse off to get a first."

Joe laughed. "I'm sure you did. Obviously, that's wonderful from my point of view," Joe continued, "but what will your parents think or say, when they find me, a strange black man, living with you in the flat."

"Probably nothing, but if I think there's a problem, I'll deal with it." Isabel leant over and kissed him.

They spent another week at Brown's, closeted in the suite, arriving at some principles for the way forward. Joe disclosed everything.

"I see you still have about five hundred thousand of the cash you nicked from the general and the share trading business is now worth, net, about two million? Wow," observed Isabel, "you have done well."

"You've forgotten the messenger business," said Joe.

"The messenger business is worth two fifths of five eighths of fuck all," said Isabel. "It should not be included in anything we discuss. I have no interest in it."

"We're going to go into the office cleaning business now. Mwangi is working on something and we'll present it to Fitzpatrick soon."

"Why do you continue to bother with it? Leave it all to Mwangi."

"I've told you why I bother with it..."

Isabel looked at Joe. "I understand all that, your colleagues are important to you. What I suggest is that you sell or give most of the business to Mwangi and the others, maybe just keep a token shareholding and act as a consultant to the business. You've done more than anyone else I know to help your colleagues."

"Good advice," said Joe, "we'll keep it separate."

"In order to make sure everything is on the straight and narrow, Ron, my dad has recommended we use a medium sized firm of Chartered Accountants and a local firm of Solicitors. Just to make sure everything is correctly documented," Isabel tried to reassure Joe.

"So, he's already involved?" said Joe suspiciously.

"He'll be providing my half of the funds for this business, so yes he has to understand what's going on. He will leave the details to me."

While Joe was getting the details of his business activities together, Isabel and her mother, Mary, scrambled around looking for furniture for a few days. When she was ready, they moved to Isabel's flat in South Kensington.

Joe now realised that to make the most of the personal and business relationship with Isabel, he would have devoted all his energies to the new venture. He would never forget his colleagues though.

Isabel continued with her MBA at the London Business school and introduced Joe to both sets of advisors in a joint meeting in a boardroom at the offices of Smith Goodwin Chartered Accountants in the City. "This is Mr Hall of Hall Wheeler Solicitors and, Joe, I would also like to introduce Mr Goodwin of Smith Goodwin Chartered Accountants, who have agreed to act as our accountants. The objective of today is to ensure that everything is kosher and above board and correctly documented," said Isabel.

"Joe Arnold," said Joe as he gave each man a firm handshake.

Hall was a tall, thin, wiry, ascetic-looking man, wearing horn-rimmed spectacles. He was dressed in what Joe could see was an expensive suit.

Goodwin was a big, overweight man, in a rumpled suit.

Both Hall and Goodwin moved uncomfortably in their seats.

"Could you tell us briefly what we are dealing with? We both know your father, Isabel, very well, but we have no idea what's involved here," asked Goodwin.

"I have a financial advisory business, which we have worked out is worth about two million pounds, and I also have about five hundred thousand pounds cash on deposit. There are no borrowings," said Joe.

"What is the source of all these funds?" asked Hall.

"Doesn't matter, now," said Goodwin. "We'll need the details of all the bank accounts anyway."

"How did the advisory business start?" asked Hall.

"I had some training in financial matters, and when I joined Higginbotham's, I started doing my own analysis, some of which I passed on to one of the senior people in the firm to see what he thought." Joe shrugged. "He submitted my analyses as his own work, without giving me any credit, so I started from there and initially invested on my own account, after which I recruited some clients, whom I advised what to buy and when to sell, and the business has grown."

"What were you employed as at Higginbotham's?"

"I run the messenger service for Higginbotham's and several other large institutions in the city," said Joe.

"A messenger service?" questioned Hall, with raised eyebrows.

"Yes. We are about to extend into an office cleaning service."

"Is that going to be included in what we are dealing with?"

"No. The proposed partnership between Isabel and me will not include the messenger or associated business. I have handed over most of my share of that business to the operators. I have agreed to act as an unpaid advisor to them."

There was a surprised look on the faces of both advisors.

"We can explain all that later," interjected Isabel, "if you want. We need to focus on the advisory business and the partnership between Joe and me for the moment."

"We will need to document everything," said Goodwin. "You may need a licence to operate such a business. What about tax? Have you submitted tax returns?"

"Oh, I have an appropriate licence and I have regularly submitted tax returns for the business."

"Who did the tax returns?"

"I did. It seemed to be fairly straightforward, although it's possible that I missed a few things. The authorities asked a couple of questions and I paid the tax. Everything is documented in my office in Bethnal Green. You will obviously have to check it all."

"Can you spell out what you want from us?" asked Hall.

"Yes," said Isabel, "we need to make sure that Joe's advisory business is fully understood by all of us. His cash needs to be incorporated into the business and then we need to have a partnership arrangement where the company, to be formed, is owned fifty/fifty by Joe and me. This company will own Joe's advisory business and I will contribute cash to bring my share up to fifty per cent."

"And then?" asked Hall.

"We will continue with the advisory business and probably expand it and we will look for other investment opportunities," said Joe.

"You also need to understand that there are some irregularities about Joe's name and his immigration status in this country," announced Isabel, having looked at Joe, who nodded.

"What sort of irregularities?" asked Hall.

"Well, he's an illegal immigrant, I suppose," said Isabel. "We are in the process of sorting that out."

Hall stood up. "Mr Goodwin and I need a few minutes to discuss the matter," said Hall, without elaborating.

They went to another nearby room, leaving Joe and Isabel where they were. "What do you think all that's about?" asked Joe.

"Just trying to make sure they want to have anything to do with us," said Isabel. "But don't worry, if there's a buck in the offing, they'll come running."

"Will they worry about the source of my funds?" asked Joe.

"They might. We'll just tell them that the accounts are legitimate. If they are that worried, I'm sure they will have a solution to bury any questions about the origins of the cash."

Hall and Goodwin returned within the hour.

"We just needed to sort out who does what, so we are happy to take it all on," announced Goodwin.

"I have arranged some extra space for you in my Bethnal Green office," said Joe. "I will take you there whenever it's convenient."

Joe now spent his time either at his Bethnal Green offices, dealing with routine matters servicing his clients and answering questions from Goodwin; or he was otherwise ensconced in Isabel's South Kensington flat. Occasionally he visited Hall's city office

Joe read every word of every document the advisors produced and questioned the professionals at great length, making sure he understood everything. Both sets of advisors were a little bemused by the attention Joe gave all the agreements.

"Just making sure they got it all right," said Joe to Isabel privately at home. "I found a few flaws, which they have corrected. They're all just like fucking vultures, feeding on meals provided by others."

"I've never seen a vulture," said Isabel.

"Hm, a pleasure yet to come," said Joe. "Also, Goodwin keeps asking me about the source of the original funds. All I have said is the bank accounts were opened legitimately and were okayed by the banks at the time. I also asked both of them if we needed a shareholder's agreement between the two of us. We will each have precisely fifty per cent of the new company – what happens if there is a fundamental disagreement between the two of us for example? The question seemed to take them by surprise."

"Not something I had thought of. What happens in that case?"

"They are now drafting a shareholders agreement. If there is such a disagreement it will be referred to arbitration and the arbitrator will be appointed by the head of the law society. Any findings by the arbitrator will have to be accepted by both parties."

"Fine. I sincerely hope it never comes to that," said Isabel.

"Same. This process has gone so far, I can't see anything that will stop us now. Joe hesitated. "Maybe it's time I met your dad."

"I've been keeping Dad in the loop. I have actually arranged for you to meet both Mum and Dad sometime in the next week or so, before they trundle off on one of their jaunts."

"I'll look forward to that. Just name the day," responded Joe. "What've you told them about me?"

"They know you are a migrant. I've told them about you starting off as a messenger at Higginbotham's and you then moving on to running your own advisory business. I have not told them anything about your relationship with Clive."

"I've done a bit of research on your dad," said Joe, "You told me he was just a builder. Very modest. But I know he established a very large construction company, which he sold for a fortune. Very impressive. Started from almost nothing. Obviously, a man after my own heart."

Isabel just smiled.

"It's all set up," said Isabel a day or so later. "Lunch tomorrow, casual," she laughed, "no suits."

The walk from Isabel's flat to the Anderson's took ten minutes. "You seem nervous," observed Joe.

"A little. I have of course told them that you happen to be black, which as I suspected did not cause a ripple of concern. I have also told them that you are the smartest person I know."

"Very flattering," said Joe.

Ron answered the door. Tall, spare, Ron was losing a bit of hair but was carrying his sixty-five years well. Joe saw a big man in his early sixties, a man still in reasonable shape.

"Joe," said Joe, before Isabel could say anything. "I'm delighted to meet you."

"Ron," answered Ron with a firm handshake. "Welcome, please come in, come and meet Mary."

They moved into the now familiar lounge area.

"Welcome Joe," said Mary. They shook hands. Mary, a slim pretty woman with white hair, also looked in good shape. Joe thought she was about the same age as Ron.

"We're having lamb and vegetables," announced Mary. "I hope that suits you. But drinks first. What can we get you?"

"Sounds lovely," said Joe. "A beer would be fine, thank you."

They initially sat in the lounge area, where a few nibbles were served, which Joe barely touched. After a short period, they moved to the dining room, where Joe could see, as promised, a delicious-looking rack of lamb and heaps of vegetables.

"Isabel has told me about your investment advisory business," said Ron.

"Yes, we're going to fold that into the company Isabel and I have now registered, and that will form my contribution to the joint venture."

"How'd you get into the business?"

"Well, I had a junior position at Higginbotham's and I just started doing my own analysis and it went from there. I then started advising some acquaintances..."

"I know Sir Oswald. How'd you get in there?"

"He was involved in some business in Kenya with a priest I used to do some domestic work for. I remembered Sir Oswald from serving him tea." Joe smiled. "Having remembered the name, I just applied for a job there."

"You seem to have come a long way."

Joe laughed, looking at Isabel. "You could say that, but our cooperation is just the start... we're hoping it will lead to great things." He shrugged.

The conversation flowed easily.

"The advisors you introduced... I check everything they do."

Ron laughed. "Very wise, hyaenas and jackals, most of them. Unfortunately, they're needed; they do all the cleaning up, so you don't get into any more trouble than is necessary. How many clients do you have now? "he asked.

"Oh, a few hundred," said Joe.

"Six hundred and fifty-three," said Isabel. "I checked yesterday."

"How long have you been in this country?" asked Ron.

"Five years or so now. As you've probably realised, I am an illegal, with a false identity."

Ron didn't bat an eyelid. "I'm surprised the people at Higginbotham's didn't pick that up."

Joe laughed. "They don't take much trouble over the recruitment of messengers. Anyway, they're out of the woods now as far as the employment of illegals is concerned, as I mentioned I now run a contracted messenger service for them. Totally legit."

"You say you came from Kenya but your English is impeccable. You sound like one of the so-called upper classes."

Joe laughed. "I spent months having daily elocution lessons, just so I could fit in properly here. It's probably why I was taken on at Higginbotham's without too many questions."

Ron looked pensive for a moment. "I don't want to interfere, but I have contacts that could probably help you legitimise your identity."

Joe looked at Isabel, who nodded.

"I have already made contact with Geoffrey Thomasoff, who you recommended," said Isabel.

"I'm looking forward to getting my original name back."

"Which is?" asked Ron.

"Njeroge wa Wacheera. I was always called Joe though. If it could be formalised as Joe Wacheera, I think I would have arrived in seventh heaven."

Ron smiled.

The three of them had a long conversation about the future and what they thought they could do with the partnership.

"With my advisory business," Joe said, "I can already see we do a better job than Higginbotham's in advising people what to do with their money, so to start with we need to really develop that, mainly because we focus solely on client's needs. Currently I do all of the research into the companies we should or should not invest in. We need to make that more professional. Relying on one person, i.e., me, puts the whole business at risk. Isabel is keen that we invest in the property market in some way. We'll see."

"What about the messenger business?"

"That's not included," said Joe. He explained the Kikuyu diaspora and how he was helping them.

When lunch was over, Ron quietly said to Isabel, within Joe's hearing, "This bloke is most unusual. I think he's great."

Eventually, Isabel and Joe agreed to set up a new company registered in England with a holding company registered in one of the less well-known cantons in Switzerland. Everything was owned fifty/fifty by Joe and Isabel. All this was completed within four months of the meeting at Brown's, once Isabel had completed her MBA.

"Why don't you want my father as a partner in the business?" Isabel had asked Joe, with considerable irritation, during one of their discussions. "Don't you trust him?"

"I trust your father totally, now having met him a few times, but I think the arrangements should just be between us, adding Ron to the picture will unnecessarily complicate the situation."

"The money for my part of the investment has all come from him."

"We can always use him as an advisor. In fact, I think he would prefer that."

"Hm, you've been talking to him?"

"Sure, I talk to him almost daily. With you being away at the business school a lot of the time."

"Okay, I think I understand. I'll work something out."

Once the agreements were finalised and signed, Isabel said to Joe, "There's a bit more cleaning up needed."

Joe looked at her, knowing what was coming.

She continued: "You no longer need to nick info from Higginbotham's."

"I know; I stopped that months ago. There's no evidence anywhere as to what I was doing. And before you mention it, the bloody accountants are having a field day in my financial advisory business. I should have that cleaned up within a couple of months. I've handed control of the messenger business to Mwangi, as we have discussed."

"You also need to get rid of that pistol and the knife you showed me, when I came to your ghastly place..."

"I ditched them in the river, during my move over here to your place."

"Nobody saw you?"

"No, of course not." Joe was irritated that Isabel thought he would be so naïve as to let anyone see what he had been doing.

"Obviously the more complicated thing to unravel is your personal history," said Isabel. "We really do need to regularise the whole bloody business and you need to help me here. I see three main problems: the murder of that ghastly General; your people smuggling business; and your British identity. I need your full cooperation with all this," Isabel added having taken complete control of the situation. "I have no intention of having any association with a jailbird and that's where you are headed unless we finesse our way out of it."

Isabel told Joe she was also under pressure from Clive, who had gradually become aware of the association between Isabel and Joe. In one of the few discussions she had with him on the subject, he had said, "Isabel, what are you doing with that fellow Joe? He's just a bloody messenger. You could do much better than that. I have dozens of contacts..." She had told him she was in love with Joe and reminded him that he wouldn't be where he was at Higginbotham's if it wasn't for the work Joe had done for him, for nothing. Clive had since been given a substantial promotion, because of many analyses emanating from Joe.

"He said something about having been the one who 'discovered' you," Isabel laughed. "That I'd now taken over. But I'm sure that will be the end of it now."

Chapter 17: Joe's Clean Up

Isabel came bundling into the flat she now shared with Joe. She was beaming.

Joe, busy poring over papers scattered all over the dining room table, looked up. "Just looking at some stuff I have found on a new potential investment," he said. "There's something odd going on here," he added, "needs more work." He smiled. "You look pleased about something..."

"Yes. As you know I've spent the last couple of weeks with Geoffrey Thomasoff, the immigration lawyer recommended by Dad, and the authorities connected with your identity. I explained your Joseph Arnold identity and why you took that route. They have now said, in view of your exemplary record here, that we will be able to get you correctly registered from the date of your entry into Britain, in your real name. So, Mr Njeroge wa Wacheera, we can now perhaps deal with the people smuggling business and the other issues," Isabel laughed. "I must say I prefer that name to Joseph Arnold."

"Thank you, thank you and thank you." He kissed her. "What I would have done without your ministrations I don't know..." Joe replied with a smile. "Hm, you'll have to practice your pronunciation a bit, especially Njeroge and don't call me Jerogi, which is what the *Wazungu* are inclined to do."

"Maybe we could pop out to dinner somewhere, just to celebrate?"

"Great, but none of this degustation nonsense or sampling. Just a real meal." Isabel laughed. "It's the latest fashion."

"Not for me," said Joe firmly.

They went to a nearby small bistro, which Isabel knew Joe would be comfortable with. Once they had ordered, Isabel instigated a very difficult conversation.

"Joe, we now need to see what we can do to sort out the other issues in your background. By the way, Thomasoff has suggested that the best thing we could do is to make contact with MI5 and tell them your story, which in my view should be of vital interest to them. This would be in return for immunity from any kind of prosecution. So where do we start?"

"The *bhang* business..."

"You told me you had handed all that over to Karanja."

"Yes."

"And then there's the demise of the general... I don't think we should go there at all. You were in Juba when he came to his unfortunate end."

"It was a mistake..."

"I believe that, but there is no purpose in raising the issue."

"Well, I did take refugees across the Med. I have considerable details of the people I dealt with, which should be useful to the British and European security services. As well as that, as I have told you, our group, at the request of British security, rescued one of their agents from a gang of Bedouin. They would almost certainly have murdered her if we hadn't done that."

"What was her name?"

"Supposedly Anne Smith. That was obviously not her name. We also had dealings with a man who called himself Michael Baker; I have a photo of the man we dealt with and a photo of a warrant card in that name. I also have many photos of the person calling herself Anne Smith."

"You can of course give them chapter and verse of the rescue mission you conducted?"

Joe looked surprised at the statement. "Yes. I planned and ran the whole thing."

"You can give them details of how you got into England?"

"If I need to. I don't think it's relevant though and I will not give them any details of the driver who brought me across."

"He tried to swindle you."

Joe shrugged. "And then we've got Ibrahim and his ghastly gang, if they are still operating."

"Ibrahim?"

"Yes. I told you all about him. They claimed they could get me British citizenship but the only plan they had was to kidnap me, if you remember. I got 'chapter and verse' from a kid that worked for them."

"Oh, yes. What about Patel?"

"They know about him already. I'm not going to go there. Thanks to you I now have my proper identity back."

Once they had finished their meal and over coffee Isabel asked, "Is that it?"

"Hm, maybe. Sir Oswald was one of a group who set up the people smuggling racket from Kenya in the first place. He helped to finance the whole thing by providing funds for Otieno to lease vehicles. I have mentioned Otieno, who owned the transport company that was used to ship refugees around – he has since died. Then we have Kigoro, the man who kicked us off our land in Ol'Kalou. The general was the last member of their group."

"Okay. I think we should pass all that by Thomasoff and he will, I am sure, help us to present it in the best possible light."

Later that week they met with Geoffrey Thomasoff in his office in Chancery Lane, near the Temple Bar and the Law Courts. Big, bluff, slightly overweight, Geoffrey Thomasoff was dressed as he often was in a well-cut beige suit, with a white shirt and tie. Joe and Isabel were dressed in smart casual clothes.

Joe, sometimes prompted by Isabel, went through all the issues they had previously discussed. No mention was made of the demise of General Kariuki. Joe brought to the meeting all his notes of the contacts he had made while in Libya, as well as his notes about the rescue of Anne Smith, which included photographs of her and the man who had identified himself as Michael Baker.

Thomasoff was not entirely satisfied with Joe's story. "How and why did you become a people smuggler in the first place?" he asked. "If we are to take all this to MI5, they are going to want to understand that. They will not be satisfied with a story that doesn't hang together."

Joe then went into detail about how his mother was forced into prostitution after the murder of his father, how and why he started the *bhang* business, including his employment with Reverend Mweleli. "It was obvious that unless I took the initiative, I would end up like many people in my position either with no job or a very low paid job. During my employment with the reverend, I served tea to a group of people who set up a people smuggling business from Kenya, they included Reverend Mweleli himself, a General Kariuki, Kigoro, the man who was responsible for the murder of my father and a man operating a transport business, a Mr Otieno Boniface, as well as Sir Oswald Higginbotham, who financed the operation by providing lease finance for Otieno's trucks – he knew exactly what he was getting into. I persuaded Otieno to take me and a number of colleagues on. Initially we shipped people from Kenya through to Juba in Sudan and eventually, still under the employment of Otieno, we joined a South Sudanese man taking refugees to Libya, with the promise of somehow getting to Europe. I and my colleagues eventually took this expedition over and sent the South Sudanese men back to Juba. All the profits went back to Otieno. We were then asked to rescue a woman, who was a member of British security, which gave all of us the funds to move on to Europe. Otieno has since died, so that contact was cut anyway, and we all moved on from there."

"You talk about colleagues. Where are they now?"

"Two returned to Kenya. Three are here in England."

Thomasoff looked shocked by Joe's revelations but he seemed satisfied with what he had been told. "As I have said to you, Isabel, the best approach is for us to make contact with MI5 and go from there. I will make the contact and let you know. Please leave all the notes and information with me and I will put a presentation together." Thomasoff smiled. "Your meticulous notes Joe, and the way you have organised them have made all the difference. There is still a long way to go, but I can see a way through to get what you want, which is complete immunity from prosecution in return for the information you will provide."

Joe smiled. "Thank you. I am hoping that the rescue of the British hostage will also be important in the scheme of things."

"Yes. Of course, it will. Anyway, I'll be in touch through Isabel." Isabel nodded, and Thomasoff showed them out.

A few days later when Isabel was out Joe opened the door of their South Kensington flat to find two policemen standing there, one in uniform and one in plain clothes. They both flashed their warrant cards at Joe.

"Joseph Arnold, you are under arrest for the murder..."

"I am not Joseph Arnold. I'll find my passport..."

"We know all about that. You are still under arrest," responded the sergeant in charge. "You will have to come with us."

"You may remain silent, but anything you say may be given in evidence..." the sergeant rambled on.

Joe was bundled into a police car and a half hour later arrived at New Scotland Yard.

As he was searched and his few possessions removed, he said, "I am entitled to make one telephone call. I would like to make it now."

He was handed a phone. "Am I entitled to make the call privately?" he asked. The room was cleared. He phoned Isabel: "Where are you?" she asked. "I've just got home."

Joe explained, calmly as always, "I have been arrested as Joseph Arnold, for murder. I am at New Scotland Yard."

"Murder!" exclaimed Isabel.

"I know nothing about what they are talking about. Must be something that occurred before I acquired the identity."

"Okay. I'll get onto Geoffrey."

At dawn the following day Isabel arrived at New Scotland Yard with Geoffrey Thomasoff. Big, bluff, bearded Thomasoff was looking none too pleased with the early start to his day. Isabel was dressed professionally in a black pantsuit with a red blouse.

"We were told," Isabel told Joe, once they were finally allowed to see him, "that we'd have to wait until the matter was brought before a magistrate. But Thomasoff here told them we were entitled to see you, Mr Wacheera, straight away, as this 'is a matter of mistaken identity, and we can save you and ourselves a lot of time if we can establish that to your satisfaction as soon as possible.'"

"Thank you. It is good to see you both." Joe explained to Thomasoff the details of how he had acquired the false identity of Joseph Arnold, most of which Thomasoff was broadly aware of.

"Can you again give me the dates of your arrival in the UK and any other information you might think is useful?"

Joe laid it all out – the date, undocumented of course, of his arrival in the country, his meeting with Mwangi. The details of the flat he rented, his elocution lessons with Mrs Braithwaite. The acquisition of the identity of Joseph Arnold, the date he was employed by Higginbotham's. He was able to tell Isabel where to find his bank statements, where it would be obvious from the dates when he started to withdraw money from one account that that was the date when he had arrived in England.

"I drew the fifty thousand to pay for the Joseph Arnold identity, from various accounts as you will see, Isabel. If you can avoid it, I suggest you leave that out of any disclosure you make to the police."

#

A day or so later Isabel and Thomasoff were granted an interview with the DI in charge of the case. In the meantime, Joe had been moved to Paddington Green police station. He was on remand pending further investigations.

"Inspector," Thomasoff said, after introducing Isabel and himself, "if you could just tell me the date of the murder that Mr Wacheera is charged with committing, I think we could save you and everyone else a great deal of time. Mr Wacheera denies any knowledge of the murder he is charged with."

"This is most irregular," said the inspector. "The date will be revealed during the course of our disclosures, during our on-going investigation, not now."

Thomasoff persisted, "My client only arrived in the UK..." he gave the sergeant the date of Joe's arrival, "so if the murder was committed prior to that date, he could not possibly have been involved."

A look of uncertainty crossed the DI's face. "He speaks English like he was born in the country," was the man's response.

"Yes," said Isabel. "He took elocution lessons after he arrived, to make sure he 'fitted in' better, to use his words."

"I have the details of the person who conducted those lessons," added Thomasoff, "and the dates on which the lessons occurred."

The policeman stood up and said, as he left the interview room, "I need to consult. I will be back. Stay here if you wish."

An hour and a half later the policeman returned and gave Isabel and Thomasoff a date.

"That's about five years before my client arrived in the country. Also, inspector, you have to understand that Mr Wacheera would only have been sixteen at the time of the murder he is supposed to have committed."

There was silence for a more than a minute, broken by Thomasoff, "Inspector, I am in a position to give you all the details you need about Mr Wacheera's arrival dates and his activities in the few years after his arrival, which I think will exonerate Mr Wacheera altogether from any suspicion that he committed the murder you are referring to. Also", he quickly glanced at Isabel, who nodded her assent, "he is about to give the security services here valuable details of people smuggling activities. This has now been suspended due to these incorrect accusations. He must be released immediately."

Isabel and Thomasoff then spent a week collecting all the information required. Initially Mrs Braithwaite would not cooperate, since she thought they were from the tax office.

At that point Isabel thought they had everything under control. But then the Detective Inspector in charge of the case suddenly disappeared.

#

Two weeks later, a Chief Inspector Branson was appointed to Joe's case. He had a brief meeting with Joe in his cell. "There have been some mistakes made in this case; I am now taking it over. I will have to re-examine everything."

Joe felt hopeful. After a week he asked to see Branson again. He was told that Branson was away on another case and was not available. He asked to see Isabel. A day later he was told that Isabel was not contactable. He asked if he could phone her directly. "No, you have already had all the phone calls you are entitled to," was the response. He asked to speak to Thomasoff. The request was refused.

Joe realised that the pressure he was being put under was completely illegal and was contrived to create distrust between him and Isabel. He knew the authorities could not continue with tactics such as they had employed for very long. He was given a pen and some paper on request. He then spent a week calmly spelling out in some detail what his objectives were for the next few years; how he could help grow the partnership with Isabel, what he thought each of their roles would be, what sort of businesses they could consider investing in.

The police insisted on reading all of what he had written. They didn't understand a word of it. "What is all this nonsense?" shouted Branson, when he eventually arrived to speak to Joe. "We are conducting a murder investigation."

"You may be doing that," said Joe. "A murder I had nothing to do with, and which was, according to you, committed five years before I arrived in this country."

After another two weeks, Isabel was allowed to see Joe. "They told me you didn't want to speak to me," she told him.

Joe shrugged. "They tried the same nonsense on me. They now know that none of that will work. Hopefully we can now get on with things."

"You seem very calm about it all."

"They know what they are doing could get them into a lot of legal strife," said Joe. "I expect they will come to their senses shortly. I have no idea what their motivation is."

"Prejudice?" said Isabel.

#

Isabel and Thomasoff then spent several hours going through with Branson all the detail of Joe's arrival in the UK, and it took a further two weeks to follow up on all the information they'd gathered. Isabel suggested that Branson speak to their contact at MI5.

"Inspector..." Thomasoff began.

He interrupted, "Chief Inspector." Branson corrected him.

Thomasoff didn't miss a beat, "Chief Inspector, we have substantial amounts of very useful information, which will be hugely useful to the security services. We cannot deal with that issue until the charges against Mr Wacheera have been dropped. I can give you the name and phone number of the person at MI5 we are dealing with, should you want to check."

Branson did eventually speak to MI5.

Very shortly after that, almost three months after his arrest, Joe was released without any charges being laid. There was no apology and no explanation from the police.

Isabel picked Joe up at Paddington Green police station.

They hugged each other for a good five minutes outside the station. "Are you okay?" Isabel asked.

"I'm fine. The whole business has given me time to think about how we can progress our partnership. I've got it all here, in my impeccable handwriting." He laughed. "I'll type it up and we can discuss. It just creates a basis for discussion. As to what sort of operations we might invest in. There's a lot of detail."

Isabel shook her head. "Rare as rocking horse shit," she laughed. "The police are trying to pin a murder on you and all you do is to look to the future."

They went home and spent most of the rest of the day in bed.

Later, over dinner Joe asked, "What do you think all that fuss with the police was about?"

"Simple. Arnold was black. You are black. One of you has to be guilty. End of story."

#

Joe and Isabel made a follow-up call to Geoffrey Thomasoff.

"Are you still happy to spill the beans to MI5?" Thomasoff asked Joe.

"You'll have to explain the origins of 'spill the beans', but yes I want to clean everything up so Isabel and I can get on with our plans."

"I'm disappointed by the way the police dealt with you. It does us, and I mean the country, no credit at all."

"No," said Joe, "thankfully all that is behind us now."

Joe also spent time catching up with developments in his investment advisory business, most of which he was happy with and it all seemed under control.

The meeting with MI5 was scheduled to be at Thames House, the MI5 headquarters. Joe looked at the large innocuous-looking building on Millbank, a few hundred metres from the British Houses of Parliament. He wondered what he was letting himself in for.

Led by Thomasoff, the trio were admitted to the building.

"We have an appointment with a Mr Giles Alison," said Thomasoff.

They were made to go through a scanner, which identified the recording machine Thomasoff was carrying.

"You can collect that on your way out," said the person in charge of security.

"Alison told us we could record the meeting," Thomasoff objected.

"No, we can't allow any such equipment into the building. Never."

The trio were then led by another security guard to the third floor where they were shown into a featureless room with no pictures or any other decoration and told to sit in chairs on the far side of the table facing the door. There was a carafe of water and some glasses on the table.

"Looks like a sound-proof room," observed Thomasoff.

A few minutes later, a man who identified himself as Giles Alison came in accompanied by a woman and two other men who came in and sat in the four chairs opposite. The door was closed.

"This document guaranteeing no action is not adequately authorised, however if you would all sign it, that should do the trick," said Thomasoff handing a one-page document to Alison.

Alison was in his mid-forties with the build of an athlete. Just short of six foot, he had a predatory, wolf-like expression on his face, and there was no hint of a smile or any kind of humour in his manner. He was well dressed. Joe then did a double take, he recognised him: this was the man in Libya, the man he had done the deal with to rescue the British hostage, Anne Smith; at the time he had called himself Michael Baker. Joe identified the same mannerisms in the man. Joe looked again. He was certain he was correct.

Joe then glanced at the woman with him. Aged in her mid-thirties, she was attractive and well-dressed in a black skirt and pale beige top. She was wearing a matching jacket, which she draped over the back of her chair. Again, Joe was shocked; he was certain that this was the woman he had rescued in Libya, who had identified herself as Anne Smith.

Joe barely noticed the other two; they were also appropriately dressed but appeared to be a couple of little grey men, who were there to take notes. With some urging from the woman, the document was signed. The other members of the team identified themselves with their alpha numeric unit identifiers.

Joe wondered if it was some kind of set-up, a thought he dismissed immediately.

Joe whispered to Thomasoff, "I need a quick word." They quickly moved to the back of the room. "What?"

"Alison is the man who made the arrangement with me to rescue the British hostage in Libya and the woman is indeed the person we rescued. Do you think we should say anything?"

"Are you quite sure of that?"

"Yes, one hundred per cent."

"Okay, then deal with it in a constructive way."

Joe nodded and they returned to their seats among some questioning glances from the MI5 people.

"There is one thing that I should mention, before we start," said Joe, "this is not meant to embarrass anyone, but it will emerge in my discourse, so we thought it better to say something now."

"Okay. Just get on with it," said Alison gruffly.

"Neither of you will recognise me and it is some years since we dealt with each other, but you, Mr Alison, was the man who made the arrangement with me to rescue a British hostage held by the Bedouin in Libya. You will recall visiting me, twice, on a boat I owned which you will remember, sir, was named the Ellen; at the time you identified yourself as Michael Baker."

Alison looked shocked, but before he was able to respond Joe addressed the woman, "and you, ma'am, are the hostage we rescued. At the time you identified yourself as Anne Smith, but also when we returned you to British security in Italy you identified yourself on the phone as 71362AD to the British. Since you were using my phone, I overheard the conversation and wrote down the identity number you quoted."

"Do you have any proof of what you are saying?" snapped Alison.

"Yes, certainly, Mr Alison. You will remember that I took a photograph of you on the Ellen, together with your warrant card. Also, ma'am I took several pictures of you in the few days we looked after you – the pictures, together with your identity, are positive proof of who you are. I have all that information with me if you would care to look at it. The originals are locked in a safety deposit box, but I have copies here with me."

Alison and the woman, 71362AD, were passed the information across the table. After a brief whispered conversation between them they handed back the documents. Both nodded, looking a little sheepish.

"This does not change anything as far as we are concerned," said Joe, "we just thought that it would be better to tell you up front. Also, it is most unlikely that you would have recognised me since at that time I had an afro hairstyle and was dressed to fit in with the local population. My English is also much improved..."

What Joe did not mention was the murder of Ali and that Anne Smith was trussed up like a chicken and pushed under a bed. He also did not mention the fact that the British obviously intended to murder him and his colleagues as well.

"We'll have to consult," announced Alison and he and the woman left the room hurriedly.

"How long do you think they'll be?" Joe asked the two others who had stayed in the room, after a few minutes of silence.

"We are forbidden to talk to you, so can't give you any information," one of the men responded.

After an hour, one of the men left the room and returned with a tray laden with tea, coffee and biscuits.

After another hour of silence, Alison and the woman returned. "We can now proceed as planned," Alison announced.

"Good," said Joe, "you both obviously know Libya and have some knowledge of Africa further south. I think that will help."

"What's that supposed to mean?" asked the woman.

"During our journey to Libya, we spent a couple of hours at Selima Oasis, filling up water containers. We saw a white woman there who was obviously a prisoner of a group of Bedouin who were passing through. We are certain that the woman was you, 71362AD."

The woman looked down. Joe thought she was about to deny it. "Yes," she said quietly, "it was me."

"Thank you. Before we continue, could we use your actual name? It seems very clumsy to keep using 71362AD."

"Alice Osborne," replied the woman with a reluctant smile. "How do you want us to proceed?" asked Joe.

"From what you have already said," answered Alice, "it seems that your entry into people smuggling started long before you reached Libya. We would like to understand where it started and what motivated you to get into the business."

"Okay," said Joe. He explained that his father had been murdered and how his mother and he, aged ten, had been forced off their property and fled to Nairobi, where his mother had been forced into prostitution by an apparent pillar of the church.

"I have some sympathy with what happened to you, but what has any of that got to do with people smuggling?" Alison interrupted angrily.

"You wanted to understand my motivations. I can assure you, sir, that piece of background is the start of what motivated me into the business," Joe replied quietly.

Alison grunted.

Joe then proceeded to tell of his clashes with Reverend Mweleli and the police, how he gathered a group of other young boys round him, his entry into the *bhang* business, and how he managed some sort of education.

Alison shifted uncomfortably in his seat at the mention of *bhang*.

"I could see that unless I did something quite different, I would end up in some sort of low paid job like many of my countrymen, or worse, exchanging sexual favours with wealthy men for whatever I could, just to get by. You don't need to know those details." Details Joe would never reveal. "At about that time I was taken on by Reverend Mweleli for some domestic duties. I was also paying him off not to go to the police in relation to the *bhang* operation, so in many ways he was a partner in the business. On several occasions I served tea to a group of people who were planning to smuggle people to Juba in South Sudan and then on to Libya."

"Names, names," muttered Alison.

Joe nodded. "Some of the names will surprise you greatly. The group consisted of a Mr Kamau Kigoro, who was the man responsible for kicking Mum and me off our land; a Mr Otieno Boniface, who ran a large transport business – he of course provided the trucks; a General Kariuki, from the Kenyan Army; and Sir Oswald Higginbotham, who as you know runs a widely respected wealth management business here in London, and of course Reverend Mweleli."

There was a sharp intake of breath at the mention of Sir Oswald's name. "How did they make money from the operation?" asked Osborne.

"Otieno charged one thousand US to take people to Juba. Kigoro, I know, provided quite a lot of people who wanted to go to Juba. He collected the one thousand US from his participants and kept US one hundred for himself, before handing the balance on to Otieno. Knowing Kigoro he probably also charged his recruits something for being included in the trip. The general and Mweleli operated in the same way as Kigoro."

"And Sir Oswald?" asked Alice Osborn.

"He provided finance by way of lease arrangements for Otieno's vehicles. He was a keen participant in meetings and knew exactly what he was getting into. I suppose he thought that part of Otieno's business was legitimate, and it would be difficult to separate the good from the bad so to speak. There also may have been a separate agreement between the parties regarding a share of the profits Otieno would make. It was briefly discussed but I don't know the details."

Sandwiches and orange juice were provided for lunch. Joe, Thomasoff and Isabel were separately escorted to the toilet.

"When I understood that Otieno's trucks were the focal point of the conspiracy, I and my five colleagues went and offered our services. We were all taken on for various trips to Juba as assistants. We were paid very little but we learnt the ropes."

"How did you get through the border? I assume none of the passengers had appropriate documentation," asked Alice.

"We walked round the border post. I found a local who, for a few shillings, guided us round the post at night."

"You found him?"

"Yes. Otieno and his people were not well prepared. The truck drivers I first accompanied had no knowledge of the people smuggling business. In fact, it was their first trip to Juba. We rescued their business on several other occasions, none of which matters here.

"By this time, I and five colleagues were in Juba and ostensibly we were still Otieno's employees, so we agreed with him that we would join a vehicle going north, again as assistants, which we did, mainly to learn the ropes. This meant that we did not have to pay the organiser of the trip anything, we were actually going to be paid something, but as you will see it didn't matter in the end.

"The man running the show was incompetent and he was systematically raping the women on the trip, which resulted in trouble with the passengers, so to cut a long story short, I and my colleagues took the trip over and we sent all the South Sudanese back to Juba. The leader's partner, who was a North Sudanese, stayed with us. He was useful because of his Arabic language skills. He tried to do the dirty on us, but we managed to finesse that and he ended up in a Libyan jail, something he had planned for me."

"Did you kill any of the South Sudanese?"

"No. The leader was injured by one of the passengers and he was hospitalised in Wadi Halfa. I paid his train trip back home."

"Where did the money come from?" asked Alice.

"Jok, the leader, had hidden it in various places round the truck. It was the money paid by the passengers. We managed to find it all."

Joe then described the rest of the trip; the ferry across the Nile, Selima Oasis, Uweinat, Al Jawf and the journey to the Libyan coast. He had a tattered copy of the map they had used to explain the route.

"With all the difficulties we had encountered I realised that people were going to do whatever they could to get to Europe, but that trying to ship them from Juba was a mug's game and dangerous for them. There also were hordes of refugees on the Libyan coast wanting to cross to Europe. Otieno still owned the business, by the way. So, I bought a boat and teamed up with a man from the Libyan coastguard, which you mentioned you were aware of, Mr Alison. We did a few trips and I paid the profits to Otieno."

"Why did you bother with Otieno anymore? By that time, you could have claimed it as your own business."

"At the time I thought it possible I might want to return to Nairobi, where my mother lived."

"What changed your mind?"

"The rescue of Anne Smith," said Joe with a brief smile. "We thought rescuing a British security operative would create a benefit for us in terms of acquiring British residence and then citizenship."

"I see. I suppose that is one of the reasons you are here today."

"Yes. I do have a lot of other information that I think you would find useful."

"What information?"

"I made notes on all the people I dealt with on the Libyan coast. How people arrived in Libya, who brought them there, what their expectations were, where they came from, what they paid to get to the coast. I have copious notes of all that. Names, phone numbers, some of the people smugglers gave me addresses in their home countries. I am in a position to give you all of that info."

"Why would they give you any of that info?"

"The smugglers needed to quickly offload the people they had shipped in. I was one of the better options."

"What did you charge?"

"Fifteen hundred US to cross the Med."

"How many people did you ship?"

"A few hundred, maybe a thousand. The assistance of the Libyan coast guard helped since in the main we were able to avoid the patrols. The patrols are not very effective anyway," Joe continued. "Some of the less scrupulous smugglers, if they sighted a patrol, would offload some of their passengers into the sea and then scoot off knowing that the patrol would be obliged to stop and pick up the people before they drowned. As I am sure you understand, a very high percentage of the people brought to the Libyan coast ended up as slaves or prostitutes because they didn't have the wherewithal to pay for the crossing. The slaves are openly sold and the prostitutes see very little of their earnings. I have some details of all that as well as the boarding houses that many of the people smugglers used."

Item by item, Joe handed over copies of all his notes to Alice Osborne. "I have all the originals," he said.

"Okay," said Alison. "We know about the rescue of my colleague here. Is there anything else? How for example did you get to England?"

"I stopped in a well-known truck stop in France and a driver offered to take me across, for a fee of course. Several of my colleagues did the same thing from Rotterdam. I am sure you are all well aware of these routes. I doubt if I can add anything to your knowledge."

There was a brief whispered conversation between Alice Osborne and Alison. "Okay. Anything else?"

"When I arrived in England, I had some dealings with people who claimed they could get me British citizenship. All they actually wanted to do was kidnap me and put me to work in one of what I think of as their slave factories."

"Slaves. Here in Britain?" asked Alice.

"Yes." Joe them gave them all his notes about Ibrahim and his organisation. "They called themselves Park Slavers. Over a few weeks I paid a boy who worked for them, who referred to himself as Jerker, and he gave me a great deal of information about the organisation. Here are copies of the notes I made from those meetings. There are names and addresses, and the boy gave me some idea of the various activities they are engaged in – slave labour and prostitution in the main." He handed over copies of all his notes.

"Why did you do that?"

"Their intention was to do me a great deal of harm, I needed to protect myself."

"Why didn't you go to the police?"

"I didn't want to draw attention to myself."

"What happened to the boy?"

"He failed to attend the rendezvous we had agreed on, for a few weeks." Joe shrugged.

"Is that it now?" asked Alison.

"Yes."

"Give us a few minutes, we'll be back," said Alison. He and Alice left the room, leaving the grey men in place.

Half an hour later, the two MI5 personnel returned.

"We will have to assess what you have provided us with," said Alison. "We will certainly have some questions."

"Do you think the information we have provided is useful?" asked Thomasoff.

"Yes. It certainly is," said Alice.

"We agreed that my client Joe Wacheera," said Thomasoff, "would be granted immunity from prosecution in any jurisdiction, particularly the United States, Europe and of course Britain, on the understanding that he provided information on the people smuggling business, which he has done in a very comprehensive way. When can we expect that formal notification?"

"As my colleague has stated, we will have some questions when we have assessed what you have told us. We should be able to provide formal notification shortly after that," Alice responded.

"We were harassed unnecessarily by the police, which delayed this meeting by some months," said Thomasoff. "Can you give us assurances that that will not recur?"

"The police contacted us during that earlier period. I don't think they have any reason to talk to you again. If they do, then please contact us and we will deal with the issue."

Thomasoff glanced at Joe and Isabel and nodded. "Any further contact should be through me," said Thomasoff.

Alison and Alice signalled their agreement.

Thomasoff, Isabel and Joe were escorted downstairs by one of the little grey men. They retrieved Thomasoff's recording equipment.

"Should we have a quick debrief?" asked Joe. "The sun, if there was one, is over the yard arm by now." He laughed. "Isn't that some sort of sign that we now have permission to have an alcoholic drink? I think I even understand the origins of that expression."

They all laughed.

"Pubs near Parliament are expensive and tend to be full of tourists," said Isabel. "If we walk up Vauxhall Bridge Road, there is a decent place called the White Swan. It's about a ten-minute walk. The Pimlico tube station is not far away."

They found seats in what Joe could see was an elegant pub with heavy wooden fixtures. They found seats easily enough. Joe bought the drinks, beer for Thomasoff and himself and a gin and tonic for Isabel.

"Joe, you did very well today," said Thomasoff, "every time you open your mouth, I learn something more about you."

Joe shrugged. "You need to understand that, in Sicily, the British, instead of handing us the money they had promised, murdered my associate, Ali, who was part of the Libyan coastguard, and they, the British, intended to murder me and my colleagues also. We escaped by the skin of our teeth. So, you will understand why I don't trust them, not one inch." He paused for a few seconds. "It was tempting to include my perceptions of that episode in what I said, but I decided it was water under the bridge and would just antagonise them, so there was no upside as far as we are concerned. That is why I left it out. They are in any event well aware of what they did and didn't do." He laughed. "I suppose one could argue that they still owe me three hundred grand!"

Joe briefly described the incident where Ali was murdered and how he, Patrick and N'guku had shoved Anne Smith under the bed, and booby- trapped the room they had occupied, when they saw the British, armed to the teeth, running towards them.

"Understanding a bit about how they work, I think we are home and dry with the no prosecution business. I also think it is likely that they will ask you to become an agent for them. Watching them, I could see that they were impressed with the way you presented all your information. Just their style," said Thomasoff.

"You'll have to explain the origins of 'home and dry'. As for an agent for MI5? Forget it. Isabel and I have bigger plans than that. We are about to take on the world, in a different way!" Joe laughed. "Anyway, responding to all Isabel's ideas is a full-time job on its own. I certainly in my wildest dreams could not imagine dealing with those ghastly people on a regular basis."

"Don't dismiss it out of hand, Joe. They make good friends and very uncomfortable enemies."

"Is there anything else we need to do?" asked Joe.

"Not really. I don't need to tell you to make certain you are completely on top of all the information you provided. They will have a lot of questions. I will see if I can make the next meeting at my offices. That place we went today gives me the creeps," said Thomasoff.

Once they were finished, Thomasoff took a taxi home.

"It's a nice evening," said Isabel. "We could just walk home."

"Great. I suppose you know the way?"

"Certainly. Embankment. Chelsea Bridge Road. Sloane Square. Sloane Street. Knightsbridge. Brompton Road and home."

"Not exactly slumming it then," said Joe.

They walked hand in hand for more than an hour with Isabel pointing out interesting landmarks.

"You were brilliant today, Joe," said Isabel.

"Huh, only today? I must pull my socks up then. What's the origin of pull your socks up, I wonder?"

"Be serious for a minute, Joe. Those ghastly people, as you describe them, were really impressed. You saved that bloody woman's life – she knows that, although she never has and never will thank you. I think we can just get on with our plans now. We have all the agreements in place."

"While we change gear, should we go away for a few days, to clear our heads, like we did after our meetings at Brown's. And I haven't thanked you enough for rescuing me. If it wasn't for you, I would still be in the shit somewhere, maybe in jail."

"Go away. Lake District again? Or somewhere else. How long for?"

"Our MI5 buddies will probably take two or three weeks. We could go for a week somewhere. I was thinking maybe Marseille?"

"Marseille. Why would you want to go there?"

"It's not posh. It has a lot of history, as I understand it. I quite liked France or what I saw of it when I made my way to England all those years ago..."

Isabel did not waste time. Joe agreed to fix dinner while she made the bookings. Joe had learnt to make spaghetti Bolognese, so that is what he served up. "Delicious," said Isabel as she tucked into her heaped plate.

"So, what have you booked?" asked Joe.

"British Airways business class Heathrow to Marseille, and I have booked a decent apartment on the waterfront."

"I suppose I should consider myself lucky that you didn't book first class!"

"Stop whining. We're going to be comfortable. I did not even think of one of those horrid cheap airlines."

Joe stood up, stepped over and kissed her. "Just pulling your leg."

The pair had a comfortable time on the flight to Marseille and booked an Uber to take them to the apartment. Isabel had the security code to let them into their accommodation.

Joe dropped the suitcases in the lounge area to admire the view of the harbour. "Magnificent," he said, "just perfect. My interest is in the old harbour. We can obviously find our way there."

They went for long walks, mostly through the old town and harbour, where Joe unearthed a small waterfront bar.

Isabel was uneasy at first. "Couldn't you have found something a bit more, er, downmarket?"

Joe ignored the sarcasm. "I feel very comfortable here. There is so much going on if you keep your eyes open. There's a drug dealer over there," he said, looking to his left, "and that fellow behind the pillar runs a gang of toughs. The well-dressed lady talking to the proprietor is almost certainly the local madam. Also, there's no chance that your friends will find me here."

Isabel grimaced. "It's nice to know we have such skills on board in our partnership. What I have in mind is a bit more on the straight and narrow."

Joe nodded. "From what I know of the straight and narrow, as you describe it, there still are plenty of sharks around."

Isabel eventually relaxed. They both enjoyed the delicious but unpretentious food.

"I was wrong about your MI5 friends not being able to find us here," Joe said on one of their regular visits to the same bar. "There's a fellow sitting at the bar who I have seen around a bit too often for my liking. He's obviously following us." Joe watched for a few minutes and, while the man was distracted, Joe sat down next to him.

Joe took several pictures of the very surprised man, who said, "Hey..."

"Just shut up and listen," said big strong Joe quietly, as he easily held the little man by the arm. "I know what you are about. Unless you want a broken leg or something worse just give me your phone. You have no business here." The man tried to get away. Joe tightened his grip. The bar owner looked up. Joe shook his head as if to say, 'Leave it to me'. Eventually the man gave Joe his phone. Still holding onto the wretch, Joe flicked through the photos on the man's phone. There were numerous images of Joe and Isabel all over Marseille, including several going into the entrance of their apartment.

"Just fuck off," said Joe. "If I ever set eyes on you again, you'll end up in the harbour."

"My phone?" said the man.

"I'll give it to your employers."

The wretch fled.

Little notice was taken by the other patrons in the bar. Joe nodded to the proprietor, who smiled.

'All in a day's work,' thought Joe.

Isabel looked shocked as Joe sat down again at their table. "What was all that about?" she asked.

"Just look at this." Joe showed her the dozens of images on the phone. "MI5?" she said.

"Who else? Don't worry. I will show it to them when we next see them. I'll make sure that all this nonsense stops."

"Should we go home?" asked Isabel.

"No. Those ghastly people are not going to spoil anything. We'll go home when we planned. I will phone Thomasoff and tell him what has happened."

They finished their meal and wandered back to the flat.

Joe phoned Thomasoff. "Joe here," he said when the call was put through. "Nothing doing yet," said Thomasoff. "I expect to hear in a day or two."

"It's not about that." Joe explained that they had decided to spend a few days in Marseille. "Just to relax. However, our MI5 friends decided to follow us here." Joe explained what had occurred at the bar, and that he had the phone of the man following them. "It has images of Isabel and me all over Marseille, from the airport until today."

"MI5, you think it's MI5?" asked Thomasoff.

"Who else would know which flight we were on, it certainly seems to be our friends."

Thomasoff sighed. "The stupid bastards. Please send me the images... I'll phone them."

"Okay, thanks Geoffrey. I'll obviously have the agent's phone when we meet them again. I'll keep an eye out, but I'm pretty sure they will back off now." Joe sent the images from the MI5 phone to Thomasoff.

Joe and Isabel then spent another ten uninterrupted days enjoying Marseille and the surrounding countryside. They also spent time fine-tuning their investment strategy.

Joe spent an hour each day talking to his investment people on the phone. "Rather than buying already existing properties," said Joe, "should we not consider actually going into the property development business?"

"What do we know about property development?" asked Isabel.

Joe smiled. "That's where Ron, your father, comes in. Maybe he'll be able to put us on the right track?"

There was a brief silence.

"You're okay with that, aren't you?" Joe continued. "As I insisted, he's not part of the business. He's exactly where he wants to be – not personally involved but acting as a consultant or adviser. If he thinks we're on the wrong track, he'll say so. As you know, I now have regular contact with him. I have also spoken to him on another issue though."

"What issue?" asked Isabel, looking suspicious.

To Isabel's complete surprise, Joe got down on one knee.

He held her hand. He had a deadly serious expression on his face. "When all this business is over, will you marry me?"

Isabel, despite herself, burst out laughing. "Marry you, of course I will. If you hadn't asked me soon, I would have popped the question to you! But what's all the drama about?"

"I thought this is how you *Wazungu* behave, I've been reading about it." There was no hint of humour in Joe's expression.

"Ah, and as part of the process, you thought you had better ask my father's permission."

"Yes, it's also part of my tribal tradition. A man would never get married without talking to the woman's father first. Normally my father would have spoken to your father, but as you know that's not possible, so I did the next best thing."

Isabel jumped up. "Time for a bit of black mamba..." She laughed.

Lying in bed later Joe said, "You will be pleased to know that your father agreed to dispense with the bridal dowry, normally about twenty cattle in your case, plus a sheep for the wedding feast."

Isabel laughed and laughed. "So, when...?"

"Your father said I should talk to you first. This is very unusual; normally the bride would just be told of the arrangements. He said you were very headstrong." Joe managed to keep a straight face.

Isabel cuddled up to Joe. "He got that one right."

A call the next day from Thomasoff brought them back to reality. "I now have all the guarantees from every jurisdiction that you asked for, so when you return, we can answer all their questions."

"All the jurisdictions?" asked Joe. "Including the USA?"

"Yes, them as well," was the answer.

Joe was silent for a moment. 'Thankfully all that nonsense is now over,' he thought.

"Right," continued Thomasoff, "I will arrange another meeting, at my office this time."

"Have they found the info useful?"

"Yes, certainly. From what I have been told, the security services are more than delighted with the info you gave them. It has put them in another realm, from what I can gather. They have shared it with the Americans and with Frontex, which is the European Union's border control operation. Frontex has been beefed up in recent times, much of their effort is centred on dealing directly with African countries where the focus has been on stopping the refugee trade at source. So, the info you have provided is invaluable."

A few days later they met in the boardroom at Thomasoff's office in Chancery Lane. Joe and Isabel arrived a few minutes before the scheduled time of 10am. Thomasoff had set up appropriate video recording equipment for what was likely to be a long session.

This time, the security service team was led by Alice Osborne. She also re-introduced the other two members of the team.

"No Mr Alison this time?" asked Joe mischievously.

Alice looked at him blankly. One of her colleagues whispered in her ear. "Oh. Yes..."

Joe nodded. "We actually know his correct name, but that is indeed what he said his name was."

"He won't be joining us today... or any other day," said Alice without the hint of a smile. "Perhaps we could now get on with what I am sure will be a very productive day?"

While answering questions, Joe also added numerous reasons, where he could, why the people he smuggled into Europe had decided to make the hazardous journey that in many cases put their lives in danger. He also discussed at length the brutalisation that many of the refugees suffered at the hands of the smugglers. "This particularly applies to people who don't have whatever the people smugglers are asking for the final trip from the Libyan coast to the island of Lampedusa or other places in Italy. Severe beatings and often rape mostly in the case of women, but not exclusively, and sometimes the unfortunates are reduced to being slaves of the smugglers. Many of the women finding themselves in this predicament are forced into prostitution."

The security trio said very little, but Joe could see they continued to be taken aback at the graphic verbal images Joe portrayed.

Joe, Isabel and Thomasoff took themselves off for lunch, to one of the many unpretentious cafés in the area, catering for the myriad of office workers.

"Joe, everything you say, it's true, isn't it?" asked Thomasoff, as they took their seats.

Joe looked bemused. "Yes, we've been through all that, yes of course. I don't see how anyone could invent stuff like that."

"Did you not get into conflict with the people smugglers?" asked Alice, during the afternoon session. "It seems that you took over when they had done what they probably considered was all the hard work."

"No, as with all the others involved in the business, we provided a valuable service in getting the refugees out of Libya and into Europe. Most of them just wanted to dump the people they had brought to the Libyan coast and disappear. We established a reputation of reliability."

"You had no conflict with the local authorities?"

"No, there are ways and means of ensuring that."

"Do you have anything further to say about that?"

"No."

She looked at him with a questioning expression on her face. "You had another question?" said Joe.

"Yes, didn't you have trouble with the Western naval patrols in the Mediterranean?"

"No. The arrangement with Ali, my contact in the Libyan coastguard, made sure of that. I have already told you what the smugglers do when they see a patrol. On the very few occasions we saw a naval vessel, they always disappeared out of sight as quickly as they could, as we did. For the reason I described at our last meeting."

"Did you throw any people into the sea, when you saw a naval vessel?"

"No. We didn't lose a single passenger on any of our trips."

Joe looked at the woman calmly, as if to say, 'don't you dare contradict me, what we did was necessary to rescue you'. Alice Osborne looked down. Joe realised then that this question was just for the record.

"What you are saying is that the naval patrols are ineffective in preventing the shipment of people across the Med?"

Joe shrugged.

Alice Osborne again looked at Joe, asking, "Is that the lot now?"

"Nothing more," said Joe.

"Did you try to assess whether the people you shipped across the Med were genuine refugees or economic migrants?" asked one of the 'grey men', one of Alice's partners. This question came out of the blue; up until that point the questions had been asked by Alice alone.

Joe had an incredulous look on his face, but before he could say anything, Alice looked at the man and said, "For God's sake, how on earth would he be able to do that?" She then looked at Joe saying, "Please ignore the question, Joe."

After a brief silence, Alice said, "You haven't told us who your principal was while you were in Libya."

"We dealt with that on the previous occasion we met. It was Otieno, who has since died. I have nothing further to add."

"Anything else?" Alice persisted.

"You could get someone to look at the Libyan Coastguard. Many of them operate legitimately but I am sure that does not apply to all of them. They sometimes have trouble getting paid, so I expect, for that reason, they take advantage of their position from time to time."

"Details?" asked Alice.

"I've told you everything I know." There was silence for a minute or two.

"We just need to consult for a few minutes," said Alice. "Can we go into another room?"

"Before you go," said Joe. He produced the phone he had taken from the man in the Marseille bar. "You already know about this," he said. "What on earth did you think it would achieve?"

"It was unauthorised. It should never have happened," was Alice's response. Joe raised his eyebrows saying nothing.

"Just a couple more questions, after which we will leave you alone," said Alice when they returned. "We have some specific questions regarding some of the info provided."

"I'll answer them if I can," answered Joe.

Most of the questions were innocuous and easy to answer, and Joe gave them full, comprehensive answers, sometimes having to dredge up the answers from his prodigious memory, after a bit of thought.

The questions then became more personal.

"What sort of crew did you have on the boat you described as 'seaworthy'?" asked Alice.

Joe looked at her with distrust. He looked at Thomasoff and shook his head.

Thomasoff said, "My client will not be answering questions of that nature. Move on please."

"Was the man Mwangi, part of the crew?"

"No, he has been resident here for more than ten years and is a British citizen."

PART 6

Chapter 18: The Partnership

Joe and Isabel returned to her flat in South Kensington. Before saying or doing anything, Joe turned and hugged her. Eventually he said, "Thank you and thank you and thank you. If it wasn't for you, I would still be stuck in some sort of limbo, not knowing what the hell to do next."

Unusually for her, Isabel had a tear in her eye when he had finished. She eventually said, "The way I feel about you, I couldn't possibly have done anything else." She kissed him. "As far as I am concerned you are the best thing that has ever happened to me. You are precious, precious."

After the meetings with MI5, they moved into an office in an old building in Finsbury Circus. They had called their operation Anderson-Wacheera Investments.

"Wouldn't you prefer Wacheera-Anderson?" asked Isabel.

Joe shrugged. "Doesn't matter to me, but I think that the community, the people we will be dealing with here, will mostly be Anglos; I suggest they might be more comfortable with Anderson coming first. It's less threatening."

Isabel suggested moving into a more modern glass and steel edifice, where Higginbotham's were established.

Joe shook his head. "The idea of bumping into 'sir' at regular intervals is not very attractive. Anyway, the older one is less expensive."

Isabel and Joe shared an office; both had large wooden desks facing each other.

Joe soon had twenty people managing their investment operation, which included the seven people from Joe's Bethnal Green set-up It serviced their own substantial investment portfolio as well as the several hundred or so clients they advised. They still traded through Fred Smiley. Joe still did much of the research himself, but he began to train three others in how he went about the research and what he expected the end result to be once research was completed.

"We could set up our own brokerage business," suggested Isabel.

"Okay, but there's no hurry. As you know, Smiley now pays us 70% of the brokerage fees he earns from the deals we put through him."

Over a few months, Isabel persuaded Joe to buy a recently renovated mews house in Kensington.

"What's wrong with this place?" he argued, referring to Isabel's flat.

"Nothing. I think we would be more comfortable in something a bit bigger."

Joe laughed. "Hm, I can see a process, where the next thing will be a mansion, and then a rural retreat and I suppose we'll finish up in a cold, unheated Norman castle on a hilltop..."

"At the moment, all I am suggesting is a mews house. What happens when we have children? We'll need more space." Isabel smiled.

"Children?" said Joe with a worried expression on his face.

"Yes. That's what happens when people get married, they have children. Apart from buying me that very nice ring, the subject of our marriage has hardly been mentioned."

"Based on your father's advice I was waiting for you," he laughed again. "Anyway, I was having trouble trying to line up a witchdoctor."

Isabel looked at him to see if this was really a serious proposal. She smiled.

"Now you've mentioned the wedding, what do you actually want?" continued Joe. "A big hoo-ha or are we just going to creep off to a local registry office?"

"Well, neither. I was talking to Mum. We've narrowed it down to a small wedding here in London and then a reception somewhere, or something more elaborate, maybe in Sydney."

"What about Kenya?" suggested Joe. "I could ask the fucking reverend to officiate. Now there's an idea." He laughed.

"Be serious for a moment." Isabel laughed. "Kenya is too complicated. Which would you prefer?"

"Probably London. Do we have time to traipse all the way to Australia? Although in time I would like to see Australia. Anyway, what would you like?"

"I think London. We need to think of inviting some of our business associates; we need to be building contacts."

"Not too many of those just yet," said Joe, "but I'm working on it."

"Do you mind if we have the ceremony in a church somewhere?"

Joe looked at her with a quizzical look on his face. "Are you serious? In all the time I've known you, you've never set foot in a church."

"I think that's what Mum would like." Joe raised an eyebrow.

Isabel just looked at him.

"Despite the considerable efforts of the fucking reverend I haven't gone through any of the Christian ceremonies, baptism, confirmation, etc.," said Joe, "and having survived so far, you would need to put me in chains and drag me off..."

Isabel laughed. "Okay, okay, point made. I'll see what I can do. Some of the Christian churches are being a bit more flexible nowadays."

Meanwhile, Isabel was engaged in researching possible acquisitions of development companies. Once she had found three or four possible candidates, as had already been discussed, she arranged for her father to join them to assess what she had unearthed.

Ron was in the office early to see Joe. He helped narrow the field down. "You have two choices," he said to Joe. "One, a very profitable bunch of 'fly-by- nights'.

Somehow, they have survived but they get themselves into an awful lot of trouble by cutting corners," he smiled. "I have some sympathy with this operation, it's how I behaved in the early days in Sydney, until I established myself. The second is a high-quality developer, possibly a bit 'stick-in-the-mud' but there's great potential there."

"You have to explain, 'fly-by-nights' and 'stick-in-the-mud'," said Joe, "but I get the picture." They continued discussing the options for another hour, with Joe anxiously looking at his watch. "Wonder where she is?" he said. "This is really her show..."

Two hours later, Isabel came bustling in.

"Oh good," said Joe, "we need your input here."

She avoided his embrace, saying to him, "I need to talk to you... urgently." At his hesitation, she almost shouted, "Now!"

Joe looked at Ron, who shrugged. They went into their office and Isabel shut the door. Joe had never seen her so angry, so he waited for her to say something.

"Have you told me everything, absolutely everything, about your past life?"

"Yes, certainly, I can't think of anything major, or anything at all that I haven't told you."

"You have a seven-year-old son. You have never mentioned that."

Joe didn't bat an eyelid. "News to me. I know nothing about a son. What are you talking about?" Joe remained calm; he had a completely clear conscience in that regard, although he had a fleeting memory of the one sexual encounter had had with Wambui. 'I can't imagine that one-night stand made her pregnant,' he thought.

"I have been approached by a woman, a Kikuyu, who claims you made her pregnant, on one of those bloody trips you made from Juba..."

"I only made one of those trips. Could you tell me the woman's name?"

"Wambui."

"How old is she?" asked Joe.

Isabel shrugged, calming down in view of Joe's quite untroubled demeanour. "Early to mid-twenties maybe," she answered.

"Isabel, I'm pretty sure I know who you are talking about, and if indeed she became pregnant during that trip, I have a fair idea who the father might be. Although, I did have sex with Wambui once."

There was silence for a minute. "Have you seen the child?" asked Joe.

"Yes, that's where I went this morning."

"You *saw* them? Where is the woman and her child? We need to sort this out, right now. I'm sorry you have so little faith in what I have told you about my past."

"I left them both in a nearby café, in London Wall," said a now contrite Isabel.

"Let's just think about this for a minute," said Joe. "We certainly don't want a public scene. Maybe you should go and fetch them, and I'll meet them here."

Isabel almost ran out of the office, while Joe sat and waited.

"They're no longer here. They seem to have scarpered," said Isabel on the phone.

"Do you know where they might have gone?"

"Yes, probably, I saw them in a small flat in Acton; that's where I was this morning."

"Was there an older woman there?"

"Yes, she said the older woman was her mother."

"Okay," said Joe. "Hail a taxi and I'll meet you downstairs."

Joe said to Ron as he left. "Just got to sort out a misunderstanding. Hope to be back soon."

Joe raced downstairs and hopped into the waiting taxi. Isabel gave the driver the address in Acton.

"You knock on the door. We don't want to scare them," said Joe. Isabel glanced at him, then did as asked.

The door was opened, and Isabel was admitted without hesitation. To the woman's surprise and horror, Joe followed Isabel into the flat. It was Wambui's mother. Joe greeted the woman in her native Kikuyu. She responded briefly, looking terrified. Joe looked around the grubby little ground floor flat, situated on one of the noisy main roads in the area. They were shown into a small living room. There was a battered dining room table with some unmatched chairs and two broken down 'comfortable' chairs and a settee in the lounge area.

The woman started to talk.

Joe looked at her, saying, still in Kikuyu, "We'll wait for Wambui and the child. Can we have a cup of tea?"

The woman nodded.

Joe followed her into the kitchen. As the tea was produced, Wambui and her son pushed open the front door. Joe moved to the front door and closed it, preventing Wambui from leaving, which she tried to. He noticed the son was very black, and he was tall for a seven-year-old.

"How much English does anyone speak?" asked Joe. There was a stunned silence for a few moments.

Isabel came to the rescue, "Wambui seems to be quite fluent and so is her son. The mother doesn't speak any English, as far as I can see."

Joe addressed the boy directly, "Can you tell me your name, please." Wambui answered for him, "We called him Joseph, after you..."

"They call me Joe at school," the boy answered.

"Okay. I would like to talk to your mother and your grandmother, just them, maybe you could play outside for a few minutes? It won't be for long."

The boy picked up a football and walked outside into a tiny, weed-infested patch of grass, visible through the front window.

"You told Isabel that I am the father of your son," Joe said to Wambui. "You know that's not true." He looked at the mother and repeated the same thing in Kikuyu. "From the look of him, I am quite sure Jok is the father," Joe continued.

There was no response from either woman.

Joe explained to Isabel, "Jok was the original leader on the trip from Juba. He is from the Dinka tribe. The Dinka are tall and have very black skin, as the child has. There is no chance in the world I am the father of the child." Joe looked out of the window.

There was no response from Isabel.

"During the trip, Jok was badly hurt during a bust-up with one of the refugees. I took over after that, but as leader he had already taken advantage of many of the refugee women on that trip. It seems that Wambui was one of his victims."

"What do you say to that, Wambui?" asked Isabel. Wambui did not answer. She looked down at her feet.

Joe translated for the benefit of Wambui's mother, who responded heatedly, in Kikuyu, "Jok was the leader, then you became the leader. You should have taken responsibility for his actions."

Joe translated into English for Isabel's benefit.

"So, Wambui, you agree that Jok is the father of your child, and not Joe?" asked Isabel.

Joe translated for the mother. Wambui unhappily nodded her head.

There was a furious response from the mother, who shouted at Wambui and ran out of the room.

Isabel looked at Joe, who said, "Somehow she thinks that I should have taken Jok's place as Wambui's lover and therefore taken responsibility for all his actions. They were clearly short of money and the mother must have traded the sexual favours of her then sixteen-year-old daughter for some sort of promise from Jok. He took no notice of course and continued to play the field. That was what got him into trouble. The mother tried the same trick on me."

An embarrassed and disconcerted Isabel shook her head. "It seems we're finished here," she said. She put her cup down and stood up.

Joe asked Wambui, "How did you find us?"

Wambui looked at Joe, saying, "We were talking to another group of Kikuyu and your name was mentioned. I found and followed you for a few days..."

"Which Kikuyu?"

"A friend of Mwangi's."

"Mwangi?"

"No, a friend of his, not Mwangi."

Joe looked at Isabel. "Okay, that's it I suppose. We should leave." They left.

Joe hailed a taxi and gave the taxi the office address. "No," said Isabel; she gave the driver their home address.

During the half hour drive back to South Kensington, Joe took Isabel's hand, saying, "As I said I did have sex with Wambui, once, on that trip. Only once. I soon realised the game that Wambui and her ghastly mother were up to, so it never happened again. Apart from Jo-Ann, we have never discussed the few women I had sex with before I met you and I didn't expect you to tell me what experiences you had had before you met me. I suppose I should consider myself lucky."

Isabel said nothing, she just squeezed Joe's hand.

As they went into their elegantly furnished mews house, Isabel shut the door and turned to Joe saying, "I'm so, so sorry. I could have played all that very differently. I overreacted. What can I do to make it up to you?"

Joe looked at her with a smile. They spent the afternoon in bed.

Before they emerged from their afternoon exertions, while they were still in bed, Joe said to Isabel, "The situation in which Wambui and her frightful mother have ended up is typical of how some of the Kikuyu find themselves in this country. We've mentioned this before. They may need help. I'll speak to Mwangi. It is a shame they are in this position; the boy too. I wish there was something I could do, to stop this nonsense in the first place. Wambui should never have had to give her body to anyone she did not want. Their options were limited, I suppose. By the way, did you phone Ron? He must be wondering what's going on."

"I did, while you were asleep."

The next two days were spent with Ron in the office. Isabel led the discussions and they finally decided to make a bid for 'Watts', the privately-owned quality developer Isabel had unearthed, based in Slough, west of London. The company's name was the name of the founder, who was ready to retire.

Joe kept himself in the background but he, Ron and Isabel, met daily during the negotiations with the owners of 'Watts'. As was his way, Joe spent hours poring over all the agreements relating to the acquisition. "We need to keep the current management in place for a couple of years at least," Joe suggested, "while we understand how the business operates. Either they keep some shares, or we develop a bonus programme for selected people."

"I wouldn't have any share minorities in the business," advised Ron. "Just go the bonus route."

"What role do you want to play?" asked Joe.

"I'll certainly keep an eye on what's going on, but there is no way I want a full-time job. One or two days a week would suit me fine. Mostly looking at the detail of building contracts."

"Okay," said Joe, "that's great. With you there the contractors won't get away with much."

Ron smiled at Joe. "They seem to be very honest to me," he said.

"They still have to prove that," Joe responded, "to me anyway. I assume we'll have a monthly board meeting."

Isabel and Ron nodded. "All set up," said Isabel.

"It's all cash, I assume?" asked Joe.

"That's something we need to discuss," said Isabel.

Ron wisely withdrew from the conversation at that point.

"Mostly cash, but I think we could easily afford to borrow a portion of the purchase price. Otherwise, we'll have to liquidate too much of our share portfolio to pay for it."

"I don't really like the idea of borrowing."

"I know how you feel," said Isabel sympathetically, "but I've had a detailed look through our portfolio and some of the stuff we've bought will only mature a few years down the track. We'd be throwing away a well-earned opportunity."

She went through the details and Joe eventually agreed with her conclusions.

"You really have done your homework," said Joe, with admiration. "We should set the maximum borrowing at thirty per cent of the purchase price."

"Yes." Isabel was relieved. "I thought the discussions on the issue would be much more difficult! I'll make an appointment with the bank."

While the negotiations were going on for the acquisition of 'Watts', Joe had one of his regular but less frequent meetings with Mwangi, who was now based in the Higginbotham offices. Mwangi had taken control of the messenger business, which now included a burgeoning office cleaning business.

"You must have heard of the nonsense with Wambui?" said Joe. Mwangi nodded. "It's that mother of hers..."

"I know, they were with me on the truck from Juba. Nothing to do with you, so don't worry."

Mwangi relaxed, knowing he was not going to be blamed for the incident with Wambui.

"You could offer Wambui a job..."

"I already did. She starts next week."

Joe explained to Isabel that Mwangi had taken Wambui on in the cleaning business.

"I thought you had bailed out of all that."

"Yes. I now have no financial interest in either the messenger or office cleaning business. I just see Mwangi every now and then to keep in touch with my crew, if you see what I mean." After a short silence, Joe said, "There is something else. A bit more significant than the messenger business."

"What's that?" asked Isabel.

"Oscar Fitzpatrick. You know the fellow, he has a senior position at Higginbotham's."

"You've mentioned him before."

"For some years now I've been aware that he's running his own operation a few blocks away from Higginbotham's. Just have a look at this." Joe indicated a screen on his laptop. "He once tried to blackmail me. Apparently, Fred Smiley is an acquaintance. Luckily, I was able to dissuade him..."

"Why should we be worrying about what Fitzpatrick is doing?" Isabel moved back to her own desk.

Joe shrugged, smiling. "I was just thinking, a few years down the track, if we ever were to think of acquiring..."

"You want to buy Higginbotham's?"

"Maybe. We're a helluva lot better than they are at managing people's money. Just a thought. I've always had my suspicions about Oscar. If we were to buy something like Higginbotham's, it would be as well to know what goes on in the background. With Mwangi in place, I have been making sure he keeps his eyes and ears open at Higginbotham's to see what he can find out about all the senior and some of the other significant employees at Higginbotham's. It's not for now: a year or two down the track maybe. After 'Watts' has been bedded down."

"Jeepers!" said Isabel smiling. "Keeping up with you really is a full time job." She hesitated for a minute. "I'm going to be very busy with 'Watts' for the time being but keep going on this. Should be fun."

Once the acquisition of 'Watts' was complete, Isabel spent every last minute working on the business, often helped by her father. She visited every construction site and got to know all the contractor's foremen and some of the sub-contractors, and within six months, despite initial reservations, mainly because they were not used to dealing with women in management roles, she had earned the respect of the entire management team of 'Watts'.

Joe kept well out of the way, except for board meetings, which were chaired by Isabel. Joe always did his homework in preparation for those meetings and made sure he kept a close eye on the financial aspects of each individual contract. He never made any suggestions at board meetings that hadn't been discussed in detail with Isabel first.

During one of the early meetings Isabel said to Joe, "Joe, you have a suggestion as to how we could progress this business."

"Should we not also have a construction business? It integrates with the development business."

There was a brief discussion.

"Ron, you're looking uncomfortable," said Joe. "What's your view on this?"

"It's tempting but is probably not a good idea. The rest of the industry will start to distrust you, especially if your own construction operation wins too many of the contracts. In the long run, you will probably feather-bed the construction operation and you will gradually become less and less competitive. Geographically expand your development business if you have the resources or expand into other sectors like commercial buildings and office blocks."

The idea was dropped.

"I've now done a bit of research on venues for our wedding," Isabel said to Joe at dinner one night, at home.

"Okay," said Joe laughing. "I'm getting the impression it's not Westminster Abbey."

"Be serious for a moment. I've found an Anglican priest who will conduct the ceremony. He's not fussy that you are not an Anglican, or even a Christian. The church is in Onslow Square, it's a branch of something bigger; they run several churches in the area. Mum and I have had a look and it will be able to accommodate the guests we invite."

"When?"

"Mid-June, just before the summer holidays."

"How many?

"A hundred and fifty or so."

Joe nodded. "I would like to invite some of my Kikuyu colleagues, about a dozen."

"None of this witch doctor business, I hope?" Joe just smiled.

Isabel went to their bedroom and returned looking quite stunning in her pristine white wedding dress, which she paraded in front of him.

Joe was intrigued with the preparations for the wedding. "What's this white wedding dress all about? Another *M'zungu* ritual I suppose," he said smiling.

He was pulling her leg, he knew perfectly well what the white wedding dress represented.

"It's traditional. It used to be a sign of virginity." She glared at him. "Don't you dare say anything about that. That's what we are having, plus four or five bridesmaids. It's tradition for the groom not to see the wedding dress until the day, but I couldn't resist."

"I'll wear my best suit," said Joe.

"No, you bloody won't. You will be wearing a proper morning coat. Either buy one or you can easily rent one. You also need a best man," Isabel continued.

"I think I'll ask Ron," said Joe, his eyes sparkling.

"He'll be giving me away. Again, don't you dare say anything about that, if you value your life."

They were eventually married in an Anglican Church in Onslow Square, with the reception being held in the Mandarin Oriental in Knightsbridge.

Chapter 19: Kenya Again

Despite their marital bliss, Joe couldn't stop thinking about Wambui and how her options had been so limited that she had given her body to Jok on that trip to Juba. There had to be something Joe could do, to prevent problems such as hers, along with every other African woman desperately fleeing poverty only to find themselves raped or, like his mother, trapped in prostitution. At least Wambui's son would now grow up and be schooled in England. If only Wambui had had that opportunity. It gave him an idea.

"How about Kenya for a holiday?" said Joe at dinner one evening. "I'd like to show you something of the place and I also have some unfinished business there."

"What! Fantastic. When?" asked an excited Isabel.

"It might take a while to get things into shape, so a few months, maybe even a year. Also, I've had an idea: of setting up a girls' school in Nairobi."

"That's a fabulous idea, Joe!"

"Luckily two of my original gang went back to Kenya, after our adventure in rescuing Alice Osborne. I am in touch, so that's where we should start. I'll introduce them to you, so you can help with the girls' school project, if that is what you want? I will also see what can be done about returning the land Mum and I were kicked off all those years ago. My friends still run the *bhang* business, with Karanja gradually taking a back seat.

"You no longer have any interest in the *bhang* business, do you?"

"No, I gave that up years ago."

Joe phoned Patrick, with Isabel on a speaker phone. Since Patrick had returned to Kenya Joe had spoken to him regularly. He always spoke to him in Kikuyu. After the usual preliminaries Joe, said, "There is a bit more to this call than before." He introduced Isabel.

"Hi Patrick, Joe has obviously told me a bit about you over the years," she said.

"Jambo," said Patrick laughing.

"Apart from wanting to catch up with you and Koinange again, I still have some unfinished business in Kenya," Joe continued.

"Such as?" asked Patrick, now speaking in English for Isabel's benefit.

"I think we should see what we can do about getting the land back that Mum and I were kicked off. I will send you our title deed as a starting point, which Mum sent me years ago. I suppose that bastard Kigoro is still running around?"

"Yes, he is," said Patrick. "Okay, the land. I have some ideas about that. Anything else?"

"We think that girls' education could be where we can contribute something to the country," said Isabel.

"Girls' education!" said surprised Patrick. "Koinange has been talking about that for a few months now. I'll talk to him about it today. Anything else, Joe? You always had dozens of ideas..."

"I'll probably see if I can scare the shit out of the fucking reverend. You still paying him off for the *bhang* business?"

"Yes. He's much the same as he always was."

"How is your father by the way? I seem to remember that you rescued him from some slave camp in Libya."

There was silence for a short minute.

"Bad," Patrick eventually answered, "he never recovered... I am able look after him and Mum, thanks partly to the *bhang* operation. Mum escaped the reverend's filthy prostitution business... Koinange and I also have a transport business, which is doing well. It's quite small still."

"Transport. Interesting. Will you get out of the *bhang...?*"

"Not yet. It's what funded the transport operation."

"Okay. Do you have any contacts with the police and the security apparatus?"

"Police, yes. Because of the *bhang.* But security people, I'll have to look into that."

"You remember that big fat *Mzungu*, Sir Oswald Higginbotham, who was involved with Otieno... Does he still visit Kenya?"

"I'll have to check. Otieno died as you know, and that oaf of a half-brother of his, Odongo, inherited the business, which he was smart enough to sell. Hasn't done him much good though. He's drinking himself to death by all accounts."

"Does the business still operate?" asked Joe.

"Certainly."

"Do they still ship people north to make their way to Europe?"

"Possibly, but now there is this European Union agency called Frontex, which has been beefed up since our day. They have people here, I think, talking to the security people, which makes it much more difficult to ship people north. I'll see what I can find out."

"Frontex, I've heard that mentioned," said Joe.

During the next year Joe phoned and e-mailed Patrick on the land issue and Isabel had her own regular contact with Koinange dealing with the girls' school project.

"I have engaged a lawyer, a Mr Lentella," Koinange told Isabel. "He can set up a trust, to be funded by you. Referring to the girls' education proposal, Mr

Lentella has arranged that the government will provide premises and we'll set up an interview process for you to select a potential headmistress."

"Okay. We agree to setting up the trust. You seem to be making progress on the rest. I'm happy with all that," said Isabel.

They both shared the results of their various communications with Patrick and Koinange.

"Patrick has also told me that, again through this Mr Lentella, he has managed to trace several of the people who owned land neighbouring that of my parents, so we are making progress," Joe reported to Isabel. "And Geoffrey Thomasoff strongly suggested that I mention the trip to MI5, Alice Osborne in particular, which I have done. So, I am a sort of unofficial agent on the trip for now. She has set me up with an introduction to one of the senior security people in Nairobi."

"I thought you didn't want to have anything more to do with them?"

"Alice Osborne has asked me a couple of questions about Sir Oswald and his people smuggling interests. I thought it might pay us in the long term to keep in with them, especially if Sir Oswald gets into strife with the security services. As we discussed I have also booked for a few days in the Maasai Mara, which has the reputation of being one of the best game parks in the world. July is the best month, if we want to witness the migration from the Serengeti in Tanzania to the Mara in Kenya," said Joe.

"Mm, lovely, I'm glad there is some holiday included in all this; it was beginning to look like all business," observed Isabel.

"Think of it as a delayed honeymoon," suggested Joe.

"Why are we going Kenya Airways?" asked Isabel. "Are they safe?"

"Just to get us in the mood," said Joe. "I'm sure they are perfectly safe; in fact, they have the reputation of being the best airline in Africa."

Isabel laughed. "That's not much of a recommendation. It's like saying it's the best wine in England."

Joe laughed.

"Hello," Joe said in Kikuyu to the pretty flight attendant, after the overnight flight had taken off. "On time," he muttered to Isabel.

"Hello to you too. Do you come from Kenya?" answered the very surprised flight attendant in the same language.

The conversation continued in Kikuyu. "Yes. I was born in Ol'Kalou."

"Where is that?"

"Rift Valley, between Gil-Gil and Nyaharuru."

The girl shrugged, though the exchange meant that they both got extra special treatment for the whole flight.

Again, Joe's language skills and his charm meant they were shuffled through the Nairobi passport and customs without any fuss.

"Did you speak to the passport officer in another language?" asked Isabel.

"Very perceptive of you. The woman was a Wakamba. I know something of their language."

"Confusing, all these different languages and tribes."

"Some seventy tribes and four quite separate ethnic groups." Joe had arranged a car from the Norfolk Hotel to meet them.

"Oh my god look at this traffic," said Isabel. "It's always like this."

"Jeepers – how long's this going to take?"

"Couple of hours, usually."

During the journey, Joe had a long conversation with the driver, mostly about poor traffic management and corrupt officials. He translated for Isabel's benefit. "The population of Nairobi has increased from about three hundred thousand to something like five million in the fifty odd years since independence. No government on earth could cope adequately with such an increase." Joe shrugged. "And it is not going to get any better."

"Is this Kikuyu again?" she asked.

"No, Swahili. The man is a Luo. Swahili is spoken in East Africa, and parts of Central Africa, but it is also understood in parts of what is now Yemen, Aden for example. What is known as 'up country' Swahili is derived from Kiswahili, which is the language of the small Swahili coastal tribe. The coastal people speak what is known as *'safi'* or clean Swahili, which is not really understood beyond Kenya's coastal fringe. The up-country Swahili was introduced by Arab slave traders in centuries gone by."

"How do you know all this? I thought you were educated in a muddy ditch."

"My education wasn't great but it was not as bad as one might think. I persuaded Mum to pay for a schoolteacher to give me private lessons. Anyway, what I've told you is more or less common knowledge."

When they eventually arrived at the Norfolk, Joe and Isabel emerged from the car and admired the colonial façade of the hotel. They both glanced around, admiring the red tiled roof of the establishment, the two fluted columns gracing the entrance and the atmosphere of relaxed gentlemanly elegance, helped by the few trees along the short driveway. Isabel took photographs, while Joe attended to the checking in arrangements.

Joe laughed. "Never got within a bull's roar – isn't that your Aussie expression – of this place in my past."

They checked into a suite Joe had booked for three weeks.

Joe phoned Patrick as soon as they were ushered into the suite. "Patrick, Joe here. We're at the Norfolk as we told you."

"Okay. Koinange and I will come over after lunch, which will give you time to settle in. Apart from your two projects, we also have a proposal which we would like your opinion on and possibly you might be able to help us with it."

"Wow," said Koinange in English as he looked around their suite. "Bit of a change from Kibera," he laughed as he and Patrick were shown around. Joe hugged them both. They were dressed in good casual clothes.

"My wife Isabel," said Joe.

They were about to formally shake her by the hand but Isabel said, "Hugs all round for friends of Joe. I've heard so much about you and how you all grew up in Kibera together."

She hugged both visitors, which broke the ice.

"You both look great," said Joe. "I'm happy to be here again after all these years. Now, down to business," said Joe, "tea, coffee anyone?" He phoned room service and while they were waiting, he asked both Patrick and Koinange if they were married.

"Married?" Koinange laughed. "No, that's miles away. We both have ambitions which marriage would interfere with."

"Marriage has helped my ambitions greatly, apart from getting me out of a whole heap of trouble," said Joe, smiling and looking at Isabel.

Soon a trolley with coffee and biscuits arrived, which Joe served.

"Maybe we could deal with the land issue first, I need to leave in about an hour. I will be back of course," offered Patrick. "Lentella has found a few of the people who shared your place in Ol'Kalou, we've found twenty people who still have their title deeds, but you say there were more than one hundred people owning plots in the area who were also kicked off. Seems like we have a way to go."

Joe nodded.

Patrick left, "I will be back as soon as I can," he said.

"About the girls' school project," said Koinange, looking at Isabel. "It's all set really and ready to go. You'll have to sign the trust deed and arrange finance, which we can do at the lawyer's office; the education department is enthusiastic. As I have told you, they will provide premises and, Isabel, I have lined up people you can interview for the headmistress position."

"Lovely. If you could just set up appointment times, I'll fit in. We are going to the Mara for a few days, I'll give you the dates."

"Okay," said Joe, "what about your own proposal?"

"We'll have to wait for Patrick to come back."

"Okay. How is your mother, by the way? She helped Mum at the Lucy Kibaki hospital when she got beaten up."

"Yes. She is still there, she worked hard, got all the nursing qualifications and is now matron at the hospital. We are all very proud of her."

Joe smiled. "That's wonderful. Remember me to her when you next see her." Koinange laughed. "She remembers you very well and often talks about you."

"I would also like to visit my mother's grave, if that's possible," Joe said to Koinange, during a brief interlude in the conversation.

"Of course."

"How is Karanja, by the way? I was thinking about going to see him."

"There is one other thing that we need to mention," said Koinange not looking at Joe and without answering the question. "Odongo Boniface, you remember him?"

"Otieno's half-brother. Yes. What about him?"

"He's running around saying you had something to do with the death of General Kariuki. Something he got from Karanja apparently. Karanja is not quite himself – dementia, I think."

"I see," said Joe calmly. He had flashes of the nightmare of the general's demise, which he tried to put out of his mind. He noticed Isabel tense up. "I was in Juba when the general was killed. Is anyone taking any notice of this nonsense?"

"I don't know. Not officially anyway."

"Okay. I'll avoid Karanja."

"You can't see Karanja anyway. He's in hospital. No visitors."

"All right," said Joe. "I do have a contact with the head of security operations here. Maybe I'll take it up with him."

Koinange looked surprised. "Head of security? Wow!" Patrick bustled in. "What's up?" he asked.

"I just told Joe about the rumours Odongo is spreading around."

"Don't worry," said Joe. "I'll deal with it."

"Head of security. He knows the head of security," Koinange threw up his hands.

There was a short silence.

"You wanted to talk about another project?" said Joe.

"Yes," answered Patrick. "I have told you that after Otieno died, his successor Odongo sold the business, Nyanza Transport, to another Luo who has completely wrecked it, not knowing much about transport."

Joe raised his eyebrows.

"We think it would be a good opportunity to buy Nyanza Transport. I'm told the man wants out at almost any price."

'Dependant on the value of the business,' Joe thought rapidly, 'Anderson-Wacheera could certainly help. Also, if we get into the detail, we will find out how many more people were smuggled out and how much money they made and how the profits were divvied up. Might help with my contact in the security services here.'

"Okay," he said aloud, "I think we can help, firstly with assessing the value of the business and then what needs to be done to fix it up, if anything. Can you get all the accounts for a preliminary look?"

"We could go over there now, that is where I was earlier. I'll call the owner, whose name is Nyamita."

Joe asked the driver of the car provided by the hotel to stop outside Nyanza Transport. "I'll call when we need you to come back," he said to the driver.

The Nyanza Transport sign on the outside of the depot looked as if it was about to fall down and, when they entered the depot, what he remembered as a well-ordered outfit had been replaced by a dirty yard with trucks parked haphazardly. Two vehicles were being attended by mechanics in the yard and not in the workshop. He looked at Isabel and raised his eyebrows.

Joe, Isabel, Patrick and Koinange walked through the depot and climbed up the short flight of steps to what Joe remembered as Otieno's office. The office reflected the chaos in the yard and behind the desk sat a very large, fat Luo, dressed in overalls. He had his top front teeth missing as is the Luo tradition. He stood up behind a mound of paper.

"Mr Nyamita, this is the man I mentioned, Joe Wacheera and his wife Isabel Wacheera. You know my colleague Koinange of course."

Nyamita shook hands with everyone.

They found a few battered-looking chairs and sat down. "So, you want to buy this business?" offered Nyamita.

"Maybe," said Patrick. "Joe will want information before we do anything, of course."

"What information?" asked Nyamita.

"Well, to start with all the accounts for the business for the last ten years. We will also need to see all the business bank accounts for the same period, and we'll ask a firm of accountants to look at everything and report back," said Joe.

"Is all that necessary?" asked Nyamita, "We just want a quick sale; what we paid for the business."

"I'm sure you do. How much did you pay for the business?" asked Patrick.
"Two million US."

"Look, for that much we are certainly going to have to examine your accounts. If that's not on, then we will take our leave and wish you the best of luck." Joe stood up and he and Isabel left the office and walked down the stairs.

They waited in the yard, and five minutes later Patrick and Koinange appeared. "Well that certainly scared Nyamita almost to death," said Patrick.

"One can see the place is a complete shambles," said Joe. "Certainly, the difference between now and the way that Otieno ran it is like chalk and cheese. You need to get some accountants in here as soon as you can. My guess is that he's haemorrhaging cash like there is no tomorrow. You should aim to get the business for a token, say one US dollar provided you take on all the debt, so that's where we should focus."

They phoned for the car.

"We could just swing by the cemetery," suggested Patrick, "you said you wanted to visit your mothers' grave."

Joe nodded. He bought a small bunch of flowers from a woman at the cemetery gate.

Patrick escorted Joe and Isabel to the grave and then went and waited in the car.

At first Joe just stood there staring at the simple gravestone, which just said: 'Ellen Wacheera.' It had her birth and death dates underneath.

After a few minutes with Isabel holding his arm, he placed the flowers on her grave. A tear slipped out. "She had an awful life," muttered Joe. "She was completely unselfish. I wish I could have done more for her."

They stood there a while longer, with Joe thinking about the life they had shared.

Isabel said nothing.

"Okay, let's go," said Joe eventually.

They walked back to the car in silence and returned to the hotel.

"Do you have a firm of accountants who can look at the business for you?" asked Joe as they enjoyed tea and biscuits in the suite.

"Yes. Probably. Small firm though."

"He won't agree to show..." offered Koinange.

"Wanna bet?" said Joe. "He has no choice. You'll hear today or tomorrow. If you need any help finding someone to dredge through the numbers, please let me know."

Two days later, Nyamita phoned Patrick. "Okay send in your accountants," was all he said.

The only partner of the firm that Patrick and Koinange were using for their own business agreed to drop everything and do a detailed evaluation of Nyanza Transport.

"I will need a day at Nyanza to look for what Otieno did with the profit from the people smuggling business," Joe said to Patrick, "after we return from the Mara. I am also going to pay a visit to the fucking reverend. I'll let you know how he reacts."

"This afternoon I suggest we will go on a little trip to Kibera," Joe said the next day to Isabel after a quick lunch in the coffee shop at the Norfolk. "A trip down memory lane, if you like, and I think we should also pay Reverend Mweleli a visit."

"I'm looking forward to meeting the famous reverend at last, having heard so much about him," laughed Isabel.

Joe had to use all his powers of persuasion for the hotel to allow the car and driver to take them to Kibera. "We would strongly advise you not to go anywhere near that suburb," the receptionist told him, "it's not safe, especially dressed as you are." Joe was dressed in a tailored suit and tie and Isabel was dressed demurely in a smart pantsuit with a beige top.

Against his better judgement, Joe eventually said to the receptionist. "I actually grew up there. We are going to see Reverend Timothy Mweleli, who runs a church there."

Despite Joe's warnings, Isabel was appalled by the condition of the suburb, the rough unmade roads, the rubbish strewn about and the stench of the usual pall of smoke, not to mention the array of poorly-built shacks, some constructed with concrete blocks, others made from corrugated iron and bits of wood and cardboard. She took several photographs.

Joe pointed out the communal toilet and the water taps each serving perhaps fifty or so households. They soon came across The Unity Wesleyan Church of God. The building was in pristine condition and the sign had recently been repainted. Isabel took a photo.

"I see the pastor, as he describes himself now, is indeed still Reverend Timothy Mweleli. We'll come back to him later. I need to show you where Mum and I lived," said Joe. Joe directed the driver the short distance to where he and his mother had lived. He got out of the car and just stood there and stared for a few minutes.

The little cottage was just as he remembered it, although it looked much dirtier and more smoke-stained than before. He tried to keep his emotions in check.

Isabel also emerged from the car and put her arm through Joe's in support. "Is that the place?" she asked.

He nodded. Within a minute, a moderately well-dressed man emerged; he glanced briefly at Joe and hurried off.

Within a further few minutes, a young woman came out of the cottage and threw a bucket of slops into the street. She smiled at Joe. "Looking for a good time?" she said in Kikuyu.

"Not today," he replied. He then quickly explained who he was and that he had lived there with his mother. He asked about Wanjiru.

The young woman shook her head.

"Do you still pay rent to the reverend?" he asked.

"Yes. Ten thousand shillings a month."

Joe nodded. "My mother charged one thousand shillings for each customer."

"Two thousand, now." She paused. "You must be Joe," she said after a few moments' hesitation, looking at him curiously. "People still talk about you, like you burnt Mutua's car or something."

"Is Mutua still there?" he asked, without responding directly to the implied question.

The woman nodded.

Joe gave her one hundred US dollars. She looked at him in amazement.

"I'm going to see the reverend now," he said. There was no response. "Can we quickly look inside?" he asked.

The woman opened the door to the cottage and Joe and Isabel stepped in. Nothing much had changed, although the place had been recently repainted, and it was all very clean and tidy. The old paraffin stove was just as Joe remembered it, and the old bed in what had been his and Ellen's room was as before. The mattress had been replaced.

Isabel gasped as they looked around. "Is this...?"

Joe looked around with very mixed emotions. On the one hand, he was proud of how far he had come since he and his mother lived there. There was also a slight feeling of resentment against the forces that had put him in such a position. 'If I hadn't been forced to come here, maybe I would still be tending a seven-acre plot in Ol'Kalou with my few cows and goats and things,' he thought. Joe nodded at Isabel "For five years or so..."

Isabel clutched his arm even tighter. "Let's go. I can't bear it," she said.

They walked outside, to be surrounded by a small group of children mostly dressed in rags.

Joe had come prepared; he gave each of the children ten shillings, before he and Isabel hopped into the waiting car. Joe directed the driver to Reverend Mweleli's mansion, situated next to the nearby church. Joe indicated that the car should be parked right outside the front door of the mansion. "I suggest you stay right here," he said to the bewildered-looking driver. Joe knocked on the front door of the mansion, which was opened by the reverend's wife.

"Yes," she said uncertainly, peering at Joe.

"We have come to see Reverend Mweleli. You may recognise me; I used to work here," he said in English.

The woman blinked, shaking her head. She led them along to what to Joe was the very familiar study. She opened the door, saying rudely in Kamba, which Joe still understood, "There is a man here, together with his *M'zungu* wife. He says he worked here."

The reverend looked a little older but was otherwise much as Joe remembered him, although he hadn't seen him for at least fifteen years. He was peering over the top of his horn-rimmed glasses.

"Do I know you?" he asked as Isabel, followed by Joe, stepped into the study. Joe shut the door. "Well, I hope so," said Joe.

The reverend looked more closely at Joe and then the blood seemed to drain from his face. "Oh my god, Joe Wacheera. What do you want?"

Joe pulled a chair out for Isabel and sat down himself. "Reverend, firstly, I would like to introduce you to my wife, Isabel."

Isabel stood up and held out her hand, which was reluctantly taken. "You just... disappeared," offered the reverend.

"I live in England now," said Joe.

"Why are you here?"

"I have a couple of projects, here in Kenya, that I think will benefit the country. As well as some issues that I think need to be cleared up."

There was an involuntary shudder from the reverend. "What projects?"

Joe ignored the question. "I understand from Patrick that he is still paying you for protection for the *bhang* business."

There was no response from the reverend, who just glowered at Joe.

"My mother, Ellen, whom you knew very well, died of AIDS a few years back."

"Hardly surprising, in view of her lifestyle," was his insensitive reply.

"Set up, encouraged and exploited by you. I have just paid a short visit to the house she and I shared. Ten thousand shillings a month, now?"

"I think you should go, or I will call the police."

"I wouldn't do that, Reverend. I think they would be most interested in some other information I have regarding your activities."

"Like what?"

"Well, we have already established drug dealing and prostitution. We could add money laundering and murder to that as well, if you like?" Joe said nothing about the people smuggling business. 'I need to make sure of all my facts, before I say anything,' he thought to himself.

"What do you want from me?" asked the reverend quietly.

"I mentioned I had some projects. One of which is the education of girls and women."

"Waste of time. As I said, what do you want from me?"

"A donation to the project would be useful, say one hundred thousand shillings a month?"

"That's ridiculous! I can't afford that."

"Fifteen or twenty women all paying you ten thousand shillings a month – I would say you can very easily afford it." Joe waited.

The reverend squirmed under his scrutiny. "Fifty thousand," whispered the reverend.

Joe shook his head.

They eventually settled on seventy-five thousand.

"Reverend, the whole project is being handled by a well-known lawyer in town, Mr Lentella; you may know of him, if you don't know him personally. He'll be in touch with you."

The reverend shuddered visibly. Joe had come to understand that Lentella was well known for his honesty and straightforward dealings.

Joe got up to go and shook the reverend by the hand. "Nice to see you looking so well, Reverend." Joe then looked him in the eye. "Please understand, Reverend, you will regret it bitterly, if you try anything on."

On the way back to their hotel, Isabel held Joe's hand, saying nothing for a few minutes. Eventually she said, "I don't know how you managed that. He's clearly terrified of you."

"From the very first minute I saw him, on the porch of that wretched church, aged only ten, I totally distrusted him. Nothing has changed. Don't worry, I've briefed Lentella; he knows all about the reverend. I will just have to give him the details of our latest conversation. Now for the Mara," said Joe when they were back in the hotel, "I've confirmed the bookings. We leave in the morning as you know."

The one-hour flight from Wilson, a small airport close to the city, took Joe and Isabel to a part of the Maasai Mara game park run by what is known as The Conservancy, separate from the area of the park run by the Kenya Wildlife Service.

"This part of the Mara is supposedly less crowded than the other side and there are fewer facilities. The roads are also much better maintained," Joe announced.

"Who are The Conservancy?" asked Isabel.

"Private investors, whose only interest is game preservation. My understanding is that they get no financial reward from their investment."

They stayed in the Serena, a luxurious hotel tastefully situated among large boulders on a hillock, in the reserve.

Isabel revelled in the early morning and late evening game drives in a four-wheel drive, with one of the guides provided by the hotel. She took dozens of photographs on a new digital camera, equipped with a telephoto lens.

Joe was less enthusiastic, although it was always Joe who spotted any visible game first. "Something to do with my historical DNA?" suggested Joe. "Our people spent thousands of years living among these animals."

Isabel was particularly entranced watching a lion kill, where lions had recently killed a zebra. There were a dozen lions, including four cubs, feasting hungrily.

There were several hyaenas and two jackals hovering and a large group of vultures.

Between them, the guide and Joe explained what was happening. "Lions only kill when they need to eat," Joe explained.

"Just watch," said the guide, "the hyaenas will grab a mouthful as and when they can and then race off. They have to be careful of the lions, who would not hesitate to kill them if they get too close."

"Just look at the vultures," said Joe. "The smaller ones in the front are Cape vultures, I think," he glanced at the guide for confirmation, as one of the lions made a half-hearted attempt to chase the nearest vulture away. "They seem to control any vulture access. Then there are other vulture types. Those with big jowls are Maribou storks, who will wait patiently for their turn."

"In the end nothing is wasted," explained the guide. "Once the lions have finished, the hyaenas and jackals will move in as well as the vultures, and they then literally clean the place up. And then the ants come. Within a week there will be nothing left but the skull and a few bones."

"You don't seem very enthusiastic about this place," said Isabel to Joe once they had returned to the Serena.

"I can see the importance of conserving the game, both from an ethical and commercial point of view, but the whole business seems to me to further emphasise the gap between the first and third world." Joe waved his arms around. "Most of the visitors here are from wealthy first world countries; they know nothing of this country and indeed have no real interest; all they want is to be able to tell their friends that they have been 'on safari', and of course post dozens of photographs on Facebook and other social media sites. It's all a bit contrived." He shrugged.

"For me it's a great privilege to be here and see all these animals in the wild," was Isabel's response. "At last, I have seen most of the big five, all except rhinos, and I have also seen lots of antelope plus jackals and hyaenas and of course, vultures," she laughed.

They happily retuned to the Norfolk.

Patrick was there to meet them after Joe had phoned him from the airport.

"How is it going with Nyanza?" asked Joe.

Patrick shrugged. "We're getting there. We've identified all the bank accounts and our man is wading through the financial figures. Everything was very orderly when Otieno ran the business, but since then it's a shambles. We'll have something in a few weeks I expect. You can spend as much time as you like there looking at the people smuggling business, just let me know when."

"Tomorrow," said Joe.

"I have planned a couple of days with Koinange, from tomorrow, to interview head mistresses for the girls' school, so that fits in well," said Isabel.

"Where are you going to do that?" asked Joe.

"The Department of Education has offered us facilities, which is perfect from our point of view."

Joe took a taxi to Nyanza transport. He took his laptop. He found his way up the steps to Nyamita's office where he found a young Kikuyu who introduced himself as Gichuru. The office had been tidied up. Nyamita was hovering uncomfortably.

"Patrick has explained what I am looking for," Joe said to Gichuru, in Kikuyu, which he didn't think Nyamita understood. "I need the details of what they earned from the people smuggling racket, about fifteen years ago."

"Patrick briefed me on the period you were looking at. There are cash books and ledgers going back that far, all neatly written up. Hope you can find what you are looking for," said Gichuru, turning to a metal cupboard, which Joe could see contained the promised accounting books.

Joe sat at a newly cleared table and spent a frustrating day wading through the cash books. He was surprised to find no trace of the money that he knew Kigoro, amongst others, had paid to Otieno. He then tried to find the London accounts, which he had set up for Otieno.

Suddenly there it all was, separately, in a small book hidden at the very back of the cupboard. All of it. The several trips that Joe and his crew had made, as well as a number of trips after Joe had taken the journey to Libya and then all the detail of what Joe had banked for Otieno from Tunisia. It even had the detail of what had been paid to the reverend, to Kigoro and Sir Oswald. Joe noted that nothing had been paid to General Kariuki or his family. Nothing also appeared to have been paid to any of the participants in the people smuggling business from the London account.

"Just check this account please," he said to Gichuru still in Kikuyu. Nyamita was nowhere to be seen.

"That's new, it not in my list of bank accounts," said Gichuru. "The access codes are listed here," said Joe. "Let's just check."

They found the account easily enough and there it all was. All the amounts Joe had transferred into the account from Tunisia were there, and there were payments, all in unnecessary detail, to the reverend, Kigoro, Sir Oswald, and the balance had been paid to Odongo in Nairobi. Again, nothing was paid to General Kariuki or his successors. There was a small balance on the account. Joe thanked his lucky stars that Otieno had maintained such detailed records.

"The balance is just to keep the account open," said Joe.

"What is this?" asked Gichuru.

"People smuggling," said Joe. "I will certainly tell Patrick. You don't have to worry about it, it's beyond your ten-year time horizon. I'm going to take this book and a printout of the London bank account," said Joe. "The book is ancient history and has nothing to do with the current business, as is the London account. How's the rest of the investigation going?"

"The business is barely surviving. They seem to have borrowed more and more money," answered Gichuru. "It will be some weeks before I have completed the exercise Patrick has asked me to do."

Joe nodded and left. Using hotel facilities Joe carefully made two copies of every piece of information he had unearthed at Nyanza Transport. Joe then phoned Patrick and told him what he had found. "I'm going to give copies of it to the security services."

He then phoned the number of the security service given to him by Alice Osborne.

The phone was quickly answered. "Code?" said a guttural voice.

Joe gave them the code again given to him by Alice Osborne. "I will just transfer you."

"Musumbi," answered a voice. Joe knew that was a Kamba name, possibly the head of security.

"I have an introduction from MI5," he said. "71362AD," he said in English "Okay. You must be Joe Wacheera."

"Yes."

"We need to meet."

"Yes. I have some information that I think you will find useful."

"Would tomorrow morning be convenient?"

"Certainly."

"A car will pick you up at 9am."

Joe was given the registration number of the vehicle that would pick him up. "Where are you staying?"

"The Norfolk."

Joe was flabbergasted when, the next day, the car took him to the gates of what had been General Kariuki's mansion. A guard questioned the driver briefly and the car was let through. The gardens were as pristine as they ever were. Joe remained outwardly calm. "Is this some sort of set-up?" he wondered. Before Joe could move, the car door was opened by a guard standing to attention next to the front door. Carrying his briefcase, Joe was ushered through the still familiar door, where he was greeted by yet another guard and escorted into what had been the general's study. Ghastly visions of the general's demise briefly flashed through his mind; thoughts that were quickly banished.

The study had been completely refurnished. There was a stout shortish man, sitting behind a modern-looking steel and glass desk, whom Joe identified as a Wakamba. He was dressed in a dark, well-cut modern suit and tie. The man leant over the desk and shook Joe's hand. "Musumbi," he said. "Thank you for coming."

Another man, also dressed in a smart suit with a tie, entered the room. 'Kikuyu,' thought Joe. He was not introduced.

"Can I offer you tea or coffee?" Musumbi asked as a pretty young woman appeared in the doorway.

"Coffee will be fine, thank you, and thank you for sending the car."

"We took this place over after the death of General Kariuki. It's very private and secluded."

Joe just nodded.

"As I told you my MI5 contact is 71362AD, who advised me you were coming and that you may have information for me."

"I hope what I have will be useful, MI5 certainly found it useful. It concerns people smuggling."

"Yes. The European Union has a presence here in the form of Frontex, whose job it is to help organisations like ours to stop people smugglers at source. It is very well funded, but any help we can provide will be mutually beneficial."

Joe then proceeded to tell Mr Musumbi the details of his experiences with shipping people from Kenya to Juba and then on to the Libyan coast. He provided much the same information he had given to MI5.

The unintroduced man was furiously busy taking notes.

"I assume that beyond Juba you have very limited interest?" Joe questioned.
"Yes. How long ago was all this?"

"About fifteen years, but I have evidence that it continued long after that. I have dates and the amounts of money that changed hands, and also who profited from the activity. I was just a *kitchen toto* doing casual work for Reverend Mweleli in Kibera," Joe continued, "and on several occasions I served tea to the group that set up this people smuggling programme. The people involved were Reverend Mweleli, Mr Kamau Kigoro from Ol'Kalou, Sir Oswald Higginbotham from England, Mr Otieno Boniface who ran the whole show with his Nyanza Transport providing the trucks, and General Kariuki. Neither General Kariuki nor his successors profited from the venture." Joe then went through every detail of what he had found at Nyanza Transport and handed over the copies he had made of all the information to Mr Musumbi.

"How did you gain access to Nyanza Transport?" asked Musumbi.

"Colleagues of mine are in the process of doing due diligence on the operation with a view to buying it. They asked me for assistance and this is what I found. I'm sure the information will be useful as far as you are concerned."

Musumbi looked at Joe with a half-smile on his face. "Here we go," thought Joe.

"Is that everything?" asked Musumbi.

Joe shrugged. "Yes, unless you have any questions."

"We may have questions later. There is one other issue though. I am surprised that you have not reacted or made any comment about this place," Musumbi waved his arms around as if to indicate the mansion.

Joe said nothing and offered a questioning glance at Musumbi.

"We know that you worked for the general over a period of years, in fact until a few days before he died. Don't you have anything to say about that? What work did you do?"

"I actually did very little work," said Joe calmly. "Here and there in the garden and kitchen, that's all. The general actually took pity on me having seen me at Reverend Mweleli's house, when, as I told you I served tea and cake to the reverend's guests. He arranged for someone to come and teach me the basics of finance and accounting, which has been personally very useful to me."

"The general had a reputation of sexually abusing young boys. Did he abuse you?"

"No," Joe said calmly.

Musumbi looked at Joe in disbelief before he said, "We have a witness, two witnesses actually, who have told us you were involved in the death of General Kariuki."

Joe forced himself to remain calm. "Can you give me a date on which the general died, and how he died?"

"He was stabbed." Musumbi also gave Joe a date on which the general was supposed to have been killed. Joe realised the date Musumbi gave was a few days before the actual date of the general's death.

Joe wrote down the date Musumbi mentioned, then looked at Musumbi. Outwardly he remained calm, although he was churning inside. "I only learnt of the death of the general when I was in Juba, on one of my trips there; about ten days after the date you mention. Could you just check that you have the correct date, Mr Musumbi, as I will?"

"Do you know Odongo Boniface and Karanja Githaiga?"

"Odongo Boniface is the half-brother of Otieno Boniface, he inherited Nyanza Transport from Otieno when the latter died, a few years ago. Karanja was my mother's husband. She died three years ago now."

"They are both saying the same thing."

Joe shrugged. "Karanja is suffering from dementia. Respectfully, sir, Mr Odongo Boniface is and always has been a liar and a charlatan. I had some experience of him during one of my trips to Juba. I am told that, having sold Nyanza Transport, he is now drunk much of the time."

"We may have to take this further," said Musumbi.

"I'm here for a few weeks. I have engaged a Mr Lentella on some other matters. So, if you wish to take this issue further, could you please deal directly with him?"

"What other matters?"

"I am keen to establish a school for girls here. My wife is talking to the Department of Education. I am also trying to see if I can get the land back that Mr Kigoro illegally and unjustly stole from us. There were also about one hundred others suffering the same fate. We have so far identified about twenty of those who were dispossessed all those years ago. I am certain that we will find most of the others; it just takes time."

"Do you have your passport with you?"

"No. I left it in the hotel."

"We'll be in touch. The car can now take you back to the hotel."

Once back in the hotel suite Joe phoned Patrick. Isabel was still out. "I have just had a meeting with people from the security service here." He explained he had given the security people copies of the information he had found at Nyanza Transport. "I suggest that you withdraw Gichuru from Nyanza transport for a few days. I am almost certain that the security people will raid the place today or tomorrow. Keep all the info you have. The raid will obviously spook Nyamita, which may make it easier for you to take the business over, if you still want to."

Joe also phoned Lentella and briefly explained the situation.

"I'm out at present. On my way back I'll come to the hotel in about thirty minutes."

In the suite Joe explained to Lentella what had occurred. "I am sure that the date Musumbi mentioned is earlier than the reported date of the general's death. Can we check that?"

Lentella made one call.

Joe retrieved both his original Kenyan passport and his new British passport from the security safe. He rifled through the Kenyan passport. "This seems to be the date that I went through the border post to South Sudan," he said to Lentella, showing him the passport. "What date do you have for the death of the general?"

They compared notes.

"From this information it looks like the general died a few days after you entered South Sudan."

"Yes."

"Why would Musumbi have given me an earlier date?" Lentella shrugged.

"Maybe we should just go home..."

"No. It makes you look guilty. Just give me the passport. I know some of the security people. I ought to be able to sort this out."

"I will give you a copy of the appropriate page, if that's okay."

Lentella nodded. "I'll be in touch," he said as he left.

Isabel, flushed and excited, returned to the suite. "I have now seen the premises for the school and interviewed several potential headmistresses. The premises are good and the people committed and wonderful. So, we're on track. How did your day go? We've agreed to call the school 'The Ellen Wacheera School for Girls.'"

Joe looked at Isabel and then got up and hugged her. "Wonderful," he said as he wiped away a tear. "She deserves that." Joe then explained what had transpired with Musumbi.

"What do you want to do?" asked an anxious Isabel.

"We'll see it through. The temptation is to bugger off home, but that means that our projects here will come to nothing. It would also mean that we probably wouldn't be able to return here again. On the other hand, they don't have a case because of the dates. Also relying on a man with dementia and a drunk with a bad reputation is not a proposition. Maybe Lentella will persuade them to drop it all. In the meanwhile, I will see what I can do to help Patrick and Koinange."

As he had promised, Joe copied all the information he had found at Nyanza Transport and had it couriered to Geoffrey Thomasoff. Included in the package was a note that asked Thomasoff to share the information with Alice Osborne at MI5.

Patrick phoned. "Two things, I'm really sorry to have to tell you but Karanja died yesterday. The funeral is tomorrow. I will come and fetch you and Isabel at ten tomorrow. Secondly, you were right, the security people have raided Nyanza Transport, they are still there and, as you thought, Nyamita is completely spooked."

Joe did not react to any of the news. He knew that the death of Karanja meant that any case against him personally would be considerably weakened.

The funeral took most of the day. It started off at Karanja's home in Westlands attended by hundreds of people. There were dozens of speeches, including one from Joe, who told the throng how Karanja had rescued his mother and himself, from the hellhole of Kibera. In between speeches there were dozens of mainly women wailing in grief. The wooden casket was then taken on the back of a pick-up truck in a very slow-moving procession to the local cemetery, where with more ceremony and demonstrations of grief, it was finally interred.

Joe and Isabel stayed to the end. Joe stood at the graveside, holding Isabel's hand, remembering Karanja and how it was the *bhang* operation that had put him on the road to where he was now. He did not shed a tear but bowed his head. Isabel squeezed his hand.

Five days later Lentella phoned. "Musumbi wants to see you again. I have arranged to take you there tomorrow."

"Would it be a good idea if Isabel came along too?"

"No," said Lentella. "It's likely to be a bit of an interrogation; she won't be allowed in the room with you."

The next day Lentella drove Joe to what Joe still thought of as General Kariuki's residence. They were ushered into what was now Musumbi's office. The same unintroduced young Kikuyu man was also there taking notes.

"I would like to review the discussion we had a few days ago about the death of General Kariuki," Musumbi started off. He knew Lentella, so there was no need for introductions or any kind of greeting. No tea or any other refreshment was offered. "As I have said we have two witnesses who attest that you were present in Kenya the day the general was murdered."

"One of the apparent witnesses," said Lentella, "Mr Karanja, has just died. His funeral was held yesterday. Also, we have irrefutable evidence that Mr Wacheera was in Juba on the day the general died. The date you gave to Mr Wacheera the other day was incorrect. I have the correct date here." Lentella had copies of the Standard, which he showed to Musumbi. "And here is Mr Wacheera's original passport showing his entry into South Sudan some days before the official date of the general's demise." He handed the passport to Musumbi, open at the appropriate page.

"This is not really proof of anything," said an irritated Musumbi. "That border is like a sieve. Like most land borders in Africa, it is easy to walk round it."

"It seems that Mr Wacheera did not walk round it. The passport was stamped."

"Border guards can easily be bribed to show any date you want."

"Mr Wacheera was only sixteen at the time. It seems unlikely that he would have known how to bribe border officials. You must remember that he was just an assistant; others were in charge."

Musumbi then changed tack. "We have evidence that General Kariuki had large sums of money hidden away in a London bank account."

Nether Joe nor Lentella responded.

"Well, don't you have anything to say about that?" He looked at Joe.

'Don't gabble,' Joe said to himself. "No, I had no knowledge of the general's personal business."

"You had the run of the house."

"No, the general kindly showed me round the house once, otherwise I was confined to the ground floor area."

"I don't believe that." Joe shrugged.

"The general's London account was raided in the weeks before his death," Musumbi continued. "It seems that the perpetrator of this crime used some sort of encryption process, which makes it difficult to identify the destination of the stolen funds."

Joe shrugged.

"Don't you have anything to say about that?"

"No."

"You told me in our previous meeting that you had overheard the general amongst others setting up a people smuggling racket."

"Yes. I have given you all the details of that."

"Was anything else discussed in those meetings?"

"Once there was a discussion about transferring money to *Ulaya,* at the time I didn't even know where *Ulaya* was."

"Did you ever transfer money to another country?"

"No. I never had enough money to transfer. My mother and I lived from hand to mouth."

There was silence for a few minutes.

"Did Mr Karanja submit his allegations in writing?" Lentella asked. Musumbi shook his head.

"Did Mr Karanja give the police any formal statement regarding his allegations?"

Musumbi shook his head. "Mr Odongo Boniface is saying the same thing. He also says that he had to rescue you on one of your trips to Juba. He says that he actually drove your truck to Juba," Musumbi changed tack once again.

Joe shrugged. "Odongo is a liar and a cheat. I went on one trip with him. He went the wrong way. Otieno had to send a vehicle to rescue him. We waited on the South Sudan side of the border with an empty truck, which had already been unloaded at the refugee camp. When he eventually drove his truck through the border, Otieno instructed Odongo to return to Nairobi with the empty truck and I took Odongo's truck to the refugee camp. I doubt if Odongo has ever been anywhere near the refugee camp in Juba; if you have a chance, ask him to describe it."

"You say you were an assistant. It seems that you drove the truck to and from the refugee camp."

"I did some of the driving, yes, by that time I had a licence."

Lentella intervened. "Is any of this relevant? What dates are we talking about?" Musumbi gave Lentella the correct date of General Kariuki's death. "I suggest you check Odongo's passport for the dates he entered South Sudan. If he still has the passport, of course," said Lentella.

"He no longer has the passport," said Musumbi.

Joe hesitated. "For what it's worth, Mr Musumbi, while I was waiting at the border post, I picked up a copy of the Standard, dated a day earlier. The headline said something about the death of General Kariuki. I had already been in South Sudan for some days by then, since I had delivered my load to the refugee camp and returned to the border," Joe added.

There was another lengthy silence.

"On one of your earlier trips to Juba you went with a man named Mbiti," stated Musumbi.

"Yes. We arrived safely in Juba and then he disappeared. I haven't seen him since."

"Who drove the truck back to Nairobi?"

"I did. On instructions from Otieno."

"His passport was found on General Kariuki's body." Joe shrugged.

"You know nothing about that?"

"No. Why should I?"

"You deny that you had anything to do with that?"

"I don't understand the question."

"Did you plant Mr Mbiti's passport on General Kariuki's body?"

"No. That's a terrible suggestion."

Musumbi then left the room for ten minutes leaving Joe, Lentella and the young Kikuyu in the office. There was no conversation.

Musumbi returned. "I will keep your passport," he said to Joe.

"No," said Lentella. "Mr Wacheera is not under arrest and as far as we are concerned in view of the unfortunate tone of this conversation, it is a critical piece of evidence. You have permission to copy it of course."

"Don't you trust us?"

"Respectfully, Mr Musumbi, General Kariuki was murdered some fifteen years ago now and you seem to be clutching at straws. Also, if any of what you have said to us is said in open court, such as references to the general's possibly fraudulently garnered wealth, references to Kenya's porous borders and references to corrupt border officials, it will do more harm than good and it will not help to convict Mr

Wacheera of anything. Also relying on hearsay evidence and relying on the dubious evidence of a renowned charlatan and drunk, will just put the whole justice system into disrepute. Please return Mr Wacheera's passport to him, once you have made whatever copies you want," Lentella said in a quietly furious voice.

Musumbi handed the offending passport to the young Kikuyu. "Make two copies please."

There was no conversation during the next ten minutes, with Musumbi sorting papers on his desk.

The young Kikuyu returned. He handed the copies to Musumbi and the passport to Joe.

"When are you returning to England, Mr Wacheera?" asked Musumbi.

"I'm not sure yet. As I mentioned earlier, I still have some unfinished business. Mr Lentella will let you know when we propose to return home."

When he returned to the hotel, Joe explained to Isabel in detail, almost word for word, what had occurred.

"They don't have any kind of case," said Isabel. After a few moments thought, she added, "I suggest you phone Alice Osborne or maybe brief Thomasoff so he can deal with her."

Joe phoned Thomasoff. He spent over an hour giving him a full briefing.

"I'll see what I can do. I can't see they have a case and you have been a very useful to both the security services here in Britain and the same in Kenya. I should add they were very impressed with the info you sent on the people smuggling business – the stuff you gave to the local security people in Kenya – it was very clear and compelling. Just their style."

A week later Thomasoff phoned Joe. He and Isabel were still at the Norfolk.

"MI5 will ask Musumbi to drop any charges, but as always there is a bit of a sting in the tail."

"Like what?" asked Joe.

"They will want you to continue to act for them, as you have in Kenya. Incidentally they are going to investigate Sir Oswald, based on the info you have provided."

"I have a major business to run, don't they understand that?"

"I will make that point to them. From the conversation I understood that they would probably want you to help them with certain specific projects. I will tell them you will agree to help them but on a limited basis."

"Okay." They rang off.

"It seems like our friends at MI5 want to keep their hooks into me on an ongoing basis," said Joe, having explained the situation to Isabel.

"You could have worse friends, having them on side could be very helpful," said Isabel.

Patrick and Koinange came to see Joe and Isabel. They met at the coffee shop in the Norfolk.

"Even before Karanja died, we were in the process of selling the *bhang* operation to another dealer," Patrick announced. "He has now paid us out and we have transferred all our street dealers to him, plus the supply avenues, which thanks to Karanja are much better than what he had."

"What are you going to do about Nyanza Transport?" asked Joe

"The business is shot. It's not a proposition. We would like to buy the premises though. It's much better than what we have at present."

"Sounds right. Do you need any help from me?"

"The *bhang* money will pay for the property. We may take over some of the truck leases though, currently financed by Higginbotham's."

"Okay, if you need any help with that, please let me know."

"I'm trying to get N'guku to come back and run the maintenance for us."

"Good idea. He may want to get his British citizenship before he returns here." Patrick acknowledged the point.

They ordered more coffee.

"Where are we at with the school?" asked Isabel.

"Well, it's all set," said Koinange. "The headmistress we appointed is busy recruiting staff, and we will get our first group of pupils at the start of the academic year. As Isabel and I have agreed, initially we will just have thirty girls for the first year of secondary school and build from there, year by year. Lentella has been very helpful, by the way, he has everything under control and he has a very tight control on all the finances."

"We are going to recruit from all tribal groups and will have at least five girls on scholarships from poor families which cannot afford the fees," said Isabel, as much for Joe's benefit as anything,

"Yes. I will initially be involved, but with the transport business hotting up, I will have to limit that over time," Koinange added.

"The business of getting our land back is progressing," said Joe, after they had all finished their coffees, "and with everything else more or less under control we will probably head back home in a day or two."

"What has happened with all those allegations Karanja and Odongo were making?" asked Koinange.

"We're dealing with the security people on all that. I expect the matter will be dropped very shortly."

After Patrick and Koinange left, Joe phoned Lentella. "What gives with the half-baked allegations against me?" asked Joe.

"I'll call Musumbi."

Sometime later Lentella phoned Joe. "Musumbi is still hanging onto his allegations," said Lentella. "He wouldn't tell me whether he had heard from MI5, which probably means that he has heard from them and is wondering how to proceed."

"As you know we have wrapped up our business here, thanks, as much as anything, to your efforts. It would suit us to go home. What do you suggest we do?"

"Hang around for a day or two. I have a few more irons in the fire. As I said earlier don't leave just yet."

The delay gave Joe and Isabel a chance to entertain Patrick and Koinange to a slap-up meal, which all parties agreed should be held in the Norfolk's elegant dining room. It was very much a 'when we were' series of reminiscences, full of laughter.

"I enjoyed all that," Isabel said to Joe afterwards. "You are either very lucky or very smart. I think you could have fallen off the perch many times in the past. Maybe we can lead a safer life in future."

"Physically, I agree, but there will be some risks going forward. It's going to be exciting," said Joe laughing.

The next day Joe had a call from Lentella. "Are we all clear?" asked Joe.

"No, I'm afraid not. Musumbi is digging his toes in, he seems to be on some sort of ego trip. He does say that he has no objection to you going home, but he is going to continue to look for evidence against you. He acknowledges that currently he has insufficient evidence to charge you."

"Should we abandon our projects here?"

"I wouldn't advise that. Musumbi is under pressure on a number of fronts. He may lose his job."

"Okay. We'll head home and keep in touch."

On the flight home, Joe said to Isabel, "You know that 'sir' is being divorced by his wife?"

"So what?"

"I am not interested in the details, but Lady Higginbotham owns twenty-five per cent of Higginbotham's, in her own right."

"I see. Again, so what?"

"Well, I thought with your charm, we might be able to persuade her to sell her shareholding to Anderson-Wacheera."

"Jesus, Joe. What's the use of twenty-five per cent?"

"It means he won't be able to sell the whole business to anyone else; it reduces the value of his holding, because of that."

"I can see what you are doing, but that brings a whole lot of other issues into play. Isn't it too big for us, anyway?"

"Just a thought. He's also in trouble because of his involvement in the people smuggling business. Makes him vulnerable."

She looked at him. "I need a bit of black mamba… helps me get used to another of your crazy ideas."

He laughed. "That may have to wait until we get home."

Chapter 20: Higginbotham's

As the front door closed on their elegant mews house, and before they had unpacked, Joe picked Isabel up, carried her upstairs and gently laid her on the bed. He quickly undressed her and then himself. They made love.

Afterwards Isabel giggled. "I thought you'd forgotten."

"I never forget demands like that. That was wonderful as always."

"Joe, I actually have some news for you."

"What news?" he looked at her suspiciously, propped up on one elbow, admiring the beautiful naked body in front of him.

"I'm pregnant. Three months."

He looked at her and was silent for a moment, then he kissed her passionately; they made love again.

"That's wonderful, wonderful," he said afterwards. "If you had told me earlier, I would have gone a bit more gently with the Kenyan trip."

"I know, that's why I didn't tell you until now."

Joe shook his head and was silent for a moment. "Boy or girl?" he asked.

She laughed. "Too soon to tell. And just one other thing, this is a perfectly natural event. I am not going to be treated like some sort of invalid. I'm going to go on as we always have done, okay? We'll get a full-time live-in nanny. We'll have to make a few adjustments here at home to accommodate everything, but that's under control. I've already engaged an architect and the alterations won't cost that much."

"Checkmate," was all Joe could muster as a response.

"You're not nervous," said Isabel. "I expected you to be nervous."

"Why would I be nervous? At Ol'Kalou, and particularly in Kibera, babies were being popped out in a number of what you would consider very unsanitary conditions. Most of them, like me I suppose, came through it all quite easily and normally. No, I'm not nervous."

The next day Joe went to the office as usual.

Isabel spent the morning with her mother, at her parents' nearby flat, to tell her the news.

"You'll have to take a few months off," said Mary. "Is there anything I can do? I know a very good gynaecologist. You really need to look after yourself."

"No, Mum, we are not going to do any of that," was Isabel's response. "I have a perfectly adequate doctor and we are booked into a nearby hospital; I have arranged a nanny. I might ask Dad to supervise the few alterations we are doing at home." She joked. "If I can, I will probably arrange to have the little bugger during the lunch break."

"Having a baby is no laughing matter. Anyway, are you going to feed the baby yourself?"

"If I can."

"You must have some time off then."

"No."

"How are you going to manage at the office and visiting all those work sites?"

"Easily. If I don't make a fuss, then nobody else will."

Once all the excitement had died down regarding Isabel's pregnancy, Joe said to Isabel one evening over dinner, "I have done some homework on the Higginbotham issue. As you know the divorce is going to be rather messy, so I think Lady Higginbotham will want to put one over on 'sir', and her ownership of those shares gives her that opportunity. We need to move quickly. The best thing would be for you to approach her directly and see what gives. You may need to brief the people who helped with the acquisition of 'Watts'."

"Can we afford to buy Higginbotham's?"

"I think so. Here, I've done a bit of homework." Joe painstakingly went through all the details of the work he had done. "This is what I think the business is worth." He took Isabel through his detailed worksheet.

"Where did you get all this information?"

"Mostly the accounts he has registered with companies house, which is in the public domain."

"Hm – mostly. Hope we're not sailing too close to the wind, to coin a phrase."

"I do have some personal knowledge of the company as well."

"Sounds a bit dodgy."

"No. There is no evidence anywhere that I acquired information illegally." Isabel was silent.

"And this is how we would finance the acquisition," said Joe. Again, he went through a detailed analysis of the resources they would need for the acquisition, then how it would be financed. "Also, as I have suggested, if we are able to acquire Lady Higginbotham's twenty-five per cent, that will give us a bench- mark of what the business is worth."

"Very good," said Isabel. She was silent for a few minutes. "Before we do anything, shouldn't we get some advice? It's a very big step. Also, Sir Oswald may get into strife if MI5 take the trouble to follow-up on the information you gave them."

Joe agreed. So, he and Isabel, accompanied by Geoffrey Thomasoff, met with their advisors in their city offices. The advisors were led by a James McDermott, who owned his own business specialising in providing advice on acquisition strategy. Joe saw a tall, spare, ascetic-looking man in his mid-fifties, dressed in a well-cut dark suit, with a suitable tie. Joe explained the situation and took both McDermott and Thomasoff through the same analysis he had shared with Isabel.

"Are you sure you want to proceed with this," asked a very surprised Thomasoff. "I think the information you supplied to MI5 could result in Sir Oswald being prosecuted, which will have a devastating effect on Higginbotham's, it may even bankrupt the company."

"Lady Higginbotham owns twenty-five per cent of the company. If we could secure that shareholding it would put us in a very good position to take the company over," Joe responded.

"Is this the smartest thing you could do?" asked James McDermott. "You have plenty of other options. I would forget Higginbotham's in view of what Geoffrey has just told us."

"I have a bit of a history with the company. I know it well, from the bottom up so to speak. I know I could make the place hum. Too much depends on one man and his ego, namely Sir Oswald."

"Hm," grunted James. "Would you consider just getting an option on Lady Higginbotham's shares? If all goes well, you could exercise the option, which would indeed put you in a good position to acquire the business. If Sir Oswald is prosecuted, the business may be worthless. As you say, the company is wholly dependent on Sir Oswald."

Joe looked doubtful; he knew in his heart of hearts that he should accept the option route but taking over Higginbotham's had been one of his ambitions almost since he joined the company. He hesitated and looked at Isabel.

"Can we have five minutes?" she said to McDermott and Thomasoff. They nodded and left the room.

"Joe," she said quietly but resolutely, "I know how you feel about Higginbotham's, but the info you gave MI5 will probably destroy the business. This could be a real watershed moment in the history of Anderson-Wacheera. If we somehow acquired Higginbotham's, you might find yourself spending the next five years trying to rescue a dead dog, not to mention the damage it could do to Anderson-Wacheera. There are plenty of other exciting prospects out there. If we manage to acquire an option on Lady Higginbotham's shares, and if Higginbotham's survives, we could then go ahead with the take-over, if not," she shrugged, "we'll lose nothing. You are not thinking straight here."

Joe stood up, knowing that for once he was wrong about Higginbotham's. A personal vendetta did not make good business sense. "Just come here," he said. "I need a hug." They hugged each other for a good five minutes. "I allowed my ego to get in the way," said Joe. "You are right, sorry, we'll go the option route. I'll call the others." Joe put his head out of the door and saw his advisors in deep conversation. They looked up. Joe signalled for them to come back into the room.

McDermott and Thomasoff sat down, saying nothing. Both had a look as if to say, 'what gives?'

Joe looked at Isabel, who nodded. "We'll go the option route," said Joe, looking at them both, "nothing else makes sense. If you can get three years, that would be ideal."

"Might cost you something," said McDermott. "I'll talk to Lady Higginbotham's lawyers and see what we can come up with. I have an idea what you think the business is worth and we'll use that as a starting point."

Over a few months McDermott, with regular consultations with Joe and Isabel, persuaded Lady Higginbotham's lawyers to grant Anderson-Wacheera an option on the twenty-five point one per cent of Higginbotham's she owned.

"They want a premium of fifty thousand pounds," McDermott told Joe. "Make it twenty-five and I'll agree," said Joe.

A week later the deal was signed and Anderson-Wacheera held an option to purchase the shares in Higginbotham's owned by Lady Higginbotham, exercisable within three years, after which the option expired.

A week after the option deal with Lady Higginbotham was signed, sealed and delivered, Joseph Ronald Wacheera made his presence known to the world, with a very loud and persistent yell.

Two days later Isabel and the young Joe were at home under the care of Joe and Rachel Clark, the middle-aged housekeeper they had engaged.

Joe was ecstatic and couldn't do enough.

Within weeks, Isabel took Joe Junior into the office for a few hours each day; and within two months, he was with her all day. She occasionally took him to worksites, but if the visit had been planned beforehand, she normally left him at home with Rachel Clark. As she had said, Joe Junior became part of routine and, since Isabel made no fuss, nobody else did.

Chapter 21: More Higginbotham's

Shortly after the birth of Joe Junior, Joe had a call from James McDermott.

"Sir Oswald has cottoned on to the fact that you now have an option to purchase the shares Lady Higginbotham owns in his company," said McDermott.

"Okay, so what?" said Joe

"He wants to talk to you, he's incandescent, says it has ruined all his plans."

"What do you suggest I do?"

"Give him a call. He can't do much."

It took Joe three attempts calling Sir Oswald before the man took his call. "Joe Wacheera here, Sir Oswald. You asked me to call."

"Yes, you thieving little crook. You have just impoverished my wife, I'll take you to court." Sir Oswald sounded as if he was foaming at the mouth.

"What did you want to discuss, Sir Oswald? You asked me to phone you"

"I want to reverse this ridiculous transaction. It will do both my wife and me an enormous amount of damage."

"I presume you are talking about the option Anderson-Wacheera has over the shares Lady Higginbotham..." He didn't finish the sentence.

"What else would I want to talk to you about, you dirty little shit. This is not a courtesy call about the weather."

"It's too late to reverse the transaction, sir. I have a legal option to purchase the shares and we paid a premium for that option."

There was silence for what seemed like an eternity. Joe waited patiently. "I'll buy the option back from you," said Sir Oswald.

"What price would you be prepared to pay? And don't forget we paid a premium to acquire the option."

"Ah you shitty little crook, I can see that all you are after is a quick and dirty deal, so you can cash in on an easy profit."

"What price would you be prepared to pay?" Joe repeated.

There was a brief silence before Sir Oswald mentioned a figure that was about half of what Anderson-Wacheera would have to pay if they exercised the option.

"Well, sir, thank you. We'll consider the offer. Could you please put it in writing by e-mail please? Could you also put it in writing on a formal letterhead signed by you please? I have just sent you my e-mail address, as well as the address to which you can send me your formal offer."

"Too clever by half," said Sir Oswald. "You'll get your comeuppance very shortly."

The phone was slammed down.

Within thirty minutes the e-mail confirming Sir Oswald's offer arrived. "Got you by the balls," Joe muttered to himself.

"I had a call from James McDermott, asking me to call Sir Oswald," said Joe at dinner that evening. Joe junior was fast asleep in his cot.

"I suppose as one would expect you had a decent, civilised conversation with your favourite person?"

Joe laughed. "He was apoplectic." Joe repeated the conversation he had had with Sir Oswald word-for-word as far as he could remember it. Joe laughed. "We've got him by the balls, Isabel, thanks to you, as much as anyone. I got him to put an offer in writing, to buy back the option we have, which he stupidly did. I have both his offer on e-mail and on his private letterhead. His offer puts a price on his own shares, which is where I'll begin as far as he's concerned."

"What are you planning to do? I still think Higginbotham's is a bum steer."

"At the price he put on his shares it would be a bargain. Anyway, if he agrees there will be months of due diligence. We'll be able to pull out at any time."

Isabel looked at Joe, then got up and came over and kissed him. "I'm not keen but let's see what gives."

Joe, Isabel and Geoffrey Thomasoff again met with James McDermott.

"I'm surprised you still want to pursue this," said McDermott in his usual low- key manner.

Joe explained what had occurred in his call with Sir Oswald. "He's effectively put a very low price on the value of his company; it obviously hadn't entered his head that we might want to buy the whole thing."

Several days were spent refining their strategy to purchase the balance of the Higginbotham's shares.

During the time with their advisors Joe received an urgent call from Geoffrey Thomasoff. "I must take this," he said as he went out into a nearby passageway.

"MI5 are going to charge Sir Oswald with profiting from illegal people smuggling operations. Much of their case is based on the info you, Joe, have provided." Thomasoff told Joe. "I will talk to MI5. You may have to go easy on this acquisition. I'll speak to Alice Osborne and get back to you. Are you certain, in view of this development, that acquiring the rest of Higginbotham's is the best thing to do?"

"If he is prosecuted it will certainly have a devastating effect on the value of his business," offered McDermott, once he had been briefed.

A day later Geoffrey Thomasoff phoned again. "MI5 will hand all the information they have over to the police," said Thomasoff. "It is certainly expected that Sir Oswald will be prosecuted. Alice Osborne said she had no advice regarding your personal situation. To quote her, 'I have no advice or interest in Mr Wacheera's personal situation. We are going to apply the full force of the law to this situation and we believe that there is a significant chance Sir Oswald will be found guilty. Mr Wacheera is likely to be the major witness in this case. He has no choice.' So that is their position."

"Geoffrey, you can tell Alice Osborne that I will be happy to give evidence, but now that I'm an official agent of MI5, would it be possible to give my evidence in camera?"

"I'll ask. The judge in the case will have to decide, based on advice from the parties to the case."

"Okay. We'll continue on that basis."

At the next meeting with the advisors, in their offices, they all looked at Joe expectantly.

"In view of the situation with the likely prosecution of Sir Oswald, are you still prepared to continue to act for us?" asked Joe.

"Yes, certainly," said James McDermott. "How do you want to proceed?"

"Sir Oswald is not yet officially aware of the position he's in. I think the right strategy will be to approach them so that they know Anderson-Wacheera is a player. We can always suspend our discussions with them at any time."

The advisors were then asked to set up a meeting with Sir Oswald.

Joe, Isabel, Thomasoff, McDermott and a bevy of advisors were ushered into the large boardroom at Higginbotham's. Five minutes later Sir Oswald and another group of advisors entered the room and were about to be seated on the opposite side of the boardroom table. When Sir Oswald saw Isabel, he said, "A bloody woman? What the hell is this? Some sort of circus?"

Joe shrugged.

Sir Oswald was about the add to his remarks, but he then looked at Joe more closely. "Don't I know you?"

"I certainly hope so, Sir Oswald, I used to work here."

Looking at Joe even more closely, he said in astonishment, "The fucking messenger – you were a messenger here. Jesus Christ!"

Joe nodded, waiting for Sir Oswald to calm down. "And you want to buy my fucking business?"

"Yes, Sir Oswald, just the seventy-four-point nine per cent of the business we don't already have options over."

"It's not for sale. Not to you anyway."

"Okay. We'll leave you to it, Sir Oswald. Thank you for seeing us."

Joe, Isabel and the Anderson-Wacheera team quietly left the premises, under a silent glare from Sir Oswald. They returned to the offices of their advisors.

"That was a completely stupid and irrational reaction," said McDermott, after they had all sat down and had been served with cups of tea and coffee.

"How do you think we should proceed?" asked Isabel.

"I will contact the Higginbotham advisors, whom I know well. From the expressions on their faces, they were horrified at Sir Oswald's reaction," said McDermott.

The next morning there was a small article in the financial press suggesting there were rumours that 'the well-respected advisory firm of Higginbotham's' was up for sale. The article went on to detail how Sir Oswald had built the firm up from scratch, and it speculated that the break-up of his marriage might have precipitated the move.

The following day the same paper published a furious denial from Sir Oswald. Meanwhile, the rest of the press had picked up on the story.

Joe had a call from James McDermott. "Joe. Forgive me for asking this, but did you have anything to do with all the publicity now surrounding Higginbotham's?"

"Absolutely not," responded Joe, "there's enough going on without that. Anyway, it's hardly in our interests that there should be any public info, regarding the possible sale of Higginbotham's."

"No, of course not."

"I need to tell you that, subsequent to all that stuff about Higginbotham's' in the press yesterday," Joe said to McDermott, "I have been sent, anonymously, in the post, copies of a number of very compromising documents relating to Higginbotham's. If these documents ever see the light of day, it would put paid to any discussions we might have regarding the acquisition of the company and would possibly eliminate any other possible suitors."

"Could you let me have copies of the documents please?"

"Yes, I will personally bring them round to your offices, now, if that's convenient."

Joe was in McDermott's office in ten minutes. They went through the sheaf of documents.

"Do you have the envelope?"

"Yes. Postmarked Southampton." Joe waved it about. "Can I keep all this please?"

"Just make copies. This is all I have."

The copies were made and Joe returned his copies to the envelope. "James, what is your advice?"

"Hang tight. I will speak to the Higginbotham advisors and come back to you. Any progress on the prosecution of Sir Oswald?"

"That could still be a while down the track. All that stuff takes time."

"The business will be worth a lot less when that happens."

"Yes."

"Another party may be tempted to put in a bid for Higginbotham's, if we don't act."

"Hm. If someone buys it now and Sir Oswald is prosecuted, they will certainly find what they have purchased is a lemon," said Joe. "Investors will flood out... Might put paid to the deal altogether. Could create an opportunity for us, either to buy the rest of Higginbotham's cheaply or we could just recruit some of the Higginbotham's investors to come to us."

"Maybe we need another meeting with Sir Oswald? It is not in the interests of Anderson-Wacheera for any of this information to emerge into the public domain," said McDermott. "I'll call you."

A week later, Joe, Isabel, James McDermott together with Geoffrey Thomasoff, met with Sir Oswald at Higginbotham's offices in the city.

"It's the bloody messenger again," said Sir Oswald, "what is it this time? You have five minutes."

"Someone has sent me information, Sir Oswald, to which I thought I would draw to your attention. I don't think it's in the interests of either you or Anderson-Wacheera for this to go any further."

"Get on with it then, get on with it. As I said, you have five minutes."

Joe had a sheaf of documents; copies of what he had received, which he started to hand over one by one. "You had a windfall from the takeover of a company called Pacific Placements. There is evidence that you had insider information relating to this takeover," Joe started off.

Sir Oswald looked stunned for a moment. "Nonsense. Our superior research had identified this prospect and we benefitted from that."

Joe handed over an internal Higginbotham document, signed by Sir Oswald, confirming what Joe had just said.

"You obviously stole this..."

"I've told you, this information was sent anonymously to me. You will notice, Sir Oswald, that the date on this note is some ten years before I joined Higginbotham's. I have several more documents that are even more compromising," added Joe. "One saying that your so-called research department at the time was purely focussed on obtaining insider information, and a second indicating that more recently, much more recently, you hugely benefitted from the takeover of another company called Technology International. A similar set of insider trading information was the basis of your windfall."

Sir Oswald remained silent.

"I also have half a dozen copies of your responses to requests for charitable donations."

"So?"

"They are all rather rude; one here says you don't support idle stumble-bums."

"I don't."

"Cancer research, stumble bums? That's an extraordinary response." Sir Oswald merely shrugged.

"I have made copies of everything, about thirty documents, just for your information, but I expect you will have no difficulty in finding the originals in your own files."

"I repeat, you obviously stole everything you've given me. I am going to prove that. This meeting is terminated."

Joe said, "If any of this information gets into the hands of the press, Higginbotham's will be worthless."

Sir Oswald just glared.

The Anderson-Wacheera team left. Thomasoff took charge of the envelope containing the compromising documents. "I'll keep these, for the time being," he said to Joe, as they walked out of the Higginbotham building.

"I'll pass all these on to Alice Osborne and see what she has to say. If there are any developments, please let me know," said Thomasoff, before hailing a taxi back to his own offices.

Two days later, several policemen headed by Chief Inspector Branson appeared at the Anderson-Wacheera offices. "I have a warrant to search these premises," said the policeman.

"What are you looking for?" asked Joe who had been called to the reception area.

"Documents. Stolen documents."

Joe phoned Thomasoff and told him what the situation was. "Let me speak to the inspector," said Thomasoff.

Joe handed the phone over.

"Chief Inspector. On behalf of Anderson-Wacheera I will apply for an immediate injunction preventing you from conducting this search. So, you will desist until the injunction has been heard."

Before he had completed the call Isabel came bustling over. "I have just had a call from Rachel Clark; the police have a warrant to search our house," she said to Thomasoff.

"The same applies to Mr and Mrs Wacheera's home, Chief Inspector," Thomasoff told Chief Inspector Branson, still on the phone. "And you will deal with me directly regarding any further developments relating to this issue."

Joe watched as Branson made a call to his people standing outside the Wacheera home, telling them to wait.

Three hours later, Thomasoff appeared at the Anderson-Wacheera premises and with Joe present gave the Chief Inspector a copy of the court order. "Chief Inspector, you may search the Anderson-Wacheera premises, but every one of your people involved in the search will be accompanied by a member of the Anderson-Wacheera staff and they may not take anything whatsoever into the Anderson-Wacheera premises, and anything you wish to take away will be copied by the Anderson-Wacheera staff. The same applies to the search on the Wacheera house. How many of your people are proposing to search the Wacheera household?"

"Three," responded a furious Chief Inspector Branson. "This is just interference in a serious and legitimate exercise."

"Generated by whom? Let me guess, Sir Oswald Higginbotham. We know what all this is about, Chief Inspector. The original documents you are looking for will all be found in the Higginbotham offices, not here," said Thomasoff.

Branson did not respond.

Isabel had already left with three members of Anderson-Wacheera staff.

The search of the Wacheera house was completed by midnight. The police were unable to find anything useful at all. Isabel saw them off the premises. She phoned Joe, still at the Anderson-Wacheera offices.

"The police have just left, with nothing," she told Joe.

"They'll be here for a while," said Joe, "the second shift has just about finished and the third is about to start. It's obvious that Sir Oswald has influence in high places. Something he may not continue to enjoy for very much longer."

Three exhausting days later, the police left having found nothing of value.

Before Branson left, at Thomasoff's insistence, he, Joe and Isabel had a quick meeting with the Chief Inspector.

"Chief Inspector, did you find what you were looking for?" asked Thomasoff.

"You know we didn't," said an angry Branson. "We did however find very detailed analyses of Higginbotham's business in both premises, which, as you know we didn't remove."

"The source of all of which you will find, is all in the public domain," said Joe. "Respectfully Chief Inspector, I was hardly likely to approach an organisation such as Higginbotham's with a view to acquiring the business, without having done my homework."

"There is also some very personal information on some of Higginbotham's employees."

"So what?" said Joe. "We approached them with a view to acquiring the balance of the business we don't already have an option on. I always believe in doing my homework."

"You have a rather strange history in this country."

"If you want to know anything more about that, speak to Alice Osborne at MI5." Thomasoff interceded. "Mr Wacheera has a guarantee of no prosecution because he provided them with a great deal of information which is certain to result in prosecutions both here in Britain and in other countries."

Branson looked surprised but didn't comment.

"Before you started this exercise, did Sir Oswald Higginbotham happen to mention that we had given him copies of some compromising documents that were sent to us, anonymously, through the post?" Thomasoff continued.

"This has got nothing to with Sir Oswald," said a furious Branson through gritted teeth.

Thomasoff shrugged. "If you do happen to bump into him, I suggest you ask him. Just a suggestion."

Branson left. He glared at Joe but refrained from saying anything further.

"As you know, I have given copies of these documents to MI5. Alice Osborne, to be precise," said Thomasoff. "You are after all an official MI5 agent, might as well earn your keep."

Joe laughed. "If I had to live on what they pay me, I'd be eating regularly at McDonalds."

Chapter 22: Higginbotham's The Aftermath

During the next few months, Isabel and Joe continued to build their own parts of the business of Anderson-Wacheera. Joe was eventually convinced by Isabel that the acquisition of a specialist builder, focussing on luxury finishes, was appropriate. Ron supported the idea.

"It should not threaten any of our other business partners," said Isabel. "In fact, it will help to quickly finish buildings, especially blocks of flats."

Joe, for his part, started to engage more staff to service their burgeoning wealth advice business. When he was satisfied that he had the people in place and properly trained, two of whom he had recruited from Higginbotham's, he started an extensive advertising campaign informing the community what they could expect if they entrusted their funds to Anderson-Wacheera. The emphasis was on the cost to the investor, which Joe knew was lower than most of the competition, particularly Higginbotham's; the adverts also highlighted Anderson-Wacheera's track record of investment success.

"You could also consider using a high-profile sportsman or something similar to advocate for us," suggested Isabel.

"Maybe, I don't want us to begin to look like a discount retailer though, or a peddler of discount health supplements," Joe answered after some thought. "What I'm experimenting with is recruitment through recommendations from existing clients."

Soon Anderson-Wacheera had to take another floor in the building they occupied.

After a year Higginbotham's had been relegated to the very back of their minds.

"I'm happy we don't actually own any shares in Higginbotham's," said Isabel, during a regular meeting examining all Anderson-Wacheera's holdings of various investments. "They seem to be going downhill."

Joe smiled. "You saved our bacon. Without you I would probably have bought those shares."

"Have you spoken to your brother Clive recently? Just to ask his impression."

"We're no longer on speaking terms."

Both Joe and Isabel kept regular contact with their projects in Kenya.

"I think another trip is needed," said Isabel. "The school is going great guns."

"Well, they've found quite a few of the title deeds of the landowners who were kicked off their land in Ol'Kalou. I'll talk to Lentella."

Joe phoned Lentella. "We were wondering when we should pay another visit to Kenya. The school seems to be thriving and we have enough title deeds now to make a case for getting our land back," said Joe.

"Musumbi has relented a bit," answered Lentella. "Revered Mweleli, Kigoro, and possibly Odongo are going to be prosecuted on charges relating to 'profiting from the activities of people smugglers' to quote him. He wants you to be a witness."

"What about Higginbotham?"

"He's going to leave that to the British."

"I can be a witness but, as with the situation in Britain, since I am an agent of MI5, I will only be able to give my testimony in camera, and I cannot be identified in public."

"I'll tell Musumbi."

"What about the business with the death of the general?"

"No change yet. I'll speak to Musumbi again about that."

Chapter 23: Back to Ol'Kalou

Two years after their previous visit to Kenya, Joe and Isabel paid another visit to the country of Joe's birth. They left Joe Junior at home, in the capable hands of Rachel Clark. This time there was no discussion about the merits or otherwise of Kenya Airways. Joe phoned Lentella and Koinange from the airport and they were both on hand to meet them when they checked in to the Norfolk.

They had a brief meeting in the hotel's coffee shop before Joe and Isabel went upstairs to unpack.

Lentella said, "As you asked, I have arranged a visit to the school this afternoon. I have told you that the school is going very well, better than expected. We have just accepted our third intake of first year secondary school pupils, and the other two intake years are doing very well. In another four years we will have a full school. The staff and pupils are all really looking forward to your visit."

Before the visit, Lentella showed them a financial summary of the trust that financed the school. Both Isabel and Joe had encouraged friends and colleagues, which included Reverend Timothy Mweleli, to contribute to the trust and all the pupils' fees were also paid into the trust. Anderson-Wacheera generously funded any deficit. The financial requirements had remained roughly the same over the years, despite the increase in the number of pupils, mainly due to increasing donations.

"The government owns some land in a nearby suburb. You will see there is a continuous building programme to accommodate the annual increase in the number of pupils. As Isabel saw on your last visit, there are extensive playing fields, which will never be built on," Lentella explained to the three of them on the drive to the school that afternoon.

They admired the large sign at the school gates, 'THE ELLEN WACHEERA SCHOOL FOR GIRLS' painted in red on a white background.

They were ushered into the large hall where almost three hundred girls were gathered.

Joe then spoke to a hushed audience for almost forty minutes partly in Swahili, since the girls were represented by the many tribes in Kenya, and partly in

English. "I was born on a small plot of land near a place called Ol'Kalou, which I don't suppose any of you have ever heard of. My father was murdered and my mother and I were chased away and spent the next few years in Kibera, here in Nairobi. A very bad start to life." He laughed. "I can laugh about it now, but it could have turned out very differently. So, if I was able to move from that little place in Ol'Kalou, to a hopeless situation in Kibera, and now with a lot of struggle and using my brains, which all of you have, otherwise you wouldn't be here, to progress on too much bigger things, then all of you, who will have the best education available, should try to aim for something bigger than yourselves. See what you can do to help your family, maybe even your country."

He sat down to a standing ovation.

Isabel was then asked to say a few words. She started off with a few words of Swahili, on which Joe had coached her, which was greeted with rapturous applause. She made her talk about the importance of educating girls and women. "Joe and I run the business as a partnership; he runs half the business and I run the other half, which is a property development business. Believe in yourselves, women can do anything," she said as the audience all spontaneously stood up and cheered her on.

Koinange was then asked to say a few words, which he did in Swahili. "I have known Joe since we were just *totos* in Kibera. We had many adventures together, which I won't bore you with here. As he has told you, Joe has moved on with his life and he could have just forgotten us altogether, but no, he has kept in touch with all his friends, here in Kenya, and also in *Ulaya.* He has helped when needed but has not interfered. And now he has returned to his roots and he and his wonderful wife Isabel have been instrumental in establishing this school, from which you will all benefit. Joe is a great example to us all."

There was another standing ovation from everyone.

At the end of the speeches, Joe, Lentella, and the staff of the school all stood up on the stage and, holding hands joined by all the pupils, shouted *'Harambee'* – all pull together. Something that had been started by Jomo Kenyatta in the early days of '*Uhuru*'-Independence.

They watched a short play, put on by some of the senior girls, on how a rural girl of ten had resisted the FMG operation and had then gone on to school and university.

They then spent half an hour talking to the scholarship girls, all of whom were funded directly by Anderson-Wacheera.

They spent a few minutes watching a netball game in the gymnasium and then exhausted, returned to the Norfolk.

"I'll leave you alone tomorrow," Lentella announced. "This Ol'Kalou business is likely to be a bit trickier. "I'll pick you up at five-thirty in the morning the following day. We can have breakfast on the way at the Bell Inn in Naivasha. It's a bit crappy – it's always been crappy – but is the best we can do. There have been a number of developments, which I will brief you on during the journey," he hesitated a moment. "I wonder if it wouldn't be wise for Isabel to remain in Nairobi for a few days, while we sort this business out?"

Isabel laughed. "Forget that," she said. "I'm coming whatever the situation."

"Okay," said Joe, looking at Isabel. "It'll all be as new to me. Mum and I left there when I was about ten."

Joe phoned Patrick to invite him to accompany them to Ol'Kalou the next day. "Kigoro will get his comeuppance if we have anything to do with it. As you know we have sixty-three land titles, all of which have been recognised by the authorities," Joe told him.

"Joe, I would love to be there but just can't leave right now. We're in the process of moving everything to the Nyanza Transport site. Anyway, Lentella has it all in hand."

"Fine. We'll keep you in the loop."

Lentella met them as promised at five-thirty outside the Norfolk in a new four-wheel drive Toyota Land Cruiser. Joe and Isabel dumped small overnight bags on the back seat. As they left the hotel, Lentella said, "I always use this for up- country trips, road conditions are not always predictable." As they drove out of Nairobi, he started his briefing: "The people involved are well established in the area and may resist any 'suggestions' we have for the return of the land to their rightful owners,"

"So?"

"We are going to need some security. I have arranged for four Moran to accompany us. They will all be armed with AK 47s, not their traditional *mkuki.* I have arranged for the Moran to go in a separate vehicle, as we may need to be flexible."

The four Moran followed in another somewhat decrepit-looking four-wheel drive.

There was room in the Land Cruiser for Joe and Isabel to sit in the front with Lentella. All three of them were dressed casually, Joe and Isabel in jeans and tee shirts. Lentella wore khaki trousers, with a casual shirt and a sports jacket. "There is nowhere much to stay in Ol'Kalou," Lentella told them, "so should the business take more than a day I have booked for us to stay in The Rift Valley Sports Club in Nakuru, which is a forty-minute drive from Ol'Kalou. It's not quite up to the standard of the Norfolk, but it's okay."

"Moran is the name of the young Maasai warriors," Joe explained to Isabel with a smile, "usually before they have permission to marry. They used to terrorise surrounding tribes, the Kikuyu in particular, before the advent of the *Wazungu* and Pax Britannia."

"I have managed to track down many of the people," Lentella said, "whose land was forcibly taken away from them, much as yours was, Joe. That is sixty-three seven-acre plots." Lentella laughed grimly. "There are now about six or seven surviving family members associated with each plot, so that means something like four hundred people. Once we have dealt with the people in Ol'Kalou, I will arrange for what I have described as 'the claimants' to be transported back to the area."

"What about people to run the show?" asked Joe.

"We should leave them out of it for the moment, until we have firmly established that our rights to the properties in question will not be challenged, either legally or illegally."

Joe barely remembered the bus trip he and his mother had made, now some twenty-five years earlier, going in the opposite direction.

Lentella pointed out the tiny chapel on the side of the road as the steep escarpment flattened out onto the floor of the Great Rift Valley. "It was apparently built by Italian prisoners of war, who originally built the road," he told them. "Do you want to stop and have a look?" Both Joe and Isabel shook their heads.

Breakfast at the Bell Inn was more than passable with fried eggs, bacon, toast and a good cup of coffee. "I phoned them yesterday," explained Lentella, smiling.

"You come here often?" asked Isabel.

"Yes. I'll explain why in a moment." During the breakfast stop, Lentella gave Isabel and Joe a further briefing on developments. "The land issue and the fate of Kigoro has taken on a life of its own," said Lentella, with Joe and Isabel listening intently. "As I have told you the authorities have recognised the titles of the sixty-three landholders who were dispossessed along with your family, Joe. When I told Musumbi that we were going to Ol'Kalou to deal with the land issue he told me that within the next day or so Kigoro, Reverend Mweleli and Odongo Boniface will all be arrested and charged with various charges relating to people smuggling."

"Should we be going to Ol'Kalou at all, then?" asked Joe.

"Oh yes. It all fits in very well, as you will see."

"What about Sir Oswald?"

"They are leaving him to the British; he will probably be charged within the next few days as well."

After breakfast they continued on their journey.

They turned off the main Nairobi-Nakuru road in the growing settlement of Gil-Gil, onto what was now a poorly maintained tarred road leading to Ol'Kalou and beyond. On the outskirts of the town there was a large sign saying 'Pembroke House'. Isabel took a couple of photos.

"That is a primary boarding school specialising in providing tuition for British common entrance exams, mainly for public (that is private) schools in that country. It now accommodates both boys and girls. It was started by the *Wazungu* some years before the second world war. Many of our better-off citizens have children at the school," Lentella informed them. "I have a son there at present, so we come down regularly. We often have a meal at the Bell Inn."

Joe said nothing. He glanced at Isabel.

"Looks like a typical English private school," she said. "I'm happy to see it has survived and appears to be thriving."

The road twisted and wound its tortuous way through the *leleshwa*. The road had been tarred since Kenyan independence, as Joe and his mother had found all those years earlier, but it had been badly constructed and, although attempts had been made to fill in the potholes, the journey was still an uncomfortable bounce from one poorly filled in pothole to another poorly filled in pothole. They passed a broken-down sign saying 'Oleolondo'.

"There was a railway station there in days gone by," said Lentella. "The branch line to Nyaharuru (Thomson's Falls) was closed when the *Wazungu* left." He shrugged. "The *Wazungu* used to send all their produce by train to the various markets. Now there is no produce to send; the people living here only produce enough to feed themselves."

"Maybe we can change that," said Joe. "Maybe," answered Lentella.

They bounced along the road in silence with everyone absorbed in their own thoughts.

Joe was to some extent coming home, at least that was what he thought, but he recognised nothing, and the place seemed completely alien to him.

Isabel continued to take photos, excited to be on such a journey. As far as she was concerned the whole area was beautiful, with the majesty of the Aberdare mountains, forming the eastern boundary of the Great Rift Valley, looming up on the right-hand side.

Lentella said very little but he eventually added, "As I told you earlier, this whole area belonged to the Maasai. All the names are still Maasai. They used it as an emergency grazing ground. That was until *Wazungu* guns chased them out in about 1910, after which the government declared it 'crown land'. It was then sold off to *Wazungu* speculators who in turn sold it to individuals. It is now populated entirely by Kikuyu – your people, Joe. So, the whole area has had a very chequered history over the past hundred years."

As they found their way into what appeared to be the thriving township of Ol'Kalou, Lentella pointed to the Aberdare Mountains, still on their right. "That is where the Mau-Mau hid out during the fight for independence. Only the Kikuyu participated; all the other tribes stood on the sidelines or were part of the British security forces. So, I suppose we have to thank your people Joe, that is the Kikuyu, for that."

They bounced over what had been a level crossing, but by now most of the rails had been removed. They entered the township amid curious but mildly hostile glances from the people hanging about. Ol'Kalou is far from any tourist area, so people were unused to seeing well-dressed strangers passing through. Lentella pointed out one of the buildings named after an Indian shopkeeper, now long gone. "The Indians were forced out after the *Wazungu* left, mainly by preventing them from selling many of the staples, such as *posho*, sugar and tea." He shrugged.

Joe thought the shops appeared to be busy.

"I think we should pay a visit to the area we are talking about, where you were born, Joe, and then I have made an appointment with the local councillor, a Mr Kigoro, here in Ol'Kalou. I think he was responsible for the death of your father, Joe, and for chasing you and your mother away." He looked at Joe.

Lentella stopped the Land Cruiser and got out to speak to the security detail following behind. "I'll just tell them to follow me," he explained.

They made their way north past a sign saying 'Ol'Kalou Country Club'. "That's where Kigoro has agreed to meet us." Lentella pointed. He drove on for a few kilometres.

Joe started to recognise the walk he and his mother had made all those years ago, when they had escaped to Nairobi.

Lentella turned off the main road and within minutes came across places that Joe recognised. "There, there," he said, "that was our hut!" He was unable to restrain the excitement in his voice.

Isabel continued to take photos.

Joe hopped out and walked over to the hut. A woman was tending a small vegetable patch; three cows grazed nearby. There was a small child playing in the dirt. Joe greeted her in Kikuyu. She gave an unenthusiastic response. "My name is Njeroge Wacheera. I was born here and used to live here."

The woman called out and a man appeared from the hut, wielding a panga.

The man shouted in Kikuyu, "We live here now. You must go away from here. Speak to Mr Kigoro in Ol'Kalou." He waved the panga threateningly, pointing vaguely in the direction of Ol'Kalou. "He put us here. This is our place now."

The security detail had parked and all four of them approached, carrying their AK 47s.

"It's okay," said Joe in Swahili to the security people. "We'll move on." They all returned to their vehicles.

"He told me to talk to Mr Kigoro."

"Yes," said Lentella.

They stopped at several more huts and had a similar hostile response from all of them.

"Hm," said Joe. "It's going to be more difficult than I expected. I suppose most of these people have been here for many years now."

"We should go to see Kigoro," offered Lentella.

As they left the area a small clearly hostile crowd gathered. They silently watched as both vehicles bounced their way out of the area, back onto the main road.

Within twenty minutes they turned onto the well-maintained track leading to the Ol'Kalou Country Club. As they approached the clubhouse, three hundred metres from the turnoff, they could see the remains of what had been a tennis court. The clubhouse looked as if it had been recently renovated. To their surprise there were two police vehicles in the small car park. There were seven or eight policemen hanging around in the car park.

"Hm," said Lentella. "It looks as if Mr Kigoro has the police in his pocket."

Lentella, Joe and Isabel clambered out of the Land Cruiser and looked around.

Then they made their way up a short flight of steps, undisturbed by the police, but not before Lentella made a quick call on his mobile phone. They walked through an open door accompanied by their security detail with Lentella leading the way to a sign saying 'BAR'.

Leaving the security detail outside, Lentella peered into the bar. The barman was quietly drying glasses. He was alone.

"Mr Kigoro?" he asked the barman in Swahili.

"Gone. Thirty minutes ago."

"Where?"

The barman shrugged. "He has an office in town."

When they went outside again, the police had disappeared. All they could see was a plume of dust down the driveway.

"I also told the police in Nairobi what we were doing," said Lentella. "I think Kigoro's police will have been instructed to return to their posts."

"I know, with all the work you have done Mr Lentella, that you have proved ownership of a very large part of the area where Joe lived," said Isabel. "But," she hesitated, "there are a lot of other people settled there now. Aren't we just going to displace another lot of poor people and replace them with our own, presumably still poor people?"

There was brief silence as the other two absorbed what she was saying.

"It's not that I don't appreciate the excellent work you have done, Mr Lentella... You have put us in a really good position to understand the situation."

"Frankly, from what I have found out in recent months, all Kigoro deserves is a very lengthy jail sentence," said Lentella, "All that together with the people smuggling charges he faces. No, we must go on with this."

Joe and Isabel glanced at each other without saying anything.

Lentella, having had two long calls on his mobile in what Joe thought was probably the Maasai language, then drove to Ol'Kalou.

"What gives?" asked Joe in English.

"Kigoro playing games," was Lentella's curt response. He drove to the local council offices, marched into reception, followed by Joe and Isabel, and asked for Kigoro.

"He's not here at the moment..."

Lentella interrupted the receptionist, "Yes he is. That's his car out in the parking lot."

The receptionist stood there with her mouth open as Lentella, again followed by Joe and Isabel, pushed past her and walked into Kigoro's office.

He was sitting at his desk talking animatedly on his mobile phone. He dropped it as soon as he saw who his visitors were, and the blood drained from his face. "Out, or I'll call the police!"

"You won't need to. It is the police and a few of your cronies..."

A minute later there was a crash and kerfuffle outside Kigoro's office and several police officers appeared; they were escorting three men, whom Joe recognised as coming from what they all now thought of as Joe's old place.

"These are not the police," wailed Kigoro.

"Show him your warrant cards," suggested Lentella. "These are not my police," repeated Kigoro.

The officer in charge said, "The people you describe as 'your police' have been suspended for accepting bribes. Until the matter is resolved I have been instructed to take over here in Ol'Kalou."

Lentella's security detail quietly crept into the room, all carrying their AKs.

There was a hush for several minutes while everybody tried to understand the new reality.

"You are not Kikuyu. This is Kikuyuland," said Kigoro.

"Mr Kigoro, you are under arrest, for bribing a police officer; you do not need to say anything...," said the officer.

A pair of handcuffs were snapped onto Kigoro's wrists and he was led away to be formally charged.

Joe and Isabel looked shocked and amazed by the developments, and the speed with which they had been implemented.

"I will explain it all shortly," said Lentella, addressing Isabel and Joe. "I must just deal with these three people here." Lentella looked at the remaining police contingent, saying, "Can I talk to these three for a moment? After that you can do what you must do. Please stay and listen to what I have to say."

"You want to come and take our land!" shouted one of the men, in Swahili.

"Kigoro misled you. The land does not belong to Kigoro or any of you, but if you listen for a moment, maybe there is a way you can stay."

Lentella then went on to explain in Swahili, that the original owners of the land had all been displaced and chased away by Kigoro and his thugs. "Many of them were killed, such as Mr Wacheera's father here. He pointed at Joe. I have now identified sixty-three landowners who each own the seven-acre plots that they purchased when the *Mzee* (Jomo Kenyatta) took the land back from the *Wazungu*. Those people will come back to the land they rightfully own. The government will make sure that happens." He looked at Isabel and Joe and nodded.

Isabel looked blank, but Joe understood what was being said; he whispered to Isabel, "I'll translate later."

"There are a number of plots where we have not been able to identify the original owners," Lentella continued. "So, if you cooperate, we will be able to make sure you can all stay somewhere in the area, and in time you may be able to own some of the property."

"What will happen to Kigoro?"

"The courts will decide, but he will probably spend a very long time in jail." The three men remained silent.

"You also have to understand that the government is determined that the area will be properly farmed," Lentella continued. "Mr Wacheera here has provided some funds, so there will be people who will come and teach everyone in the area what to do, including you if you wish. There will be tractors and general farm equipment to help. We are going to get the boreholes running again. The government has electrified the whole area, so there will be electric light, and power for the boreholes and anything else that's needed."

"We just want to be left alone and live as we do now," said one of the three men.

Lentella shook his head. "The land was stolen from its rightful owners, so you won't be able to do that. Land that was secured for them by *Mzee*."

After a short discussion, the three men who had accompanied the police were released and not charged with any offence. The remaining police left. Lentella's security contingent waited outside.

Isabel, Joe and Lentella sat in Kigoro's comfortable office.

The receptionist crept in uneasily and asked if any of them would like tea or coffee. They all asked for coffee.

"Mr Lentella, this whole thing has taken on a life of its own, a new dimension, if you like. Maybe you could explain what's going on? I'm not uncomfortable with where we seem to be at, by the way," said Joe, once he had given Isabel a brief explanation of the developments and what Lentella had just said.

Lentella smiled. "I involved the government a lot more closely with this proposal than I told you, over past years. The Ministry of Agriculture is very concerned that almost all the land recovered from the *Wazungu* has become unproductive, and they see this project as the start of a way of restoring it to productive use. I also had to involve them to make sure the titles to the land would be recognised, based on the deeds I have in my possession. You can also be sure that there will be a significant police and security presence until everything settles down, so that is one worry out of the way."

"It seems that the government has almost taken over the project," observed Isabel.

"Not really; all they have done is to provide the support necessary for it to succeed. We will run it as we have planned to all along. We will appoint and pay the management and will run the finances."

"So, the original financial commitment from Anderson-Wacheera still stands?" asked Isabel.

"Yes. My recommendation is, once everything is in place, we approach a number of aid agencies and possibly the World Bank. Frankly, if the project is half as successful as we have forecast, they will all be falling over each other to be involved."

"What do you suggest we do now?" asked Joe.

"We need to let everything settle down a bit. There is a contingent of police, who will be stationed here to make certain there is no trouble. We should return to Nairobi and can now interview the people I have lined up, and hopefully make appropriate appointments to come and run the show for you."

"They have all completed the tests I recommended?" asked Isabel.

"Yes."

"You have been busy," observed Joe.

"As I have said before I find it interesting and exciting," said Lentella. "Your activities here should encourage others of the Kenyan diaspora, to come back and invest in the country.

It's still early," said Lentella. "I suggest we return to Nairobi a slightly longer way, which should be interesting for you Isabel and it may provoke other memories for you Joe."

Lentella retraced his steps past the Ol'Kalou Country Club. "We go due west from here," he said. Lentella had told the security detail to return to Nairobi.

Joe and Isabel, both thanked them personally in Swahili.

They drove along the well-constructed tarred road, which climbed up several steep hills. "Some of the *Wazungu* farms along here were divided up into fifty- acre plots; a bit larger than the place your father owned," offered Lentella. After about seven or eight kilometres, Lentella stopped the vehicle at a vantage point on the road, looking eastwards towards the Aberdare mountains.

"This gives you a great view of the Wanjohe valley," he said as they all got out of the vehicle. There were a number of people standing around waiting for the Nakuru bus. "That's Sattimma over there," he pointed, "the highest point of the Aberdare range; and to the right is Kipipiri. This whole area was settled by the *Wazungu*. Kenyatta persuaded the British government to buy all the *Wazungu* farms, here and all over Kenya, as part of the Independence settlement in the early sixties; this was one of the first areas to be resettled. This area is now entirely settled by Kikuyu."

"It really is beautiful," said Isabel, "quite stunning." Lentella nodded.

"I can see why they wanted to live here," said Isabel, "it's like bloody paradise."

Another few minutes were spent admiring the view. Joe chatted to some waiting bus passengers.

They continued on their journey. "People seem a bit unsettled," said Joe. "They complained about the poor bus service, although they were pleased with the upgraded road."

"What are they unsettled about?" asked Isabel.

"Most of them are labourers. They don't always get paid on time or at all. I suppose it's a method the landowners have, many of whom live in the cities, of keeping the people on their land, by making sure they, the owners, always owe their employees something," Joe answered. "Also, the whole area produces very little, just enough for the people living here to live on. I am sure we can change that."

Lentella glanced at Joe but added nothing to the observation. Soon they passed through an area of intense activity.

"This used to be what was called the Bahati forest," said Lentella. "Pristine rain forest, with old cedar trees. All burnt for firewood. As you can see there is not a tree in sight now and the name Bahati has altogether disappeared. The Colobus monkeys, pretty creatures, have disappeared of course. They were mostly eaten, I suppose. The people just came here and settled down and nobody could stop them. It's the population explosion."

As they descended towards Nakuru, Isabel remarked, "That pink line round the lake there. Are those the famous flamingos?"

"Yes, indeed," said Lentella. He stopped the Land Cruiser at a suitable vantage point and they all got out to admire the view.

It was new to Joe as well, he had never seen Nakuru from this perspective, although he had been through the city on his trips to Juba.

Isabel got busy with her camera.

Joe reflected on what he had seen that day. 'It's like a foreign country,' he thought, 'what do I really know of this place?'

Isabel was fascinated with the busy, crowded streets of Nakuru. She took a few photos. "Any chance of a visit to the lake?" asked Isabel.

"I wondered about that," said Lentella, "so I checked. There has apparently been a lot of rain recently and the park is closed at present. Sorry. I believe it's worth a visit." He explained that he had very little interest in the numerous wildlife attractions in Kenya that seemed to attract western tourists.

They returned to Nairobi.

Both Isabel and Joe interviewed the people who had been selected by Lentella for the Ol'Kalou land. Over two weeks they made several appointments.

"I think you can leave me in charge, with you two perhaps paying an annual visit?" suggested Lentella. "As with the school I will send you and Koinange periodic reports, every two or three months, and if there are any difficulties there is the phone and e-mail, of course."

By this time both Joe and Isabel had come to trust Lentella and his motives, so they agreed to the suggestions, including the fees he would charge for all his services.

"Any reservations?" Joe asked Isabel when they were alone at the Norfolk. "Nope. We control the purse strings."

"By the time our projects get into full swing, every cent that I stole from General Kariuki will have been returned to the country," Joe added wistfully.

Isabel said nothing, just held his hand.

Joe caught up with Patrick and Koinange, mainly to tell them about the developments following their trip to Ol'Kalou. "You should also know that Reverend Mweleli, Kigoro and Odongo have been charged with various offences relating to people smuggling. Mweleli will also be charged with money laundering, profiting from the results of prostitution and murder. Kigoro will also be charged with murder, bribing police officers and many other offences yet to be determined. Odongo will probably get off lightly." Joe laughed. "Stupidity is not yet an official offence."

"How far have you got with Nyanza Transport?" asked Joe.

"We bought the property, as we told you we would, and have moved in; there were many complications that delayed us. The business is worth nothing. Over time we identified all Nyanza Transport's customers and have mostly been able to win them over to us. So, we are much better off than we were. All your advice was very useful, critical in fact."

"We can continue to provide lease finance for new vehicles."

"Yes. We are dealing with the man you put us in touch with at Anderson-Wacheera. N'guku is coming back. Now that he has his British citizenship."

"We'll be back too, every now and then, but the projects are well looked after by Lentella. He is a great find by the way."

Later Joe received a call from Thomasoff. "Just to let you know that Sir Oswald has been arrested and charged with money laundering offences, as well as numerous insider trading offences. All as a result of information you provided. I understand from Alice Osborne that MI5 officers are currently all over the Higginbotham business and are unearthing new stuff all the time. Sir Oswald is out on bail."

Shortly after that he received a call from James McDermott. "You won't be surprised that I have had a call from Sir Oswald, wanting to resume your acquisition proposals."

Joe laughed. "In the nicest possible way, you will of course tell him to get fucked, won't you."

"I already have. The business will go bankrupt when all this leaks out, which it will in a few days. There is some value in the data they have accumulated and possibly in some of the people. Your options will put you in good order with the administrators, when they are appointed, to access all that. You won't of course be exercising the option," said McDermott more as a statement than a question.

"No of course not. My thoughts exactly on the data and the people; nobody else will be able to understand its value anyway. We'll be back in London within a week or two. If there are any developments, you'll let me know of course."

Isabel was witness to the calls. "What was all that about?" asked Isabel. Joe told her.

"So, I suppose, instead of the fucking reverend, we'll now be hearing about Sir fucking Oswald." She laughed.

Lentella phoned. "Musumbi wants to see you again."

"Okay, when? This time Isabel will come with me."

"Tomorrow. I'll pick you both up."

As Lentella's car drove in through the gates, Joe was not able to blank out faint images of the general's demise.

On this occasion Musumbi was more accommodating and offered coffee and biscuits to his guests.

"Thank you," said both Joe and Isabel almost in unison.

"You will be subpoenaed to be a witness in the trials of Reverend Mweleli and Mr Kigoro," Musumbi announced.

"I will willingly be a witness." Joe answered. "There is no need to subpoena me."

"There is just one thing I request of you."

"What's that?"

"There should be no mention in your testimony of General Kariuki. He did not benefit from his apparent participation in the people smuggling racket you have reported to us on."

"I don't need to mention his name in my testimony, but his name was mentioned in my original report. Also, what happens if I'm asked a question by the defence, if anyone else was at the meetings run by Reverend Mweleli?"

Musumbi nodded.

"Mr Wacheera is now an official agent of MI5. As such he needs to be able to testify in camera," added Lentella.

"We have already agreed with the British that Mr Wacheera's testimony will be in camera," said Musumbi.

"Mr and Mrs Wacheera will be returning to England shortly. Can his testimony be via a video link?"

"Yes. Probably. The judge will have to agree to that. Anything else?"

"I presume Odongo Boniface will get a slap on the wrist. He was never a major participant in the people smuggling scheme anyway."

Musumbi nodded. "The court will decide. Anything else?"

Joe shook his head looking at Lentella. "Well, if that's all," said Joe, "we'll take our leave."

He and Isabel got up, shook Musumbi's hand and left.

Musumbi indicated that Lentella should wait behind for a moment.

Joe and Isabel walked out into the front garden, just as well kept as it ever was.

Lentella appeared after a few minutes. "Musumbi was surprised that you didn't raise the issue of your supposed involvement in the death of the general," said Lentella as they drove out of the gates. "He said you were a cool customer."

"So is he," said Joe. "Anyway, they don't have a case."

"He said they will not be pursuing the matter. I have got him to agree there will soon be a letter exonerating you for any culpability in the death of General Kariuki. He also said that you were putting so much back into the country, it would be a pity to jeopardise that."

"Interesting. I've never thought of it in those terms."

"What's that?" Isabel laughed. "Something you *haven't* thought through?" Joe smiled. She knew him so well.

AUTHOR BIOGRAPHY

Guy Hallowes has lived in many different countries: born in Kenya, and qualified as a Chartered Accountant in the UK, he has also lived in South Africa, Botswana, and Canada whilst settling with wife Diana and their four children on Sydney's leafy north shore.

A Senior Executive in a major international publishing company for twenty years, Guy always harboured a wish to write – a wish that has now been more than fulfilled with six novels published and now a seventh one: 'Joe'.

Web-site: www.guyhallowes.com

OTHER GUY HALLOWES NOVELS:

Set in Africa

'Winds of Change Trilogy':
No Happy Valley
What the Crocodiles Don't Eat, will be washed into the sea
No Peace for the Wicked

'Other Africa'

Rough Diamonds

Books set in Sydney

'Dystopian novels relating to the consequences of Climate Change':
Icefall Beyond Icefall